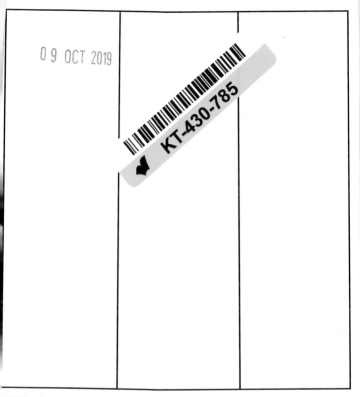

KT-430-785

This book should be returned/renewed by the latest date shown above. Overdue items incur charges which prevent self-service renewals. Please contact the library.

Wandsworth Libraries
24 hour Renewal Hotline
01159 293388
www.wandsworth.gov.uk

Wandsworth

Discover more at millsandboon.co.uk

REDEEMED BY PASSION

JOSS WOOD

MONTANA SEDUCTION

JULES BENNETT

MILLS & BOON

First Published in Great Britain 2019
by Mills & Boon, an imprint of HarperCollinsPublishers,
1 London Bridge Street, London, SE1 9GF

Redeemed by Passion © 2019 Harlequin Books S.A.
Montana Seduction © 2019 Jules Bennett

Special thanks and acknowledgement are given to Joss Wood for her contribution to the *Dynasties: Secrets of the A-List* series.

ISBN: 978-0-263-27189-8

0819

MIX
Paper from
responsible sources
FSC
www.fsc.org
FSC™ C007454

This book is produced from independently certified FSC™ paper to ensure responsible forest management.

For more information visit: www.harpercollins.co.uk/green

Printed and bound in Spain
by CPI, Barcelona

REDEEMED BY PASSION

JOSS WOOD

One

Liam Christopher tipped his head up and tracked the winking light of a jet above him. That could, for all he knew, be Brooks Abbingdon's jet carrying Teresa away from him. The image of Teresa curled up in Brooks's lap, him comforting her as she cried—because, hell, if anyone deserved to cry it was Teresa St. Claire—flashed on his retina and his grip tightened on the crystal tumbler in his hand. He heard a sharp crack and a second later, expensive liquor ran over his palm and under the wristband of his watch.

Liam opened his hand and looked at the cracked glass and its sharp shards. Surprisingly, there was no blood. Transferring the broken glass from his hand to the coffee table on the balcony, he shook the droplets of his Manhattan cocktail off his hand before reaching for his pocket square and wiping the liquid away.

Well, that was a waste of good booze. Liam looked back

into the luxurious Presidential Suite of the Goblet Hotel
and saw his friend Matt Richmond pacing the area between
the designer sofas and the dining table. Matt was pissed
and he had a right to be. His gala evening was ruined and
would be long remembered for all the wrong reasons.

And it was all Teresa's fault. Well, not her fault exactly—she hadn't known that her brother would show up
and ruin months of work—but as the event planner, the
buck stopped with her.

Would her company recover from this? He doubted it.
Would she? Teresa was tough but she'd had a couple of
hard knocks lately. When Matt asked her to leave the retreat immediately, taking her brother with her, Teresa knew
that her reputation was about to take another beating, and
Liam understood why she felt the need to run. Why would
she want to stay and witness the pitying looks, the cruel
smirks, hear the caustic comments?

She also wanted to run from him. And that, he understood most of all.

Seeing movement in the room behind him, Liam turned
his head to watch Nadia approach Matt, her eyes on her
man. Matt was still on the phone but he held out his hand
and Nadia tucked herself into his side, her arms encircling
his waist. Matt dropped a kiss on her head before con-
tinuing his conversation. Liam's stomach cramped with
what he thought might be jealousy. He'd never believed
in true love—hadn't been exposed to it growing up—but
maybe it did exist; maybe it was just as rare as hell. Matt
had found his Holy Grail in Nadia but Liam wasn't naive
enough to believe that everybody, most especially him,
would be that lucky.

Love, he was convinced, wasn't for him.

Matt threw his phone onto the sofa behind him and
pulled his wife into his body, burying his face in the crook

of her neck. Although Nadia was a foot shorter than Matt, Liam knew that he was sucking strength from her, that Matt was leaning on her. They were a unit, taking turns to lead and to follow, to give and receive strength. They were two trees growing together, sharing soil and water, their branches and roots intermingling.

It struck him that he and Teresa were two separate pine trees planted in a regimented row. They both stood tall, took the wind, never bent. They'd been planted too far apart—and too much had happened between them and to them—to bridge the gap to be able to even start to explore anything deeper than flash point sex.

Liam turned away and walked to the edge of the balcony, gripping the balustrade with tight fingers. Maybe Teresa's leaving, her breaking it off for good, was—as she'd said—what was best for her, him, Christopher Corporation. For everybody involved.

And if that was true then why did he feel like week-old crap?

Hearing Matt's footsteps he turned his head and saw Matt approaching him, a bottle of bourbon in his hand. Matt raised his eyebrows at the broken glass and, without words, handed Liam the bottle. Liam took a hefty sip before dropping the bottle to his side, holding it in a loose grip. By the time dawn broke, he was going to be best buds with this bottle.

"Where's Nadia?"

Matt leaned his butt against the railing and rolled his head from side to side to release the knots in his neck. Liam didn't bother; his knots were now permanent residents. "She went to bed," Matt replied. He glanced at his watch. "It is almost three in the morning."

"It was a hell of a night." Liam took another hit from the bottle, ignoring his still-sticky hand. He glanced up, saw another jet and forced himself to meet Matt's eyes. "I feel like I should apologize."

"For what?" Matt asked, his eyes and tone weary. "You didn't cause Teresa's brother to ruin my gala evening."

"Neither did Teresa," Liam responded, needing to defend her.

"Tell me about her brother," Matt said, moving to the sofa and dropping down. He immediately tucked a pillow under his head and propped his feet up onto the coffee table.

Ordinarily, Liam would never consider divulging someone else's secrets but this was Matt, his best friend, and he trusted him implicitly. He also needed Matt's sharp brain to help him make sense of what was, at this crazy hour, the senseless.

"It's a tangled mess but I'm going to tell you what I do know, gathered from what Teresa has told me, along with what my investigator dug up.

"So years ago, Joshua, her brother, liked drugs and alcohol a little too much and got himself in debt with some unsavory characters. They offered him a job to pay off the money. He became a chauffeur—"

"And he, knowingly or unknowingly, ferried drugs," Matt finished for him.

Matt was, by far, the sharpest tool in the shed. "Yep. He was busted and was jailed. Via Mariella Santiago-Marshall, Teresa employed the talents of The Fixer—"

Matt whistled his astonishment. "I've heard of him. He's—"

Liam raised an eyebrow. "Effective?"

"I was going to say *ruthless* but that works, too."

"Anyway," Liam continued, "he got Joshua's charges dropped, him out of jail and across the country. The kid didn't learn and has raked up another huge gambling debt.

A mafia-type organization has bought that debt from the original crew and it's rocketed to an impossible sum."

"How much?"

"Seven million dollars," Liam replied. "Several weeks back Teresa was told that he'd been kidnapped but that turned out to be BS. Teresa's been informed that she needs to repay his loan, but she doesn't have that kind of cash, and they've never called her back, as far as I know."

"Pay it for her, offset it against the cost of the shares you are going to buy from her when she's completed her yearlong mandatory stint on the board of Christopher Corporation," Matt suggested. "As per the terms of your father's will."

"Teresa is hoping that she can delay repaying them until she's sold her shares. She wants to keep me out of the equation. Hell, maybe she's shopping around for a better deal for the shares." The thought of Teresa selling those shares to anyone else made his stomach whirl. If she did that, he would no longer have the thin sliver of control over Christopher Corporation he did now.

"Nobody has given Teresa, or Joshua, a firm deadline for the repayment of the debt."

"Weird," Matt agreed. "So it should be imperative that he keep his head down, even stay out of sight. Then why would Joshua crash a highly visible, live-streamed event?

"What does Teresa think?" Matt asked, after a moment's silence.

"I don't know since she blew me off and hightailed it back to Seattle in Abbingdon's private plane," Liam muttered his sour reply. He pulled his cell out of his pocket and hit the speed dial number that would connect him to Teresa. It didn't mean anything that he'd moved his personal assistant, Duncan, to number two on his list and Teresa to number one. It meant nothing. At all.

Liam listened to her phone ring and urged her to pick up. He needed to know that she was okay, that Joshua was okay—God, the kid hadn't looked, or sounded, good. And he wasn't talking about the bruise his fist made on his jaw. Her phone went to voice mail and he dropped a hard "Call me" order into her message system.

Liam placed the bourbon bottle on the coffee table, sat down in the chair opposite Matt and rested his forearms on his knees. He released a series of low but intense f-bombs.

"That kind of sums up my feelings about this evening," Matt commented. "I've been doing damage control but there's not much spin you can generate when everything is caught on video and then live-streamed."

Liam winced. "How many views?"

"Far too many." Matt lifted his glass in a sarcastic salute. "I've got to admit, when Teresa messes up, she does it properly."

"She didn't know her brother was in town, never mind that he was going to do that," Liam retorted.

"So defending her seems to be your default reaction tonight," Matt commented, hitting the nail on its head.

Liam sent his best friend a hard stare. "What's your point, Matt?"

"It's been one drama after another with her, starting with the fact that you thought she had an affair with your dad."

"She explained that. My father was her mentor and good friend."

Matt rolled his eyes. "They had to be very good friends for him to leave Teresa a twenty-five-percent stake in Christopher Corporation worth millions."

When Matt put it like that, all his fears and insecurities about their relationship floated to the surface. Was he being conned? Could he believe Teresa's version of what happened? In his final hours, Linus did confirm that there had been nothing between them but friendship and Liam wanted to believe him, them. But he'd been raised to believe that everyone lied so how the hell could he trust anything they said? Anything anybody said?

He thought he could, at least, trust his parents to some degree but their latest lie had been the biggest of his life. As his father lay dying, he realized that it was scientifically impossible that his parents, with their blood groups, could produce a child with his blood group. Ergo, either only one of them was his biological parent or he was adopted. Hell of a thing to realize at the age of thirty-two.

Was it any wonder he was so messed up when it came to relationships?

It was late and Liam was done with talking. He wanted this conversation to end so he told Matt that Teresa wanted nothing more to do with him. Liam caught the look of relief on Matt's face. "You're happy about that?"

Matt shook his head. "*Happy* is the wrong word..." He sat up, swinging his feet off the table. "It's just that relationships shouldn't be this hard, bud. Over the past few months you've thought that she's a liar, a gold digger and an opportunist. You've slept with her and then slept with other women."

No, he hadn't. "I tried to sleep with someone else to get her out of my system."

Matt waved his explanation away. "Whatever. She hit the tabloids, dragging you along with her. Those scumsuckers informed the world that she had an affair with your father and that she only slept with Linus to get her hands on the company."

He knew this. He'd goddamn lived it. "Do you have a point and are you going to get to it in the near future?"

"My point is that, while I actually like Teresa—"

"You could've fooled me." Liam's interjection was bone-dry.

"I do like her," Matt said. "She's smart, super-organized and she's an amazing event planner. Yeah, I'm mad as hell that tonight ended the way it did, but intellectually, I get that it wasn't her fault. But her career did not need this and if she was boycotted before, it's going to be nothing like what's going to happen to her now."

Liam gripped the bridge of his nose. God.

Matt's long sigh was audible. "But at the end of the day, my loyalty is to you. And, as your friend, I am telling you that I don't think she is good for you because, frankly, you look like crap."

Well, that wasn't news.

"Are you in love with her?"

Liam's head shot up and his eyes slammed into Matt's. His throat closed as panic crept up. In his sappier moments lately, he'd flirted with the idea of love, but that was just a result of hormones and stupendous sex. No, of course he wasn't in love with Teresa; he didn't believe in love. But he was attracted to her, stupidly so. And attraction was easily confused for that other emotion. He croaked a "No."

Matt stood up and gripped his shoulder. "Can I then just point out that this woman you profess not to love has the innate ability to mess with your head and your life? That's an enormous amount of power for someone you just like to sleep with."

Craphelldammit.

"Go to bed, Matt."

Matt smiled for the first time that evening. "Yep, that's where I'm heading. Into the arms of the woman who, instead of messing with my head and life, actually makes my life better and brighter."

Liam glared at his friend as he walked back into the

hotel room and thought about returning to his own suite, to the empty king-size bed waiting for him. But the night was mild, this sofa was quite comfortable and he had a bottle to keep him company. And really, he had too much on his mind to sleep.

Liam lay back and tucked a pillow under his head and watched the light of airplanes move between the stars.

Right, exactly what level of hell had she reached?

Teresa St. Claire had experienced hot—Liam Christopher believing that she'd had an affair with his father—and knew what blistering felt like when her face was plastered over the front pages of the tabloid press accusing her of stealing Liam's fortune.

But tonight she'd stood inside the flames, her skin melting.

Now, as Brooks Abbingdon's jet cut through the dark night, Teresa felt frozen, her heart encased in dry ice. Maybe true hell was this dead-on-the-inside, will-never-recover feeling.

Teresa flopped down into the chair opposite Brooks Abbingdon and eyed her brother through half-closed eyes. A bright blue bruise colored his jaw, and his lower lip was swollen. She loved Joshua, but right now she didn't like him even a little bit. The only man she felt remotely charitable toward was Brooks Abbingdon, who'd offered her a ride out of the nightmare that was her latest professional disaster zone. He was also sitting across from her, ankle on his knee, deep in thought.

Teresa swallowed down a groan and felt her stomach cramp. Her reputation, along with her company, had been dancing on the knife-edge of ruin for weeks but her brother gate-crashing her most illustrious clients' gala evening and, worse, grabbing the mic from singer Jessie Humphrey and placing himself front and center while ranting about rich losers and liars had pushed her off that sliver-thin edge.

And since she would be, if she wasn't already, person very non grata by morning, why had Brooks Abbingdon, CEO of Abbingdon Airlines, rushed to her rescue? He was rich, successful and gorgeous so she had no idea why he'd offered them a lift on his plane heading back to Seattle. But she wasn't complaining; she needed to get Joshua back under the radar as soon as possible and Brooks had offered her a way out.

Joshua was hunched over in his seat, mumbling to himself. Thank God he'd stopped ranting, his words and sentences not making any sense.

Teresa couldn't pull her eyes off his face. Joshua had been a pain in her ass, especially these past few years, but he was her baby brother; she'd always looked after him. Initially, she'd blamed his actions on a combination of drugs and alcohol, but earlier she'd touched his left arm and he'd cried out. Teresa rolled back his sleeveshirt to see a small but distinctive puncture mark on his forearm. In a place where it would be difficult for him to self-inject. Like so much else about this night, nothing made sense.

But hell, why was she surprised? This was her insane life; everything and anything was possible.

Teresa looked from Joshua to Brooks and found his eyes studying her. Teresa waited for the kick of attraction, for a spark, and sighed when nothing happened. Maybe she wasn't responding to him because she was exhausted and overwrought because Brooks was everything she normally found attractive in a man. At six-four or so, he was tall but perfectly proportioned with wide shoulders, narrow hips and long, muscular legs. His voice, carrying the accent of an expensive British education, was deep and luscious, his face masculine and sexy, and his skin the color of old sepia photographs.

But he wasn't, dammit, Liam.

Gah!

As if she'd summoned him, Teresa heard the discreet beep of her phone and there was his name, flashing on the screen. Her heart whimpered and her stomach clenched. Nope, she couldn't talk to him, not tonight, possibly never again. For the past few months, since she'd stumbled back into his orbit, she'd felt off-kilter and was constantly uncertain about what she'd face on any given day. She'd been a duck, serene on the outside but paddling like hell under the water. As a result, she was utterly drained on just about every level. Tonight she'd bled out every pint of energy she'd ever possessed.

Teresa simply did not know if she'd be able to pick her head up, struggle on. Curling up in a ball and weeping sounded far more fun than fighting another day.

She was done. Possibly for good.

Brooks cleared his throat and Teresa lifted her head to see him holding out a tumbler of whiskey. Taking the glass, she glanced at Joshua. He'd fallen asleep, his head between the edge of the seat and the wall of the plane. Tossing back her whiskey, she lowered the glass and met Brooks's sympathetic eyes.

"Would you like another?" Brooks asked, his words holding the snap of Eton and Oxford.

Teresa shook her head. "If I do, I'll collapse in a heap and then you will have two St. Claires to deal with."

Teresa blew out her breath and gestured to Joshua. "I am *so* sorry. I know I'm repeating myself, but I don't know how he found out where I was working or what prompted him to—" She hesitated, looking for words. *Destroy my career? Embarrass the hell out of me? Bankrupt my business?* "—do what he did."

Brooks lifted his shoulder in a quick shrug. When he didn't respond, Teresa took a deep breath and bit the bullet. "I will absolutely understand if you want to rescind your offer to have me plan your wedding."

Brooks stared at her for a long time and Teresa resisted the urge to squirm. She wouldn't blame him if he pulled his offer for her to plan his wedding; he'd floated the offer earlier that evening, back at the gala, before her carefully planned event went to hell on horseback.

Unbidden, snapshots of the evening jumped onto the big screen of her mind. Joshua ripping the microphone from Jessie's hand, his incoherent screaming. Liam, bigger and stronger than her lanky brother, tackling him to the ground, his fist connecting with Joshua's face. And all of it streaming live to Jessie's fans around the world.

Teresa placed her hand on her heart and tried to rub the pain away. But nope, it wasn't going anywhere.

Brooks tapped a long finger against the Waterford tumbler and shook his head. "Up until your brother's unfortunate interruption, the gala evening, and the weekend, was going well. I'm intelligent enough to see how much work you put into the preparations and how dedicated you are to your job. What he did wasn't your fault."

At the unexpected vote of support, Teresa felt her eyes sting. "Thank you."

"Let's discuss my wedding."

Teresa frowned. It was close to three in the morning, she was exhausted and, after a crappy evening, Brooks wanted her to talk flowers and food? Teresa slapped back her frustration. He was offering her a lifeboat as she treaded water in a stormy sea.

Okay, then. She'd talk weddings. "Sure."

Then she realized that she had no idea who Brooks was marrying and, come to think of it, was still surprised to hear of his engagement. She'd pegged him as a confirmed bachelor, someone who wasn't interested in settling down. She pulled a smile up onto her face. "Who's the lucky lady?"

Brooks stared at her for a moment, his eyes not leaving hers. "You will be informed in due course."

Okay, then. That was a super-weird response. Teresa worked hard not to show her shock, to react in any way other than polite acquiescence. Why the secrecy? Wasn't the bride supposed to be part of these discussions? What was going on here?

Her thoughts scrambling, Teresa linked her hands around her knees and tried to corral her thoughts. Right, moving on. "Do you have a preference on where you would like to marry? When? How many guests? What's your budget?"

Brooks held her eyes when he dropped what Teresa hoped would be the last bombshell of the evening. "You have an unlimited budget and I'm offering to pay double your normal fee."

"What's the catch?" she asked, not sure that she wanted to know.

Brooks smiled. "I need you to organize the wedding of the year so that it can take place on the thirtieth."

"Of what month?" She needed at least six months to prepare; six months was tight but doable.

Brooks held her eye and didn't flinch. "I'm getting married on the last Saturday of this month, Teresa."

Two weeks?

Frick.

Teresa held out her glass and nodded to the whiskey bottle. "Can I have another? And, respectfully, are you insane? There is no way I can plan a wedding in two weeks."

Brooks pulled out his phone and dialed. "She said she can't do it," he said to the person on the other line. He then handed her the phone. "He wants to talk to you."

Two

There was a method to his madness…and a madness to his methods. Shakespeare's quote, Brooks Abbingdon thought, had never been more apt. His particular method of madness was to marry.

In two weeks' time.

Teresa hung up the phone and looked at him with wide, defeated eyes. "I'd be…" she hesitated "…happy to do your wedding. Two weeks is no problem."

Another success for The Fixer and that meant that another hefty bill would be landing in his Brooks's inbox soon. Fact: sometimes you had to pay for things to go your way.

Seeing that Teresa was at the end of her rope—it was the early hours of the morning and she'd had a hell of a day—Brooks told her to rest and Teresa immediately dropped her head back and closed her eyes. She'd been shocked by his time frame; hearing that he had yet to choose a bride might cause her brain to explode.

Because, really, who planned a wedding without se-curing a bride?

Apparently, he did.

Brooks stretched out his legs and jammed his hands into the pockets of his suit pants, mostly to hide the small tremor in his fingers. Married? Him? He'd always believed, still did, that wedding rings were the world's smallest, strongest pair of handcuffs. But here he was, about to get hitched because his grandfather refused to listen to reason.

Stubborn old bastard.

Lester Abbingdon desperately wanted to invest in a friend's yet-to-be-developed chain of luxury boutique ho-tels. Brooks wasn't convinced that the investment would provide a decent, or any, return. But Lester rather fancied the idea of being the world's next hotel mogul and, since he couldn't take money from the swimming-in-cash Ab-bingdon Trust, he was determined to raise the money he needed by selling his personal stake in Abbingdon Air-lines. Brooks had no intention of dealing with a new part-ner, of having to justify his decisions or, far worse, ask for permission to do what he wanted, when he wanted, with his company.

No, the only option was to buy his grandfather's shares from him and in order to raise the cash needed—with-out having to get banks or other investors involved—that meant, *yippee-doo-dah*, getting married.

Brooks stared out the window into the inky blackness and remembered his first visit to the stuffy offices of the Abbingdon Trust's lawyers. He'd been twenty-one and in their wood-paneled offices, they told him that, as the only Abbingdon heir, he was entitled to a sizeable monthly in-come from the trust but he was also set to inherit a crap-ton of cash on his twenty-fifth birthday. *If* he was married.

The offer would only be renewed every five years and

at twenty-five, using Lester's money to buy his first two cargo planes, he'd opted not to marry—he'd been having too much fun playing the field and had no intention, and no need, to sacrifice his freedom. Ditto at thirty but at thirty-five, Abbingdon Airlines was worth the inconvenience. He wanted control and for control he needed cash; to get the cash he needed to marry...

He'd established and grown Abbingdon Airlines; it was his hard work that had made the company one of the most trusted and respected companies in the country. His clients knew that they could rely on him to get them, or their goods, where they needed to go in the shortest time possible. But Lester wanted to go and play Monopoly with real-life assets and had placed him between a rock and a hard place. Shouldn't ninety-year-old men be smoking cigars and playing bridge?

And of course, every time they spoke about this deal, Lester never failed to remind him that he was ecstatic that he was being forced to marry and that maybe, God willing, he'd get a much-desired great-grandchild, preferably a grandson, out of the deal. Lester then launched into his oft-repeated lecture on his lack of commitment to providing an heir to continue the Abbingdon line, that if he didn't hop to it—his words—six hundred years of DNA-soaked history would cease to exist. The art and furniture collected over twenty-four generations would scatter to private collectors all over the world. Abbingdon Castle and its surrounding land would be sold to the highest bidder. The Abbingdons weren't royalty but they were damn close.

And it all rested on Brooks's shoulders...

Or in his loins.

He'd have a kid, one day. Not now. Right now all he wanted to do was save his company.

Brooks took a sip of his whiskey, staring past young

Joshua St. Claire—sleeping now, thank God—to the inky night beyond the window of his Global 7000 jet. The kid was so out of it, he barely registered that he was on a private jet and hadn't noticed the rich leather seats, the fine wood veneers and the stylish carpets and stonework. This jet had just hit the market but he owned one and, being aviation crazy, it annoyed him that neither of his two guests appreciated their luxurious mode of transport.

And his annoyance had nothing to do with the aircraft's hefty price tag, which was upward of half a billion dollars. This plane was superbly designed, exquisitely manufactured and brilliantly engineered. It was, in its way, a masterpiece. And his guests, like his grandfather, didn't share his passion for anything with an engine and two wings.

His business was damn good. And his life, up until two weeks ago, had been friggin' amazing.

Yet, here he was, planning his wedding. And because the Abbingdon Trust paid for all Abbingdon weddings, he was going to take full advantage and turn his wedding into a massive networking event, inviting all his present clients and anybody he thought could be a potential client. If he was going to put his head in a hangman's noose, then he was going to swing in style.

All he now needed was a bride.

Brooks looked at the cool beauty in the chair across from him and cocked his head. Teresa St. Claire was beautiful; there was no doubt about it. Tall and slim, she rocked an old-school Grace Kelly vibe, classy as hell. Despite the rumors and gossip swirling around her she'd held her head high and he'd yet to see her unhinged, to break into a sweat.

He liked calm women, women who could keep it together when their lives were falling apart. That showed a strength of character few women—hell, few men—possessed. Teresa St. Claire was beautiful, sexy and smart. What more could he want in a wife? The Fixer had also suggested her as a candidate to be his wife; said that she was a possibility and that he could, possibly, make that happen.

Marrying Teresa would've been an elegant, and quick, resolution to his current problem. Except for the little problem that she was crazy about Liam Christopher... He wasn't the most perceptive guy in the world but even he noticed the way she looked at Christopher. Part exasperation, part denial, part annoyance but mostly like all she wanted to do was strip him naked and do several things to him that were X-rated. Brooks knew that he was marrying for convenience, as a means to an end, but he certainly didn't need to watch his wife pine for someone else. Or wish he was someone else.

So he refused The Fixer's offer and settled for his arranging for Teresa to organize his blowout wedding.

What could The Fixer have on her to (a) think that he could get her to agree to marriage and (b) to get her to undertake such a massive event on such short notice? It had to be something...

But Teresa's past didn't concern him and he had bigger worries. Like who might say yes to his crazy-ass proposal to marry him.

In two weeks' time.

Happy bloody birthday to him.

Teresa leaned back in her chair and stared out the high-arched windows of her waterfront office in Seattle, just a few blocks from Pike Market. She loved her view, her open-plan office with its high ceilings, industrial lighting and its hardwood floors. But today all she could think about was the look of betrayal on Joshua's face as she left him at the tightly controlled and monitored rehab facility two hours away. He understood that he had to lie low but, damn, his tightly crossed arms and the emotion washing in and out of his eyes nearly dropped her to her knees.

She wanted to believe his denials about his addictions, she really did. But she still didn't know how to explain that small puncture mark on his arm. Had someone injected him and then, in his woozy and hazy state, manipulated him to take a flight across the country to Napa to gate-crash Matt's party? Was that possible or was she overreacting, allowing her imagination to run wild because she so badly wanted to believe him?

All her anxiety about Joshua would simply evaporate if she could pay off Joshua's debt. Then they'd both be free. She'd been such a naive fool to believe that when the drug-running charges against Joshua were dropped—thanks to The Fixer—he would get his life together. Silly her.

Most women in their late twenties were concerned about their careers, their young children or their new marriages—and, frequently, a combination of all three—but no, she spent her time stressing about unpaid debts to criminals, her inconvenient attraction to a man who blew hot and cold but whom she couldn't avoid, and rocketing from crisis to crisis. It was times like these that Teresa wished she had a mother to turn to but her mom, like her brother, relied on her. Since her father's death, she'd been the glue holding their family together, the strong one, the capable one, the one who could always make a plan.

It would be so nice to rely on someone else, to have someone in her corner loving and supporting her but she was terrified that that person would, just like her father had, fade on her. Sharing the load meant opening up, allowing herself to be vulnerable, exposing herself...

What if that person left, disappeared on her, leaving her to waft in the wind? No, it was better to hang tough…

Besides, there was only one person who'd scaled her walls to peek inside her soul—she hadn't told anyone else but Liam about Joshua and the stress she was under—and he was even more closed up and messed up than she was. They were a hell of a pair…

Teresa heard a throat clear and lifted her head to see Corinne hovering by her partly open door as if deciding whether to knock or not. Teresa dropped her hands, swallowed her sigh and gestured her assistant inside. Corinne's face reflected the grim mood of the rest of her colleagues: they were worried about the future of Limitless Events, and Teresa didn't blame them. For any event company, Saturday's events would be a death knell and she had no doubt that most of her people were brushing up their résumés.

Teresa gestured for Corinne to sit. When Corinne's eyes met hers, she saw her curiosity and knew a dozen questions were hovering on Corinne's tongue. Teresa's respect for her increased when Corinne just powered up her iPad and asked a simple question. "So, what's the plan?"

Teresa tucked a strand of hair that had fallen from her loose bun behind her ear. "The plan is that we arrange Brooks Abbingdon's big blowout wedding."

Corinne's brown eyes widened. "He's getting married? To whom?" Corinne read the social pages and entertainment magazines with utter dedication and Teresa knew that she was wondering whether she'd missed a crucial piece of gossip.

"He didn't say."

Corinne looked at her like she was, finally, losing it. "I'm sorry? I don't understand."

Yep, crazy. "Brooks didn't tell me who he was marrying. I suspect it's someone very famous and intensely publicity-shy. And that's okay. We don't need her input because Brooks was very explicit in what he wanted."

Corinne leaned forward, her expression intense. "So what does he want?"

Teresa half smiled. "He wants me to recreate Delilah Rhodes and Alex Dane's wedding. With one crucial difference…"

Corinne bounced up and down and gestured Teresa to keep talking. "What? What's the difference?"

"Delilah and Alex had a massive budget."

"Our budget is smaller? Dammit. Okay, we can get creative."

Teresa shook her head. "No, we have an unlimited budget. We can spend what we like, how we like, but it's got to be blow-your-socks-off amazing. But we only have two weeks to get everything organized."

Corinne pulled a smile up onto her face in an effort to appreciate the joke. "Ha ha."

"I wish I were joking. But I'm not. Brooks has thrown Limitless Events a lifeline. Minimal time is the cost of that lifeline." Teresa forced a smile of her own. "But, if we work every hour of the day, maybe we'll all still have jobs at the end of the month."

Teresa watched as confusion and disbelief flew across Corinne's face and gave her assistant a minute to take in the news. She'd come into her office thinking that the company could not possibly recover from Saturday night's fiasco but instead of getting pink slips, they were going to organize the wedding of the year.

How did this happen? Why was this happening? Teresa couldn't answer Corinne's questions, not without explaining that she owed someone a favor and that this was his way of collecting. The Fixer had told her, when he checked on Joshua to see if the $7 million debt was real, that she owed him a nonmonetary favor and she was finally being asked to cough up.

She'd always worried that The Fixer would ask her to do something illegal, something below board—she wasn't an idiot; she knew that he wasn't a law-abiding angel—and she was so relieved that he was asking her to use her skills to repay her debt. Yeah, Brooks's time frame was totally ludicrous but, compared to some of the scenarios she'd imagined, this was child's play. And, thank God, legal.

And best of all, Brooks was still going to pay her. Bonus.

Teresa couldn't help wondering how Brooks had heard of The Fixer and whether asking for help on organizing his wedding was all he'd asked of the man who, it was reported, could arrange anything, anywhere. She'd heard of The Fixer through her previous boss, Mariella Santiago-Marshall, but how had Brooks connected with her sure-his-hands-are-dirty angel? It had to be word of mouth, whispered over boardroom tables or over glasses of five-hundred-dollar whiskey. But unlike hers, The Fixer's fee to Brooks was sure to be hard cash.

Hey, she didn't care. She was ridding herself of one debt. And she'd use the enormous fee Brooks had offered her to pay some of Josh's debt, hoping to placate Joshua's money lender and buy them some time.

But nobody would be getting paid if they didn't get to work. Teresa looked at Corinne and issued the first of many instructions. "I'd like you to make up a mood board of all our most expensive weddings to show to Brooks, to get an idea of what he does and doesn't want. Focus on the Newport Bridge wedding."

When Corinne left the room, Teresa stood up and walked over to her window and watched the Seattle-Bremerton ferry cross Elliott Bay. She placed her hand on the window and sighed at the wet, miserable day. Normally, the weather didn't bother her but today it just reminded her of her soggy heart, her tear-soaked soul.

She missed Liam…

Get used to it; you're going to be missing him for a long, long time.

Never again would she feel his mouth on hers, the scratch of his two-or three-or four-day stubble on her skin. Her body wouldn't hum in pleasure as he traced her lips with his, drawing out the anticipation of his tongue moving into her mouth to tangle with hers. She doubted that she'd ever again experience the flood of wet, warm heat between her legs as his hands tightened on her hips and he laid siege to her mouth.

Memories of how he made her feel rushed over Teresa. He'd slowly, too slowly, pull her shirt from the waistband of her trousers or skirt, his fingers drawing bright, bold patterns on her skin. Liam loved to turn her around in order to trace the bumps of her spine, his hard and rigid cock pressing into her butt. No matter how much she begged, Liam treated her like a present he wanted to take his time opening, slowly removing her clothes, one feminine piece at a time. His words burned her skin—"You're so pretty," "God, I want you," "Can't wait to watch you come"—and with a flick of his tongue across a lace-covered nipple, he'd have her hovering on the edge of an orgasm, desperate to take flight.

He'd take his time, too much time, before slipping his fingers into her panties, to find the heat between her slick folds. He always knew how to touch her, whether it was with a flick of his finger or a swipe of his tongue. He'd bring her to orgasm, sometimes once, a couple of times twice, with his fingers and his tongue, not entering her until she was limp and languid and so very, very well loved.

Then he'd push inside her, hot and long and devastatingly masculine and build her up again. And again. And yet again before allowing her to crash and burn and flame.

None of that would happen again.

The thought made her want to cry. But she didn't because she was Teresa St. Claire, and when had tears helped with anything? No, the best she could do was to soldier on because that was what she did best.

Like brightly colored pieces of a shattered mosaic pile, Teresa always picked up all the pieces she could and rearranged them to make a new pattern or picture. But damn, it was getting harder and harder to do.

In his office at the Abbingdon private airport on the outskirts of Seattle, Brooks lifted his head to watch an ACJ—an Airbus Corporate Jet—land on the runway to the left of his office on the top floor of the office block that housed Abbingdon Airlines' headquarters. The jet was exquisite and the touchdown perfect on the slick runway. Brooks looked at his watch and yep, the limousines were leaving their hangar to pick up the twenty guests who had flown in, as he'd heard, for *Carmen*, playing at the Seattle Opera House. He'd been offered tickets to attend but couldn't remember by whom.

Brooks shrugged. It didn't matter since he didn't have time to waste attending the theater when he had a wife to find, a future to secure.

Pulling his eyes off the ACJ and its fluid, feminine lines, Brooks looked at his computer monitor and opened the email he'd received while he was salivating over the jet. Brooks read the two-word correspondence:

For consideration.

Knowing, without a smidgen of doubt, that the message was from The Fixer, Brooks double-clicked on the first of three files. A photograph of a raven-haired beauty popped up in front of him and Brooks lifted his eyebrows in appreciation. Beneath the photograph The Fixer had a brief paragraph detailing why she was a suitable candidate to become the first Mrs. Brooks Abbingdon. In Mari Ruiz's case, she was a divorcée who'd been skinned by her husband, leaving her with a taste for high living but with no one to fund it. She had two degrees, was a champion ballroom dancer and spoke three languages. She was also a gourmet cook.

Mmm, interesting. Brooks opened the next file, a sultry redhead, who was a young widow looking for a dad for her three kids, all under the age of seven. Brooks dismissed her immediately; this situation was messed up already without adding kids to the chaos. Sighing, Brooks opened the third file and sucked in a surprised breath.

Well, well. Nicolette Ryan wasn't someone he'd expected to find on his computer at nine thirty in the morning. He knew Nicolette, had been introduced to her once or twice and he'd had her microphone pointed in his face on various occasions. She was intelligent and witty and, holy hell, with her long black hair and petite frame, and those expressive, brown-black eyes, as sexy as sin. He liked her. She was the one journalist most of his friends and acquaintances found tolerable.

But why was she on his list of prospective brides? Intrigued, Brooks read The Fixer's report. Nicolette Ryan was, per his comments, brainy and ambitious and wanted to make a break into serious reporting. Apparently, she'd been floating a documentary film to any producer who'd listen but nobody was taking her seriously. The project was important to her—personally important and related to something in her past—and The Fixer was convinced that there was little she wouldn't do to see the project on the big screen.

Brooks scrolled down, annoyed to realize that The Fixer hadn't explained his cryptic comment about her past. Brooks touched the reply button and banged out a quick message asking for an explanation. He was about to hit the Send button when the thought occurred that, had The Fixer wanted him to have that information, he would've given it. A demanding email wouldn't change his mind.

The point was: Nicolette Ryan wanted something and if he could provide her the means to achieve that goal, she might be amenable to a temporary marriage.

Brooks flipped back to look at the picture of the sultry brunette but, compared to Nicolette, she looked over-the-top, too high-maintenance.

He'd met Nicolette; he liked her and there'd been a buzz of attraction when they spoke. It wasn't love at first sight—who believed in that anyway?—but something definitely arced between them.

He was hopeful. After all, everyone had their price—his was Abbingdon Airlines—and he just needed to find out whether her documentary was important enough to her to sacrifice her single status. God, he hoped so.

He was running out of time.

Three

Nobody in Seattle refused to take his calls and Teresa St. Claire wouldn't be the first.

Liam stepped into the large open-plan office and met the wide eyes of the young receptionist sitting behind a sleek desk. Early twenties, first job out of college, wide eyes and desperate to please. Child's play.

"I'm on my way to see Ms. St. Claire."

Liam had to give her credit; she did jump up from her desk and did try to run after him, but his legs were longer and her headphones were connected to her laptop. Besides, he was a foot taller, bigger and broader; how on earth could she stop him?

Walking across the open-plan offices, he ignored the buzz of chatter his presence generated and ignored the eyes boring into his back. Limitless Events occupied one corner of the top floor of this building and high, arched windows flooded the office with natural light. He flicked a glance outside; it was still raining, and he thought that Teresa had a hell of a view. Slowing down, he approached a messy desk in front of the only self-contained office and growled when he saw that the doors were closed. He looked at Teresa's PA, surprised to see her leaning back in her chair, legs crossed, a smirk on her pretty face.

"To what do we owe the honor of your illustrious presence, Mr. Christopher?" Oh, yeah, there was a ton of snark under the sweet smile.

"Cut the crap, Corinne. You know damn well that I've left six messages and that I've been trying to talk to her since early Sunday morning," Liam retorted. "She's avoiding me."

"So you thought the best way to deal with her was to show up at her place of work?" Corinne had the audacity to roll her eyes. "Do you know anything about women, Mr. Christopher?"

Obviously not. Up until Teresa appeared in his life, he thought he had. He could charm them into bed, show them a good time and when he was bored, extracted himself quietly, easing his way out of their lives with flowers or perfume or more expensive gifts, depending on the woman and the situation. Once, when that Russian ballet dancer refused to go quietly, he'd needed to say goodbye with a holiday in Cannes and a diamond tennis bracelet. But generally, women weren't difficult.

And then there was Teresa…

"Can I go in?"

Corinne bared her teeth at him. "Let me see if she has time for you."

Before Corinne could connect the call, Liam turned at the sound of a door opening. Teresa stood in the open doorway, looking beautiful but fragile. Her creamy complexion was two shades paler than usual, her sexy mouth was pulled tight and the bags under her eyes were a darker blue than her irises. But as he was coming to accept, Teresa could look like a ghoul and she'd still manage to turn him on.

"What are you doing here, Liam?"

Since there was only one answer to that question— he wanted to speak to her, dammit!—he shook his head and took two steps in her direction. When he stood close enough to her to inhale her sweet breath, close enough for his chest to flirt with hers, he placed both hands under her elbows and lifted her off her feet. Hell, his woman, *this* woman, needed to eat more! Walking her backward, he deposited her inside her office, back on her two-inch, ice-pick heels—black today to match her severe black suit and, probably, her mood—and kicked the door shut with his foot.

When he heard the snick of the lock, he shoved his hands into the pockets of his suit pants. His hands, stupid things, desperately wanted to pull that black sweater from her skirt and lift it up and over her head. Would her bra be black, too? Her panties? He thought so but he sure as hell would like to make sure.

"I do not appreciate you barging into my office," Teresa told him, trying to sound snotty.

"I do not appreciate you not taking my calls," Liam whipped back, not fazed by her cool eyes and her tight mouth. He knew her well enough to see the pain lurking beneath all that liquid, velvet blue, knew that she was fighting the urge to weep or scream.

She had a right to.

Liam couldn't resist running a thumb over her cheekbone, skirting the edges of her eye sockets. "Have you slept at all since the weekend?"

He knew that her pride had her wanting to lie but at

the last minute she shook her head. "No, I've dozed here and there."

"Things will seem better after you've slept."

Teresa stepped away from him and walked away, dropping into the sleek office chair behind her desk. She placed her hands on the table and her amazing eyes flashed blue fire. "So if I sleep, will I wake up and find that my brother didn't gate-crash Matt's party, you didn't hit him, he wasn't seen on YouTube and I didn't have to force him to stay in rehab, with him insisting that he's not an addict? Will that just all go away with some sleep?"

She had him there. "No."

"Exactly." Teresa scratched her forehead and she released a long stream of air and her shoulders fell from somewhere near her ears. "I don't want to fight with you, Liam."

"I don't want to fight, either."

"But I can't deal with you right now. Right now I have another commission, an event to organize, and everything is riding on it." Teresa picked up a pen and rolled it between her palms. "I can't be distracted and I need to focus. And I really do believe that it's better that we not see each other anymore."

"BS," Liam shot back. "You're just feeling overwhelmed. Possibly scared."

Teresa nodded. "Sure I am. But maybe I am also trying to protect you. I'm not good for you, Liam."

Liam slapped his hands on his hips, anger coursing through him. She sounded too much like his mother, who'd made her own disparaging comments about Teresa over the past few weeks. Not good enough, a tart, so little class. They were both wrong but there was only one person whose mind he wanted to change. "I'm a big boy. I don't need you protecting me."

"No matter what I say, there are people out there, including your mother, who believe I had an affair with your father, who think I've only latched on to you because I have my eyes on your company."

He didn't give a rat's ass what other people thought and, honestly, he didn't care much what his mother thought. "So? Let them think what they want."

A pencil hit his chest and dropped to the floor. Liam looked at it, raised one eyebrow and returned his eyes to Teresa's face. On the plus side, she had color in her cheeks. She also looked like she was about to blow.

"Liam, *listen* to me. You and me, it's… Whatever the hell we had, it's over! Whatever it was, it's done."

Liam sent her a steady look. "I'm not trying to be a jerk, Teresa, but it's not as easy as that."

"Just go, Liam. Please."

God, this woman was as stubborn as a boulder. He could tell her that their attraction hadn't died, that it would take more than her calling it to end this craziness between them. They couldn't just switch off the taps and walk away. Like her, he couldn't define what they had but it sure as hell wasn't something that could be simply and easily dismissed. He'd tried that several times and it never worked. But that argument wouldn't work with her so he latched on to what was tangible. "Linus's will stipulates that we still have to work together at Christopher Corporation for a whole year."

His statement detonated fireworks in her eyes. And not the good kind. "The corporation? That's what you are thinking about?"

Well, no. He was thinking about taking her to bed but knew that if he made that suggestion he might leave her office minus a few of his essential body parts.

And that thought pissed him off, big-time. And once he

acknowledged his anger, it took on a life of its own. He'd been worrying about her for days and he had to storm her citadel to check whether she was okay.

Teresa placed her fingertips on her forehead. "We can't keep doing this, Liam. At some point we have to accept that we are bad for each other."

Liam surged to his feet, walked over to her chair and placing his hands on her waist, pulled her up. He gripped her luscious butt and yanked her into him, allowing his hard erection to push into her stomach. "Feel that? That isn't bad, dammit!"

Teresa looked up at him and he could see her body warring with her brain, each equally stubborn. He dipped his head down and slapped his lips against hers. Her mouth immediately opened beneath his and he swept inside, determined to show her that desire like this was worth fighting for, holding on to, keeping. Yeah, they weren't great at communicating but this, this they could do. This they couldn't fake, lie about, deny.

As for the other stuff, they could work on it...

Liam felt Teresa soften and when she pressed her breasts into his chest, he slowed his kiss down, needing to savor her, to explore her intense combination of flavors. He could taste her hazelnut-flavor coffee, toothpaste and a tart sweetness that was all Teresa. Pulling her jersey up, he placed his hands on her lower back, easily spanning her slim waist. The smell of soft, fragrant, heated skin drifted up to his and he felt his knees soften, his head swim. This was the only woman who'd ever managed to create fog in his brain, remove the saliva from his mouth, shut down his thought processes.

Not for the first time Liam decided that she scared the crap out of him.

Liam pulled back from the kiss and lifted his hand to

hold the back of her head, his fingers pushing up and under the loose bun she habitually wore. Risking her ire but needing to see her hair down, he pulled out her pins and her thick blond hair cascaded over his hands, down her back. With her hair down she looked softer, more vulnerable and younger and, if that were at all possible, sexier.

Teresa rested her cheek on his pec and lightly placed her hands on his waist as if she couldn't decide whether to hold him or not. "Stop fighting me, Teresa, and let me hold you."

Teresa stiffened in his arms and then he heard her long sigh and slowly, so slowly, her arms moved around his body and she buried her nose in his shirt.

"Everything is so messed up, Liam."

And she was, as she always did, trying to handle everything herself. "I know, honey."

"I can't let you help. I don't know how to accept help," Teresa said, her voice so low he had to bend his head to hear her soft words. "I need to sort this out myself, Liam."

He dropped a kiss into her hair. "Why?"

Teresa took her time answering. "Because people have told me, all my life, that they would be there for me. Then they left."

"I won't do that to you, Teresa."

Teresa pulled back, pulled her teeth between her lips and when Liam looked into her eyes, the pain within them nearly dropped him to his knees. "Maybe, maybe not. But I can't take that chance because you, disappointing me again, is a step too far, a bridge that will blow up once I cross it. I'm not strong enough to cope with that, as well as the rest of my life falling apart. Frankly, Liam, I'm starting to believe that I'm not very strong at all."

Teresa walked over to her desk, stared down at it and tapped her finger on the sleek wood. He watched her profile as her eyes moved from her desk to the window to right at the view of Elliott Bay. When she spoke again, he heard her uncertainty and, dammit, the fear in her voice. "I need some time, Liam, probably quite a bit of it."

"I can't give that to you," Liam replied.

Christopher Corporation, and the terms of his father's will, demanded her presence and involvement in the company. And besides, if he gave her the space she demanded, wouldn't he be doing exactly what she expected, running when she needed him to plant his feet and stick?

"My brother owes money to dangerous people. Money that I am in the process of trying to find. I have a high-society, over-the-top wedding to organize in two weeks' time so that I can save my company's reputation and buy us some time with those previously mentioned mobsters. And I still need to face Matt Richmond and apologize once again for ruining his gala evening."

"While organizing a wedding isn't in my skill set, I am thrilled you have work and I know you will do a fantastic job. I will bring you late-night pizzas and early-morning coffee if that's what you need me to do." She was listening to him so he took the opportunity to float a few options available.

"Allow me to lend you the money to pay off your brother's debts. I have the money and we can work out a repayment plan because I know that you are too proud to take a handout. Yeah, apologizing to Matt is something I can't do for you but I can hold your hand while you do it."

Teresa closed her eyes and Liam desperately wanted to rub away the single tear that dared to escape. But he knew that if he acknowledged her emotion, he'd lose her. So he just kept his eyes on her face and waited for her response.

"Please go, Liam. Go before I take you up on one or all of your sweet offers. Go before I start to believe in you."

To hell with that. Instead of walking to the door, Liam wrapped his arms around her and held on tight. Resting his chin in her hair, he held her until he felt her body stiffen, until she started to push away. Knowing he'd pushed her far enough today, he decided to retreat so he placed a kiss on her temple and released his grip. "I'm going to go. But I'll call you later, okay?"

Teresa nodded.

Liam tipped her chin up with the side of his thumb and waited until her eyes met his. All that deep, velvety blue was a sharp smack to his heart. "And when I do, take my damn calls."

Four

Teresa watched her office door close behind Liam's rather fine back view—oh, who was she kidding, viewed from every angle Liam was sexy—and she staggered to her chair and dropped into it, feeling like a leaky balloon. She could fight with Liam, roll around the sheets with Liam but Liam being kind, sensitive? Generous? She hated him acting like that.

But only because you want to curl up in his arms, in his strength. You hate it because it tempts you to take a breath, to allow someone else to take the wheel, to steer the ship. And God forbid that you let go for one minute. Who knows what could happen? The world might stop turning!

Teresa frowned at her inner sarcastic self and picked up a pen, thinking that it was high time she went back to work, that she paid some attention to saving her business.

But as hard as she tried, she couldn't concentrate.

Was she that much of a control freak? Possibly. Handing

over control to anyone on anything made her feel twitchy and disoriented. Yes, she kept a tight control on her life, and her emotions, because if she didn't, people side-winded her because she made the mistake of trusting them to do what they said they would. Her father had told her, time and again, that he'd always be there for her, that he'd never leave her, that she was "his girl," but when he needed to make a choice, he'd left the country and never returned. She shouldn't be angry at him for dying but, dammit, she was.

Her mother was also skilled at making promises she couldn't keep. "I'll get a job next week, honey."

"Yes, I promise I'll come to your school recital."

"I will stop drinking, smoking, staying out late."

Words, to her mom, were cheap, and promises weren't ever something that were meant to be kept. To her taking the easy way out was always the better option and that words were easily forgotten. Joshua followed in their mother's footsteps but Teresa went in the opposite direction.

Because words spoken did have consequences, and promises were supposed to be kept. She refused to cut corners and she never made excuses. And she owned her life, her choices and her mistakes. But maybe because her childhood and teenage years had been such a tumultuous time, maybe she did now try to control every little thing so that it wouldn't come back to bite her in the butt.

So yeah, she owned that she was a control freak and wasn't able to roll with the punches. But punches hurt, dammit, and why should she have to experience the pain if she could avoid it altogether?

Teresa heard the brisk knock on her door and then Corinne pushed it open. "Hey, you have an unexpected visitor."

Corinne's emphasis on *unexpected* made Teresa sit up straighter. "Who?"

"Me."

Oh, hell, no! Teresa watched as Nicolette Ryan brushed past Corinne to stand just inside her office. Teresa looked past Nicolette to Corinne, who lifted her hands in a "what-could-I-do?" shrug.

So far this morning, both Liam and this entertainment reporter had pushed by her gatekeepers and barged into her office. If this was going to be a trend, she'd need better security.

Teresa narrowed her eyes at Corinne before transferring her gaze onto the petite woman standing in front of her. She was gorgeous; she'd always thought so. With her black hair hitting her waist and brown-black eyes, even features and a spray of freckles across her nose, Nicolette was a combination of vamp and girl-next-door and, as a result, had millions of fans of both sexes. She wore a tight, deep navy skirt and a white, long-sleeved, plain silk shirt that skimmed her curves and the most amazing, quirky pair of bright red heels.

Teresa, reluctantly, felt herself tumbling head over heels in love with her shoes.

"I do like your style."

Teresa winced, wishing she could pull the words back. She was supremely annoyed with this woman—her ongoing coverage of Saturday night's suck-fest had kept Matt's disastrous gala in the news—and she didn't want to admire a damn thing about her.

But to be fair, she liked Nicolette's dress sense. She always managed to look classy despite wearing tight and short dresses and sky-high heels. Yeah, she showed a bit of cleavage and a lot of leg but she never stepped over the line into trashy. And the same could be said of her reporting; she never made sly innuendos or flirted with the truth. She reported on what she was told and didn't embellish.

And maybe that was the only reason Teresa hadn't tossed her through her partially open window to the street below.

"You have a lot of cheek showing your face here," Teresa stated, pleased with her calm voice.

"It's been said that the one attribute I don't lack is cheek." Nicolette gestured to the seat on the opposite side of her desk. "Do you mind if I sit down?"

"If you've come to ask me for a follow-up interview, then I really wouldn't bother. I don't have anything to say."

Nicolette sat down, crossed her legs and swung her foot. "I'd love you to give me a comment, or better, an interview—"

Teresa growled and Nicolette grinned. She held up her hand. "As I was about to say, that's not the reason I'm here."

Teresa didn't believe that for a minute but okay, she'd hear her out. "Then why don't you get to the point and tell me why you are here?"

Nicolette inhaled and Teresa noticed the panic in her eyes and her tight grip on her handbag. "I'm getting married and you, apparently, are planning my wedding."

No, she wasn't. Teresa knew that it had been a tough couple of days but she was pretty sure that she'd never agreed to organize Nicolette Ryan's wedding.

The girl was crackers, possibly delusional. "Okay, so who are you marrying?"

"Brooks Abbingdon."

Yeah, it still didn't make any sense.

And Teresa St. Claire looked as gobsmacked as she still felt. Because, really, Nic was still waiting for a camera crew to pop out from behind a door or a screen, yelling "just kidding" and "you've been pranked."

Nic turned her head to look at the closed door to Teresa's office but it wasn't opening; she could hear no movement behind the door. Nobody, dammit, was there and nobody was about to return her life to normal, to tell her that this was a big mistake, a dream, a crazy prank.

"You are marrying Brooks?" Teresa said after another minute of stunned silence.

Nic nodded.

"Okay, wow." Teresa stood up, placed her hands on her desk and pulled in a deep breath. "I didn't know that you and Brooks were seeing each other."

They hadn't been. In fact, up until yesterday evening, she'd just admired—okay, lusted and drooled over—Brooks from afar. His visit to her apartment last night changed everything. No, his proposal had upended her life and sent it spinning in a whole new direction.

And it was one she needed to take.

"Take every opportunity to tell Jane's story, Nic. Promise me."

"I promise, Gran."

Did that promise cover marriage? Surely not. But a big and bright opportunity came with the marriage and that was covered by her promise to her dying grandmother ten years before. So there was no, or very little, wiggle room. And Brooks had been clear; marriage meant funding for her project, guaranteed distribution and the opportunity to make a difference. If she didn't marry Brooks, her project—the one that was dear to her heart and the one she spent every spare minute she had working on—would never see the light of day. And she couldn't let Janie, or her grandmother, down.

Teresa stood up straight, shook her head and looked bemused. "I don't know what to say. And when I find myself without words, coffee normally works. Would you like some?"

Nic thanked her and Teresa left the room, muttering something about it being a helluva day. Nic dropped her bag to the floor, uncrossed her legs and stared at the old, original hardwood floor. She couldn't believe that she was sitting here, in Teresa's office, talking about her upcoming wedding to one of Seattle's most eligible bachelors.

A man she thought sexier than Idris Elba and hotter than Charlie Hunnam. A man who'd, for some odd reason, wanted to marry her. In a couple of weeks' time.

Was this really happening to her? She hadn't dreamed everything that happened last night?

It had been a normal Tuesday evening and she'd been in her apartment, working on Jane's project, something she did whenever she had a free moment. She'd also been waiting for a pizza delivery and muttered "Hallelujah" when her intercom buzzed. Thinking it was her regular pizza man, she told Pete to come on up, hitting the button to open the front door downstairs. Knowing that Pete ran up the stairs, she waited a minute before heading to the door, flinging it open. God, she was hungry…

Instead of a classic margherita pie, Brooks Abbingdon stood in the hallway, his fist raised.

"You're not my pizza." But damn, she could've taken a bite out of him as easily.

Brooks's grin was slow, sexy and machine-gun lethal. "Sorry to disappoint you."

Instinctively, she knew that she couldn't give this man an inch or he'd take her a thousand miles. And she might let him. *Get yourself and, more important, your hormones under control!*

"You should be sorry because I'm starving and while you smell good, my pizza smells better."

Brooks's mouth twitched with amusement and those eyes, an unusual shade of gold, lightened. "Care to share?"

Nic deliberately attempted to look and sound bored. Difficult when her stomach was doing loops under her rib cage. "Care to tell me why you are standing outside my door?"

"Share your pizza and I will."

He might have a story he wanted covered, a piece of hot gossip. While most of her sources called her on her private number or emailed her, one or two had asked to meet her face-to-face. Though none had, admittedly, had the balls to show up at her door.

Should she take a chance and let him in? Or should she insist that they meet in a public place? What the hell could Brooks Abbingdon want to tell her? She'd never once thought he was the type to dish dirt.

But why else would he be here?

Nic quickly recalled what she knew of Brooks Abbingdon, immediately discounting his wealth and good looks. All his ex-girlfriends, and they'd been a few, had only good things to say about him…he was a nice guy, a gentleman, that he'd make a great husband if he ever chose to settle down. Because he treated his exes well, Nic thought she'd be safe enough if she let him into her apartment.

"My sharing my pizza depends on why you are here." Nic stepped back into her hallway and jerked her head to tell him to come inside. She closed the door behind him and sent him a cool smile.

By the time she'd put a beer in his hand and invited him to sit, her pizza had arrived and Nic, above Brooks's objection, handed Pete his money and carried the box back into the living room. She placed the box on the coffee table in front of Brooks and walked into her kitchen to choose plates and silverware. It annoyed her to realize that she'd chosen her best plates and had dug two linen napkins out of a drawer. Was she really trying to impress Brooks?

Irritated, Nic dumped plates next to the box and handed Brooks a napkin. She opened the box, slid a piece of pizza onto her plate and tucked her feet up under her bottom. Brooks surprised her by picking up a slice of pizza and putting the pointy end straight into his mouth. He swirled a piece of melted cheese around his finger, sucked it off and Nic felt a wave of hot heat surge between her legs.

Do not jump him, do not stand up and slap your mouth against his.

"Good pie," Brooks said in between bites. "Where do you order from?"

"A little Italian place on the next corner," Nic replied. Because she hated feeling so out-of-control attracted to him, she put a whole bunch of spice into her voice. "I thought the deal was that you tell me something good and *then* you share my pizza."

Brooks rested his arms on his muscled thighs, his hands dangling between his knees. Then he looked her dead in the eye and when he spoke his voice was heart-attack serious.

"Okay, if you insist. I want you to marry me. In two weeks' time. If you say yes, I will provide you the funding to produce your documentary project and I will open doors to you so that it can get the widest distribution possible. I have enough money and connections to make sure that happens."

Nic laughed at his absurd statement and rolled her eyes. She was about to tell him to stop wasting her time and then his words sank in. He knew about her project…

He knew.

About her project.

Nobody, apart from a handful of people she'd spoken to about Jane's Nightmare, knew how she spent her free time. How on earth had Brooks found out?

"How do you know about my documentary?"

Brooks waved her words away. "I just do. And it can happen, if you marry me."

Honestly, this was too bizarre, like a scene out of a B-grade movie. Who shows up on a Tuesday evening and starts proposing to a random woman? And, despite their meeting once or twice before and some very mild flirting, she was very random indeed.

"This is a good opportunity for you, Nicolette."

Yeah, first time she'd heard marriage described in those terms. Nic tipped her head. "Okay, I'll play your ridiculous game. What if I say no?"

Remorse flickered across his face but it was quickly chased away by determination. "Then I kill your project. I have enough money and contacts in the entertainment world to do that, as well. And by kill it, I mean it will never see the light of day. *Ever.*"

Brooks reached for another slice of pizza but Nic was quicker. She whipped up the box and pulled it onto her lap. She stared at Brooks, wondering if behind all that sexy was insanity. "Are you mad? You're talking crazy, and crazy talk does not get rewarded with pizza!"

Brooks simply pulled the box from her, helped himself to another piece of pizza and, in between bites, explained his offer. They'd be married in name only, for a period of time yet to be determined, but the marriage had to, to keep the gossip to the minimum, last longer than a year.

In addition to funding her documentary, she'd also get a significant amount of money for one year as his wife. For every additional year they remained married, she would receive a large sum of cash. If, after a year, she wanted out, he wouldn't contest the divorce.

Children weren't a prerequisite but he wasn't opposed to fathering a child. Should she choose to have one with him, he'd pay her living expenses, post-divorce, for the rest of her life. But that meant them sleeping together and while she wished she could emphatically state that would only happen when hell iced over, honesty had her admitting that she'd have difficulty avoiding his bed.

Really, what hot-blooded—or even moderately warm-blooded woman, wouldn't? He was hot. As in blistering.

"Why do you need to get married?"

"You don't need to know that."

"And why do you need to be married by month's end?"

"You don't need to know that, either." Brooks's reply left her with more questions than answers. He'd given her until this morning to decide—a scant eight hours!—and she'd spent all of last night pacing her apartment, both intrigued and pissed that she was considering saying yes to his ridiculous offer.

Oh, she didn't care about the money and, while she did want kids sometime in the future, she didn't need to marry to get one. So the only reason to consider Brooks's offer was related to how important it was for her to tell Jane's story and to highlight human trafficking. She owed it to her sister. She needed to tell the world about her because maybe, just maybe, it would save one girl's life.

She worked with street girls, spoke to at-risk teenagers, but her documentary would reach so many more people, might save more lives. And, on screen, Jane would always be remembered.

When Brooks called her at half past seven this morning, she'd agreed to his crazy proposal. The man, damn him, hadn't seemed surprised to hear her reluctant "yes."

It was almost as if he knew her better than she knew herself.

Nic heard footsteps behind her and watched as Teresa placed a tray on her desk, the smell of freshly ground beans wafting her way. Since last night she hadn't been able to eat or drink and her tongue started to salivate. It took all her willpower not to grab that mug of coffee and suck it down.

Teresa leaned her butt against the edge of the desk and crossed her feet at her ankles. Cradling her cup in her hands, she looked at Nic over the rim. "I'm not very happy with you right now."

Honestly, she had bigger worries than gaining Teresa St. Claire's approval. "Because of my coverage of Matt's party? Or my reporting on the ensuing chaos?"

"The latter." Teresa lifted one slim shoulder. "Wouldn't you be?"

She wouldn't lie. "Sure. But any journalist worth his or her salt would've covered the story."

Teresa started to argue, hauled in her words and Nic's Spidey sense quivered. She slowly lowered her cup from her mouth and looked at Teresa. Why was she acting squirrelly?

"You organized Matt's event. You didn't have anything to do with that guy crashing the party," Nic stated and saw Teresa's eyes flare at the mention of the young man. "Nobody could blame you for the bad ending."

"Of course they can't," Teresa quickly replied. Too quickly. Why did she think Teresa was lying? Oh, hell, yes, there was much, much more to this story than she was privy to. And, while she wanted to push and pry, to get to the heart of the matter, she couldn't because she wasn't here as a reporter, she was here as Brooks Abbingdon's fiancée.

And how bizarre did that sound? But maybe she could be both...

Before she could formulate her first probing question, Teresa pulled up a big smile that was as fake as the plastic surgery she routinely saw on the red carpet. "So you're going to marry Brooks."

Apparently so.

"That's so exciting! How long have you been seeing each other?"

Nic wished she could tell her that they'd met fourteen hours before but knew that would be placing a match to a flame of gas. "Long enough."

Long enough to decide to sacrifice her freedom for her career and for a project she'd promised her gran she'd complete.

"Brooks told me that he wants an over-the-top, blow-your-socks-off wedding. He's given me an unlimited budget and no instructions except to tell me that it will happen in two weeks' time, venue to be decided."

Nic pulled in her breath, shook her head and nailed Teresa with a hard glare. "That's not going to happen. It will be a small, understated wedding with minimal fuss, preferably in court."

"Okay," Teresa muttered. "Flowers?"

This was a business arrangement not a parade. "None."

"Do you have a dress?"

"I have a white pantsuit that would be suitable," Nic lobbed back.

Teresa looked like she'd swallowed a bug. "Guests?"

"Him, me and whoever is authorized to marry us," Nic said, her tone final. "Do we need anyone else?"

Leaning back, Teresa picked up her phone and tapped the screen with fast-moving fingers. Nic heard phone ringing and realized that Teresa had put the phone on speaker mode. Brooks's deep "Hello" sent a shiver of awareness down her spine. She was stupidly, ruthlessly attracted to her wretched blackmailer!

"Brooks, we have a problem," Teresa calmly stated.

"I'm paying you an extraordinary amount of money for there not to be problems, Teresa," Brooks stated.

"Well, I have no problem spending your money but your fiancée definitely does. You both seem to have very different ideas on what you want from this wedding and I am, not surprisingly, confused."

"Is she there with you?" Brooks demanded.

Nic answered before Teresa could. "*She* is. And *she* is not happy about any of this."

He was a smart man; he'd understand that she was talking about more than the wedding. "You've made that clear, Nic."

Nic? Nobody but Jess and Gran called her Nic. Coming from his mouth her name sounded feminine and, dammit, sweet. Almost tender.

"What I suggest," Teresa said in her no-nonsense voice, "is that you two meet and decide what you want. Bearing in mind that I have minimal time, I need you to get back to me by tomorrow morning on exactly what type of wedding you want. And I need you to cover everything: flowers, music, guests, type of food, potential venues, budget. *Everything.*"

"What a nightmare," Nic muttered. She was still getting used to the idea of getting hitched; now she had to make definitive decisions around her wedding day? Could she take a breath first?

"All right," Brooks agreed. "We'll meet up tonight and thrash it out."

"Good. I need everything you come up with by tomorrow morning," Teresa said, her tone crisp. "And Brooks?"

"Yeah?"

Teresa smiled at Nic and Nic sensed a warming of her polar-cold attitude. "If you want people to take this engagement seriously, you should buy your fiancée a ring. Preferably one that can be seen from space."

Five

Later that day Teresa, shaky with hunger and exhaustion, heard the sound of a heavy masculine tread outside her office door and barely had any energy to react. If the person outside her door was a burglar, he could take what he wanted. If it was someone with nastier ideas, well, then, she didn't much care. She was *that* tired.

But really, logically, it was probably just Dan, the night janitor, waging the war on dust bunnies and trash baskets.

Pushing her glasses up onto her nose, Teresa stared at the figures on her Excel spreadsheet, trying to make sense of the data on the screen. She'd been crunching numbers all afternoon, building cash flow forecasts and up-to-date financials. She needed accurate information regarding her company, boiled down to how much she had (x) and that would last her how long (y)?

Without Brooks's commission, she was looking at weeks, not months. With his project she had another six months. But what happened after that? Would she have work? Would her reputation recover? Had it taken too many hits?

What then? What the hell would she do?

Teresa placed a hand on her stomach, felt the room spin so she turned sideways and dropped her head between her knees. For the first time since she was a kid she felt truly scared, utterly vulnerable. She couldn't lose her company, it was what she did, who she was. This was all she had.

And she hadn't even addressed the issue of sucking money from the company to make a part payment toward Joshua's debt.

Teresa felt the energy in the room change and one of the many ropes wrapped around her lungs loosened. When Liam placed a large hand on her back, another rope dropped away and she felt like she could suck in a tiny breath.

Damn him for making her feel better, stronger, more in control. "Take a long, deep breath and try to relax."

Teresa wanted to lift her head to send him a "get real" look but her head felt like it weighed the equivalent of a baby elephant. And if she could relax, she wouldn't have her head between her legs and the room wouldn't be spinning. But her dizziness might also be a result of not eating for the last forty-eight hours. Coffee didn't have the nutritional value of vegetables or protein. Frankly, coffee really needed to up its game.

When Teresa felt like her lungs could function, she lifted her head and was happy to find that the world had stabilized. Liam, wearing faded jeans and a cranberry-colored sweater, was on his haunches in front of her, looking all handsome and hot. She leaned forward to kiss him but he just placed the back of his hand against her forehead.

"You don't have a fever. Do you have a stomachache?"

Teresa swatted his hand away. "Stop fussing, Liam. I'm fine. What are you doing here?"

Liam placed his forearm on his knee, innately at ease as he rested on the balls of his feet. "You are not fine. You are exhausted, hungry and stressed out. Overworked and at the end of your rope."

Teresa rolled her eyes, uncomfortable with exactly how accurate his diagnosis was. "I needed to run some figures."

"At nine at night?" Liam retorted. He stood up and placed his hands on his hips. "It couldn't wait until tomorrow?"

Probably. But she would not have been able to sleep until she had an accurate view of where she stood. Then again, she probably wouldn't sleep now that she did have an accurate view of the situation. Facing bankruptcy was an excellent reason to stay awake worrying.

Teresa leaned back in her chair, raising her head to look into Liam's frustrated face. "Why are you here?"

Liam picked up her phone and waved it from side to side. "You're not answering your phone. Again."

Teresa snatched it out of his hand and tapped the screen. When it remained stubbornly black, she grimaced. "It doesn't have any juice."

"Which is an accurate description of you."

Liam bent over, rested his hands on her knees and Teresa felt lust, and warmth, dance across her skin. "We need to talk about the next Christopher Corporation board meeting and your expected attendance."

Teresa opened her mouth to argue but Liam squeezed her knee. "But not tonight, honey. Tonight all you need to do is eat and then sleep."

Throw a bath and sex into that scenario and she would be in heaven. Actually, maybe just a bath because, as talented as Liam was and however much she craved his touch, she simply didn't have the energy for anything more.

Liam stood up, took her hands and pulled her to her feet. Teresa looked at her monitor and hesitated. She had a few more scenarios to run, figures to input. "It'll still be there in the morning."

She should stay here. Teresa tugged her hand from Liam's and shook her head. "I think I should stay."

"Well, that's not going to happen," Liam said, picking up her dead phone. He tucked it into the back pocket of his jeans. Teresa accepted that her reactions were super-slow because, before she could figure out what he was doing, her tote bag was over his shoulder and her car keys were clutched in his fist. He gestured to the door. "After you."

Not happening. Liam Christopher had no right to barge into her office and order her around. Who did he think he was? Who did he think he was dealing with? Some weak-willed female whose knees would buckle at his display of dominance? Okay, her knees were a bit jelly-like but that had more to do with lack of food than his caveman approach to an argument.

"Do you really think your bossy attitude is going to work with me?"

Liam had the cheek to grin at her. He shook his head. "Not at all. But I am stronger and bigger and this will." He bent his knees, placed his arm under her thigh and another around her back and Teresa found herself cradled against his broad chest.

By the time her shock receded enough for her to speak, they were inside the elevator and heading to the basement parking garage. And when the elevator doors opened, she was yawning and thinking that this position wasn't too uncomfortable, and conceding that she neither had the energy to protest his high-handed tactics or his bossiness. Really, this was the second time he'd used his physical strength on her and she should protest...

She *would* protest. Sometime soon.

But the leather seats of his expensive car were heated and comfortable and if she turned her head and pulled her knees up, she could pretend she was in her bed...

Brooks had seen Nicolette in tiny lamé dresses, rocking three-inch heels and in short skirts and tight tops, so to discover that she was just as sexy in loose-fitting yoga pants and an old T-shirt came as a shock. Her face was also makeup free and she looked a lot younger than her twenty-eight years.

Brooks ran a finger around the open collar of his shirt and wondered if he was making a mistake, not sure if Nicolette was the right person for this crazy venture. Barefoot, her long hair pulled up into a ponytail, she looked softer, vulnerable and nothing like the sophisticated reporter he'd encountered a few times before.

"Are you going to stand in my doorway or are you going to come inside?" Nicolette demanded.

Brooks stepped into the hallway of her apartment and shrugged off his jacket, relieved to hear the acerbity in Nicolette's tone. Acerbity he could handle.

"Good evening, Nicolette," he said, hanging his jacket on a coat hook.

"For goodness' sake, call me Nic." Nic waved him to the couch. A pair of glasses stood on the coffee table, as well as a bottle of red wine. He picked up the wine and examined the label, surprised to see it was from a small winery in South Africa. He might be mistaken but he thought he might have toured the winery when he visited that country a few years back. He picked up the bottle and poured wine into two glasses and, before taking his seat, handed a glass to Nic. "Take a seat."

Nic narrowed her eyes at his bossiness but curled up into a single chair, tucking her bare feet under her luscious ass. She sipped her wine before resting the glass against her forehead.

"Tough day?" The words slipped out before Brooks could pull them back. It was a stupid question; he was blackmailing her into marrying him. How could she be having a good day?

Nic, thank God, chose not to respond. "So let's talk about this farcical arrangement we are entering."

Okay, then, straight to business. "Absolutely, since Teresa needs some answers."

"So do I," Nic replied. "I know why I am sacrificing my freedom and my single status but why are you doing this? What's prompting you to marry a woman you don't even know? Are you gay?"

Brooks grinned, not at all offended. Some of his favorite people were gay. "Nope."

His eyes dropped to her cleavage, to the soft skin on display, and lust shot straight to his groin. He was very not-gay. He started to swell and didn't really care if she noticed. The sooner she got used to the idea that he was intensely attracted to her, the sooner he could take her to bed. And, judging by the way her cheeks flushed at his blatantly sexual stare, she'd had a sexy thought, or two, about him.

Good, one less mountain to climb.

"Just like you, I need to marry to reach a goal."

"What goal? What are you trying to achieve? You didn't tell me anything last night," Nic demanded, and Brooks could see why she was such a good reporter. The woman was tenacious.

What harm could it do if he told her? He didn't think she would turn his words into an article but, just to cover his bases, he tossed out the question, "Off the record?"

Nic's sour expression conveyed her annoyance at his question. When he didn't speak again, she lifted her hands in frustration. "Of course it's off the record. I'm not going to write a story about my fiancé!"

She had the reputation of playing it straight, of not repeating stories told to her in confidence, so Brooks allowed himself to relax a fraction. "In order to access a lot of cash from Abbingdon Trust, I need to be married. And I need to marry either on or before the last day of the month, which is my birthday."

"I thought that you are wealthy. What do you need money for?"

Yeah, her curiosity wasn't easily satiated.

"I own a forty-nine-percent share in Abbingdon Airlines," Brooks explained. "The remainder of the shares are owned by my grandfather, in his personal capacity, and he wants to sell his stake. If I am married on my thirty-fifth birthday, I inherit a load of cash via the Abbingdon Trust and I can buy complete control of Abbingdon Airlines."

"Are you certain your grandfather will sell to you and only you?"

Brooks knew that his smile was a little self-satisfied but he was still proud of himself for inserting clauses into his agreements with his grandfather that provided for such an eventuality.

"As per our agreement, he has to sell me shares if and when I have the cash. I would've been happy for him to keep the shares if he wasn't dead-set on using his shares as collateral on another silly, guaranteed-to-lose-his-shirt business proposition."

Nic took a healthy sip of her wine. "What would happen

to the cash if you weren't married by thirty-five? Would you lose it?"

Brooks shook his head. "Nope. Every five years the offer is made, with the same conditions."

"So why didn't you get married at thirty?" Nic asked.

"Didn't need the money, hadn't met anyone I wanted to marry, there was no urgency to." Brooks shrugged. "Now there is."

"And I'm the sacrificial goat."

Brooks felt a spurt of annoyance and the acid taste in the back of his throat. Was he that bad a catch? Was this really the worst thing that could happen to her? He had all his teeth and hair, wasn't a complete jerk and intended to keep her in a style any woman could easily become accustomed to. He was going to fund her documentary, introduce her to influential people who'd make sure her film received the exposure it needed.

And when they parted, he'd inject a significant amount of cash into her bank account. Why was *she* acting like she was headed toward the hangman's noose?

And why did he care? Why did her approval matter so much? Generally, he didn't care what people thought about him but Nic's approval, for some insane reason, seemed to matter to him.

Nic put her wineglass down on the coffee table and lifted her arms to tighten the tie holding her long, thick hair off her face. Her breasts lifted and Brooks sucked in his breath as he saw the freckles on her chest, a hint of her lacy white bra. God, anyone would think that he hadn't had a woman in years instead of weeks...

But he'd never had Nic.

And why that should make a difference he had no damn idea.

"Let's talk weddings," Nic said, her tone brisk and her

eyes cool. "Why the big push for something wildly over-the-top?"

"It's an opportunity to throw a helluva party on someone else's dime." Brooks placed his ankle on his opposite knee. "And also because it will generate publicity. For me, for Abbingdon Airlines and for you."

Nic frowned. "For me?"

"Sure. You're an entertainment reporter and your marriage to me will generate a lot of interest and grow your profile exponentially. That will help you generate publicity when you start publicizing your documentary. You want as many people to see your documentary as possible and the higher your profile, the more that will happen."

Nic reached for the bottle of wine and dashed some liquid into her empty glass. "You haven't asked me about my documentary or inquired why it's so important to me."

Brooks had thought about it, had wanted to commission a deep background check on her but stopped himself. For some strange and probably asinine reason, he wanted Nic to tell him herself, to open up to him when she felt comfortable to do so.

"When you want to, you'll tell me without coercion."

He wanted to get to know this woman who was going to become his wife. She fascinated him on levels he found disturbing.

And if he had a choice, he'd probably run as far as he could from her, and this marriage. She made him think about what it would be like to marry, to have a smart and gorgeous woman as his life partner.

And now he felt like he had a noose around his neck.

Teresa, feeling renewed after nine hours of sleep, walked into the open-plan living area dressed in an old boyfriend's T-shirt. Stepping into her living room, she glanced out her living room window and looked down the street to the narrow view of Elliott Bay. The sun was out, the sky was blue and she swore that, if she opened her window, she'd hear birds chirping.

It was amazing how much a beautiful day and nine hours of solid sleep could improve her mood.

And, yeah, seeing Liam Christopher leaning against her kitchen counter, shirtless and with the top two buttons of his jeans open, revealing his sexy happy trail, was guaranteed to lift her mood even higher. Unnoticed by him, she leaned against the wall and waited for him to finish his call, perfectly happy to spend a couple of minutes checking him out.

Messy hair, a three-day growth on his cheeks and chin and easing down his thick, strong neck. The muscles in his broad shoulders were well-defined and flowed into sexy biceps that were big and, well, bitable. A light dusting of black hair covered his upper chest and a fine trail of hair bisected his six-pack, another part of his body she loved to nibble. Teresa pouted at the jeans covering his long legs but she easily remembered the muscles in his thighs, his strong calves and yep, she even liked his bare feet.

And that was the problem: she wasn't only half in love with Liam Christopher—she *liked* him. Love would be easier to ignore if she wasn't as attracted to his personality and his brain as she was to his body. God, why couldn't they have met at a different time, been different people? What if she had just bumped into him at a coffee shop and they dated like normal people? Why did Linus have to leave her shares in Christopher Corporation? Why did their pasts have to be so damn complicated?

"I need you to dig as deeply into the past as you can. Don't be scared to turn over rocks."

It took a minute for Liam's words to sink in and she

frowned. Who was he talking to and why would he need anyone to investigate his past? What was going on here? Peeling herself off the wall, Teresa continued walking to the kitchen and watched as he turned his head to observe her approach. His green eyes darted over her face, down her body, and her nipples puckered in response to his appreciative look. His eyes hovered on her breasts before sliding down her thighs and over her bare feet.

"Oh, and can you suggest a reputable lab who can do genetic testing? I'm prepared to pay a premium for some rushed results."

Curiouser and curiouser.

Liam ended his call and tossed his phone onto the kitchen table and then gripped the counter behind him. The action made his stomach ripple and his biceps flex. It also sent heat to her core and she felt the slow burn between her legs. Oh, God. How was she supposed to resist him looking so sexy, and a little sad?

"Everything okay?" Teresa asked. She desperately wanted coffee but her coffee machine was behind Liam and if she came within a foot of him, she'd start begging him to do her on the floor.

You are not going back to that make love, fight, break up circle again. Enough now.

"Yes, no. Sort of."

Well, that was as clear as mud. Before Teresa could push him to explain, he spoke again. "You look much better this morning. You slept like the dead."

"And how would you know that?"

Liam's smile could heat up the sun. "Within two minutes of leaving your office you were out for the count. So I brought you here. I carried you from the car to your bed and you never woke up once." His grin turned naughty. "And, God, you weigh a ton."

Since her doctor kept telling her that she could do with picking up a pound or two, Teresa didn't react to his teasing. She just lifted her brows and tried to look haughty.

"I undressed you, put you to bed and, after showering, crawled in after you."

"You could've gone home," Teresa pointed out.

Liam lifted one shoulder in an easy shrug. "I was tired and I like your place. I always have."

Teresa looked around her light-filled condo and nodded. She liked her place, too. It was filled with natural colors, comfy furniture and luscious plants. She could relax here, be herself. There weren't many places she felt comfortable enough to shed her cool-as-a-cucumber persona, and this apartment, and her office, when she was alone, were probably the only two in existence. And Liam was the only person who'd ever seen her emotionally naked.

And that made her feel vulnerable. And weak. And scared.

And because she was feeling off-kilter, she lifted her nose in the air and put ice into her voice. "You do remember that I broke up with you, don't you? That I told you I didn't want to have anything to do with you, that we were unfixable?"

"I do. But I'm ignoring you."

Teresa's mouth dropped open at his insouciant reply. How dare he dismiss her feelings? And that reminded her. How dare he pick her up and lug her around like she was a bag of cement? "You can't just ignore me and we need to address your caveman antics, as well."

Liam sent her a get-real look.

"Seriously, Liam, this isn't going to work. You and I, we don't work. We make love, we think we might have a chance and—" Teresa made her hands explode, mimicking a bomb detonation "—*boom*! It all blows up. We try again, another explosion. We don't talk, we don't trust. I think life is trying to tell us that we aren't supposed to be together."

Liam surprised her by nodding his agreement. "Maybe. But I'm thinking that it might be telling us to slow down, to take it easy."

"What are you talking about?"

"It's just been problem after problem with us, drama after drama. Maybe if we were better friends we wouldn't be very volatile. Everything wouldn't be such a production. We'd stick around instead of bolting." Liam rubbed the back of his neck. "Because that's our default reaction when things fall apart. We try and put distance between us and the problem."

"And you don't trust me."

"I don't trust anyone, Teresa. But I'm going to work on that," Liam said, his voice somber. "And you have to accept that there are some things that can't be fixed according to your timetable. Or at all."

Because a part of her still believed that her father didn't fight hard enough to get back to his family when his visa expired, Teresa knew that she tended to go overboard in pushing for what she wanted. She simply never wanted to live with regrets, with "what if I'd done that" thoughts. And yes, because she couldn't go back and understand her father's inability to come home, and his subsequent death, she did try to fix situations and people.

But trying to fix her and Liam was a lost cause. Even she knew that.

Didn't she?

"We bolt, Teresa, when things don't go our way or turn out the way we want them to. It's a fault we both share."

They'd both been scarred by their pasts and it was second nature to protect themselves. And they both recognized that the other had the power to hurt, to scald and to scour. But how would being friends help, and how on earth would they manage to ignore the passion that always flared between them? They could barely be in the same room without wanting to attack zippers and buttons.

God, she couldn't have this conversation without coffee. Teresa walked over to the counter to stand next to him, pushing him to the side with a nudge from her shoulder. Her bare arm brushed the skin of his and heat flashed. Goose bumps also danced on her skin.

Teresa threw up her hands in frustration. "That! That's the problem right there! You touch me and I want to fall into your arms and kiss you stupid."

Teresa dropped her eyes to his crotch and she noticed his erection starting to swell, straining the fabric of his jeans. "And look! It's not just me."

Liam groaned and rubbed his hands over his face. "I will admit, it's…inconvenient!"

"It's uncontrollable." Teresa placed both her hands on his shoulder and pushed him to the edge of the counter. "Stand over there! And put a damn shirt on!"

"Bossy," Liam muttered, a small smile touching his lips.

"You're only figuring this out now?"

Teresa turned her attention back to the coffee machine and darted a look at Liam's back as he walked across her living room to the hallway and then, she presumed, to her bedroom where he'd left his shirt and shoes. He was gone but a minute and Teresa wished it were five, or ten. She needed to wrangle her libido, to get blood to her brain. Damn Liam Christopher for having this effect on her.

Teresa watched coffee drip into her mug and considered putting her mouth to the spout to get some caffeine into her system. Hearing Liam's footsteps, she turned around and he was fully dressed, thank God. But only looking slightly less sexy. She still wanted to jump him.

"You can go now," Teresa told him, waving toward her front door.

"Yeah, that's not going to happen," Liam said, walking over to her and filching her cup of coffee from under the spout.

Teresa stared at him, thoughts of stabbing him between the eyes with a rusty fork dancing across her brain. "Do you want to die?"

Liam sipped before handing her cup back to her. Teresa placed her lips where his had been and thought that she could taste him. She was losing it, it was official. Not bothering to add milk or sugar, she pulled out a chair and dropped into it as Liam reached for another mug on the shelf above her machine and tapped the side of his fist against the start button.

"Let's go back to what we were discussing."

Teresa groaned. "Let's not."

Liam glanced at his half-full cup under the spout before picking up hers and taking another sip. Teresa growled but didn't have the energy to argue. She was saving her strength for bigger battles. She could not allow Liam to persuade her to try again, to be drawn back into his life and his orbit. Yeah, the highs were fantastic but the lows had the ability to drop her to her knees. She'd walked away from him in Napa Valley and she needed to keep on walking.

They were bad for each other...why wasn't he seeing this?

"Just go, Liam."

Instead of listening, Liam dropped into a chair and tapped his fingers against his coffee mug. "I want to apologize for not telling you that I hired an investigator to look into your life. He's still digging and has been, for several weeks. I ordered him to find everything and anything."

Teresa immediately noticed that he was apologizing for not telling her, not apologizing for hiring the detective. "I told you that I would tell you anything you needed to know about me!"

"The thing is… I don't think you know what I need to know."

Say what? It was still too early to have such a convoluted conversation. Liam's eyes darkened. "I can't move on. I can't go forward until I know why Linus left you those shares."

This again! "For the millionth time, I did not sleep with your father!"

Liam held up his hand. "I know that, *I do.* But there has to be a reason why he left you the shares worth millions. I want to know what that reason is because I'm tired of living in darkness, constantly wondering and waiting for information. I'm done with it. I want to pull all the skeletons, dirty or not, out of the cupboard and damn well deal with them!"

Teresa stared at him and saw the determination to find the truth in his eyes. Not sure what this meant, for him or them, she remained quiet.

"I feel like we are trying to build something, you and I, on shaky ground. We need all the facts about everything."

"I told you about Joshua, about the debt that he owes," Teresa responded. Didn't he realize what a huge step that was for her?

"And I appreciate you doing that," Liam said and after some thought, spoke again. "According to my guy, Joshua's debt was sold on to an outfit in Vegas. This new group specializes in hard-to-recover debt. They are, according to his sources, looking for Joshua and there's no doubt that they now know he's back on the West Coast."

Liam tapped his finger against his coffee cup. "Did you ask your brother why he gate-crashed that party?"

Of course she had. "He said that he was in a bar back east and he vaguely remembers some girl offering to buy him a drink. That's when his memory goes fuzzy.

"He remembers thinking that I was in trouble and the only way to save me was to go to the Goblet and confront my enemies. That's what he was trying to do by standing up and making a fool of himself."

"So he got drunk on the East Coast and six to eight hours later he still hadn't sobered up?" Liam asked, skeptical.

Teresa hadn't had a proper conversation with Josh in weeks and she had no idea about his mental state. Should she tell Liam about the puncture wound on his arm?

Before she could decide, Liam leaned forward, his expression intense. "He was drunk on the East Coast, so drunk that he couldn't remember what he did or said, but he bought himself a ticket, got himself on a plane and still made his way to Napa Valley and found you? And if he did manage to do all that while pissed, don't you think he might've sobered up at one point and wondered what the hell he was doing?"

She'd had this thought a few days back but she'd dismissed her suspicions. "He had help," she stated.

Teresa told Liam about the injection mark on his arm and he frowned. "Well, I think that confirms our working theory that he had help."

"But why would somebody track him down, liquor him up and escort him across the country to ruin an event you were organizing?"

Panic closed her throat and Liam immediately reached for her wrist, his thumb tracing patterns on her skin. Te-

resa immediately felt her vocal cords loosening, air flow-
ing into her lungs.

"Breathe, honey," Liam ordered her, his voice soft. But
his eyes and expression were anything but tender. "Somebody has it in for you."

"Or maybe for Matt Richmond?"

Liam shook his head. "Then why use Joshua? No,
honey, this is all about you. Maybe it's the loan shark trying to force you to cough up but I don't think so."

"Why not?"

"Because they don't play around by ruining events. No,
they are more likely to cut off little fingers or break a knee-
cap to get someone to pay. Trust me, they'd go straight for
the jugular."

She was sorry she'd asked. Teresa felt her stomach
lurch. "Oh, God."

"There's no doubt about it. You need to pay that debt,
Teresa. As soon as possible."

"When he called me, telling me about the debt, a part
of me thought that it was a mistake, like the kidnapping
was a mistake."

"They are being deadly serious, Teresa."

"I don't have the money…" Teresa saw the offer on
his lips and his next sentence confirmed her assumption.

"I can loan you the money. It'll take me a day or two to
get it together but I have it, Teresa."

She was so conflicted, her pride and her protective instincts at war. She couldn't risk Joshua getting hurt, not
when Liam was providing her with a reasonable alterna-
tive. Since she'd be selling her Christopher Corporation
shares to him at the end of the year, it would be a temporary loan.

Borrowing money from Liam made sense. Dammit.
But…not yet. "Thank you for the offer…"

"But?"

Teresa shook her head. "No buts, well, maybe a small one. I am just going to wait until they contact me again, making demands for the money. I don't know how to get in touch with them and they told me not to try. When they do, *if* they do, I'll ask you for the loan."

Relief made Liam's eyes greener. "When they make contact again, you need to tell them that you want proof that, if the debt is paid, no one else will come after you later. They need to give you a guarantee."

Teresa nodded, feeling lighter. "Thank you. I owe you. Joshua owes you."

Liam smiled and his eyes dropped to her mouth, and Teresa knew that he was no longer thinking about money and debts and lenders. He leaned forward, his mouth so close to hers that she could smell his sweet, minty breath, count the individual hairs in his scruffy beard, see the small scar on his bottom lip. She wanted him to kiss her, to take her to bed and away from thoughts of debt and mobsters and inheritances she didn't want. She wanted him to take her to bed where there was only his touch and his taste and the way he made her feel.

Teresa lifted her hand and rubbed her thumb against his bottom lip, surprised at how soft his lips were. Was he ever going to kiss her?

Liam gently pulled the tip of her thumb between his teeth and bit down. Teresa sucked in her breath at the spark of pleasure-pain and sighed when Liam gently sucked her digit. How could she be so turned on by him kissing her thumb?

"Teresa?" Liam whispered.

"Mmm?"

"Can we try and be friends? Can we also try to work together to get to the bottom of why Linus left you shares?"

Liam's teeth scraped the side of her thumb and she shivered. "Mmm-hmm."

"Oh, so I'll expect to see you at the Christopher Corporation shareholders meeting the day after tomorrow? I should also have the seven million ready for you by then."

"Okay."

Teresa heard her response and something about it sounded wrong. Wait, what had he said? She pulled back and stared at him while rewinding the conversation in her head. Her mouth dropped open, then closed and then opened again.

"You're catching flies." Liam leaned back, folded his arms and smirked. Teresa wanted to smack him sideways.

"You were trying to seduce me to get your own way!" Teresa accused. "That's a crappy thing to do! That's not playing fair."

Liam laughed. "Honey, nobody ever said life was going to be fair." Standing up, he dropped a hard, openmouthed kiss on her lips. When he pulled back, he smiled at her and Teresa felt her stomach, and her liver and her kidneys, do backflips. "But damn, it can be fun. Later."

Liam walked out of the kitchen toward her front door and Teresa tried to think of something cutting to say. The "I hate you" she tossed in his direction fell well short of the mark.

At the door, Liam turned and smiled again, causing her poor organs to take flight once more. "No, you don't."

No, she didn't. Not even close.

Six

Liam lied.

The board meeting was as horrible as she'd thought it would be. As Liam guided her out of Christopher Corporation's ultra-modern boardroom, Teresa glanced back into the room to check that the blond hardwood floors weren't, actually, blood-stained.

Because it felt like she and Liam had been drained of a pint or two.

Teresa glanced up at Liam's hard face and grimaced at the anger she saw blazing from his eyes, the tension tightening his jaw and the frustration thinning his mouth. How he'd held his temper, kept so even and calm, while his father's contemporaries attacked him from all sides, Teresa had no idea. He'd remained calm when their ire was directed at him but when one of the members turned his vitriol on her, Teresa saw the first crack in his seemingly impenetrable armor. As long as she lived, she'd never forget his cold, hard words spoken in defense of her.

"You can criticize me, criticize my leadership and my work ethic and my decisions but Ms. St. Claire is off-limits. Am I clear?"

Teresa shivered at his ice-cold, CIA-interrogator voice and she'd watched, reluctantly fascinated, as the board members leaned back as if to avoid the wave of Liam's ire. When nobody made a counter comment, Teresa knew that she could, fractionally, relax.

And she tried to, she did, but then one of the members passed a motion suggesting that Liam be removed as CEO. Teresa knew that Liam didn't expect the meeting to go well but that was a rocket he hadn't expected to be launched, nor detonated. She was seriously impressed by his self-control.

Teresa watched as he simply smiled, leaned back in his chair and loosened the button of his immaculately tailored suit jacket. He tapped the point of his capped pen on the surface of the sleek table and locked eyes with his opponent. Liam's quiet words, his sensible response, knocked that rocket right out of the sky.

"Ladies and gentlemen, we are all getting ahead of ourselves. Yes, it's been a rough couple of months. Yes, things have happened that haven't placed the company in the best light but I have a contract and you cannot fire me without cause. And if you do, I will sue the pants off you and, trust me, that will not be in the company's best interest.

"Now, may I suggest that we all take a deep breath and start thinking instead of reacting emotionally?"

"Your father wanted you to be CEO, Liam. Not all of us agreed with that," the chairman of the board pointed out.

"Noted. But according to company policy, I am entitled to some time to prove myself," Liam replied, looking unfazed and even bored. Teresa, furious for him, sat on her hands and clenched her teeth in an effort not to defend him. He wouldn't appreciate it and she respected him enough to allow him to fight his own battles. This was, after all, his arena.

"And we will be watching you. And may I suggest that you distance yourself from Ms. St. Claire, Liam?"

Liam's face hardened further and Teresa saw his fist clench. "You're out of line, Bosworth."

"I am protecting this company."

"Christopher Corporation is my responsibility, mine to protect."

Bosworth smiled and gestured to the rest of the board members. "Actually, with this new distribution of shares, it's all of ours to protect, look after, to steer. And should Ms. St. Claire decide to divest her shares to someone other than you, this situation will become very interesting indeed."

Like that would happen. She had no idea why Linus left her his shares but she'd never consider selling them to anyone but Liam. They were his. Did he know that? With all the other craziness happening around them, had she even explained that to him? Could he be in doubt of where her loyalties lay?

Teresa raised her hand to speak and Bosworth gave her a condescending smile. "I think we've wasted enough time on this subject. Moving on to item six…"

"But—" Teresa protested.

"Moving on, Ms. St. Claire."

She'd been dismissed and disrespected and Teresa had to exert a substantial amount of self-control not to demand to be heard. Besides, it didn't matter what the board thought, as long as Liam knew that she would never sell her shares to anyone but him. That was all that was important.

But jeez, she wouldn't mind educating Bosworth and his cronies about equality and fairness.

Teresa felt Liam's hand on her back as he guided her down the long hallway to his executive office in the corner of the building. When they reached his office, Duncan, his PA, jumped to his feet, his expression worried.

Liam stopped by his assistant's desk and the two men exchanged a long look. "Was it as bad as you thought?" Duncan asked.

"Worse."

Duncan ran his hand over his mouth before defiance sparked in his eyes. "Screw 'em. What do we need to do?"

Liam's mouth finally kicked up at the corners in the tiniest of smiles. "They are a necessary evil."

Duncan folded his arms and rocked on his heels. "They," he stated, looking annoyed, "are a bunch of rickety old geezers who should've been put out to pasture decades ago."

Teresa grinned. She really, really liked Liam's young PA.

Liam briefly clasped the younger man's shoulder before opening the door to his massive office and gesturing her inside. "Coffee would be good. It might help me maintain my 'haven't killed anyone yet' streak."

Liam closed the office door behind him and Teresa, rested his forehead on the door and banged his head against the wood, releasing colorful combinations of curses. In his own office, away from prying eyes, he could release his iron-tight grip of control and allow the rolling waves of anger to consume him.

Folding his arms above his head and resting his forearms on the door, Liam closed his eyes and tried to make sense of the past two hours. Oh, he knew that the board wouldn't be happy about the recent events. He and Christopher Corporation had received some negative publicity but he genuinely believed that the dip in share price was mostly due to current economic conditions and nothing to do with his leadership or Teresa or the shares. But the board members were using it as an excuse to oust him, to put someone else behind his desk. Why?

Why didn't they want him running the company his father created?

Because, unlike his father, he wasn't a negotiator; neither was he easily swayed. He did things his way, set a course, and the board either came along for the ride or was left on the sidelines. He wasn't a yes-man and he wanted autonomy. His father ran the board like a democracy; he had no intention of allowing a bunch of, mostly, doddery old fools charting the course of his modern, technologically rich company. They feared what they couldn't understand and Liam wanted to take the company into places and markets they didn't understand and couldn't relate to.

They were scared, and scared men did stupid things. Like firing him from his own company.

But Jesus, they'd crossed a very big line when they attacked Teresa. Yeah, he had a million unanswered questions about her but she knew that she'd never do anything to harm him or Christopher Corporation. Despite everything she'd been through, she'd held her head high and marched on through the flames. Today she'd been polite and brave and kept her dignity while those around them lost theirs. She was an asset to the corporation and, yeah, to him.

He couldn't let her go, wouldn't let her go. When he'd first seen her seven years ago, sitting across the family dining table, he'd instinctively recognized that she was important to him, to his happiness.

He'd known her, recognized her. He wanted to claim her, to make her his. He wasn't that young man who saw everything in black-and-white anymore; he knew that life was a lot of gray. But his possessiveness toward Teresa remained as strong as it always had been.

And he was damned if he'd allow anything else to happen to her. From this day on, she was under his protection. And protect her, he would.

Liam pulled away from the door and walked over to his desk that sat at right angles to the floor-to-ceiling windows. If he looked south, he could see, on clear days, Mt. Rainier; north, the iconic Space Needle and west, West Puget Sound. If he looked east, the view was of his door and Teresa, staring at him with big, round eyes.

With her hair pulled backed into a loose bun and dressed in a tight black skirt and a tailored, open-neck white shirt she looked every inch the corporate drone. But if one looked at her feet and noticed her tangerine heels, that impression of a tightly wound, composed woman was blown out of the water.

But really, he just had to look into her expressive blue eyes to see what she was thinking. Her eyes reflected every emotion lodged in her soul and yep, confusion and concern reigned.

"Would you like to explain what just happened in there?"

Teresa was a bright woman; she knew he'd just been put on notice. She was really asking whether he had a plan. He didn't need one; his position was safe for at least six months and by then, he would've completed a few deals and seen some projects come online, like the joint Sasha Project with Richmond Industries. The share price would be up and those fickle bastards would be satisfied. He wasn't worried about the company; he was worried about Teresa.

Her company was in dire straits; she needed to secure her brother's safety; she looked like she was on the edge of falling apart. Except that she wouldn't because she was too damn strong to do that.

She needed someone to stand in her corner, to show her that she wasn't alone, to be there for her.

That could all be easily accomplished if she married him.

Liam swallowed, tried to push the thoughts of being married away but couldn't dislodge the thought. As his wife, Teresa would be quickly accepted by the highest echelons of Seattle society. That acceptance would translate into business for Limitless Events and his business associates would also funnel their events her way.

If she married him, he'd have a reason to immediately pay off her brother's debts—he'd tell her that he couldn't afford for anyone to discover that his brother-in-law owed mobsters money. Quickly settling her debt would ensure her safety and that was intensely important to him.

And if they married, she wouldn't be alone anymore.

Was he in savior-complex mode? Liam heard Matt's question in his head and pulled his eyes off Teresa to look out his window. Matt often accused him of wanting to save everyone and everything because that was what his mother demanded of him, and his father, growing up. Linus had refused to rush to her rescue, to pay attention to her every want and need, so Liam provided her with the attention she craved.

Matt was convinced that he was conditioned to wanting to help if someone was in crisis. It was, his best friend told him, his biggest weakness and his most powerful strength. Matt also frequently told him that his savior complex would come back to bite him on the ass.

So be it. Teresa needed help and he was going to give it to her. But how best to do that? Was marriage the only answer?

"Take a seat," Liam told her, gesturing to his sleek white couch she was standing behind.

Teresa sat down and tucked one orange heel behind the opposite calf. She was so very graceful, every movement fluid. He just wanted to take her to bed. Hell, a bed wasn't even necessary; he could lock the door and make love to her in the late-morning light, stripping her naked as the world went on outside without them.

A sharp knock on the door and Duncan walking into the room dissolved that fantasy. Duncan placed a tray holding a carafe of coffee, cups and cream and sugar on the coffee table in front of Teresa and lifted his eyebrows at Liam. After a beat, Duncan nodded briskly. "Enjoy your coffee. I'll make sure that you aren't disturbed."

Liam squirmed, thinking that the younger man might be able to read his mind. When Duncan left the room, he took his seat opposite Teresa, linked his hands and waited until her eyes met his. There was one way to get her under his wing, to put a message out there that she was off-limits, that she was under his protection.

"I think we should get married. As soon as possible."

Teresa thought she heard Liam asking her to marry him. Which wasn't possible. *Was it?*

Before she could force her tongue to form words—not that she had the vaguest idea of what she should say, apart from "are you nuts?"—Liam stood up and loomed over her, one hand on the arm of the sofa, the other behind her head, caging her in. She stared into his beautiful eyes, fringed with those dark, thick lashes, and lifted her fingers to the scruff on his square jaw.

She'd go back to harsh reality in a minute—a freakin' marriage proposal?—she just needed to touch him, inhale his sexy scent, lose herself in his forest-green eyes.

Teresa watched as his mouth descend toward hers and she pushed away the thought that they should be talking about business, that she needed to respond to his crazy suggestion. She didn't want to be sensible or businesslike or strategic; she just needed to feel.

Kissing Liam, touching his wonderful, masculine body, made sense; nothing else did.

Confusion and lust warred for dominance in Liam's eyes. "I shouldn't be kissing you—" he said.

Screw that.

"The only thing you should be doing right now is kissing me." Teresa whispered the words against his lips.

Liam released a harsh swear before his mouth covered hers and as his tongue swept into her mouth, Teresa, for the first time in days, relaxed. Here, in Liam's arms, was where she felt safe, protected, totally at ease.

Teresa wound her arms around Liam's neck and stumbled to her feet, needing to be closer to him, wanting, if possible, to crawl inside his skin and stay there. She pushed her breasts into his hard chest, mentally cursing the fabric barriers between them.

As Liam's hand moved from her head, over her back and down her ass, Teresa gripped the fabric of his shirt at his hips and pulled it out from the waistband of his suit pants. Pushing her hands up and under the fabric, she finally found hot, male skin covering long, sleek muscles. Heat and need and warmth soaked her panties as she pushed his shirt up his chest, wrenching her mouth away from his to place hot kisses on his right pec, flicking her tongue across his flat nipple.

Above her head, Liam cursed and she felt his hands pulling at his tie and undoing the top button of his shirt. Then he lifted his shirt up and over his head and she had easy access to his wide chest and ridged stomach.

"You're so hot and it's been so long and I want you so much," Teresa told him as she dropped her hands to his belt buckle and pulled it apart, her fingers struggling to undo the clasp of his suit pants.

If she didn't get him inside her, filling her and all those empty, bleak places, she might just cry…

"Hold on a sec," Liam muttered.

Teresa ignored him and when he pushed her hands away, using one hand to loosely clasp her wrists behind her back, he used his other hand to tip her chin up. His eyes met hers and his sweet smile liquefied her knees. "Slow down a sec, honey. I need to get you caught up."

Teresa stared at him as he dropped his hand to flick open the buttons of her silk shirt and when he spread the fabric apart and stared down at her barely there bra, passion flashed, hot and bright, in his eyes. "You are so beautiful."

In that moment, watching Liam as he looked at her, Teresa felt beautiful. Thoughts of marriage and mergers and machinations fell away and she knew that he wanted her. Liam's long finger traced her breasts above midnight-colored lace and when his thumb drifted over her nipple, she sucked in her breath and wobbled on her heels.

Liam released her hands, hoisted her skirt up her hips and spun around, dropping to sit on the sofa behind him. Her skirt, now up around her hips, was no longer a barrier to movement so he spread her knees across his thighs and positioned her so that her hot core was directly positioned over his rock-hard erection. Teresa felt her eyes cross and her breathing became shallower as she rocked against him.

It wouldn't take much for her to come…

Pleasure spiked when Liam pulled the cup of her bra down and sucked her into his mouth, his tongue winding around her tight nipple. Teresa held the back of his head and whimpered, the hurricane of pleasure whirling and swirling around and within her.

Liam pulled away from her and looked up, his eyes slamming into hers. "This is truth, Teresa. This is the only truth. The way you make me feel...this is where truth lies."

Unable to take in his words, to discern what he was trying to say, Teresa arched her back, only concerned that he give her other breast the same attention. When he did, she ground down on his cock, needing to feel him, every hard inch of him.

"Tell me you want me," Liam muttered, pushing his hand between them to pull down his zipper, his knuckles brushing against her clit. Teresa gasped, demanding more.

Between her legs, Liam's hand stilled. "Tell me."

Teresa forced her eyes open. "I want you, Liam." She pushed against his hand. "Can't you tell?"

Liam kept his eyes on hers as he lifted his hips, pulling his suit pants and his underwear down his hips. Teresa sighed when she felt his heat and hardness, stroking her core up and down his long, lovely length.

Liam did a half sit-up and reached for the clasp of her bra, flicking it open. He pulled it off and, still arched, bent down to suckle one breast, then the other.

Teresa pushed her hand between them and gripped his cock, moving so that his tip was positioned at her entrance, delaying the pleasure of feeling him slide into her for as long as possible.

"Condom, Teresa."

She couldn't wait and what was the point? "I'm on the pill."

Relief flashed across Liam's face and, two seconds later, he lifted his hips and surged into her in one hard, soul-touching stroke. Teresa sighed, sank deeper onto him and wrapped her arms around his shoulders, conscious of his face in her neck, his breath against her skin. This was a curiously intimate position. She wasn't sure who was cradling whom but it didn't matter... Liam was inside her, where she needed him to be.

"You feel amazing," Liam muttered, rocking his hips with small movements and sending bursts of pleasure coursing through her. But she needed more; she needed everything. She needed hard and long and intense...she needed *him*.

This.

Teresa pulled back, held his face in her hands and met his foggy-with-pleasure eyes. "I need you, Liam. I need hard and hot and long and rough. I need you to make me forget everything but how you make me feel."

Liam dropped another curse. "I'm holding on with everything I have, honey. If I take you hard, I'm not going to last a minute."

"I'll be with you every step along the way," Teresa assured him.

He looked at her for a moment, silently questioning her, and something in her face must've convinced him because he surged to his feet, easily picking her up. Ignoring the pants around his hips, he put her on her feet and turned her back to him and placed a hand between her shoulder blades, forcing her to bend over the arm of the sofa. He stepped out of one trouser leg and used his knee to nudge her legs apart. His hands kneaded the bare flesh of her ass, and Teresa heard the snap of the thin cords of her thong breaking and, out of the corner of her eye, saw the dark blue fabric flutter to the floor.

Liam crowded her, his erection resting between her butt cheeks as his hand traveled across her flat stomach and his fingers brushed the thin strip of hair. Expertly, knowingly, his fingers found her clit and Teresa gasped and instinctively lifted her ass. Taking her massive hint, Liam slid into her from behind and Teresa placed her forearms on the sofa arm and buried her face into the crook of her arm.

"No, I need you close," Liam muttered, wrapping his arm diagonally across her chest and pulling her into him, her back to his front. His other arm wrapped around her waist and she felt his mouth on her shoulder, in the crook of her neck.

Needing more, Teresa turned her head and his mouth met hers, his tongue echoing the smooth slides of his cock as he pushed into her and pulled back.

Pleasure, hot and white, shot with silver and white, started at her toes and sprinted up her calves, her thighs, and lodged itself in her womb. It grew brighter and bigger and bolder and when Liam pulled back and placed his hands on her hips and slammed into her, that ball of brilliance shattered and a million sparks danced across her skin. Liam groaned and shuddered, his forehead on her spine.

Teresa closed her eyes, wanting to hold on to the dream for as long as possible. But when Liam kissed her shoulder blade, when he pulled out of her, she knew that reality, and her life, was about to smack her in the face again.

Liam bent down and picked up his suit pants and her bra and shirt. As she took her clothes from him, Teresa flushed when she realized that her skirt was still up around her hips and her heels were still on her feet.

"My private bathroom is through there," Liam said, his voice low as she held her garments with a shaking hand. "And when you come back, we can discuss getting married."

Teresa stared at herself in the mirror above the sink and shook her head. Judging by her foggy eyes and her swollen mouth, it was obvious to see that she'd just been thoroughly ravished.

Ravished...

It was such an old-fashioned word but it really captured the essence of the moment.

Teresa gripped the edges of the basin and stared down at the white porcelain. As wonderful as making love with Liam was, she had to concentrate. Liam wanted them to get married...

She'd rather stab herself between the eyebrows with a rusty fork.

Oh, she couldn't imagine spending her life with anyone but him, but she was damned if she'd use marriage, even marriage to Liam Christopher, as a business solution, as a logical solution to a sticky situation!

Who did that?

Apparently, good-looking billionaires who wanted to save their jobs and their company. While she didn't want Liam to get ousted as CEO of Christopher Corporation— he was the company and it needed him, no matter what those dinosaurs said earlier—she wouldn't sacrifice herself to the cause. She respected herself too much to settle for less than true love and can't-live-without-you. And she needed trust.

He didn't believe in her. And he still didn't trust her.

And, to be honest, did she fully trust him? Could she ever fully trust anyone again, to trust that he'd stick by her through thick and thin, sickness and health, all that richer and poorer stuff? She didn't know, she didn't think so... people simply didn't do that anymore but she more than wanted that sort of commitment. Having grown up without any support system, she *needed* it.

And then her thoughts started to spiral. Why did he want to marry her, why now? What was driving him? Liam

wanting to marry her might also be an easy way for him
to get his hands on her shares…without paying for them.

And if he did that then she wouldn't have a way to bul-
letproof her business and, more important, to pay Joshua's
debts so that he would forever be free of those cretins in
Vegas.

There were a million reasons why she couldn't marry
Liam but at the heart of it was the fact that he didn't love
her, didn't trust her and never would. She was already
mostly miserable without being married to him; getting
the legal system involved would make her feel a hundred
times worse.

Through the thick wooden door Teresa heard him clearing his throat. "Teresa, we need to talk."

She really didn't want to. She'd far prefer it if she could
walk out of the bathroom and keep moving until she left his
office, his building, Seattle and her life. Until she reached
the white sands of Bali…

Teresa opened the door and slowly walked back to his
sofa, trying not to remember how amazing she felt not ten
minutes before. She picked her tote bag up from the floor
and slung it over her shoulder. She looked at him, now
fully dressed, his tie loosely slung around his neck and his
hair messy from her fingers. For a minute he didn't look
like the calm and always-in-control Liam Christopher she
knew and fought with. He looked like a man waiting on a
woman's answer, uncertain and a little worried.

A small part of her wanted to say yes, to give him the
answer he needed. Then she remembered that he didn't
love her and he didn't trust her or believe anything she said.

No, as great as the sex was—and it was fan-freaking-
tastic—she couldn't give him the answer he wanted. She
wanted love. Was that too much to ask for?

"No, Liam."

It took a moment for her words to make sense and when they did, shock passed across his face and lodged in his eyes. "What?"

He'd heard her; he just didn't want to accept what she'd said. "No, I won't marry you."

Not for a business. Her self-respect, her happiness, her soul, wasn't for sale.

Seven

Nicolette flashed a smile at Brooks's driver as he opened the back door to his limousine. She slid inside and surreptitiously pinched herself. Taking her seat, she looked past Brooks's broad shoulders as he followed her inside the vehicle and caught a glimpse of the elegant, discreet sign to the left of the red door. Paul's was, if not the best restaurant in Seattle, within the top three. Sitting down for a meal in the twelve-seater restaurant was more difficult than booking a flight to space, but when Brooks asked her where she wanted to eat, she'd tossed out the name of the restaurant as a joke. He'd made it happen.

Brooks. Made. Stuff. Happen.

Brooks settled in beside her, looking utterly masculine in a charcoal suit and an open-neck, white button-down shirt. She looked at his big hand resting on his thigh and wished that it was on her leg, that he was turning to face her, about to lean in for a kiss. Nic swallowed once, then twice. She really, really wanted to kiss Brooks, had from the first moment they met.

How was she going to live with him, in his house, share his life and not jump him on a regular-to-often basis? She was a red-blooded woman in her late twenties and she liked sex; she *needed* sex. And she desperately wanted to get naked with her soon-to-be husband.

Nic sighed and flicked the diamond-and-emerald engagement ring Brooks placed on her finger earlier that evening. It was ridiculously big and stupidly expensive and she couldn't help wishing that the ring came with a heartfelt "I adore you" or "I'm so glad that you are mine."

Gah!

The limo pulled away and Nic turned her head to stare out the window, annoyed at the burning sensation in her eyes.

This is a business arrangement. Why are you allowing yourself to feel all gooey? Stop it right now.

She had to remember why she was doing this, what she was trying to achieve. If she could save one girl…

"My sister and I were close as kids but when she hit her teens, things started to go wrong."

She felt Brooks's eyes on her, could feel his gaze tracing her features. She didn't need to see his face to know that his entire focus was on her. She needed to tell him why her documentary was important, *imperative*, partly so that he would understand why she'd agreed to marry him and also to keep her feet firmly on the ground. This wasn't about love, it wasn't about money…she was doing this to tell Jane's story.

Nic felt Brooks's hand on her thigh, his touch comforting and not sexual, and she sucked in a deep breath. She could trust this man with her secrets; she was sure she could.

"My older sister and I were raised by my grandmother. My mom..." God, how could she say this?

Brooks squeezed her bare thigh in silent support. Nic forced the words through her teeth. "My mom liked booze a little too much and men even more."

"Your dad?"

Nic lifted one shoulder. "Jane and I had different fathers. She met hers once, I think. Mine was long gone before I was born."

Brooks lifted his hand from her thigh and pushed his hand between the seat and her back, sliding his arm around her waist. He pulled her into him so that her back was against his chest, her head against his shoulder. She felt him kiss her hair, so softly, so...kindly.

Kindness was, she decided, so very underrated.

"Jane, like my mom, liked alcohol and men. She started using both when she was about fourteen. My grandmother put her into rehab a few times but it never took."

Behind her, Brooks tensed but then his hand came up to stroke her hair, his silent support tangible. "At sixteen she met a guy, someone a lot older, and she ran away from home to be with him."

"Oh, honey."

"When I was eighteen and she twenty, we were informed that she'd died of a drug overdose. The investigator from the Medical Examiner's office told us that she'd been working the streets to feed her addictions. When I asked about the guy she ran away with, she told us that Jane lived with her pimp and, by his description, I knew it was the same guy she left with years before."

"Why didn't she make contact?"

It was a fair question. "Embarrassment? Fear of rejection? Coming home would also mean failure and she would've known that Gran and I would've made her face her demons."

Brooks ran his fingers up and down her arm and his light touch gave her the strength to carry on with her explanation. "The investigator handed over her personal effects and there wasn't much. A few clothes, a couple of photos of us as children and an expensive smartphone she'd hidden under a floorboard. I was surprised to see the phone because I thought she would've sold it for crack but she didn't. I went through the phone and on it were twenty, thirty videos, some long, some not."

Tension rippled through Brooks and she turned abruptly, immediately realizing that he'd jumped to the wrong conclusion. Facing him, she linked her fingers in his, needing the connection. "No, they weren't sex videos. It was, I suppose, a diary of sorts. She told her story, her struggle with drugs and addiction, why she ran away. She detailed how her boyfriend and pimp forced her to have sex with multiple men for money in different hotels daily. And that she did it because she felt she owed him, that without him she was nothing. That she, in a warped way, loved him.

"It's a story that plays out a thousand different ways for a hundred thousand girls daily in America, millions across the world. Trafficking doesn't always mean sex rings and forced captivity. Sometimes, most times, it can be just one girl, one guy. And drugs and prostitution and trafficking go together like a hand in a glove."

"And that's why you want to do the documentary," Brooks said, tucking a strand of hair behind her ears.

"That's why *Janie* wanted me to do the documentary. She knew that I was studying journalism and she made the videos for me, hoping that I would tell her story and save another girl from experiencing what she went through.

"My first attempt at the documentary happened in my

final year of college but it wasn't very good. I put it aside
for a few years and when my grandmother died, she made
me promise to do it properly," Nic said, keeping her voice
low. "To do that, I need funds."

Brooks was quiet for a long time, but his eyes remained
on her face and Nic felt like she could see into his soul. "If
you didn't need my money, if you didn't have a story to
tell, you'd never consider marriage, would you?"

She wanted to be able to tell him that there was no way
in hell she'd be marrying if it wasn't for Jane and the promise she made to her gran, but she couldn't deny the truth.
There was a very good chance that, even without any in-
centive, she might've still said yes.

She was that attracted to him; her need to be with him,
around him, superseded her good sense and any rational
thought.

Instead of answering him—how could she admit that
to him? It was hard enough facing the truth herself!—Nic
leaned forward, her eyes on his lips. Placing her hand on
his cheek, she rubbed her thumb through his stubble, loving the feel of his scruff beneath her fingers. Was she brave
enough to kiss him, to find out how he tasted?

"Nic, would you have considered marriage to me?"

Knowing that he would push her for an answer, but not
knowing why, Nic lowered his mouth to hers and when
their lips met, a powder keg exploded beneath them. One
minute she was kissing Brooks, her tongue gliding over
his lips, and the next, she was straddling him, his hands
on her bare ass and his tongue wrapped around hers, taking and giving and sucking...

And a minute later she was lying under him, his long
form pressed into hers, her leg curled around his calf, her
arm hooked around his neck as he kissed her and kissed
her and kissed her...

Nic was lost in a vortex of need and passion and flat-out desire, but over her pounding heart she heard his soft whisper. "Would you have still considered marrying me, Nic?"

No, yes, she didn't know. Not having an answer, Nic just kissed him as the limousine made its way through Seattle's rain and fog to her front door.

After fleeing Napa Valley in Brooks's jet with Joshua, Teresa solemnly promised herself that she wouldn't sleep with Liam again, that she wouldn't allow him to mess with her head again.

Fail and fail.

When would she learn? Never, it seemed.

At the venue for the Ryan/Abbingdon wedding Teresa stepped onto the lavender-edged path that would take her to the bridal cottage and trailed her hand through the fragrant bushes.

Where was Liam now? What was he doing? She hadn't spoken to him since she'd stormed out of his office and while she had a bunch of questions for him—why had he proposed? Was his offer to loan her money against her shares still on the table? Did he really want to marry her?— she knew she had to stay away from him. Liam took up too much brain space and she'd needed to concentrate on Brooks and Nicolette's wedding. So she'd spent the past ten days working her ass off and the big day was finally here.

It was the most important day of her life, career-wise, and she couldn't afford to be distracted by thoughts of Liam Christopher and how much she missed him. Neither could she allow herself to be sidetracked by wondering and worrying about when she'd be contacted next about repaying Joshua's debt, trying to figure out why Linus left her the shares in the first place or the future of her business.

She could only worry about what she could control and this wedding should be—was, dammit!—her entire focus.

As she passed the groom's cottage, and the old-fashioned gazebo placed between the two cottages, she thought about Brooks's strange call the day before.

"There's something else I need you to do for me, Teresa."

Her toes had curled—not in a good way—at his greeting.

"Okay." Think about the money; think about the fact that organizing this wedding is a way to reestablish yourself.

"Can you delegate some of your pre-wedding duties to one or more of your minions, and help Nic dress?"

Nope. She liked Nicolette but they hardly knew each other. "I don't think Nicolette would want me to intrude..."

"She has no family and she works too hard to make friends." Yep, Teresa could relate. "I need you to be there, Teresa. I don't want her to be alone."

Hearing the concern in Brooks's voice had her, despite the millions of things she had to see to, saying yes.

Teresa looked over her shoulder toward the main buildings and sighed at how picture-perfect the venue looked. Using Brooks's money and influence, she'd persuaded the owner of The Two Barns, a fantastically exclusive wedding venue on the outskirts of Seattle, to speed up the last few renovations so that Brooks and Nic could hold their wedding in the newly converted, cathedral-like barns.

The smaller barn was a chapel and the bigger barn would hold the reception. The venue, with its old bridge, babbling stream and a profusion of weeping willows, was ridiculously pretty and also housed an award-winning restaurant on the premises. Joaquin, the Michelin-starred chef and owner, had also added two small cottages, places where the bridal parties could dress.

She'd love to wander around the grounds, sit next to the brook, dip her toes in the cool water. Pretend that her life wasn't going to hell in a broken-down wagon. She wanted a minute to catch her breath, to zone out, to center herself before she faced the madness of the next six to eight to ten hours. But because Brooks asked her to, she was going to check on the bride, hold her hand. See if she was okay...

The thing was, *she* wasn't okay. She was stressed and tired and unhappy, feeling isolated and a little scared, and very much alone, but she'd never, not in a million years, let Nicolette see that. This was her day to feel like a princess and she didn't need to know that her event planner felt like her nervous breakdown was waiting for her around the corner.

Teresa dug deep for her courage—that well was starting to run dry—and knocked on the cottage door. When she heard Nicolette's call to enter, she stepped into the exquisitely decorated room. Mint green and cream, feminine furnishings, sophisticated art. An unopened bottle of champagne stood in an ice bucket, and a plate of chocolate-tipped strawberries sat next to the bridal bouquet on the coffee table.

The room also contained one of the most beautiful brides she'd ever seen.

Teresa stopped, placed her hand on her heart and simply stared at the vision in front of her. Beaded silk flowers bloomed down a low bodice and along illusion tulle sleeves. The material gathered at her tiny waist, and expensive lace fell in a waterfall of fabric hand-beaded with pearls, beads and stones. A dramatic train completed her fairy-tale look.

Nicolette turned and lifted her eyebrows. "Do I look okay?"

"You look absolutely amazing," Teresa replied, feeling a little weepy. She'd done hundreds of weddings and rarely felt emotional, but Nicolette's ethereal, natural beauty took her breath away. And, truth be told, she was a little envious. She wanted to be Nicolette, who had an amazing career and was about to embark on this amazing life with a sexy, nice man. Nicolette didn't have to worry about her brother, his debts or deal with inconvenient feelings for a complicated man.

She wanted this, Teresa reluctantly admitted. She wanted the pretty dress, the flawless makeup, the bouquets of lilies sitting on the coffee table. She wanted a new start with a strong man...

She didn't want a half-assed proposal, nor did she want a marriage based on convenience and protection and money and shares.

Teresa shook off her blues. "Brooks asked me to check on you. He wanted to make sure that you were all right."

Nicolette's eyes softened. "He's a good guy."

Teresa flashed her a grin. "And he's sexy as hell."

Nicolette smiled. "Isn't he just?"

Teresa sat down on the arm of the sofa and crossed her legs. She glanced at her watch and realized that it was later than she thought, fifteen minutes before Nicolette had to walk down the aisle. But they had time for a quick chat, a small glass of champagne. When she made the offer to Nicolette, she shook her head. "With my luck, I'll probably pour it over my dress."

Teresa looked longingly at the imported, expensive bottle of champagne. "And I'm working. Damn."

Standing, she walked over to the table and picked up a strawberry and popped it into her mouth. She moaned as the flavors hit her tongue. Ripe, juicy berries and dark, rich Belgian chocolate. Could she just stay here for the rest of the day and drink champers and gorge on strawberries and chocolate and pretend the real world didn't exist?

She wished.

"Those look amazing," Nicolette commented, looking at the strawberries with undisguised longing.

A girl should be able to eat whatever the hell she wanted to on her wedding day. Teresa picked up a berry by the stalk. "Open wide," Teresa commanded her.

"My dress, my makeup," Nicolette protested.

"Just bend forward and open up wide."

Nicolette did as she was told and Teresa popped the berry into her mouth, watching as her eyes fogged over with pleasure. "Aren't they divine?"

She nodded enthusiastically, chewed and opened her mouth again. Teresa fed her strawberries until Nicolette indicated that she'd had enough. "Thanks, I didn't have breakfast," Nic said. "Nerves."

"Can't think why you are nervous. You're only getting married today," Teresa quipped.

"I'm such a wuss." Nicolette's tone was desert-dry.

Teresa checked her watch again and tapped her foot. She shouldn't ask her this, she really shouldn't. "Nicolette, how did you know Brooks was the one?"

"Please call me Nic."

Her eyes flashed with an emotion Teresa couldn't identify. Then she dropped her eyes and looked away. Curious.

"I think that love, true love, ferocious love, doesn't roll around often and that, as a society, we are in love with the idea of love."

So that was a helluva complicated answer to a simple question.

"Love doesn't have to be the only reason for marriage,

Teresa." Nic lifted one lovely, creamy shoulder. "I'm a practical person, Teresa, as I suspect are you."

Oh, damn, that had to mean that Nic was marrying Brooks for a reason other than love. Sadness swept over her. She liked Nic a lot and she liked Brooks, as well, and if they didn't marry for love, would they spend the rest of their lives feeling cheated? Because, if she had to marry Liam without love, her life would be sheer hell.

She'd saved herself; maybe she could save Nic, as well. "Please don't, Nic."

Nic lifted perfectly arched eyebrows. "Please don't what?"

"Marry him."

Realizing what she was putting at risk—her reputation as a wedding planner, the plans she had for that money, Joshua's hide—Teresa suddenly felt sick. What the hell was she doing? Was she certifiably insane?

But just like she and Liam did, Nicolette and Brooks deserved the ferocity of love, deserved happy-ever-after happiness. "You don't need to get married today. You can take your time, think this through."

Nic smiled softly. "Teresa, we have hundreds of guests waiting for me. We have spent a ridiculous amount of money—your fees included—to throw this function together in two weeks. Brooks is expecting me."

Teresa chewed the lipstick off her bottom lip. "It's the rest of *your* life, Nic. The rest of *his* life."

Nic ran her hand up Teresa's arm. "I'm not asking you to get married."

No, she wasn't, and she had no right to project her fears onto Nic. To judge her for what she was doing just because she couldn't marry without love and commitment and trust. She wanted it all; maybe Nic didn't need it. Nic took her hand and squeezed. "I know what I'm doing, Teresa."

"Of course you do. I'm sorry. I was out of line."

Nic cocked her head, her smile a little cheeky. "Why, Teresa St. Claire, I think you are a bit of a romantic."

"Maybe," Teresa reluctantly agreed.

Nic laughed softly and picked up the heavy skirts of luscious wedding dress. She nodded toward her cascading bouquet. "Can you grab that?"

Dammit, she was doing this. She really was. Nic walked toward the door and Teresa followed.

Teresa ran her hand across her eyes and sighed. *Not your circus, not your monkeys.* If Nic wanted to sacrifice herself on the altar of a marriage for any reason at all, big or small, it had nothing to do with her.

But she wouldn't do it; she couldn't do it. She'd love to marry Liam, but not like this. Never like this.

At the door, Nic took her bouquet and smoothed down her skirts. She sucked in a big breath and looked Teresa in the eye. "I'll be fine."

Teresa nodded. Leaning forward, she placed her cheek against Nic's. "I know."

Nic put a camera-ready, confident smile on her face. "Let's go give Brooks his birthday present."

It was Brooks's birthday? "It's his birthday today? What are you giving him as a gift?"

Nic's answer was short. And to the point. "Me."

Eight

If he never had to attend another wedding again it would be too soon. Liam, having arrived too late to watch the ceremony, walked into the reception and released a low whistle. He'd grown up with wealth, had attended far too many society events and weddings, but this venue was impressive.

The recently restored barn boasted clear grain cedar wallboards, high cathedral ceilings with polished beams and what he thought might be an original fir floor. The warmth of the wood was contrasted with a floor-to-ceiling glass wall on one end. The wood and glass effect was softened by a profusion of multicolored and massive flower arrangements and fairy lights. It was soft and elegant and pretty and, yeah, romantic.

Teresa was good at her job.

Liam ordered a Manhattan from a passing waiter, greeted an acquaintance and looked around for someone he'd like to talk to. Matt was across the room, waiting to issue his congratulations to the bridal couple. Brooks looked like another guy in his tuxedo and solid black tie but Nic, Liam admitted, looked like a fairy-tale princess in her gown. No wonder Brooks couldn't keep his eyes off his beautiful bride…

It was all so damn pretty and perfect. But marriage seldom was. Hadn't he seen this, not only with his parents, but also with dozens of acquaintances over the years? He'd attend the engagement parties and the weddings and six months later, a year, sometimes five, he'd hear that they were splitting, that they'd made a mistake. That divorce was inevitable.

And then he'd hear about the vicious divorce proceedings, the custody battles and he'd remember the pretty and perfect. It was all such…crap.

He'd watched and learned and rarely—okay never—allowed emotions to factor into his brief relationships. He'd never intended to get married, to put his head in that noose…

Yet, that was exactly what he'd proposed—marriage—and Teresa had been clever enough to say no. Marriage would never work between them; he was too reticent and Teresa was too independent. They were both too scarred and too scared.

Over the past ten days he'd spent a lot of time thinking about his crazy suggestion. Wondering why he'd made the offer. He finally, reluctantly, admitted that while he wanted to place Teresa under his protection—the protection of the Christopher name—he'd also wanted to save himself from being alone.

During that board meeting, with Teresa sitting in the seat next to him, knowing that she was there and solidly on his side, he'd felt stronger and more confident than he had in years. He'd felt invincible and he wanted the feeling to stick around.

If they married, he'd never have to attend another wedding or event alone; he wouldn't have to come home to a cold, silent, empty house. He'd have access to amazing sex with a partner he craved, whose body he adored.

He wouldn't be alone...

Nope, not a good enough reason to get hitched.

Liam looked around for the object of his thoughts and dreams, and the reason for his confusion. He doubted he'd find her; there were over five hundred people here and she'd be working behind the scenes to make sure that this event went off smoothly. Because, honestly, any mishap today would end her career. She'd had a few chances but if something happened to throw the wedding into disarray—whether it was her fault or not—Teresa would be persona very non grata in Seattle. Forever.

Liam looked around again, checking for threats he couldn't, admittedly, identify. He saw a young man to the left and his heart rate picked up. Was that Joshua, Teresa's brother? Looking again, Liam realized that the kid was too young, too fair, and he told himself to calm the hell down.

Taking his drink, he stared out the glass wall to the trees beyond the stream and thought that it would be a wonderful place for the paparazzi to hide, telescopic lenses poking out from between the branches of the trees. Had Teresa thought about that? Brooks would be pissed if unauthorized photos of his wedding hit the wire...

"Will you please stop scowling?"

Liam turned to see Matt with Nadia, as per usual, tucked into his side. They looked happy, content. Maybe, just maybe, Matt and Nadia would avoid the separation and the contentious divorce. He really hoped so. He liked them both, liked the way they looked together.

"Are you okay, Liam?" Nadia asked after kissing his cheek.

"Fine, thanks, Nadia." Liam forced some joviality into his tone and decided to tease Matt. "When are you going to ditch this this ugly and poor dude, Nadia? You can do so much better."

Nadia's mouth pursed and she looked like she was considering his suggestion. "Tempting but…no." Nadia looked across the room, waved at someone and stepped away from Matt. "I'll leave you two to chat. I've seen someone I want to have a word with."

Matt watched Nadia walk away with a sappy look on his face. The man was toast. And he looked happy being toast. God help him.

"Quite a party," Matt commented.

"Yep. I hope everyone enjoyed watching Brooks while he had his spine and balls removed. Hope he gets some kick-ass presents for his trouble."

Matt narrowed his eyes. "Hell, that's cold and cynical, even for you, man."

Remorse rolled over Liam, cold and greasy. Sighing, he rubbed the back of his neck and softly swore. "Sorry. Being here makes me feel scratchy."

He and Matt were best friends but he couldn't tell him that he wanted what Matt had, having a woman in his life who was there for him, only for him. Someone whom he could trust, love, rely on.

Liam couldn't look at Matt—he didn't want to see the pity on his face and looked toward the glass end wall and there she was, dressed in a halter-neck emerald jumpsuit, looking tall and willowy and so sexy it hurt. Liam immediately felt the ache in his heart and the hitch in his breath. Teresa's hair was pulled into a loose knot at the back of her neck—no surprise there—and, because she was holding an iPad, everyone knew she was working but she still looked effortlessly classy.

He wanted her. Would there ever be a time when he didn't? Liam doubted it.

Teresa's eyes met his and even though they were so far apart, he could see the sadness in her eyes. Why couldn't they make this work? Why was it hard? Why wasn't sex enough?

Why did he, more than anything, want to take her in his arms and slow-dance her around the room? For the rest of his life?

And because the thought was knock-him-off-his-feet powerful and equally terrifying, Liam handed Matt his drink and walked toward the exit and toward the valet parking. Ten minutes later he was in his car, speeding back to the city.

Nicolette swallowed another yawn and resisted the urge to lean her head on Brooks's very broad, very comfortable shoulder. They were seated at the wedding table and Nic thought that she finally, finally, had a minute alone with her, *gulp*, new husband. Before either of them had a chance to speak, Brooks's grandfather—white-haired, white-mustached and bearer of the plummiest of plummy English accents—pulled up a chair next to them and Nic swallowed her frustrated growl.

"Happy birthday, son."

Nicolette placed her elbow on the table and her chin in her hands. At the altar, she'd whispered a quiet happy birthday to Brooks when she reached his side and, as long as she lived, she'd never forget the emotion in his Cognac-colored eyes: lust and pride and...affection?

"You're the best birthday present I've ever received,"

Brooks told her and then he smiled at her and she all but melted at his feet.

Nic gave herself a mental slap and reminded herself that he'd most likely been thinking about the money that was, probably, already lodged in his bank account. The money he needed to take complete control of Abbingdon Airlines.

This wasn't a fairy tale and Brooks wasn't about to pluck stars from the sky and hand them to her. Despite her glorious dress and the pretty flowers and the amazing food and venue—Teresa had cemented her reputation as one of the best event coordinators in the city—this wedding was still a sham, a short-lived arrangement. She couldn't afford to forget that.

And she couldn't allow her full-blown, very grown-up and kick-ass attraction to her brand-new husband to complicate this imbroglio any further. Imbroglio, what a lovely word...

"So marriage plus your birthday must mean that you have liquidated your trust fund," Lester said.

Brooks's expression turned inscrutable and Nic noticed his grim smile. "As we sit here, a formal offer to buy your shares in Abbingdon Airlines is winging its way to your inbox. In terms of our agreement, you have to accept my offer."

"Yes, I saw that."

Brooks pushed his hand through his hair. "I don't mean to bring up an old argument but I really think you investing in that hotel chain is a very bad idea."

"So you've said." Lester sipped his drink and regarded Brooks over the rim. "Okay, I'll take your advice and not invest."

If she wasn't absolutely wiped and feeling equally overwhelmed, Nic might've smiled at Brooks's astonishment. She figured it didn't happen very often. "What?"

"You're better at business than I am. Since I no longer need all your millions, would you like them back? As a wedding present?"

Brooks's mouth fell open and he glanced at the glass in Lester's hand. "How many of those have you had?" he demanded.

"Enough." Lester drained his drink and pushed himself to his feet. Ignoring Brooks's suspicious expression, he picked up Nic's hand and dropped an old-fashioned kiss on her knuckles.

"You are truly lovely, Nicolette. I look forward to getting to know you better." Lester squeezed her hand and sent her a soft smile. "You've married the best of us, my dear. Welcome to the family."

Lester drifted off and Brooks's eyes followed his progress across the room. When Lester disappeared, he looked at Nic, lifted his hands and shook his head. "What the hell—"

Nic lifted her hand to her mouth to hide her yawn. "Problem?"

Brooks frowned. "On the surface, no. But I think I've just been thoroughly outmaneuvered by that wily old fox."

Okay, she was battling to keep up. "I don't understand."

His smile was a mixture of ruefulness and amusement. "I don't think he ever intended to invest. This was all about getting me married."

Nic wanted to pay attention, she really did, but she felt her eyes closing and when Brooks cupped her cheek into his hand, she sighed. If he just held her head, just like that, she could probably sleep. Yeah, that would go down well with his friends and business associates. She could see the headlines…

BORED ALREADY? ABBINGDON'S NEW WIFE FALLS ASLEEP AT WEDDING TABLE.

Nic straightened her spine and rolled her head to release some knots. She knew that Brooks was staring at her but she couldn't meet his eyes, fearing that he would see how much she wanted him, how much she ached to take this evening to its natural conclusion. Back to business, chick. "Right, who else should we talk to?"

Brooks gripped her chin and tipped it up, forcing Nic to meet his eyes. Warm eyes, eyes the color of burned sugar. "I just want to sit here and look at you," Brooks said, his deep voice soft and sensuous. "You look absolutely exquisite, Nic."

Nic's hand drifted over her full skirt. "Thank you. You look pretty good yourself."

He snorted. "I'm just a guy in a tux. You, on the other hand, look perfect."

She wanted to believe him, she did, but she didn't want to set herself up to feel disappointed. She liked Brooks. God help her if she fell in love with him.

Brooks pushed back the sleeve of his jacket to reveal the simple face of what she assumed to be a very expensive watch. Brooks lifted one strong eyebrow. "Want to get out of here?"

She very much did. She wanted a hot shower, to wash her hair and brush her teeth and collapse in a heap. Nic just nodded.

Brooks stood up, took her hand and pulled back her chair. Nic rose and sighed when she saw a well-known, very charismatic senator heading in their direction. Brooks ran his thumb over her cheekbone and placed his hand on her hip, pulling her close. Nic held her breath, thinking he was about to kiss her and ignored her disappointment when his lips brushed her ear. "Excuse yourself to go to the bathroom. Wait five minutes and when you leave, turn right down the passage instead of left. There's an emergency exit and there's a car waiting there for you."

Oh, that sounded like heaven. She could, absolutely, do that. But…what then? Where would she go? Where should she go? Back to her house, back to his? Nicolette hadn't thought of what would happen after they said their I-do's but she didn't want this evening to end.

Brooks brushed her lips once, then twice, and Nic heard his frustrated sigh. "Bathroom, emergency exit, limo."

Nic took the moment—she shouldn't have but she did—and slapped her lips on his in a hard, desperate kiss. As she walked away, she felt his eyes on her back and forced herself not to turn around and bellow her burning questions across the room.

What now? Where am I going? Am I going to see you later?

Nic wrapped her arms around her pillow and, smelling the sea, opened her eyes. A sheer curtain fluttered in the window as a warm wind rushed over her face and shoulders, before picking up and blowing the fabric to one side. Nic gasped as she caught a glimpse of a sparkling infinity pool and beyond that, a blue-green ocean. Sitting up, Nic looked down and saw that she was dressed in an oversize T-shirt. Then she saw the wedding band on her finger and her eyes darted to the ring finger on her right hand to the spectacular ring Brooks placed there when she agreed to marry him.

She was married to Brooks; she remembered the wedding. Nic wrapped her arms around her knees, yawned and recalled Brooks sliding into the limo next to her and his brief order to his driver to take them to the airport. Fighting sleep—by that point she'd been beyond exhaustion—she'd asked her new husband where they were going.

She vaguely recalled him saying something about a no-strings honeymoon, that she should sleep and when he'd tapped his shoulder, suggesting that she rest her head against it, she had. He'd carried her on his plane and placed her on a bed in the private cabin. She'd apparently, somehow, slept through the flight and the drive from the airport to…wherever this was.

Flinging back the sheet, Nic padded across the room to the veranda and stepped onto an expansive balcony. Walking past the infinity pool, she stopped at the tempered glass that served as a wall and looked down. Nic sucked in her breath at the thirty-meter drop on the other side of the barrier. The cliff ended in a small, white, what looked to be private, beach.

And then beyond that, a hundred yards of shallow, crystal-clear, blue sea. So…

Wow.

"Morning, sleepyhead."

Nic smiled at his low, deep voice and slowly turned. Brooks was lying on a lounger under the shade of an umbrella, wearing designer sunglasses and a pair of plain black swimming shorts. He was also wearing miles and miles of tawny skin covering big, defined muscles. Oh, God, she'd known that he was in shape but hadn't thought he'd have such muscled legs, big arms and a washboard stomach.

Nic pushed her hand into what she knew was messy hair and wished that she'd taken the time to shower, to brush her teeth. He looked like chocolate-covered sin and she…

Didn't.

"Hi." Nic sent a longing look to the room she left and wondered if he'd think she was nuts if she bolted back inside and hit the shower. Probably. Definitely. Nic, knowing that she couldn't keep staring at him—oh, how she wanted to!—looked at the blindingly white house behind them before gesturing to the sea. "Where are we?"

"St. Barts. This is one of the Abbingdon vacation homes."

One of their homes? "How many do you have?"

Brooks pushed his sunglasses to rest on top of his head. "A few." Those rich eyes drifted over her in frank admiration. "You're looking so much better. You were totally out of it for a while."

Nic colored. "I haven't slept much lately. I suppose it all caught up with me. And when I did sleep, I didn't get any rest."

"Did the thought of marrying me give you nightmares?" Brooks asked, swinging his feet to the floor.

She couldn't tell him that she was terrified of falling in love with him, petrified that one day, probably sooner rather than later, she'd have to walk away from him after sampling a taste of what life with Brooks was like. Oh, the wealth was…nice, she supposed, but if he lost everything tomorrow, she knew that she'd still want to wake up to his beautiful eyes, that hard body, that slow smile.

Man, how was she going to resist him? Seeing that he was still waiting for an answer, Nic shrugged. "Change is always scary."

"It can be. It can also be exciting and thrilling and life-changing," Brooks quietly stated, standing up. "Well, we're here for a week and there's not a hell of a lot to do besides tan and swim and snorkel. I need to work for a few hours but I could also do with some downtime."

A week on the beach? It sounded like heaven. There was only one thing that would make it better…

Don't, Nic, it's not a good idea.

He said that it was a no-strings honeymoon, that he didn't expect anything. Actually, she remembered hearing

a great deal of hope in his voice but that might've been ex-
treme tiredness causing her imagination to run riot. There
was only one way to find out...

*If you sleep with him, it'll be so much harder to walk
away.*

But if I don't sleep with him I might lose my mind.

"Do you want me?"

Oh, God, she'd intended those words to come out
smooth and a little carefree, not desperate and demanding.
He was going to think she was as gauche as a teenager...

When it came to Brooks Abbingdon, she was.

Brooks tensed and his head snapped up and his gaze
pinned her to the floor. He swallowed and when he spoke,
Nic heard the rough edge in his normally smooth voice. "I
want you so much I can barely breathe."

Phew. Well...

Good.

Brooks stayed where he was, his arms folded against
his chest, his fingers digging into his biceps. Why wasn't
he moving? Didn't he understand what she was offering?
Nic lifted her thumb to gnaw the edge of a nonexistent
cuticle. "Um...well...crap, I don't know what to say now."

"You could say that you want me, too," Brooks stated
but Nic heard a touch of insecurity underneath his evenly
stated words.

"I thought that was as obvious as a sixty-foot flashing neon sign," Nic admitted. "That's a big part of why I
haven't been sleeping."

"Because you've been thinking about me?"

Nic blushed but nodded. "There have been a couple of
dreams that have been real and I wake up, hovering on the
edge of..." She stumbled over her words and waved her
hand. "Oh, God, shut up now, Nic."

"I'd really prefer that you didn't," Brooks said, amusement in his eyes. And then he, finally, started to move. Nic watched his long-legged stride, saw the erection pulling his trunks tight, and wondered where all the saliva in her mouth had gone.

When he was a few feet from her, Nic held up her hand. "This has nothing to do with anything else, our fake marriage or our business arrangement."

"We left that behind in Seattle," Brooks agreed. "All of it. It's just me, Brooks, desperate to kiss you, Nic."

She wanted that, too, wanted his mouth on hers…oh, yuck! Her mouth! Ack!

Nic slapped her hand over her mouth and saw Brooks's eyes widen. He stopped and lifted an eyebrow. "And now?" he asked.

"I need a shower and to brush my teeth." Nic mumbled the words against the palm of her hand.

Brooks smiled at her and he looked ten years younger. Bending his knees, he placed his shoulder against her stomach and wrapped one arm around her bare thighs. Hoisting her up and over his shoulder, he patted her satin-covered butt and walked her down the veranda toward the far end of the house. As he stepped into an expansive master suite, Nic saw that the room was at the end of the house and was open on two sides. The view from this room was more stunning, if that was at all possible, than the view from her room.

Her heart pounding and her temperature rising, but that could be because Brooks's hand had sneaked between the tops of her thighs, she was carried by Brooks as he walked her past a massive bed and into an open-air bathroom. Allowing her to slide down his body, oh, wow, he was hot and hard…everywhere, Brooks turned her to face one of the two basins. Rummaging in the cupboard below, he pulled out a brand-new toothbrush and removed it from its packaging. Handing her the brush and a tube of toothpaste, he told her she had two minutes.

Fascinated by the need in his eyes, and the way he kept looking at her mouth, Nic obeyed. She couldn't wait to kiss him…

Brooks left her and walked over to the open-air double-headed shower, encased by the same tempered clear glass barrier she'd seen earlier on the entertainment area. Her mouth full of toothpaste, Nic looked past Brooks onto a thick forest below and realized it was totally private.

Yay, because she had a feeling that her back and ass were going to be wedged against that glass as Brooks slid into her.

Damn, she really couldn't wait. Like not for one second more.

Nine

She was absolutely not going to get naked with Liam this morning. This was a business meeting, a follow-up meeting—as he'd stated in his email, asking her to carve out some time for him—not a let's-get-naked meeting.

Not that she had many—or any—problems getting naked with Liam Christopher.

"It's nine o'clock on Monday morning for God's sake," Teresa muttered to herself.

Duncan, Liam's sharply dressed PA, looked up from his monitor and lifted a perfectly groomed eyebrow. And that reminded her; she needed to book a facial and a brow shaping, a mani and pedi. With her hectic schedule lately organizing Brooks and Nic's wedding, she hadn't had any time for herself.

Oh, and a bikini wax was also needed. Now, there was a very decent reason why, when she was finally admitted into Liam's inner sanctum, she'd keep all her clothes on.

Duncan leaned back in his chair and offered a pleasant

greeting. "Liam said you did a spectacular job organizing the Ryan/Abbingdon wedding. He was very impressed."

Teresa felt like she'd won the lottery and had to stop herself from dancing on the spot. Then cynicism rolled in... Liam wasn't the type who handed out praise easily. "Did he really say that or are you just being nice?"

Duncan rolled his eyes. "He really said that."

Oh.

Oh, wow. Liam liked what she did. And if he liked it, then maybe the rest of Seattle did, too, and she'd start picking up work again. Because she still had her brother's hide to save and his debt to repay.

Duncan stood up and walked around his desk. Taking Teresa's arm, he pulled her over to his desk and pointed at a small box with a green and a red light on it. "When the green light flicks on, you can go on in." Duncan straightened his tie. "I'm going to organize coffee because I'm pretty sure you're all going to need some." He pulled a face. "That or a fire extinguisher."

Teresa watched him walk away, conscious of the fire in her cheeks. She hoped that Duncan wasn't referring to what happened the last time she and Liam were alone together. How would he even know that they'd made love? Had the words "just got laid" appeared on her forehead as she left Liam's office?

Now, there was just one more reason why no clothes would be shed during this meeting. Not a tie, not even her jacket...it was a slippery slope and she had no intention of ending up in a tangled, bruised and bloody heap at the bottom of the hill. Because, yeah, that was exactly what was going to happen if she didn't get her feelings for Liam under control. Though, honestly, that horse might've already bolted.

Like, weeks ago...

The light on Duncan's desk flashed green and Teresa strode over to his door, pushing down on the ornate handle. It would be better to get ahead of their attraction, to remind him this was a business meeting and that it was Monday morning. It was the most sensible, businesslike time of the week and that was what they had to be. Businesslike.

"I have half an hour for you, and all of those thirty minutes will be spent with our clothes on."

Teresa saw Liam's grin and out of the corner of her eye she saw a flutter of a cream silk skirt, the flash of a peach blouse.

Oh, shit, they weren't alone.

Teresa, her cheeks flaming, turned her head and…

Yep. Liam's mother, her expression perfectly haughty, sat on his expensive sofa, the same sofa on which Liam had loved her so well.

Gah.

"Mrs. Christopher, I didn't know…ah…" Teresa sent a helpless look at Liam, looking stupidly sexy in a deep gray suit and bottle-green tie.

"Teresa, you remember my mother, Catherine," Liam smoothly stated, walking around his desk to gently grip her biceps. "My mother stopped by but she's about to leave."

Feeling steadier, she was shocked when Liam's mouth drifted across hers. "Hi," he murmured.

Teresa's eyes immediately flew back to Catherine's eating-a-sour-lemon face.

Deep in her tote bag, her phone rang and, deeply thankful for the interruption, Teresa dived into it, keeping her face down to give herself time to think. It was obvious that Catherine Christopher still blamed her for the breakup of her marriage, and was, obviously, still incensed that Linus left her twenty-five percent of his shares in this business. As for her baby sleeping with her archenemy? If looks could kill, she'd be a tiny pile of ash on Liam's expensive carpet.

Teresa uttered her standard greeting. Hopefully, it would be a client and she could use him, or her, as an excuse to skedaddle.

"Teresa, they've found me!"

Dammit, dammit, dammit. She'd left her phone on loudspeaker and her brother's voice bounced off Liam's office walls.

"Josh, hold on," Teresa commanded him, punching the button to make their conversation private.

Turning her back on the mother and son duo, she walked past Liam's desk to the window, placing her hand on the glass and keeping her voice low. "What happened?"

"I got a call at The Bridge. We're not supposed to have them but they let me take it," Joshua shouted, his voice sounding like a hundred decibels in her ear. Teresa's blood froze. She'd booked Josh in under an assumed name, paid in cash. He shouldn't have been found, not this quickly.

Stay calm, Teresa. You have to think. "What did they say?"

"That I had a week to pay up. That if not, I was dead, and you were, too."

Teresa closed her eyes and rested her forehead on the glass. She sent Liam a quick look and caught the concern in his eyes. "Okay, that's doable. I can raise the money and we'll put an end to this."

"Where will you get the money?"

Did it matter? "Where are you now?" Teresa asked, avoiding his question.

"I snuck out and am back in the city. I went by your apartment and picked up my phone," Joshua replied. "Where are you going to get the money, Teresa?"

"Why does it matter, Joshua? The debt will be paid."

Joshua waited a beat before replying. "Because I was told that if you take the money from Liam Christopher, we'll still die. And so will Christopher."

Teresa felt her knees buckle, her throat tighten. "That makes no sense," she whispered. "Why do they care where the money comes from?"

"I don't know but they do," Joshua replied. "So guess we are back to square one, right? What are we going to do...run?"

Liam was her only option for money and if she couldn't borrow it from him—and there was no way that she'd put his life in danger—they'd have to. "I'll meet you at home, Josh."

"Yeah. But later." Josh disconnected the call and Teresa released a howl. Frustrated beyond belief, her stress levels climbing, Teresa banged her phone against the window.

Liam plucked the phone from her grasp and pulled her into his arms, cradling her head against his chest.

Teresa wanted to wrap her arms around his waist, sink into his strength but she couldn't. He was now in the cross-hairs of the same people targeting them, and she would not put him in danger. There had been too many casualties in this war; she was damned if Liam was going to be one, too. She could not risk his life by borrowing money against her shares, by having anything more to do with him. He was too precious, too important...

Liam had been her only option for quick money and now there was no way she'd be able to raise seven million in less than a week. And judging by the threats, it seemed that the people holding Joshua's marker weren't interested in a pay-back-in-installments arrangement.

By calling Josh, threatening him, they were telling her that they could find him, them, if they tried to hide. If they wanted a shot at safety, they'd needed another plan.

As Joshua suggested, they'd have to run, to leave the west coast, find new identities and get used to a life on the run. It was the only way they'd survive.

If they survived.

Teresa's mind raced. She had the money Brooks paid her; she hadn't paid her suppliers yet. Yeah, if she didn't pay them, she'd be stealing, defrauding them, but she needed every cent of that payout from Brooks to get them new identities, to purchase a car for cash, to pay for flights to somewhere else…

Her business, and her reputation, would never survive but if they didn't run, neither would they.

It was the only option they had left. Teresa, sucking in every last bit of courage she possessed, placed her hands on Liam's chest and pushed herself out of his arms. Without looking at him—she couldn't because if she did, she'd beg him for help and then he'd be in danger—she held out her hand for her phone.

"I've got to go. I'll call you in a few hours."

"Stay here, Teresa. Let me help you," Liam said, his voice low and persuasive.

"I'll reschedule," Teresa lied. What she'd do, once they were on the road, is find a lawyer and sign over all her shares to him even though the year wasn't up. Yeah, she'd lose the money but it would sever the tie between them. He'd be safe and if she and Josh wanted to survive the next few months, years, decades, she needed to cut her ties with everyone.

Giving up everyone and everything would be the price she'd have to pay for her, Josh and, most important, Liam, to stay alive.

So be it.

Teresa stood up on her tiptoes and brushed her mouth against Liam's, leaving it there for a moment longer than appropriate. How could she walk away from him? Where was she going to find the strength? She wanted to tell him she loved him, that he was everything she'd ever wanted, or needed. That his was the head she wanted sharing her pillow, the body she wanted to wake up beside, the smile she wanted to see when she was eighty. The hand she wanted to hold when death came calling.

"Let me help you," Liam repeated, his fingers digging into her hips.

Teresa forced a smile on her lips. "With what, Liam?" she said, keeping her voice chirpy. "All is well."

"Don't lie to me," Liam said.

Teresa bit her bottom lip, cursing the tears that filled her eyes. "Then don't ask me questions that require a lie." Teresa stood on her toes, kissed his cheek and pulled back. "Bye, Liam."

Teresa forced herself to walk to the door, forced her leaden feet to move. Ignoring Catherine, who watched their interactions with undisguised glee, she finally—finally—reached the door.

"Don't make me come after you, Teresa," Liam warned.

Teresa looked back at him and the tears she'd tried so hard to contain, rolled down her face. "Please don't, Liam. I'm just going to say no."

Liam wore his stubborn expression and Teresa knew what to say to stop him from chasing after her. She would have to force the words out but they were words she knew would keep him away, words that would keep him safe. Because his safety was all that mattered.

Teresa tossed her hair and prepared to utter her biggest lie ever. The one she knew would burn every bridge between them.

"I should never have slept with your dad."

Teresa saw the pain flash in Liam's eyes and forced herself to remain upright. She couldn't fall to the floor; she had too much to do.

Forcing a smile onto her face took everything she had. "He was good but you are better."

"You bitch! You slutty, skanky trollop. I was right! I am always right!"

Teresa pulled the door closed on Catherine's vitriol, knowing that Liam's mother would never be a fan.

What really hurt was that, after today, Liam wouldn't be, either.

That was good for his safety, bad for her.

As long as Liam was safe, she could live with just about anything.

She was lying through her pretty, pearly teeth. And badly, at that.

Liam looked at his closed door and shook his head. Teresa hadn't slept with his father; any fool could see that she'd uttered those words to distance herself from him, to put an insurmountable barrier between them. She'd only say something like that to make him so mad that he'd wash his hands of her.

Well, tough crap, lady. It wasn't working. He wasn't that thick or that easily manipulated. Or weak.

"I told you she slept with your father! Why won't anyone listen to me?"

Catherine's high-pitched scream pierced his what-the-hell moment and Liam pulled his eyes off his door, resisting the urge to go after Teresa. Oh, she thought he was done, but she wasn't getting away from him that easily.

And he was done with her being stubborn, was sick of her pride and her need to fly solo. This situation needed to end. And it would, today.

Ignoring his mother, who'd moved on to her well-rehearsed diatribe about his father's unfaithfulness and how awful her life was, he pulled his phone from the inside pocket of his jacket and stared down at the screen. Relief rolled over him as he saw the text message on his phone. Somehow he'd had the presence of mind, while he'd had possession of Teresa's phone, to forward her brother's contact number to his phone.

And he knew just the guy who had the skills to tell him where exactly Joshua St. Claire was, right at this moment. Jeremy Dutton was more than just a private investigator. *Investigator* barely began to describe all the things Dutton was capable of.

Teresa wasn't the only one with a Fixer.

When Dutton answered, Liam didn't bother with niceties. "I need you to ping this number and find out exactly where this phone is," Liam said.

"How soon do you need it?" Dutton asked.

"Five minutes ago," Liam retorted.

"Okay, working on it."

"Also, I also need you to front me seven mil. I'll pay you back in a few days." Dutton was one of the few people who had tens of millions in cash he could easily access. Handy when people like him needed a lot of cash quickly. Dutton charged exorbitant rates for the temporary loan but Liam could afford it.

"Unmarked bills?"

"Preferably." Liam gripped the bridge of his nose, his mind turning over at warp speed. He quickly laid the bare facts on the table, reminding Dutton of Teresa's circumstances. He'd done the investigation on her, but Liam wasn't his only client, so a reminder brought him up to speed.

"I need you to contact the head of that organization and make arrangements for this debt to be settled. I want it done this afternoon. You will pay them directly and I want a guarantee that the association between them and the St. Claires will be terminated once that money changes hands. I want them to forget they ever heard their names."

"Why don't I secure world peace and reverse climate change while I'm at it?" Dutton grumbled.

"Are you not up to it? Shall I call The Fixer?"

Desperate times meant desperate measures and Liam knew that mentioning his competitor's name would motivate Dutton.

Liam saw his mother's shocked face and ignored her waving hands, her gestures to get him to stop talking. "I'm offering you another hundred thousand, on top of the interest you're charging on the loan, to make this all go away. But I want it done by this afternoon."

"Two-fifty."

Greedy bastard. "Two."

"Done. I'll let you know when the deal is completed."

"And get me the location of that phone."

"On it."

Liam disconnected the call and looked at his mother, who sat on the edge of her chair, looking ashen. "What's wrong with you?"

"You believe her," Catherine said, now sounding calm and utterly disconnected.

"Who are you talking about?" Liam demanded. He didn't have time for his mother right now. He needed to stop Teresa from doing whatever she was planning. Because she sure as hell was planning something.

"You are just like your father."

Liam's fingers returned to grip his nose as he looked for calm. There was a good chance that he might lose it with his mother today and it wasn't going to be pretty. Long overdue maybe, but not pretty.

Liam didn't have time to pussyfoot around Catherine. "What she said about sleeping with Dad, it was a lie, Mom. She never slept with him."

"She just admitted it!" Catherine screamed, pointing at the closed door.

"She was lying." Probably to protect him but he wasn't sure why. He didn't need it. But whatever her reasoning, her inability to ask for help annoyed and hurt him. But why was he surprised? Teresa did everything solo.

"I can't see the attraction! She's a piece of skirt, a tramp—"

"Be careful, Mother."

"No matter what I do, she still comes out smelling like a rose!"

Liam was about to ask his mother to leave when her words sank in.

He tensed as icy fingers of dread tap-danced on his spine. "What do you mean, no matter what you do?"

Please let her have misspoken; please let it not be what he was thinking.

Liam stared at Catherine and noticed the malevolence in her eyes. This was going to be a lot worse than what he thought.

Catherine, as defiant as hell, met his eyes. "She got her hooks into your father. I absolutely wasn't going to let her get her hooks into you."

"What did you do?" Liam dropped his voice, knowing that he had to keep a cap on his anger because, if he let it loose, it would roar and claw and eviscerate.

Catherine stood up and lifted her shoulders in an elegant, indifferent shrug. "I was the source of the tabloid rumors. I've been telling my friends, and encouraging them to tell their friends, not to hire Teresa St. Claire, that she's just not our sort."

Yeah, that was the truth; it just wasn't all the truth. "What else?"

That shrug again. He didn't want to think, or face it, but he had to ask. "Did you have any interactions with her brother, Joshua?"

Catherine inspected her nails. "Not directly."

She wanted to tell him, he realized; she wanted him to know. To brag? He wouldn't put it past her. Liam remained quiet and waited her out. It didn't take long for her to start talking.

"When I heard that she was working for Matt, I knew that you'd run into her and I knew that there was a chance that you'd still find her attractive. I was soon proved right. I was not going to let her back into our lives."

Oh, shit.

"I'd always kept tabs on her. I thought it necessary. I knew exactly who she was, what her brother had done. I made contact with the people who bought her brother's debt and I encouraged them to inflate the interest, to apply pressure. I made certain financial contributions to make her life hell."

"Did you have anything to do with Joshua's flight across the country, him gate-crashing Matt's party?"

"A little ketamine, two thugs and a thousand dollars will go a long way," Catherine admitted without a shred of remorse. "I also fed the tabloids information and photographs about her affair with your father but I have to admit, that girl is harder to scare than I thought."

Liam realized that he'd never been this angry before. Right now he absolutely hated his mother. Loathed her with every fiber of his being.

He still had so many questions but he was running out of time. "How did you contact the people holding Josh's debt?"

"The same way you did. People in our social circle, people with serious money, all have people who take care of things like that for us," Catherine replied, bored. "We don't do it ourselves, darling."

"The Fixer?"

"Someone like him." Liam fought the insane desire to laugh. People like them never got their hands dirty; they directed proceedings from afar. Plausible deniability, wasn't that the term? No more. He was done with trying to keep his hands clean. If fighting dirty was what was needed to save Teresa from his mother's machinations and, as scary, the criminal underworld, that was what he'd do.

Picking up his phone, he redialed the previous number he'd used.

"I just sent you the coordinates," Jeremy stated. "Since you're in your office, it should take you about ten minutes to get to him."

"I want to be in on those conversations. I want to be in on that meeting. I want to be the one to hand over the cash. Make it happen."

Liam looked at his mother and narrowed his eyes at her. He tossed his phone on his desk and sent his mother a hard look. "I want you out of my life, Catherine, but right now I'll settle for you leaving my office."

Catherine, for the first time in her life, left without further argument.

Ten

It took a few hours to track Joshua down as the kid kept moving through the city. When he did, Liam sat on the park bench next to Teresa's younger brother, watching him out of the corner of his eye. Joshua looked as relaxed as a rabbit on speed and at any moment he expected him to bolt. Liam, on hearing that Joshua was in Cal Anderson Park, was surprised to find him on one of the first benches after entering the park.

"Did my sister send you?" Joshua demanded.

"No, the world has to stop turning before your sister asks me for help," Liam muttered, still annoyed. "So, what's the plan? How are you going to deal with this situation? How do you plan on repaying the money?"

Joshua's expression turned grim. "We're not. If we can't borrow it from you it leaves us only one option and that's to run."

Liam felt his heart constrict. Running was the stupidest

idea ever. "Wait, back up. What do you mean if we can't borrow it from me?"

Joshua looked at him like he was thick. "Because if we do, we all die. Including you."

Nice. So that was the reason Teresa issued that stupid lie. She'd been trying to protect him.

Liam forced himself to push the thought of his imminent demise away. "That makes no sense. They shouldn't care where the money comes from, just that they get it. Unless…"

Unless his mother put that bug in their ear.

Oh, that sounded like something she'd say. Liam wanted to believe that she didn't mean it but, having seen what lengths she'd go to get Teresa out of his life, and hers, he wasn't so sure.

Dutton's voice flowed into his ear. "When I spoke to the boss, he made it clear that he's only concerned about getting the money asap. If that was a condition, he would've said something so I think it's safe to assume that they don't give a damn who pays and that it was an empty threat."

"Awesome," Liam replied to Dutton, who was monitoring his conversation through some fancy spy gear. He had a bud in his ear and the pen in his inside pocket was operating as a microphone and recorder. He was also somewhere around and when he met with his contact, Dutton would video-record the transaction. There was no way anyone would be able to dispute the payment.

Liam put his hand on the leather knapsack, needing to keep contact with the cash that had been delivered to his office an hour ago. Newish bills, packets and packets of them.

He was carrying around seven million dollars in cash and in thirty minutes, he was going to hand the rucksack over at a coffee shop not far from here. He was trying to play it cool but he hoped Joshua couldn't tell that his heart felt like it was about to beat out of his chest. It wasn't every day one met with the lieutenant of some mafia-like organization. Okay, he met with sharks all the time—his board members were an excellent example—but these were streetwise sharks and they had a history of drawing blood.

Joshua's phone rang and the kid leaped a foot out of his seat. He pulled it out of the deep pocket of his stupid, low-hanging pants—had he never heard of a belt?—and squinted at the display. "It's Teresa again. She's flipping out."

Liam hated the thought of Teresa worrying and could easily imagine her pacing her apartment, wondering where the hell Joshua was. But if she, and Joshua, were kept in the dark about what he was doing there was no chance of either of them messing up his plans. And Teresa wouldn't run without Joshua and he intended to keep Joshua with him until the very last minute.

This needed to end and he intended to do exactly that.

Joshua stared at his heavy biker boots. "Why are you doing this? Why are you helping me?"

Liam thought it better that there was no misunderstanding between him and Teresa's brother. "I'm not doing it for you."

Joshua frowned and for the first time, his eyes met Liam's. "Uh…you're not?"

Liam folded his arms across his chest. "Nope. I'm doing this for your sister, so that you can stop being the biggest pain in her ass."

"I…um… I know I messed up," Joshua hedged and his voice took on a whiny tinge that Liam despised.

"You are in your twenties, St. Claire. When are you going to stand on your own two feet and stop expecting your sister to bail your skinny ass out of trouble?"

"I didn't mean to—"

Liam plowed his fist into Joshua's biceps and the kid skidded down the park bench and nearly fell off the end. "Stop lying to yourself. You act first and think later or you ask Teresa to think for you. That stops here. And it stops today."

"I guess," Joshua muttered. "You're hella protective over my sister. Why are you doing this?"

"God alone knows."

Joshua tipped his head to the side. "Have you told my sister that you love her?"

Liam turned his head slowly and he saw Joshua inch down the bench, away from him. He wanted to deny his words but he couldn't; neither did he have an answer to his question. He hadn't told Teresa because, as of two seconds ago, he wasn't completely sure that he did. Now he was. Sure, that is. She was his; she always had been since that evening they first met all those years ago.

He loved her.

That had to be the reason why he was handing over seven million dollars to some assface at lunchtime on a Monday morning.

"Well?" Joshua asked. "Does she know? Are you ever going to tell her?"

Not yet, not quite yet. Maybe never. There were so many gaps in his life, so many blanks he still needed to fill. He needed those missing puzzle pieces to be filled before he could go to Teresa and hand his heart over. There were so many questions he needed answered—about his parents, about why Linus left her his shares—and he would also need to tell her about Catherine's machinations.

His mother had messed with her and Joshua's lives, had tried to ruin her business, caused her untold worry. How would she be able to look past that to a life with him?

She'd thought that she was bad for him but today's events proved that he wasn't good enough for her. They didn't have a hope in hell.

"Are you going to ask her to marry you? Are you going to get her name tattooed on your butt? Are you going to make her a playlist with a whole bunch of love songs on it?"

Right, the kid was now starting to annoy him. Liam lowered his glasses and when Joshua met his eyes, scowled. "Remember that fist I planted on your jaw a few weeks back?"

Joshua rubbed the side of his face. "Yeah, you came close to breaking it."

Not even close. "Well, if you don't shut the hell up, I'll try again."

"Relax, Liam," Dutton cautioned via the tiny bud in his ear. "By the way, I've just sent an email through to your phone with regard to that DNA testing."

Liam felt his heart shrivel and his lungs collapse. This? Now? "I'm about to hand over a crap load of cash to a known criminal and you want to discuss this now?"

Dutton had the audacity to laugh. "You can do two things at once. Do you want me to give you the highlights?"

"Give me a sec." Did he? Liam knew that whatever Dutton was about to say next would change his life, on a fundamental level. He wouldn't be the same person he was right now; he might not even be, he suspected, a Christopher. Did he really want to know? Could he live with himself if he didn't find out?

No, he was done with lies, half truths and obfuscations. He needed the truth, no matter how hard it was to hear. The truth was always better than a lie…

Maybe.

No, it was. Truth *had* to win, every time. And if he wasn't a Christopher he'd deal with the ramifications—his father's will, this position on the board, in society—later.

"Tell me," Liam said, pushing the words through clenched teeth.

"Your mother is your biological mother. Your father is not."

Liam took a moment to digest his words. Hold on, what did that mean? It didn't take him long to figure it out since he knew that his parents had been married for a few years before he was born.

So that had to mean that his mother had an affair.

A bubble of hysterical laughter formed in Liam's chest. Catherine had bitched and whined and moaned and cried buckets over his father's supposed affair with Teresa. But she was the one who'd colored outside the lines and not only had an affair—she also passed off her lover's son as her husband's.

Priceless.

Liam picked up his phone and walking just far enough away from Joshua so that he couldn't hear his conversation, dialed his mother's cell.

"I do hope you've called to apologize."

Not in this lifetime.

"So, Catherine, would you like to tell me who my biological father is?" Liam asked. It was a strain to keep his voice calm and even but if he started shouting, there was a solid chance that Catherine would hang up. And he needed answers and he needed them now.

"I have no idea what you are talking about. Have you been drinking, Liam?"

Nice try, Mom. "I noticed Dad's blood type in the hospital, and I knew that people with his blood type can't produce a kid with my blood type. When I asked you about it at Dad's funeral, you said it was a typo."

Catherine's silence was hot and heavy.

"So I ordered some genetic testing done and those results came in a few minutes ago. You're my mother, but Linus wasn't my father."

"He was your father in every way that mattered—"

"Cut the crap, Mom. You had an affair—ironic, giving how much you've had to say on Dad's perceived infidelity—and pretended that I was Dad's."

"You have been drinking!"

He'd definitely inherited his stubborn gene from Catherine. "Are you denying it?"

"Until my last breath."

"Science doesn't lie, Mom, but you sure as hell do." Liam waited a beat. "I will find out."

"It's not going to change anything, Liam!" Catherine said and for the first time, Liam heard the edge of fear in her voice.

"Maybe not. Then again, it might change everything."

Liam disconnected the call and gripped the bridge of his nose. With a mother like Catherine, who only saw what she wanted to see, it was no wonder he had trust issues. Would Catherine ever tell him the truth? He doubted it. So then, how to find out who his real father was? And why did he need to?

Liam stared at the green grass beneath his leather shoes. He needed to know because he now didn't know who he was, where his real place in the world was. Was he a Christopher? What parts of him were a result of nurture and not nature? There were too many puzzle pieces of his life missing and he needed to find them, to get a clear picture of where he came from and who he was.

Until he was clear about that, he couldn't know for certain how he felt about marriage and love and...

Teresa.

He needed to know everything, to be able to show Teresa exactly who he was so that, when—if—he ever found the guts to tell her he loved her, she'd know everything. The good and the bad. It was vitally important that there was nothing between them but cold, hard truth.

Lies corroded and if he kept anything from her, whatever they had would be eaten from the inside out.

"So do you want me to dig into who your biological father might be?" Dutton asked.

Dammit, he'd forgotten about his own Fixer, listening to every word he'd uttered.

Oh, well, what was done was done. "Yeah."

"Can you give me a starting point?" Dutton asked. "Where were your folks living at the time? Please don't tell me here in Seattle."

Linus wasn't his father; Linus wasn't his father... Who was? Liam forced himself to think about Dutton's question.

"Uh... I think I remember my mom saying that I was conceived in Hawaii. My dad was building a hotel out there at the time. Before he started with tech products, he was into real estate," Liam replied. "They sold the hotel decades ago but it's still there. It's now called The Poseidon Inn."

"I'm on it. Well, I will be when we're done here."

Liam looked around, trying to act casual. "Where are you?"

"Around."

Liam walked back to the bench and sat down, resting his forearms on his thighs. He felt Joshua's eyes on his face. "You look as white as a sheet. What happened?"

Liam shook his head. "Nothing to do with you."

Joshua nodded. "Fair enough. But if you are stressed, you should talk to Teresa. She's good at listening and finding solutions."

Yeah, she was. But Liam wasn't going to burden her with his ugly past. Teresa had had too many people dumping their crap on her; he wouldn't be another one in a long line who looked to her for a solution. He was a big boy; he'd work it out for himself, his way. "There's a lot to be said for independence, Joshua. You should try it sometime."

Dutton spoke in his ear, informing him that he needed to leave if he was going to meet his contact on time. Standing, he placed a hand on Joshua's shoulder. "By the end of today your life is going to be very different. You're about to get a second chance, so don't mess it up. That being said, can you do me a favor?"

"What?"

"Wait here for me, maybe for twenty minutes, a half hour? Then we'll tackle your sister together."

Joshua nodded and Liam picked up the rucksack and walked away, trying to act like he wasn't carrying several fortunes over his shoulder.

Teresa was about to climb the walls by the time she heard a knock on her apartment door. Flying across the room, she hurdled the two suitcases she'd packed—the absolute essentials she couldn't leave behind—and yanked the door open. Her brother, looking tired but unharmed, lifted his hand in a half wave. Teresa, conscious of Liam behind him looking grim, wrapped her arms around Joshua's waist and burst into tears.

"I thought you were dead. Why didn't you answer my calls?" Teresa demanded between hiccups and sobs.

Joshua steered her backward into the room and awkwardly patted her back.

Aware that Liam had followed them into the room, she stepped away from Joshua and wiped her eyes with the balls of her hands. Teresa was so glad to see him one more time, for the last time, and she wished she could throw herself into his arms and ask him for help. But this was her mess. Well, Joshua's actually, and while she might, emphasis on the *might*, consider asking him for a loan to help her out, she couldn't ask him to risk his life.

No, her only option was to run, as soon as they could and as far as they could. Mexico? Alaska? God, it was all so overwhelming. But first, she had to get Liam to leave.

Liam nudged a suitcase with his foot. "Going somewhere?"

She didn't want to lie to him, she really didn't. But she had already once today—and such a huge one—so the damage was done. "I'm taking Joshua on a short trip."

"No, you're bolting," Liam stated, folding his arms over his chest. "Why didn't you ask me for help instead?"

Joshua opened his mouth to speak but a hard look from Liam killed whatever he was about to say. He lifted his hands. "I'm going to give you some privacy."

Liam waited until Joshua had left the room before speaking again. "Well?"

Teresa lifted her head. "I don't need your help, Liam. I can handle whatever happens in my life."

"By running away? When did that ever help?"

It would help him to stay alive! But she couldn't tell him that! Why was he pushing her? He should be at home, cursing her name. "Why are you here? After what I said today, I never expected to see you again."

"You're a really bad liar, Teresa, and I know the truth, because I know *you*. You did not sleep with my dad and you only said that to create some distance between us. So that I would let you go."

Dammit, dammit, dammit. Teresa glanced down at her bags. "I'm going anyway."

"You're staying exactly where you are," Liam stated, his face implacable. "It's over, Teresa."

What was over? Their relationship? Yes, she already assumed as much. "I know. There's been too much craziness between us to make us work."

"That's not what I was talking about," Liam said, pulling a small flash drive from the pocket of his suit. He handed it to her and Teresa frowned as she took the drive.

"What is this?"

"That is proof that Joshua's debts have been paid, that he is no longer in danger from any criminal element, anywhere." Liam narrowed his eyes. "But if he finds himself entangled in that world again, I will not be pleased."

Teresa heard his words but they didn't make any sense. Feeling her knees turning mushy, she sat down on the arm of her sofa and stared up at Liam. "I don't understand. How did this happen? What did you *do*?"

Liam picked up a wooden sculpture of a hummingbird on a stand and ran his thumb down its smooth back. He replaced the sculpture before jamming his hands into the pockets of his pants.

"If you'd just put your stubbornness aside and asked for my help, this could've been handled weeks ago."

"But the money…it's a lot of money. And they threatened *you*, Liam."

"The threat was an empty one and we would've figured that out together if you'd just talked to me. And it's just money, Teresa, and I have a lot of it."

But how would she ever pay him back? How would Joshua? But before she got to that, she needed to know how her life went from falling apart to…not. "Tell me everything."

Liam hesitated as if he was trying to decide where to start.

"You know I also have a guy who does things for me, someone I have on speed dial. He has connections that you and I—" Liam hesitated "—do not. He helped me arrange to pay off the debt. It's done. But as Nicolette suspected back in Napa, it was more personal than we realized, Teresa. Somebody went to a lot of effort to make your life hell."

Teresa sucked her bottom lip between her teeth. She didn't want to hear this, and she knew that Liam didn't want to tell her this part of the story. "Do you know who?"

He nodded. Liam met her eyes and in the green depths, she saw pain and mortification. "My mother."

Teresa's mouth fell open. *"What?"*

"My mother blames you for the breakup of her marriage. She refuses to accept that you didn't have an affair with Linus. She was behind the tabloid stories, the rumors, the escalation of the debt. She was also, I am mortified to admit this, behind today's threat to have me killed. She didn't mean it but she knew it would be effective."

"Your mother?" Teresa spluttered.

Liam's cheeks flushed with embarrassment. "I can't tell you how sorry I am." Liam pushed his hand through his hair and rubbed the back of his neck. "I'd completely understand if you want to press charges against her."

Teresa's brows flew up. Have his mother arrested? Was he nuts? "Could I prove anything?" she asked.

"Probably not," Liam admitted.

Teresa forced herself to think, to distance herself from her anger. "That would create another scandal that Christopher Corporation doesn't need right now."

"I don't give a flying...fig how it affects the company." Liam pushed the words out between clenched teeth.

"Yeah, Liam, you do. And you should," Teresa said. She made a quick decision. "I'm not going to take this any further. Your mother is a sad woman and I think she is living her own type of hell."

She couldn't miss the relief that she saw in his eyes. Catherine was, after all, his mother, and although she was pampered, spoiled, narcissistic and a complete bitch, he didn't want to see her humiliated. Teresa, who'd always protected her own mother, could see that from a mile away.

Teresa stared down at her hardwood floor and allowed herself to relax, finally starting to believe that it was all over. She felt like an elephant had been lifted off her chest, like her mind had been vacuumed. Laughter, relief and joy bubbled up inside her. She wanted to throw herself into Liam's arms, express her gratitude in the most basic way she knew how...naked and horizontally.

But Liam, when she looked at him, still looked as remote as he did when he walked into her apartment. "Why do I feel like you are about to drop another bombshell?" she asked, not sure if she wanted to know.

When he just looked at her without saying anything, she shrugged. "I don't have to marry you today to save Christopher Corporation, do I?" she joked, hoping to see humor flash in his eyes.

Liam just held her eyes. "Would you? If it came down to that?"

She would. Today she'd realized that there wasn't anything she wouldn't do for him. She'd been prepared to run to save him and his reputation, to give him a life that, she'd assumed, was better without her in it. She'd given him everything and anything she could, in any way she could.

"If you wanted me to..."

Emotion as bold as a lightning strike and as fragile as a butterfly wing flashed in his eyes and in that moment,

Teresa released all resistance to what she was feeling. She loved him and while she was intensely grateful that he'd saved her brother's life, her career, her home, she was not confusing gratitude with love. She loved him—intensely, passionately, forever.

What was the point of keeping her heart, that useless organ that now only thumped for him, to herself? Wasn't love—especially something so rich and wild and desperate to be free—meant to be shared?

"I love you."

She dropped the words into the quiet space between them, and she immediately felt his body tense. His eyes lightened and darkened and, for one brief moment, she thought he might reach for her, pull her into his arms, but he just stood there, his eyes locked with hers.

"I'm sorry if that's not what you want to hear but I do. I think I always have. I know I always will."

Liam ran his hand over his head, obviously agitated. "Dammit, Teresa."

Not the reaction she wanted but also not one that surprised her. She never expected Liam to drop to his knees, overcome with emotion; that wasn't his way. Besides, her love had nothing to do with his response; it just *was*.

Teresa stood up and placed her hands on his chest, looking up into his face. "You and I have had a rocky road and have dealt with things no couple should be forced to face. It's been rough and hard and tough. And that's okay. I can handle anything with you standing next to me." Teresa stroked the fabric of his shirt, feeling his hot skin beneath it, felt the *thump thump* of his heart beneath her palm. "But love, true love, grown-up love, isn't based on what you get back. It's judged by how much you give."

"I don't understand."

Teresa's smile was sad. "I know. I didn't, either. I loved

my mom and protected her, loved and protected Joshua, and all I wanted was for them to love and protect me as much as I did them. I wanted something back. Maybe, initially, I wanted that from you, too.

"But now I don't expect, can't expect, you to love me just because I love you. Love is not conditional. I understand that now."

"I don't understand any of this," Liam muttered, his rigid arms still at his sides. "I've got things to work through, stuff I need to find out."

Teresa saw the confusion and misery in his eyes but knew that there was so much he wasn't telling her. He still couldn't trust her. And she couldn't blame him. With parents like his, trust was impossible. Teresa placed her hand on his cheek. "I'll always be on your side, Liam. No matter what."

Liam covered her hand with his and closed his eyes. After a minute he told her, his voice rough with emotion, that he needed to go.

Teresa dropped her hands and blinked back her tears. "I know."

And she needed him to go before she begged him to stay.

Because love, she thought as Liam left her apartment and her life, could not be demanded.

Eleven

Teresa, dressed in yoga pants and a tank top, walked down her hallway and into her kitchen, squinting at the bright sunlight streaming in from the open windows. She loved her apartment and she was so grateful to Liam for providing her the means for her to stay in it and for, obviously, saving her brother.

While she waited for her coffee to brew, Teresa placed her elbows on the granite counter and her face in her hands. Four days had passed since Liam handed her the flash drive and their freedom and she and Joshua had spent that time getting used to the idea that they were free.

Since she'd repaid The Fixer by organizing Brooks's wedding, Teresa was also free of him. Corinne was fielding a bunch of queries for her to organize events and had already delegated some of the smaller, less high-profile events to her staff. Corinne had also declared that Teresa needed a few days off so, not having the energy to argue,

Teresa opted to stay home. But she'd had enough of doing nothing except missing Liam.

Thinking about Liam.

Needing Liam.

Teresa tried to ignore the knife in her heart, the barbed wire wrapped around her stomach. She should go back to work; she wanted her life to go back to normal, but most of all, she wanted to go back to Liam.

Teresa heard her front door opening and walked through to her living room, frowning. Joshua slept late as often as he could and frequently didn't surface until around noon. God, she needed to do something about her brother and soon.

She loved him but she couldn't live with him.

Joshua walked into the living room, his body sweaty. What was going on? Joshua didn't exercise. Ever.

"Are you feeling okay?" she asked.

Joshua ran a hand towel over his glistening face. "Fine, why?"

"It's not even seven thirty and you've been exercising. What's up with that?"

Joshua rubbed his head with his towel and Teresa thought she heard something about Liam and boxing. Yanking his towel away, she glared at him. "Say that again?"

"Liam told me that I had to be at his gym at six this morning," Joshua told her, heading in the direction of the kitchen. Teresa followed him, trying to make sense of his words. Joshua pulled a bottle of water from the fridge and Teresa grabbed the edge of his T-shirt as he tried to edge past her to go to his room. "Hold on there, Josh. You went to the gym with Liam?"

"Yep."

"Why?"

"Because he told me I had to. I started two days ago," Joshua replied, holding her intense stare. Okay, so that was new. It had been ages since Joshua had managed to maintain eye contact.

"And why are you listening to Liam?"

Joshua lifted a thin shoulder. "Because I owe him."

Teresa started to protest but Joshua slapped his hand over her mouth. His sweaty, recently-been-in-a-glove hand. Yuck. Teresa shuddered and slapped it away. She pointed to a bar stool next to the counter. "Sit. And explain."

"I can never repay Liam the seven mil, I know that," Joshua said.

"I'll repay him when I sell the shares back to him."

Joshua smiled. "He said you'd say that and he said to remind you that he doesn't want your money." Joshua took another long pull of water before carefully placing his bottle on the counter. "Besides, the money has nothing to do with you."

Teresa frowned at him. "Maybe so but you don't have the money to repay Liam."

"I know that. So does Liam," Joshua said, sounding irritated. "But it doesn't change the fact that it's my problem, not yours."

Okay, technically true but she'd looked after Joshua all his life.

"Liam says it's time that I act my age, that I take responsibility for my actions." Joshua lifted his chin and Teresa saw her own stubbornness in his eyes. "I'm working it out with him."

Oh. *Ohhhh.* She narrowed her eyes, not pleased. What was Liam up to? She loved the man but she'd still go to war with him over Josh. He was still her baby brother.

"Liam expects me at the gym four mornings a week," Joshua replied. "I'm also starting work at Christopher

Corporation next week Monday. And I'm going to school at night." Teresa opened her mouth to ask how he was going to pay for school but Joshua beat her to it. "Apparently, Christopher Corporation has a few interns who work shorter hours for a smaller salary and study part-time."

So, wow. "What are you going to study?"

Joshua ducked his head. "I'm really interested in computers. Maybe software engineering?"

"That sounds great," Teresa said, still needing to know more. "How long do you have to work for Liam?"

"He didn't say. He just wants me to give it a decent shot. He says that he believes that I can do anything I want to, if I started to trust myself and if I made decent decisions."

Teresa placed a hand on her heart, thinking it might beat out of her chest. Man, Liam was such a good man. A good man who was keeping his distance. She could just slap him. Why were they being miserable apart when they could be happy together?

"I'm proud of you, Josh. I think you're going to be just fine," Teresa said, patting his hand. She wanted to hug him but she'd do that after he'd showered.

Joshua rocked the bottle of water from side to side. "You both have the same look in your eyes. Both of you are so damn unhappy but trying to be strong."

Well, that was what adults did. "I'm glad you get to spend time with Liam, Josh. He's a really good man."

"A good guy with a hell of a right hook," Joshua said, rubbing his jaw. "Did he tell you that his mom paid some guys to drug me, and that they suggested that I crash that party and insult those people?"

Not exactly but she'd figured that was what happened. "Catherine is convinced that I slept with Liam's dad and she wanted to punish me."

"She's nutso."

Teresa agreed with him. "Liam explained everything to me. His mother is a loon, his father isn't his father and that's why he's off to Oahu this morning," Joshua said.

What?

"Whoa, back up. What did you say?"

"Liam flew to Oahu."

"No! What do you mean that his father isn't his father?"

Joshua looked guilty. "I don't know if I should've mentioned that. It wasn't like he *told* me that."

She was going to wrap her hands around his throat and squeeze the information out of him. "Tell me exactly what he said, Joshua David."

Josh winced when she used his full name. Good, she was not playing around. "Yesterday I told Liam that I was heading straight home but I changed my mind and headed to the showers. I think Liam thought they were alone—"

"Who is *they*?" Teresa demanded.

"Oh, his friend Matt joined us for a workout."

"Go on."

"I only got bits and pieces of what he was saying. He mentioned DNA testing and that someone called Dutton had tracked down his real dad. And that he was still in Hawaii." Josh pushed his wet hair off his forehead. "Then today Liam tells me that he's flying his plane to Oahu, that he has some business there to see to. It wasn't difficult to add two and two together."

Teresa stood up, needing to pace the small area between the living room and the kitchen island. Typical Liam, determined to do everything by himself. When would he realize that she was on his side? That they were stronger together than they were apart? She'd tried to give him space, to give him time to reach the conclusion she had but she was running out of patience.

Stopping abruptly, she sent Joshua a hard look. "Do you know where he was going in Oahu?"

Joshua shook his head. "Nope. Why, are you thinking of joining him?"

Teresa slapped her hands on her hips and narrowed her eyes. "I don't care if you think it's a bad idea. I'm going anyway."

Joshua shook his head. "I think it's a great idea. You love him and he, I'm convinced, loves you. It's stupid to be apart. You might run out of time."

Just like their parents had. Teresa nodded. She and Joshua both understood how important it was to live in the moment, yet she was here and Liam was not. She was over it.

"How are you going to find him?" Joshua asked, genuinely curious. "Oahu is a big island."

Happy to have something to do, a direction to follow, Teresa flashed him a grin. "Watch and learn, young one." Picking up her phone, she punched in the number and put the device on loudspeaker.

"Liam Christopher's office."

After greeting Duncan, Teresa demanded to know where Liam was.

Duncan, being the professional he was, refused to tell her. "I'm sure if Liam wanted you to know his whereabouts, he would've told you himself, Teresa."

"Duncan, don't make me turn mean." Teresa kept her tone pleasant.

"Threats won't work on me but feel free to try your luck," Duncan said, a hint of laughter in his voice.

Teresa winked at Joshua. "Really? Tell me, Duncan, how much of a pain in the ass is Catherine Christopher?"

"Huge. Massive. Freakin' ginormous."

"All that and she's only Liam's mother."

"And what is that supposed to mean?" Duncan asked, all humor now gone.

"I fully intend to be Liam's wife and I can either be utterly wonderful or so obnoxious you'll think Catherine is a pussycat. You telling me exactly where Liam is will help me make that decision."

"You're too nice to be a bitch."

"But do you want to take that chance?"

Duncan replied something inaudible and muttered out an address. Teresa grabbed a pen from the container and wrote the name of the hotel on her hand. "Thanks, Duncan."

"Sure. It'll be your fault if he fires me," Duncan said.

"Duncan, if he fires you, I'll hire you. Deal?"

"At a ten percent salary increase and an extra week vacation time," Duncan stated, as quick as ever.

She could never afford Duncan. He was too highly paid for her company but it was a moot point because Liam would never let Duncan go. Ever.

She didn't think.

"Thanks. I owe you," Teresa told him before disconnecting the call. She looked at Josh and allowed him to see her sudden uncertainty. "Am I doing the right thing?"

"Are you asking me?" Josh clarified and when she nodded, he shrugged. "I don't have a clue but at least you're trying. That's got to count for something."

Man, she sure hoped so.

Nic wound her arms around her knees and watched as the Caribbean sky turned from blue to pink as the superhot day faded away. She looked down at her arms, thinking that she couldn't remember when last she looked so tan, how long it had been since she'd had a proper vacation. When last had she felt so utterly relaxed?

That would be…never.

But time was running away from them and tomorrow they would be on an Abbingdon jet and heading back to Seattle and real life. Except that she had no idea what her real life entailed. Over the past week, she and Brooks had laughed and loved and talked but they'd both avoided talking about the future. It was as if they were both trying to circumvent what came next, living utterly and absolutely in the moment. But Nic needed to know where she was going to sleep tomorrow night, whether she'd be in her own bed or his. She was legally married to him but their marriage was, despite spending every moment together lately, one of convenience. They were both getting something they needed from the deal and that was all that had been promised.

She was such a fool for wanting more, for wanting everything. She'd been raised by a tough cookie grandmother who refused to feed her a diet of princess and happily-ever-after stories. Life is what you make it, she'd said. It's hard and tough and cold and there isn't a prince out there who is going to hand you a shoe or awaken you from a deep sleep with a kiss.

You buy your own damn shoes and don't put yourself in a position where you require rescuing.

Except that she did, sort of, have a prince and he did own jets and luxury vacation houses with private beaches.

But everything good comes to an end, Nic. You know this. Do not expect anything from Brooks but his contacts to get your documentary flighted because if you do, you will get your heart broken.

You don't need him; you will be fine on your own. Always have been, always will be.

Nic felt the air move and looked up to see Brooks dropping to the sand next to her, stretching out long legs and digging his heels into the sand. He dumped a silver ice bucket containing a bottle of Moët between them and she saw the two flutes in his other hand.

Champagne on the beach. It was, Nic supposed, the perfect way to end a perfect week.

Brooks didn't say anything as he popped the cork and poured the pale liquid into her glass. Nic waited for him to pour champagne into his glass before clinking hers against his. "Thank you."

Brooks took a sip of champagne. "For what?"

"The best week of my life. I've loved every second," Nic said. She sipped and smiled when the champagne bubbles popped on the back of her tongue. That was what happened to her skin when Brooks kissed her, well, anywhere.

"I love it here," Brooks admitted. "I try to come as often as I can. Which isn't, I admit, nearly often enough."

Nic felt the hot flash of jealously. Who else had he brought here and had he loved those women in the same bed, in the shower, in the damned Jacuzzi? *Ack.*

"This has always been my bolt-hole, the place I come to be alone. You're the first person I've brought here."

"Oh."

Brooks nudged her with his shoulder. "I saw that streak of jealousy, Mrs. Abbingdon."

That title sounded weird but right. So damn right.

"Admit it. You were jealous thinking of me sharing this space with someone else."

Play it cool, Nic. Shrug his comment away. He was just teasing her. She wanted to utter something pithy, something horribly sophisticated but she couldn't form the words. So she went for the truth. "Yeah, I was, am, jealous."

Brooks was quiet for a minute and when Nic looked at him, she saw something in his eyes that made her heart stumble and the champagne-flavored moisture in her mouth disappear. "What?" she asked.

"The thought of you being anywhere, with any other man, makes my head want to explode. Hell, the thought of you, being with anyone else, ever, makes my skin crawl."

What was he trying to say? Nic pulled her finger through the sand. When she realized that she'd drawn a heart, she hastily swiped her palm across the sand. The sky was now shot with tangerine flames but all Nic's attention was on Brooks. "What happens tomorrow?"

"We go back to Seattle."

Nic sent him a don't-be-obtuse look. "I mean with us. We discussed getting married and what we wanted out of it but we didn't discuss how we were going to live in this arrangement."

"Yeah, it did get a bit mad," Brooks admitted, scratching his left shoulder with his right hand. Nic watched his muscles ripple and told herself to concentrate. This was not a good time to get distracted; who knew what she might find herself agreeing to next?

"What do you want to do, Nic? We can live together or apart. It's up to you."

"If we lived together, would we be living together? I mean, sleeping together?"

"Damn straight," Brooks answered in his typical, no-nonsense way. "There is no way I could live in the same house as you and have you sleeping in another bed."

"Oh." Nic waved at the sunset. "I thought that you might want to leave this all here?"

"Why would you think that?" Brooks asked, his voice tender.

"Because this is pretend, Brooks. This is warm seas and good food, no worries, no stress. This is a vacation thing. It's not real life. You haven't lived with me when I have PMS, when I'm on a deadline, when I'm so tired I get super-bitchy."

"And you haven't lived with me when I've had a bad day or am arguing with my grandfather or I've lost a deal. I understand that this isn't real life. Real life is messy and hard and gritty and generally crazy."

"And you still want me in yours?"

Brooks leaned sideways and placed a kiss on her temple. "Yeah."

Brooks wrapped a strong arm around her shoulder and Nic leaned into him, immediately finding that super-comfortable spot to rest her head.

"Nic?"

"Mmm?"

"I'm not telling you that I love you—" Nic pulled away and looked up into his masculine face. In the fading light his eyes turned lighter and brighter. But it was his words that transfixed her, that kept all her attention on his beautifully masculine face "—but I'm not telling you that I don't, either. I like you. I like you more than a lot. More than any woman I've ever known. I want—"

Brooks pulled a face and Nic was charmed by the sudden redness in his cheeks. "I want you in my bed, for you to be there when I come home or to be waiting for you to come home if you are late. I want to share showers and breakfasts and my body with you. But—"

Oh, God, here it came, the big *but*.

"But a part of me also wants you to go back to your place so that I can pick you up for a date. I want to take it slow so that I can seduce the hell out of my wife. I want to take you to Paris for the weekend or skiing in Tahoe. I want it all and I want it all right now."

Nic released the air she was holding, feeling like every part of her was smiling. Turning, she swung her leg over

Brooks's thigh and when she faced him, wound her arms around his neck. She pressed her forehead against his and crossed her eyes, making him laugh.

"Well, Mr. Abbingdon, then I have a proposal for you. I'll live with you over weekends and I'll date you during the week." She kissed the tip of his nose before pulling back. "And if you're very, very lucky, and if you play your cards right, I might, sometime in the future, agree to marry you."

The corners of Brooks's sexy mouth lifted. "Let me think about that, Mrs. Abbingdon. It's a big step. A lot of factors should be considered." He brushed his mouth across hers, lifting his lips to murmur a "Hell, yes" against her lips.

"Yes to what, Brooks?"

"Everything, darling. For the rest of our lives."

Twelve

Liam sat down at a table situated on the balcony of The Veranda, the trendy meeting place just off the lobby of the luxurious Kahala Hotel. He glanced over the beach, pool and dolphin lagoon and wished Teresa was here, knowing she'd get a kick out of this luxury hotel located just a few minutes from the famous Waikiki Beach.

Liam ordered a Manhattan from a waiter and wiped his hand on his thigh. He couldn't remember when last he'd been this nervous. This was nerves on a whole new level. Damn, he really wanted Teresa here. Somehow, she had a way of calming him, of silently reminding him that it was okay, that he was okay. That he mattered…

Liam thanked the waiter for his drink and picked up the brown envelope he'd placed on the table earlier. He'd spent hours looking at the photographs Dutton sent him, had read his report a dozen times, maybe more. His father was John Hamilton. He'd been born and raised on the island, and had three college-aged daughters. Liam paused, thinking that he had three sisters. He'd always wanted a sibling—someone to help share the burden of his mother's cloying love, protectiveness and general craziness. Now he had three. Well, intellectually he had three; he didn't know if he'd ever get to meet them.

He had to meet his father first, and John Hamilton had agreed to meet him here, at The Veranda, in, Liam glanced at his watch, three minutes.

Liam lifted his hand and grimaced at his trembling fingers. This was big, this was huge, this might all blow up in his face.

What did he want from John? What did he need? Would they keep in touch or would this one meeting be it? Would he meet his wife or would he want to keep Liam separate from his real family? Would he want money? Was he only meeting with Liam because he was loaded? God, maybe this wasn't such a great idea…maybe he should go.

"You're Liam."

Showtime. Liam hauled in a deep breath and stood up, giving his hands one last swipe. He turned slowly and saw himself, plus thirty years. Gray-flecked dark hair, lined eyes and the same long nose. Liam stared at his father for a minute and eventually lifted his hand for a handshake. John gripped his hand and Liam thought, just for a fraction of a second, that he wanted to pull him in and hug him. But grown men seldom did that, and Christophers never.

Liam gestured for John to sit and they stared at each other. John was the first to break the awkward silence. He rubbed his chin as he propped his foot on his opposite knee. "I never expected to hear from you."

Liam reached for his Manhattan and then realized that John probably needed something to drink, as well. He called over a waiter.

"I think this conversation calls for some liquid courage," Liam said as the waiter approached him. "What would you like?"

"Whatever you are having."

When the waiter left, Liam spoke. "Did you know about me?"

"Yeah. Initially, your mother refused to admit it but I knew that you were mine. The dates worked." John dropped his knee and leaned forward. "First off, you need to know that I am not proud of myself. She was married and she should've been firmly off-limits but damn, she was entrancing."

"How did you meet?" Liam asked.

"Linus was building a hotel here and I was working for the landscaper who was building the gardens. Your mother loved horticulture and your father gave her free reign to do whatever she wanted in the grounds. God, she changed her mind a million times and it made us crazy. Eventually, the boss couldn't deal with her and handed the project over to me. One thing led to another…"

"How long were you together?"

"Nearly a year. Linus wasn't always around. He was establishing the tech arm of your company at that point and he was consumed by that. Catherine was about five months pregnant when he sold the hotel and she left the island."

"Did you want her to stay?"

John winced. "Honestly? Probably not. But I sure as hell wanted you. But Linus was her husband. He could give her, and you, everything I couldn't. Then."

"Then?"

John's smile held a hint of pride along with sadness. "If she'd just been prepared to hang tough for a few years, I could've given her most of what Linus could. I opened my own landscaping business and then a garden supply store. Within five years I had ten. Now I have a lot more."

Liam's agile mind connected the dots. "You're the Hamilton of Hamilton's Home and Garden Stores?"

John nodded. "I handed the day-to-day running of the company over to a group of young, sharp business people and I spend my days surfing or in my garden. Or bugging my wife." John smiled. "I'm keeping the business for a couple of years to see if any of my kids want to run it but none of my girls have shown any interest. Do you want it?"

Liam jerked back, shocked. "You can't give it to me!"

John cocked his head. "Why not? You're my kid, too."

Wait, this was madness. "You don't know me, John."

John picked up the rucksack he'd walked in with and pulled three bulging files from the bag. He put them on the table and slapped the top cover. "Part of the deal with your mom to keep my mouth shut about you was that she send me all your school records, achievements and a monthly report. There's thirty-plus years of info on you in there, most of which you've probably forgotten. I might not have raised you but I know you."

Liam rubbed the back of his neck as he flipped open the cover of the top file. His Apgar scores jumped out at him, as well as a picture of him a few minutes old, looking like a pissed-off monkey. Liam flipped through the file, reports, his first karate belt, a spelling bee he entered. More photos. John wasn't lying; this was his life, in three files.

"Why didn't you contact me when I was older?" Liam quietly asked.

"Catherine promised to tell you who your real father was when you turned eighteen. We agreed that it would be your choice as to whether you reached out. You didn't so I assumed that you weren't interested in meeting me," John said and Liam heard the hurt in his voice.

"Yeah, my mother isn't great at keeping her word," Liam replied. "I only recently figured out that someone with my blood group couldn't be a product of their combined DNA." Liam blew air over his lips. "My mother is a piece of work."

John nodded. "Am I allowed to say, as respectfully as possible, that I know that I dodged a bullet? Heidi, my wife, who knows about you by the way, and I have been married for twenty-six years and we're ridiculously happy."

Liam's mouth curved up. "That's wonderful. And encouraging."

John tapped his finger against his tumbler. He smiled knowingly. "Who is she?"

Liam thought about lying but decided he didn't have the energy. "Teresa St. Claire. We've had this crazy, crazy relationship, thanks in part to my mother's interference and machinations. It's been…complicated."

John frowned and clicked his fingers, something Liam realized that he also did when he was thinking. "Teresa St. Claire. Didn't she inherit a large portion of your father's shares of Christopher Corporation?"

"Twenty-five percent and how do you know that?" Liam asked, surprised.

John nodded to the folders. "When you turned eighteen your mother cut off my supply of Liam-related information. I hired a PI to keep me informed." Liam wanted to think that was creepy but he just felt…treasured. Cherished. Like he had a father who really, really cared about him.

"St. Claire, damn, that name sounds familiar."

Liam frowned. "Teresa's dad briefly worked for my dad but that was before I was born."

"That's it! I remember Catherine talking about him ad infinitum."

Liam leaned forward, immediately interested. "Do you remember those conversations?"

John gave it some thought. "I remember her being in a snit, for days, because Linus wanted to pay him a whack of cash for something—a formula?—and Catherine objected because Linus had what he needed from St. Claire already. I remember arguing about who owned the rights to intellectual property, the individual or the company."

Holy, holy smokes. Around the time he was born, his dad had launched the tech division of Christopher Corporation, the division that eventually became the heart of the company. And Nigel St. Claire must have developed the code for their biggest selling product, a software program that revolutionized web security. The software that made the Christophers rich beyond belief.

"What else do you remember about him?"

"St. Claire? Mmm, let me think. He left the country for some reason and I think that one or both of your parents made it difficult for the guy to come back to the States. Something about knowing someone in Immigration and St. Claire's expired visa, I think. Catherine mentioned something about him not being able to sue them if he was out of the country."

Liam gripped the edges of his nose, trying to control his anger. His parents kept Nigel from his kids. Man, his image of his parents was tarnishing minute by minute. But his father—Linus—obviously felt guilty about it because he'd tried to make restitution to Nigel's family by leaving Teresa the shares.

Crap, what a tangled, complicated mess.

When he told Teresa why her dad didn't come home, why he couldn't come home for so long, she was going to flip. Catherine had already tried to mess with her life, to ruin her reputation and torch her business, but Teresa had handled that. But Catherine, or Linus, or both, had conspired to keep her father from returning to the States. That she wouldn't forgive. Everybody had issues with their partner's families but this was beyond what was acceptable.

He'd have to tell her but he knew that it would be the mortal blow that would fracture their already fragile relationship. How would she be able to live with and love the man whose family destroyed hers?

"Liam, look at me."

Liam forced his eyes up, surprised at the forceful note in John's voice, the determination in his eyes.

"What your parents did does not reflect on you. You are only responsible for the things you do and the things you say. You are your own man."

"But I'm dealing with the consequences of their actions," Liam pointed out.

John grimaced. "For that I am sorry. I'm also sorry I didn't fight harder for you. I genuinely believed that they could give you what I couldn't."

Liam felt a surge of anger, for the reserved, scared, frequently overwhelmed kid he'd been. "Yeah, John, I had the latest toys and the brand-name clothing and the holidays in exotic places. But you know what I didn't have? I didn't have a father who came to my sports matches or who spent any time throwing a ball. Praise was given when I achieved an A and withdrawn when I messed up. I handed my mother tissues when she cried over something my father would or wouldn't do and I handed him the whiskey bottle when he bitched about her."

Liam stood up, unable to deal with any more, feeling emotionally shattered. "But you know, I had the toys and the clothes and the holidays."

John scrambled to his feet and placed his hand on Liam's arm. "Don't rush off, Liam. Let's talk."

Liam stared at a point behind his shoulder, not seeing the gold and pink sunset, the soft sea. He stepped back and shook his head. "I can't. Not anymore."

Liam picked up his brown envelope, sent another look at the files and shook his head. He needed to go; he couldn't take any more and he definitely needed to leave. And God, he needed another drink. Or ten.

"Am I going to see you again?" John asked, his green eyes worried.

"I don't know, John," Liam replied, walking away. All he knew for sure is that he needed some quiet, some peace and to stop thinking.

But more than anything he needed Teresa.

Teresa ran her hand over her hip and looked down at the satin material below her hand. The designer dress, the one she last wore at Hunter and Jenna's wedding, was the purest shade of daffodil yellow and the color, along with its deep neckline, body-skimming shape and shortish skirt was a weapon set to stun. She knew that the yellow brought out the blue of her eyes and she'd deliberately applied more eyeshadow than normal, creating a deep and sexy smoky eye effect. She'd contoured her cheekbones and swiped a thin layer of pink gloss over her lips. Under her dress she only wore ludicrously expensive French perfume.

She intended to seduce the hell out of Liam Christopher.

She wanted him cross-eyed and naked. And, preferably, so discombobulated that he'd drop his guard and tell her how much he loved her and how he couldn't live without her. She wanted him to tell her about meeting his father, and how he felt about the past.

Though, in all honesty, if she just got him to forget to ask how she knew he was in Hawaii, she'd take that as a minor win.

Taking a breath, Teresa knocked on the door to the presidential suite and when he didn't answer, knocked again. If he wasn't in his suite, she had no idea how to find him. And she didn't have a place to go since she hadn't reserved a hotel room. She supposed she could go and hang out in the bar and try again later. But what if Liam had left and was on his way back to Seattle?

No, she refused to accept that she'd wasted the flight and this dress. Teresa banged on the door again and nearly wept when she heard male footsteps on the other side of the door.

"I didn't order room service—" Liam said as he opened the door. Teresa had planned on saying something sexy like "Let's misbehave" but her words dried on her tongue. A wet Liam, wearing just a white towel around his hips, glowered down at her, acres and acres of tanned skin just waiting to be touched. His eyes were wide with shock and he placed a hand on the door frame as if to steady himself.

"Teresa? You're here?"

"I'm here," Teresa said, ducking under his arm. Inside the suite, she sucked in a breath at the luxury furnishings—damn, she always forgot how rich Liam was—before turning around to see Liam stalking toward her.

"Aren't you going to ask me why I'm here?" Teresa asked, then did a mental facepalm. She didn't want him asking questions, not yet anyway.

Later, when she'd loved him so thoroughly and fried his brain, she'd tell him that their being apart was ridiculous and that they were supposed to be together. She'd ask him about his dad…

"I don't give a rat's ass why you're here. I was in the shower, wishing you were with me," Liam growled. He reached her and cupped her face, his fingers pushing into her hair, which she'd left to flow down her shoulders. Liam picked up a strand and ran it through his fingers. "I always forget how long it is. How silky."

Teresa placed her hands on his waist and drew circles on his bare skin with her thumbs. She turned her mouth to kiss his palm and kept her eyes connected with him. "And just what were you doing in the shower while you were thinking of me?"

"You know what I was doing," Liam muttered, taking her hand and placing it on his hard cock. He felt hard and full and desperate beneath her hand and Teresa released a low hum of approval. Liam placed his forehead against hers and sighed. "You're really here."

Teresa briefly wondered why he kept saying that, why he was acting like having her here was like a dream he expected to be jerked from. Teresa's eyes connected with his and saw misery and confusion and a whole bunch of regret. Dammit. Needing to chase his ghosts away, Teresa linked her arms around his neck and stood on her tiptoes— her nude high heels, as sexy as they were, still didn't give her the height she needed—and rested her mouth against his. Speaking softly, she whispered the words against his lips. "If you need me, Liam, take me."

"You might regret saying that," Liam muttered as his hand drifted over her ass.

"I'll never regret anything to do with you," Teresa told him.

Liam released a short, harsh laugh but before she could comment on his cynicism, he covered her mouth with his and twisted his tongue around hers. His strong arms pulled her into him and her breasts pushed into hard chest, instantly dampening her dress from a combination of heat and lust and shower droplets.

Liam held her head so that he could possess her mouth, pulling her bottom lip between his teeth. As if he couldn't get enough, he yanked his mouth away to nibble her jaw, to that sexy place where her jawbone met her ear and then down the cord of her neck. Teresa felt her eyes cross and she grabbed his chin, wanting more of his mouth, his lips, his tongue. Liam fed her what she wanted, what she craved: long, hot, drugging, push-reality-away kisses.

Conscious of her swimming head, Teresa whimpered when he pulled away from her to run a finger down the deep vee of her neckline.

"Love this dress but it would be so much better on the floor."

The thought—that the dress was too expensive and too precious to end up on any floor—whispered past her and evaporated when Liam turned her around and placed his fingers on the zipper. She felt his breath on her back following the zip down her body and shuddered when his mouth kissed her lower spine. She was already wet and pulsing. It wouldn't take much for her to come...

Liam straightened, brushed the dress from her shoulders and Teresa heard his appreciative gasp when he realized that she was come-take-me-baby naked beneath the dress.

"I'm liking that dress better and better," Liam said, his hand coming across her torso to cup her breast. He lightly pinched her nipple and Teresa bucked, more from pleasure than pain.

"You are so beautiful. You're everything I want."

Liam murmured in her ear as he lifted her hair to kiss the back of her neck. She felt his mouth moving down her spine again, his hands sliding over her stomach, over her thin patch of hair and down the front of her thighs. Needing him, needing more, Teresa spun around.

Liam, now on his knees, looked up at her. "Perfect. You're exactly where I wanted you."

Teresa stared down at his dark head as he spread her

folds and gently kissed her mound. Teresa felt her legs wobble and locked her knees, sighing when Liam's clever fingers slipped into her heat. Teresa pushed her fingers into his hair, tugging him closer, silently demanding more. When Teresa didn't think she could take his teasing any longer, Liam licked her, his hot tongue creating a blazing trail. A finger, then another, slid inside her and Teresa whipped her head from side to side. It was too much; she'd wanted to love him like this; she'd wanted to drive him crazy, take him outside himself, but she was on the receiving end.

She wasn't strong enough to ask him to stop.

Liam's tongue flicked her clit, his fingers twisted inside her and Teresa felt herself spinning away, a hot, whirling dervish of pure sensation. Teresa peaked, sank, peaked again and as she was falling back, Liam grabbed her ass, boosted her up his body and entered her with one long, hard stroke. She was so wet, so turned on, that her eyes rolled back in her head and her inner muscles clenched, wanting more. Wanting it all.

Again.

Liam moved her dead weight as if she were a piece of lint and sank down onto the closest chair. Teresa used her knees to lift herself up so that she just had his tip inside her before sliding back down again. Opening her eyes, she looked into his foggy gaze and thought that this was love. This perfect jumble of sensations—lust, excitement, passion, trust—this was love.

Love was also waking up with him every morning, giving him a child, making him feel like he was the most important part of her day, that he was her world.

Because he was. Tears filled her eyes and rolled down her cheeks and Liam brushed them away with his fingers. "Teresa? What's wrong?"

Teresa just shook her head.

"Do you want to stop?"

Teresa shook her head and pushed down on him, making him groan. Her man...only Liam would offer to stop at the sight of her tears, even though he was so deep inside her she wasn't sure where he ended and she began, that he was trembling as he tried to keep control.

She loved him. Up until that moment, she never understood how much, but now she could feel it in every cell, every heartbeat, every look and stroke and kiss.

"Let go, Liam," she murmured, gently touching his face, running her thumb along his jawline. "Let go and take me with you."

Liam launched himself upward and using his core muscles picked her up and whipped her off the chair. The floor was the closest horizontal surface and he laid her on the Persian carpet, picked up her one leg and slammed into her.

"Not going to be able to wait."

Teresa felt that delicious curling sensation deep within her and knew that she was a heartbeat behind him. She felt Liam tense, heard his guttural moan and then his hand was between them and his thumb flicked her bead and her soul shattered.

This, this was love and it was wonderful.

So, in fact, were her multiple, earth-shattering orgasms.

Liam ran his hand down Teresa's spine, feeling every bump and dip. Her skin was utterly flawless except for three freckles perfectly placed under her right shoulder blade. Maybe there were more on her body; he'd have to check. But not, unfortunately, now. They needed to talk.

He didn't want to but he was an adult and adults did what they needed to do. Adults like his parents did what they wanted to do and damn the consequences. He would not be following in their footsteps. But Linus and Catherine weren't his only parents; he also had John, whose shoes, from the little he knew of him, might be worth stepping into.

Or maybe he could just wear his own. Create his own path, strike out on his own, be exactly the person he was. The thought was liberating. And thrilling. But would he be walking that path alone? Teresa had said she'd loved him but, after hearing about the role his family played in her father's life, would she still?

There was only one way to find out.

As if she'd heard his silent plea for her attention, Teresa rolled over and sent him a soft smile. "We made love for most of the night so I suppose I must pay the piper."

"What do you mean?"

"We need to talk, Teresa."

They, very unfortunately, did. Teresa sat up and pulled the sheet up, covering her beautiful breasts, a crime beyond comprehension. Then again, there was no way he could concentrate on any conversation while she was naked.

Hell, even knowing she was naked under the bedclothes was messing with his head.

"Let's order some coffee and take it onto the balcony," Liam suggested, rolling out of bed. He yanked on a pair of boxer shorts he'd left on the chair and fished in the chest of drawers for a T-shirt, which he tossed her way. Leaving the bedroom, he walked into the lounge, knowing that if he stayed, they'd be making love again. The longer she stayed, the harder it would be for him to watch her walk away.

And she'd walk away. That was a given.

Liam ordered coffee from his personal concierge and opened the floor-to-ceiling doors that led onto the private balcony. He gripped the railing and sighed when Teresa wound her arms around his waist and buried her face in the hollow of his spine. She felt so tiny against him, so feminine.

"Please don't fire Duncan for telling me where you are."

Liam frowned and turned around. He almost laughed at Teresa's face, her expression a perfect combination of guilt and mischief. "I threatened the hell out of him if he didn't tell me."

Okay, this was going to be good. Duncan was not a pushover and he knew the rules. "Okay. What did you threaten him with?"

Teresa drew patterns on the tiles with her big toe. "Your mother. Well, not precisely your mother." She blushed, which he found adorable. "I told him that if he didn't tell me I would make his life a living hell, acting ten times worse than Catherine, after we were married."

His heart bounced at the thought of marriage. "I should fire him," Liam teased, happy to have a moment of levity before the storm crashed over them. "My privacy is sacrosanct."

"But if you fire him then I have to hire him and give him a ten percent raise. I can't afford him!" Teresa wailed.

Liam threw his head back and laughed. Nobody but Teresa could amuse him and make him as happy and horny as she did. What if he didn't tell her about her dad? What if he took this moment, told her he loved her and took every other moment from here on out to be happy? It was so damn tempting but Liam knew that a relationship could not be built on a foundation of lies.

It wasn't really a lie but an omission...

And he was splitting hairs. His self-respect and his immense respect for her, for everything she'd done for her family, demanded that she know the truth.

Liam heard the door to the suite open and he pushed Teresa behind him, hiding her with his bulk as the concierge pushed a trolley laden with a silver coffeepot, bone china cups and a pile of fresh-baked pastries and a bowl of refreshing fruit salad. Coffee, thank God.

Once the concierge left, Teresa immediately picked up a croissant and lifted it to her nose. "Heavenly."

Liam poured coffee while Teresa pulled small chunks from the croissant and lifted them to her mouth. Liam handed her a cup of coffee and gestured for her to take a seat on the lounger.

Sitting opposite her, he cradled his cup in his hand and thought that her eyes were the exact color of the Pacific Ocean below them.

"I met my dad yesterday, my biological father."

Teresa immediately put her croissant on a plate and placed her cup on the table between them. She crossed her legs and leaned forward, every strand of her DNA focused on him as he explained the recent events.

"And?" she asked. "What was your biological father like?"

Liam shrugged. "He was…nice. He looks like me or I look like him."

"Was he happy to meet you? Did he know about you? Why didn't he contact you?"

Liam explained the circumstances of Catherine's infidelity, and John's reasoning around letting him be raised as a Christopher. Her eyes welled up when he mentioned the scrapbooks. His Teresa, under her capable attitude, had a very tender heart.

"Are you going to meet him again?" Teresa asked.

Liam lifted both shoulders to his ears. "I don't know. I left in a mood."

Teresa's eyes sharpened and the fingers clasping her knee tightened. "A mood?"

"I was pissed off."

"Because he didn't try to find you? Because your sisters had what sounded to be a great childhood and you didn't? Because of your mother's I-can-judge-but-don't-judge-me view of life?"

All of those, he supposed. "I was most pissed off about what I heard about your dad."

"My dad? How did the subject of *my* father come up?" Teresa asked, genuinely confused.

Liam sat his cup down and rested his forearms on his knees. "John, my biological dad, filled in a missing puzzle piece, something I couldn't work out."

"Which is?"

"The real reason Linus left those shares to you," Liam said. Oh, her shoulders were already tensing, her mouth tightening. They were wandering into stormy weather here.

Liam lifted his hand. "Just hear me out, please?"

"I thought we'd moved past this," Teresa muttered.

"Look, as much as Linus liked you, and I do believe he liked you and appreciated your fine mind, he was not the type of man who would leave his shares, worth millions, to someone outside the family, no matter how fond he was of that person. He lived for Christopher Corporation. And if you didn't sleep with him—" Teresa growled and Liam ignored the sound, pushing on "—and I believe that you didn't, then why would he bequeath you those shares?"

Teresa threw up her hands, obviously irritated. "I don't know, Liam. If I knew, I'd tell you."

"But I *do* know, Teresa."

Teresa frowned, stared at him, and her frown deepened. "Okay, you know. So are you going to share?"

Liam felt like a free diver, standing on a ninety-foot cliff, unsure whether there were rocks below in the water or not. He had no option but to dive.

"Your father, Nigel, worked for my father when he was

an intern. He developed code for super-secure web-based encryption and that discovery catapulted our company into the big leagues. From there we were able to hire some of the best minds in the world and we have diversified into artificial intelligence. But that code, that was how we got our start."

Liam pulled on his earlobe. "Your father created that code, and the policy at the time was that any developments made at Christopher Corporation remained our intellectual property. When we listed on Wall Street your father must have deduced that our growth was being built on his work. He was right."

Teresa placed her fingers over her mouth, her eyes wide with shock.

Liam plowed on. "According to my investigator, your father started some sort of legal proceedings against the company, demanding a profit share. My investigator couldn't find any trace of proceedings reaching court so the legal proceedings didn't get very far, because your father ran into trouble with Immigration."

Teresa nodded. "He got deported back to the UK. It happened so fast. I was only six, but I remember. One minute he was there, then gone."

Liam swallowed, hoping he'd be able to get these next words over his tongue. "I think your dad got into trouble with Immigration because my parents put him on their radar. To Dutton and me, it sounds like something someone like him, a Fixer, would do. Your father was trying to sue and they dug into his life and probably found out that his visa was expired or that he was here illegally and they got him hustled out of the country. It's difficult waging a court case in a foreign country when you're not in the country or a citizen of that country. Your credibility is also diminished when you've been deported from said country.

It was an easy solution to a very expensive, in their eyes, problem. Dutton also thinks a note in your dad's personnel file at the company was planted. It said he'd taken a leave of absence for a family issue. No one ever questions those so no one asked when he was coming back.

"Did your mom ever talk about your dad?" Liam asked.

Teresa shook her head. "My mom didn't like to deal with anything hard, or inconvenient. If dad was having problems, I doubt he would've shared them with my mom, especially since she was pregnant with Josh at the time." Teresa grimaced. "My mom doesn't handle stress well and he would've tried to protect her."

Liam waited, and watched, as Teresa digested this latest revelation. He watched her beautiful and much-loved face as she stared past him to the sea beyond, her eyes full of sadness. His heart nearly shattered when her eyes glistened with tears.

"I thought he didn't come back because he didn't want to."

"No, he didn't come back because I think they were actively trying to keep him out and then he died in a freak accident." Liam rubbed his forehead with his fingertips. "I am so sorry, Teresa. I am ashamed and mortified and horrified at what they did."

Teresa nodded and didn't say anything and Liam felt cold fingers gripping his heart, about to start that agonizing rip.

"But I'm convinced that's why Linus left you the shares, why he took an interest in you. I think he knew that it was wrong, that he should've treated your father better. He, in his ham-fisted way, tried to right a wrong. And it also explains my mother's antipathy toward you."

Teresa dropped her head to stare at her bare feet and Liam knew that, for as long as he lived, he'd remembered her like this, blond head bowed and her arms wrapped around her waist to comfort herself. He wanted to wrap his arms around her, to hold her as she made sense of this new information, but he didn't think she'd appreciate his touch.

"I don't know what else to say, to tell you how sorry I am," Liam said, hearing the desperation in his voice. "Again."

Teresa sucked her bottom lip between her teeth and when she released it, he saw the impression they'd left there. Straightening, she lifted her head and Liam couldn't identify all the emotions swimming in and out of her eyes. "I would never have known this if you didn't tell me."

Liam could only nod.

"You know how I feel about you and we could've carried on, had a relationship, and you could've swept this under the carpet, treated it as something that never happened. I wouldn't have had a clue. You had to know that telling me this would put what we have at risk…"

He knew that. God, he was living it! Liam just held her steady gaze and waited for her to continue. It was her turn to speak and his to wait for her verdict.

"Why did you tell me?" Teresa demanded.

Liam knitted his fingers together and squeezed. "Because I didn't want there to be any lies between us. Our pasts, my parents, caused so much trouble, for you—"

"And you."

"They lied and they manipulated and they used and they lied some more," Liam said, his voice rough. "I don't want there to be any more lies between us. And withholding truth is just another form of lying. I'm done with it and I'm done with them and what I thought was normal. Normal is not a cold marriage between two people who were more concerned about money and power and status than the people who worked for them and, to an extent, me.

Normal is not a cold, quiet house with no affection and no laughter. Normal is not keeping everything bottled up to the point you think your head might explode. I want normal, Teresa. I want normal so much it hurts."

"And how do you define normal, Liam?" Teresa softly asked.

He had to say this before she walked away, before those fingers tugging on his heart ripped it apart. "Normal is you, with me. Normal would be you and I married, both working at our separate careers, supporting and loving and learning from each other. Normal would be calling you to ask you for input when I have a problem, and vice versa. It's doing the best we can for ourselves, our kids and, I know this sounds corny, the world." He lifted one shoulder, his throat tightening and his eyes burning. "There is nobody I trust more than you, and that now feels normal. Finally, normal is me loving you for as long as I live. But I know that's a long shot."

"Sometimes long shots pay off," Teresa softly said. Liam frowned at her, not sure of her meaning.

"I don't understand."

A small smile tipped her sexy mouth up. "Okay then, what if I just said yes?"

It had been a tough morning, he got that, but he was losing track of this conversation. "Yes to what?"

Teresa touched her tongue to her top lip and Liam's heart stopped at the brilliant blue of her eyes. "Yes to everything. You, me, the work thing, the kids thing. The marriage thing that has absolutely nothing to do with shares and everything to do with us."

"Uh—"

Teresa leaned forward and placed her hands on his knees. "Are you with me, Liam?" she asked.

Barely. He was pretty sure that joy had just drowned out

his ability to speak so he just nodded. But because there was still a kernel of doubt—this was too damn easy!—Liam forced himself to construct a sentence. "Say that again?"

Teresa rubbed his thighs with her thumbs. "I love you, darling. I want to spend every minute of my life with you."

"Are you sure? Did you hear what I said about what my parents did to your dad?"

Teresa nodded. "Yeah, I did. I'm still going to need some time to process that and I will probably never have a relationship with your mother—"

"Completely understandable," Liam jumped in.

"But what they did has nothing to do with us. What they did, what your dad did to try and make amends, brought us together. We triumphed, despite having everything but the kitchen sink thrown at us. I'd be a fool to walk away from a love that stubborn, that persistent."

Liam's fingers touched her cheek. "You really do love me."

"I really do," Teresa said, her lips curving under the pressure of his thumb.

"I love you so much, Teresa," Liam said as she lifted her chin to receive his kiss. He wanted to dive into her, to lose himself in her and her warmth and beauty and love but there were one or two issues that still needed to be cleared up. "Going forward, can we agree on a couple of things?"

Teresa lifted her eyebrows. "What things?"

"First, can we remove the contact numbers for any and all Fixers from our phones? From now on, we live exceptionally boring lives that don't require the dubious talents of men with connections to pave the way for us."

Teresa nodded, her eyes sparkling. "That's a great idea. What else?"

"Will you marry me, as soon as possible?" Liam asked. "Like within the month?"

Teresa looked at him as she considered his question. "Liam, you know how long it takes to organize a wedding. Yeah, I managed to do Brooks and Nic's in record time but it nearly killed me."

Dammit, he was going to have to wait. But it was a long shot anyway. "Okay, two months? Three?"

Teresa smiled. "How about three days, on a beach at sunset? That'll give our friends enough time to get here. We won't invite Catherine but we will invite your biological dad and his family. How does that sound?"

Liam knew that he was doing his best goldfish look. "But you are a wedding planner. I thought you'd want a fairy-tale wedding."

Teresa's mouth was soft against his. "Liam, you are my fairy tale. I don't need anything else." She kissed him again and pulled back to hold his face. "Shall I meet you on the beach in three days' time?"

"Anywhere you are is where I want to be," Liam said, hauling her into his arms.

Epilogue

Teresa rather liked the way that Liam's eyes kept returning to her leg and she deliberately toyed with the ruffle that ended very high up on her left thigh. She knew that, with the smallest hint, his hand would be under the asymmetrical folds of her ball gown and heading north.

She rather liked his hand there and welcomed his touch day or night but they were on their way to the first of what they hoped would be a yearly event—the Christopher Ball—and she'd spent a fortune on this hand-beaded gown.

Liam squinted at her as their limousine moved slowly through the traffic to the red carpet. "Is it just me being romantic or does that gown look a little wedding-y?"

Teresa wasn't surprised he'd noticed. Her husband was ridiculously astute.

On hearing that she was to marry at such short notice, Corinne, brilliant friend and personal assistant that she was, found her a rose-patterned lace dress, with spaghetti straps and a fitted bodice. It was a perfect dress for a perfect beach ceremony witnessed by Matt and Nadia, Liam's fantastic new family, Joshua and a handful of friends who could rearrange their schedule on short notice. As wonderful as the ceremony and the joyous dinner afterward was, she'd still yearned for a one-off designer gown, something utterly extravagant. This ball that she and Nic conceived was the perfect opportunity to have something designed that was utterly unique and breathtaking.

Her off-the-shoulder, backless dress with its hand-beaded bodice and frilled skirt bordered on the edges of being bridal but Teresa didn't care. As the wife of Seattle's most influential man, hell, as Teresa St. Claire-Christopher, she didn't give a hoot. Liam loved it and that was all that mattered.

"You look beautiful. I'm so lucky to have married you," Liam murmured.

Teresa, not caring about her lipstick, leaned forward to receive his kiss. "Glad you like the dress."

"I love it. But as always, it would look so much better on the floor," Liam commented, making Teresa smile. Yeah, no. This was a twenty-thousand-dollar dress; the only place it was going was back in its plastic bag and back into her walk-in closet.

The limousine stopped. "We're here."

Teresa looked out the tinted windows and saw Nicolette standing on the red carpet, and behind her, and behind barriers, were the photographers, cameras already pointed their way. Nic looked fantastic in a long, red boho-inspired ball gown. She was talking to the camera, and Teresa wondered where Brooks was, knowing that he couldn't be that far away. Nic lowered her mic, handed it off to someone and headed for their limo. Liam opened the door for her and Teresa scooted up so that Nic could sit down next to her. Kissing Teresa's cheek, she took the bottle of Evian Liam handed her and took a grateful sip.

"Wow, this is hard work."

Teresa cocked her head. Nic was looking a bit tired and pale. "Are you okay? I know how hard you've been working, helping me to arrange this ball—"

"It was the least I could do since it's raising funds for our foundation."

A couple of months after their wedding, Brooks and Nic set up a foundation to raise funds for the prevention of human trafficking and, on hearing about it, Teresa immediately wanted to arrange an event to raise funds for the cause very dear to Nic's heart. Her film was also premiering tonight and Teresa knew she was as nervous as hell. Add that to her covering the event for her day job, Teresa understood that Nic was burning the candle at both ends.

"Where's Brooks?"

"Inside. Raising money for us." Nic softly smiled and when she touched her stomach Teresa knew exactly why she was so tired.

"Oh my God, when?" she cried, wrapping both her arms around Nic's shoulders.

"It's new so not for a long time," Nic said, grinning.

"What's going on?" Liam asked, confused.

"Nic's pregnant!" Teresa told him, ecstatic for her friend. She and Liam weren't quite ready for kids but they were having a bunch of fun practicing how to make one. "What does Brooks think? Was it planned? Are you going to find out the sex?"

Nic laughed at her questions. "You and I are going to have a long lunch and we'll discuss this to death but right now we need to get to work."

"But this is so exciting!" Teresa said, clasping her hands. "You're happy, all our friends are happy and I love that!"

"I just heard you're planning Shane and Isabel's wedding. Isabel told me that she loved your proposal and now that The Opulence is reopened, it seems perfect for their wedding," Nicolette told her.

Teresa clapped her hands in delight. "Yay!" Then she mock-pouted. "I'm still a bit cross with Jessie and Gideon for eloping."

"They both made huge donations to this event and Jessie is performing for free so you have to forgive them," Liam reminded her, laughter in his gorgeous eyes.

Teresa winked at him. "Maybe. Okay, let's get this done."

Nic nodded and glanced at the discreet bangle watch on her wrist. "Give me a few minutes, and we're going to live-feed your arrival. I'll give the signal to your driver when we are live."

Nic slipped out of the car and the door shut behind them. Teresa turned to Liam and her smile faded at his serious face. "What's wrong? What's the matter?" she demanded, placing her hand on his thigh.

Liam shook his head as he pulled a folded piece of paper out of his tuxedo jacket. "Do you know that six months has passed and in another six months you can divest yourself of your shares in Christopher Corporation?"

Time flew when you were happy. Teresa shrugged as she took the paper he held out. "I was thinking about keeping those shares for our kids."

"I love that idea," Liam told her. He nodded at the paper. "That was delivered by Linus's lawyer this morning. It's a letter from my...dad. Linus." Teresa caught the look he sent toward the entrance of the venue and saw the guilt on his face. He and John had become exceptionally close these past few months and she knew that he battled with the idea that he'd never been close to Linus. "Read it..."

Teresa slowly opened the letter.

Liam,

I've never been a great one for writing letters and I'm even worse at love letters. But in its way, this is one, and it's the best I can do.

I was always proud of you, proud to call you mine. No matter what you hear, what you discover, I wanted you to know that.

I'm sorry I never warned you about giving Teresa the company shares. I have no idea what she will do with them when the year is up. I hope they remain in Christopher hands but I can't control that. Giving Teresa the shares was my way of making up for a grievous error in my past. I also like the girl, very much. In my more fanciful moments, I think she'd be an excellent daughter-in-law.

But I'm not there and you know your own mind and I trust your choices. With the company, and more important, for your own happiness.

For God's sake, be happy in love, son. It's all that matters.

Dad

Teresa folded the letter and handed it back to him. She arched an eyebrow. "Are you happy, darling?"

Liam's driver opened the heavy door and the sound of the excited, noisy crowd rushed toward them. But Liam's eyes were steady on her face. "Exceptionally. You?"

"Indescribably. But Liam?"

"Yeah?"

Teresa waved her finger in the direction of her chest. "This dress, seriously, it can't end up on the floor."

Her husband helped her out of the car and sent her a rakish smile. "Oh, but we both know it will."

* * * * *

MONTANA
SEDUCTION

JULES BENNETT

To Lori Foster,
who spoke at the first writer's meeting
I ever attended *a few years ago* and
has turned into a great friend.
Thank you for everything!

One

Getting dumped only days before the wedding and spending the romantic mountain honeymoon at a fantasy adults-only resort by himself was humiliating. What could be worse than going on a honeymoon riding solo?

Or at least, that was the response Dane Michaels was counting on.

Sympathy could be a powerful tool, and he planned to use it in his favor. No one would have the slightest suspicion about the poor, abandoned man staying at Mirage Resort and Spa—and by a combination of laying on the charm and playing on everyone's solicitousness, he should be able to get all the information he needed.

So did it really matter that Dane had never actually had a fiancée—never intended to marry? The lie had embedded itself so deep in his head, he was more than ready to play the part of the jilted groom.

Dane pulled his truck to the front of the resort. The four-story lodge seemed suspended on the side of Gold Valley Mountain and with each guest suite having one-way windows from floor to ceiling, nearly every angle offered a breathtaking view of the valley below.

Gold Valley, Montana, had been his mother's first choice when opening Mirage. She'd had a vision, a life plan. But before she could fulfill her dreams, she'd suffered a fatal stroke, and her bastard husband, Robert Anderson, had taken over the two Mirage resorts and left Dane and his brother, Ethan, penniless and alone.

Dane exited the vehicle before the valet could assist him with the door. Dane wasn't here for the amenities or the secret rooms designed to fulfill couples' fantasies. He was here for one purpose and one purpose only—to find his opening to get this resort back in his name where it belonged, so he could honor his mother's memory.

Slipping the attendant a couple of Benjamins, Dane headed up the stone steps leading to the grand entrance. Nostalgia threatened to suck the breath from his lungs, but he pushed on, determined to get exactly what he came here for.

He hadn't been back in so long for several reasons. Mainly because he didn't want to return until he was sure he could secure this place for himself. The time had come.

Ignoring the pain of being back nearly two decades after his mother's death, Dane steeled himself against any emotions. He hadn't gotten this far by being soft and sensitive. Dane had been smacked with a dose of reality at the age of eighteen and life had been a giant kick in the ass since.

Everything he'd done, he'd crawled and fought for until he got back the money, the power due to him... there was just one thing left.

Without a glance to any of the couples milling about in the open lobby, Dane headed straight to the front desk to check in, reminding himself to remain constantly aware of those around him. There was no room for error and no time to waste.

Dane had a nearly twenty-year-old promise to fulfill.

Mirage manager Stella Garcia had no clue who he was, had no idea her world was about to change. Mustering up charm and sex appeal wasn't exactly Dane's area of expertise anymore, he left that to his playboy brother. But right now, and for the foreseeable future, Dane would use every other tool in his arsenal to pull those family secrets from this stranger to get back what belonged to him.

Once upon a time, a seduction would have been Dane's method of choice for an operation like this. Back then, he didn't have to try to get a woman into bed, they were more than willing to follow.

Fighting overseas in Iraq had changed him, hardened him, made him even more hell-bent on getting what he deserved.

It had also left him scarred and horrendous.

Getting close to anyone, let alone being sexual, had been practically impossible ever since. He wasn't stupid or naive. He knew what he looked like, knew doctors said there was hope if he wanted to go through painful surgeries in an attempt to cover the scars.

He didn't need to cover them. They went far beneath the surface of his skin so some vain attempt at erasing the past was a moot point.

And that had been the sole reason as to why he'd
been reluctant to follow through on this plan. But when
he couldn't think of another way to get what he wanted,
Dane realized this might be the only way to gain full
control of Mirage.

Besides, he needed a distraction from his own mind,
the prison he'd been trapped in since coming home from
Iraq. He'd thought getting his hands dirty and working from dusk till dawn at his ranch would exorcise the
demons away, but they were still waiting every single
night.

From the photos he'd seen of Stella, flirting with and
charming her certainly wouldn't be a hardship. "Charming" wasn't his default mode, but he could turn it on if
he needed to. And presenting himself as an abandoned
groom seemed tailor-made to winning her sympathies
and softening her reserve.

He sure as hell hoped his act of vulnerability and
loneliness got her to trust him, to open up and give
him a glimpse of exactly how he could use her to get to
her father. Presenting himself as some woman's reject
chafed at his pride, but he'd put up with it so he could
gain the information he needed. Then he'd head back
to his ranch, make this deal a legal thing and no one
would even care about his initial plan.

Of course he'd have to hire someone to run the resort. That person would have to be trustworthy and
loyal. Dane would accept nothing less than the best for
his mother's place.

Dane kept his sunglasses firmly in place and quickly
checked in, turning down the offer to have his bags
taken to his room. He knew the way. There was nothing
about this resort he didn't know. A few things may have

changed—the decor, the staff—but the layout hadn't. He'd practically grown up here.

Dane had booked the largest luxury penthouse, the one he knew matched the owner's penthouse. They were the only two suites with a mini pool and oversize hot tub off the enclosed bedroom balcony. Lovers could literally take just a few steps from their bed and sink into the pool or hot tub while overlooking the beauty of the mountains and valleys.

All of the rooms were top-notch, but Dane wanted the best. After all, wouldn't any groom plan the most romantic getaway and spare no expense?

As he stepped into the elevator, Dane removed his glasses and pocketed them. Once he put his things away, he had every intention of going out and "accidentally" running into Stella. He knew her schedule, knew every single thing about her thanks to the investigator he'd hired. Dane's knowledge of her schedule and her personality were the keys to gaining her trust.

Dane was well aware that her father treated her like shit and that he'd given her only six months to prove to him that she could run this place and show a profit—a mammoth undertaking after years of mismanagement had nearly run Mirage into bankruptcy.

Getting Mirage for himself was the main goal, but besting the arrogant bastard who treated his daughter like some bothersome employee was going to be icing on the proverbial cake. Victory was always sweet but victory over assholes was just plain fun. Dane was willing to admit he wasn't exactly an angel himself, but at least he was a smart and careful devil.

Dane left his bag in his suite, taking only a moment to admire the open view and spacious room. The wall

of windows made it seem like he was suspended above
Gold Valley. The curved pool was just as inviting as
he recalled.

Later he would fully take in the beauty of the room
his mother had designed. The stone fireplace, the balcony, the high beams stretching across the ceiling.

For now, though, memories would have to wait. He
had a woman to find.

"What do you mean he didn't show up?"

Stella Garcia attempted to tamp down the migraine
that threatened to further sour her already stressful,
overloaded day. She stared at one of the hostesses for
their main dining area and Stella thought for sure the
poor girl was going to burst into tears.

Tears solved nothing—a life lesson Stella had
learned from the start. Her mother had died after com-
plications giving birth, ultimately leaving Stella with
the most unloving father.

For reasons Stella still tried to wrap her mind around,
she wanted his approval—craved it even. Would do
anything to earn it, even if that meant taking on impossible tasks.

Which was how she found herself in the current situation—running a top-tier resort with a crowd of hungry patrons about to descend for dinner…and no cook.

Maybe if she'd had her mother, maybe if she'd had
just one parent who pretended to actually care…

"He called and said he quit, effective immediately,"
the hostess said, nervously tucking her short blond hair
behind her ear. "He said something about moving back
home to his wife in Oregon."

Stella pulled in a deep breath and wished she could

fast-forward to midnight when she could go up to her suite, pop open the prosecco and unwind.

Unfortunately, at this rate, she didn't even know if she'd get to bed tonight. All-nighters were depressingly common with this job. Some days were certainly more difficult than others, but she had to keep reminding herself that she'd inherited a mess from the previous manager and her father thought her incapable of fixing it. Those were two highly motivational reasons to prove to the whole damn world that she could and would make Mirage the greatest, most talked about resort on the globe.

"Our guests will start rolling in within an hour," she stated, tapping her finger on her chin as she thought out loud. "I'll need to see if there's anything already prepped or if we have to start from scratch. I know zilch about cooking."

But she could make a spreadsheet on the financial analytics of nearly any type of business and never break a sweat. She actually loved business and numbers. Damn, she was such a nerd. Too bad her hobbies hadn't included donning an apron and sizzling steaks.

Her young hostess shook her head. "I burn Pop-Tarts, so don't look at me."

If Stella had the time, she'd call up her now ex-chef and verbally shred him. But using her energy to get angry wouldn't solve their problem. For now, she simply had to push that employee out of her mind because at this point, he was irrelevant.

Really, it was better that he was gone. She didn't want anyone working for her who wasn't loyal. There was no room for mistrust or laziness, especially when she was on the verge of getting Mirage back on its feet and finally taking charge of her own life.

"Maybe Martha could help," the girl suggested.

Stella shook her head. "No, she's off because her sister is getting married. Damn it. She would've been able to salvage this evening. She's an amazing chef. I don't even think Raul is coming in until Friday. I may have to call him in because we are in a bind. But I doubt he'd get here in time."

Employees' names raced through her mind. It was hard to think of any options. The kitchen staff had the perfect rhythm down and worked like clockwork…well, they did until someone decided to up and quit. But the synchronicity meant no one really stood out as someone who could be trusted to take over the kitchen, even just for one night.

"Okay," Stella stated as she tucked a wayward strand of hair behind her ear. "We can do this. There's a logical solution, I just have to figure it out."

"Excuse me?"

Stella jerked her attention to the double wooden doors leading to the bar and private seating area. She was about to say they weren't open yet, but her words died in her throat.

Hello, cowboy.

That charcoal-and-red-plaid shirt tucked into well-worn jeans did nothing to hide the beautifully muscled bulk of the mystery man in the doorway. Those shoulders stretched the material of his shirt and his silver belt buckle shone with some emblem she couldn't quite make out.

Well, she could if she wanted to get caught staring at his junk, which wouldn't really be the classiest move.

Not to mention it would be totally unprofessional of her since he was a guest…and likely here with his significant other.

Shame, that. This man might be worth the risk of forgetting her duties and obligations, but she preferred her men to be available…unlike the jerk who thought she was his ticket into the family money—and that she was too dumb to uncover that he actually had a girlfriend with a kid on the way.

Yeah, no thanks, asshole.

Stella pulled her mind from the nauseating memory and opted to focus on the living fantasy standing in the doorway.

But that man would just have to stay a fantasy— along with every other man for the time being—because anything or anyone taking up her time would mean failing at her job, and her father was just waiting for one little slipup to sell this place out from under her. Her sole focus had to be on Mirage.

Smoothing down her button-up shirt-style dress, Stella took a step toward the striking man with dark eyes. "Our dining room doesn't open for another hour. Did you need to make a reservation?"

Which he totally should, because there was plenty of divine food prepared by an experienced chef. Part of Stella wanted to laugh at the snarky comment inside her head, because she'd realized over the past few months that if she didn't laugh, she'd have a nervous breakdown.

But at this moment, she worried that her laughter might border on manic or deranged. She was so, so close to getting what she wanted. There was no way she'd let a rogue chef thwart her plans.

"I couldn't help but overhear that you're in a bind."

That whiskey-soaked voice had her shivering and the vivid fantasy she'd tried to push to the back of her mind kept rushing to the front. Wasn't there some resort rule about lusting after a guest? After all, this was an adults-only resort so he probably wasn't here alone. A man who looked like that likely never slept alone… while she knew no other way.

Oh, she wasn't innocent, but she never stayed the night in someone's bed, and over the past year she'd barely dragged herself into hers. She'd been working her ass off for her father, wanting to gain his approval, wanting…hell, something from him other than disdain.

Getting Mirage running like a dream was her last chance at some type of parental nod.

"I might be able to help," the stranger added.

Stella crossed her arms and smiled. "Oh, well, that's not necessary, but thank you."

"Do you have someone else to cook?" he asked.

Oh, that dark arched brow that accompanied the question had her belly quivering with unwanted arousal. She must be sexually deprived if a brow and a voice turned her on. Well, the whole rough, manly-man exterior also gave a healthy punch of lust.

Maybe she should examine that belt buckle a little closer.

"Are you a chef, Mr…?"

"Michaels. Dane Michaels." In two strides he was in front of her and offering a half grin that drew her eyes down from his perfect teeth to the dark stubble covering his jawline. "I'm not a professional chef, but I'm a damn good cook. Ask any employee on my ranch."

His ranch. Of course someone this rugged and mysterious had a ranch. Montana had no shortage of cowboys, but this guy…he was the real deal and no doubt hands-on with his work if those weathered lines on his face were any indication. Likely the emblem on his buckle was that of his ranch.

"Mr. Michaels—"

"Dane," he corrected and had her toes curling in her boots with that full-fledged smile. "And you are?"

"Stella Garcia. I'm the manager of Mirage." Soon to be owner…she hoped. "Dane, I can't ask a guest to come into the kitchen where food is being prepared."

He propped his hands on his narrow hips and held her gaze. "You didn't ask and I don't see that you have many other options right now. Do you?"

Well, no, but that didn't mean this was a good idea. She couldn't let a stranger just come in and ride to her rescue. Good heavens, if her father heard of that, she'd definitely be reprimanded.

"Stella."

She turned to the Mia, the hostess Stella had completely forgotten was even in the room. "Yes?"

"We just got three more reservations and that booked us up for the night. That doesn't include the fantasy rooms and the room service." Mia chewed on her lip and stared over Stella's shoulder to the fantasy man. "I mean, you should at least think about his offer, but do it fast because in forty-five minutes, people will start coming in."

Stella rubbed her head and tried to remind herself that she wanted this job, that she loved Mirage. So far she'd had one headache after another, but for the most part she'd been cleaning up the mess left by the previous manager. Apparently he'd been a jerk to the employees and now Stella was paying the price of the resulting

disloyalty. Loyal employees didn't leave without giving notice.

But she did want to own Mirage. True, she wanted
her father to see her as a valuable businesswoman and
a capable daughter...they were all the family each other
had. But more so, she wanted this place because she'd
heard of the woman who built it. A single mother who
branched out to create something spectacular all on
her own.

How could Stella not admire that and strive to be as
strong as the original owner, Lara Anderson? When
her father had acquired the resort, Stella had done her
research on the place before her father let her in this
position. She did that with each of his acquisitions, but
this one had always stuck out to her and she'd had her
sights set on it for years.

"I can't believe I'm considering this," Stella muttered
as she spun back around to Dane.

Had he just been checking out her ass?

Well, well, well.

No. That should not excite her. She'd been in a relationship several years ago with a guy whose eyes, and
other body parts, wandered a bit too much.

Stella cleared her throat. "I couldn't pull you away
from your significant other."

"I'm actually here alone," he countered.

"Alone?"

"It's a long story," he added with another slight
grin—this one looked a little pained. "I'll tell you about
it while we prepare dinner. Deal?"

Stella shouldn't go along with this. The idea of letting a stranger, a *guest*, into the kitchen was preposter-
ous, but at this point, she wasn't sure what other option

she had. She needed help and she'd be in there the entire time watching to make sure nothing lawsuit-worthy
happened, so what could go wrong?

The worst choice would be to do nothing and stand
here and have a mental debate with herself. If her father
happened to find out what she'd done, she'd be more
than happy to defend herself and be proud that she'd
pulled this ill-fated night out of despair…so long as this
stranger could do all he'd promised.

Stella nodded toward the kitchen. "Follow me, Mr.
Michaels."

"Dane, remember?"

As she led the way through the dining room, she felt
very aware of the intriguing stranger following closely
at her back. She worked with men every single day. Her
father was one of the most powerful men in business
and had a slew of minions in suits that worked for and
with him. None had her in a fluster like this one.

There was certainly something to be said about a
mysterious, attractive man riding to the rescue at the
eleventh hour. It was like fate had planted him right in
her path.

And the fact he was here alone had her even more
intrigued. Stella couldn't imagine there wasn't a line of
women with lingerie packed and ready for a getaway
to a fantasy resort with this guy.

"There should be several starters made up in advance," Stella began as she pushed on the swinging
kitchen door. "Let's hope that's the case tonight."

"Either way, it will all work out," he told her.

When that velvety voice washed over her, she wanted
to believe him, but considering they were coming from

two different positions, she wasn't sure she should be so quick to let her guard down.

"The menu is set up two weeks in advance so we can have enough supplies ordered in—that means we have a direction on where to go." Stella pointed toward the wooden board hanging outside the walk-in refrigerator. "I know we'll have everything for tonight's menu, it's just putting it all together like it should be that's the challenge. And well, I'm not known for my kitchen skills."

Dane stepped around her and placed a hand on her forearm. That warm, rough palm slid over her skin and had her wondering just how those hands would feel over other, more neglected parts of her body.

Now was not the time for her dormant hormones to come rushing back to the surface.

"I promised it would all work out, right?" he asked. Those dark eyes held her in place. "Trust me."

"That's a bit difficult since I don't know you," she stated as she stared into those midnight eyes framed with heavy black lashes. "But for now, I'm going to have to trust my instincts and roll with this plan."

His thumb stroked over her arm. "I'll make sure this all works out. For both of us."

Suddenly, Stella wondered if he wasn't just referring to dinner.

Two

Dane had originally thought his plan was going to be easy, but getting in the door had taken charm and a little flirting. He was usually so good at getting information he needed.

Both actions painfully outside of his comfort zone these days, but he'd taken a page from his younger, more social brother, Ethan.

For now, Dane would act like he was the most confident, suave man Stella had ever seen. There would be no cause for her to be suspicious. Soon, she'd trust him with all sorts of secrets, and after that, the resort would be his in no time. Finally, after all of these years.

And all he had to do was get close to a striking, sexy woman. Cooking was going to be the easy part, and hopefully this instant foot in the door would give him that extra boost he needed when it came to capturing her trust and attention.

She'd certainly captured *his* attention with no trouble at all.

That first glimpse of Stella when she'd turned around had nearly rendered him speechless. Thankfully, he'd remembered why he was here and that any distraction, no matter how sexy, could cost him everything.

Just because he was here to get close to her, didn't mean he could lose sight of the prize.

But then the rest of the kitchen staff started milling in and Stella went to work and took charge. While Dane figured out what the hell he needed to do to create a dinner for one hundred–plus people coming in and out over the next few hours, he also managed to watch Stella in action, knowing that would give him insight as to how to handle his next steps with her.

Damn if she wasn't even sexier when she focused on her own goal. He knew she wanted this resort for herself, he also knew her father wouldn't let that happen. The old bastard was stringing her along and had no intention of giving his daughter anything.

While Dane had never met the man in person, watching him from a distance and hiring an investigator to dig up details had shown that Ruiz Garcia was the biggest male chauvinist jerk Dane had ever heard of.

But that was just one more weapon in his arsenal—a point of connection between them he could use to create sympathy and trust. They both had bastard father/ stepfathers and they'd both lost their mothers.

Once all was said and done, and he'd secured Mirage, Stella would see that he'd actually done her a favor by getting her out from under the thumb of her controlling father.

Until then, well, Dane would have to do a little more

socializing than he'd planned. The pleasure of spending time with a sultry, alluring woman would make up for the comfort zone he'd stepped so far from. She was responding to him nicely so far—he just had to make sure that he kept up the act…and that he didn't let her expose the ugly, scarred parts of him, whether they were visible or not.

There was one obstacle after another, but that end result…

Several hours and countless dishes of pork roast with mashed potatoes later, Dane worked on the cleanup. The rest of the staff had been dismissed and Stella was out in the dining room straightening everything.

Dane certainly wasn't a star chef, but being raised by a single mother had given him an edge in household tasks. Lara Anderson had been adamant that her boys do every bit of work deemed for "women" and she swore she'd make them good husband material. His mother wasn't here to see that neither of her sons had any intention of being a husband, but Dane was still thankful he'd paid attention when she'd shared her special recipes and guided him through basic preparation steps.

Most of the dishes were washed and put away. From the checklist, it looked like all Dane needed to do was prepare a few things for the breakfast crowd. The fruit needed to be cut and placed into separate bowls. The bread was all ready to go, it just had to be put out at room temperature.

The more Dane did, the more he missed his ranch. Being alone and feeding just one was more his speed. His cattle could fend mostly for themselves and the horses were like his best friends. Aside from his ranch hands, those animals were about the extent of anyone or anything he wanted to care for.

Soon, though. Soon he'd be out of here, with the property in his name and then he could figure out how much time to spend at the ranch and how much to spend here. The penthouse he'd gotten for this stay would be a perfect suite for him to keep, but he knew the owner's suite was even more spectacular. His mother had spared no expense when she had brought her dream to life.

"Well, you saved my ass."

He'd admired said ass quite a bit since first stepping through the dining room. The sway of her little dress as the hem hit the back of her knees. Those tiny buttons that ran down the middle of the front had teased him all night. He'd stared at the one just between her breasts as if willing it to slide right open.

Dane wondered what she wore beneath and opted to use his own imagination. He figured Stella to be a lace type of lady. Someone like her would want to be all business on the exterior yet all woman beneath.

His body responded instantly to the image of her with the dress stripped away, her dark hair around her shoulders and her breasts bound by lace.

Dane slid the sharp knife through the juicy strawberry, but didn't glance up at Stella. She came to stand on the other side of the stainless prep area and rested her palms on the flat surface. If Ethan were in his place he would've cleared off this island and had her beneath him in seconds.

Dane wasn't Ethan. Revealing his body by taking Stella to bed wouldn't seal the deal—it would sour it, once she saw what he was hiding under his clothes. No, there wouldn't be sex—just flirting. Teasing. Winning her trust slowly and carefully. Well, as slowly as his sanity would allow. He wanted Mirage in his name right now, but he knew he had to be patient.

"Happy I could help," he finally replied, attempting to get control over his hormones. He needed to pace himself. "I'm just going to get this fruit cut up and set in the fridge. What time should I be here tomorrow?"

"Oh, no," Stella retorted. "You've more than helped. I called in our part-time chef and offered an exorbitant amount of money if she would cover for the next few weeks."

Dane stopped slicing and set the knife down as he lifted his gaze to hers. "That wasn't necessary. I would've helped while I was here."

Stella smiled. Not the flirty smile he often got from women when he ventured out, but the type of smile that contained a sense of…pity.

Damn it. He'd seen enough of that from his staff at the ranch when he'd get lost in his war nightmares. He'd let the majority of them go because he did not need sympathy and he didn't want anyone in his house hearing his cries. He refused to take pity from anybody and he sure as hell couldn't afford to have it from the woman he was trying to get close to.

But pity from Stella was a bit easier to handle. She didn't even know the real reason to pity him, so technically her emotions toward him right now were null.

"It's not like I had anything else to do," he replied. "Besides, it wasn't bad and I got to help a beautiful woman."

Stella pursed her lips, but she didn't even blush. He'd have to reconsider his verbiage. Clearly she was either used to compliments or she wasn't interested in them.

Either way, he had to tread carefully and keep working to build a connection between them.

"I'm sure you could've done just fine on your own," he amended. "I can't imagine you would've let a rogue chef ruin the night."

Stella crossed her arms over her chest and cocked her head. "I don't let anyone ruin my plans once I set them into motion."

Perhaps they had even more in common than he'd initially thought. Which would make this entire process that much easier…once they got over this initial get-to-know-you phase.

"That attitude is why this place is so successful." He flashed her a smile and picked up a strawberry, extending it across the island toward her. "You're an admirable woman."

She kept her eyes on his as she took the fruit from his hand. "I've already comped your room for the duration of your stay. Flattery isn't necessary."

Comped his room? Wasn't that adorable. He had enough money to buy this entire resort and not put a dent in his finances, but the fact she'd done so just proved she was sincere in her commitment to Mirage… and her father didn't deserve such loyalty.

"That wasn't necessary," he replied.

With a shrug, she bit into the strawberry. The second her lips closed around her fingers to clean away the juices, Dane was pretty damn thankful he had a barrier between his waist and her eyes.

Was she purposely taunting him? She'd been so all-business before, he'd thought he'd have to be the one to initiate all the flirting. Only one of them could take the lead and he'd already signed up for that position. No way was he going to be sidetracked.

On the other hand, if he'd already gotten her curiosity piqued, his work here could be over sooner than he'd planned.

"I believe you owe me a story," she told him after she finished licking each finger and driving him out of his mind with want. He wanted that mouth on him. "We got so busy you didn't get a chance to tell me how someone like you is at an adult resort all alone."

At least this part he'd rehearsed and prepared for. He didn't know how to hide his actual arousal because that sure as hell wasn't an act and not planned...at least not standing in the resort kitchen.

"I'm on my honeymoon."

Stella stared at him a moment before she let out a sharp laugh. "And you left your wife at home?"

"Actually, my fiancée opted to leave me a couple days before the wedding."

Her smile vanished as her brows shot up. "You're serious."

Dane nodded, pushing forward with the lie that rolled easily off his tongue. "Humiliating as this is to admit, yes. Apparently ranch life wasn't for her and she decided to reconnect with her ex. I thought about canceling the reservations, but I figured I deserved a getaway so here I am. I hope that's not against any house rules."

Stella pulled in a deep breath and made her way around the prep island. Dane shifted to face her as she came to stand before him.

"Not at all. We don't usually get singles, but there's no rule." Stella's dark eyes held him, captivated him.

"Your fiancée is either a moron or undeserving. You're better off without her."

"You don't even know me. Perhaps she's the smart one."

Stella reached over and plucked a cut berry from the chopping board and held it out to him. "I realize we just met, but I'm a good judge of character. I'd say you're pretty noble and loyal."

Loyal? Hell yes, he was loyal—to a very select few. There were only two people in this world he'd do anything for: his twin brother, even though their personalities were completely opposite and they rarely saw each other, and his mother.

His mother was the sole reason for this charade and his brother…well, they each had their own thing going in trying to track down the bastard who stole everything from them once their mother passed. Yes, he knew plenty about loyalty. But he was about as far from noble as he could get.

His plan to take her father down and reclaim what belonged to him might be devious; it might be cruel, even. He wasn't proud of that. For all his faults, he'd never been selfish, he'd never purposely been deceitful. But he was about to do a hell of a job now because the future of his mother's legacy was on the line. With honor on one side and loyalty on the other, his choice was clear. There were no rules for him.

"Looking back, we could best be described more as friends than anything," he added. He didn't want to come off as a complete prick for flirting with Stella right after ending an engagement. "I'd gotten used to the idea of not being alone and being a couple was more habit than anything. She found someone and they're in love. She's happier now."

"And you?" Her question came out in a slight whisper. "Are you happier now?"

Dane swallowed the strawberry and licked his lips. Her eyes darted to his mouth and he wondered if seduction really could be this easy. No wonder Ethan always had a new woman. Still, this wasn't Dane's typical behavior. There was no going back now, though.

Not with the chemistry crackling between them even though he hadn't even laid a finger on her. Damn...he wanted to get her into bed. Even though it wasn't in the plan—even though it might ruin everything—the temptation was growing stronger with every passing moment. Something shifted, something he couldn't quite place a finger on.

Lust. He hadn't expected this strong of a pull. He hadn't wanted a woman in so long. Well, he had natural urges, but to actually feel the desire and the ache...he couldn't recall the last time. Granted, avoiding people in general probably contributed to his lack of sex life. But sex or getting close to anyone would open the door to questions he wasn't ready to answer.

In the last several hours, Dane found he actually wanted to get closer to Stella. That could be the lack of sex in his life talking, though.

"I'm happy that the marriage didn't happen," he stated. "When I marry, I plan for it to be a one-time thing."

He nearly laughed at that statement because he rarely left his ranch, let alone dated anyone. Dodging people and any social activity had been his new normal since leaving the army, deepening the seclusion that had started with the untimely death of his mother, when he'd opted to keep to himself instead of talk to anyone—even Ethan.

So, no. Marrying was certainly off the table because he'd never let anyone get that close to him. Besides the fear of abandonment again, he wouldn't subject anyone to his nightmares.

"So you do want marriage?" she asked.

"Maybe. Eventually. I'm not in a hurry."

He leaned his hip against the edge of the stainless steel and reached out to push her long inky hair over her slender shoulder. There was no reason for him to try to avoid touching her.

He also needed to get away from this topic because the last thing he wanted her to believe was that he was ready for some fictitious happily-ever-after. The attraction clearly had a place here and that's what he'd hone in on. Any sort of romance had to be left behind.

"You're staying for a week." She smiled and every nerve ending sizzled at that tiny dimple nestled against the corner of her mouth. "Consider every upgrade and meal on the house."

"I can't do that." He shook his head and laughed. "You've already settled the bill for my room. That's more than enough for just helping out over a few hours, though no thanks were necessary."

"Thanks was very necessary," she countered. "Considering I'm riding a thin line and I have someone waiting for me to fail… Well, that's a story for another time."

"So there will be another time?" he asked, not pressuring her on the topic of her father.

Her eyes held his and her smile remained. "As much as I'd like to, I work what seems like thirty hours a day."

"All the more reason to take a break."

"Breaks could cost me everything," she murmured as she glanced away. Then she adjusted her shoulders and returned her focus to him. "It's late and I'm sure you'd like to get to your room and relax."

Only if she came with him.

"I'd relax more if I had some bourbon. Pappy Van Winkle would do the trick, but that's not an option right now," he half joked. "What do you do to relax, Stella?"

Her lids fluttered just a second when he said her name. Good. He wanted her thrown off. He wanted her to be flustered and aroused, thrown off guard enough to let things slip.

"I don't even know what relaxing is," she stated, but he knew she wasn't joking.

"Have a glass of wine with me."

Stella raised a brow. "And what about breakfast prep?"

"I'll finish up afterward," he told her. "I've seen the list and once I get this in the fridge, the rest has to be done in the morning."

"I can't leave a stranger in my kitchen."

Fair enough. "Then help me and we'll get out of here and have that wine."

When she started to shake her head, Dane reached out and gripped her chin with his thumb and forefinger, pulling her gaze directly to his. Those dark eyes held so much emotion. He wondered if she even knew that the pain and the worry inside them was projected to anyone who looked closely.

Had anyone ever looked? Was there someone who took the time to care how much she ran herself ragged? Sure as hell not her father...and Dane wasn't volunteering for that position, either. But she deserved someone. People like Stella worked hard and had great aspirations, but they could get run over.

"Breaks can cost me everything, too," he told her, needing her to know they really weren't all that different, also silently warning himself that he needed to tread lightly for his own sanity. "But I'm willing to take the chance. Are you?"

Three

What was she doing here? Stella had more pressing things to do than to stare at the seam of the closed private elevator doors leading to Dane Michaels's penthouse suite…with a chilled bottle of prosecco in hand, no less.

Maybe she should've brought a nice cab instead? Or bourbon. Hadn't he mentioned a bourbon earlier?

"This is the most ridiculous thing I've ever done," she muttered.

What was she thinking? Just because one mysterious, sexy rancher sauntered in to rescue her, she got all excited and aroused and suddenly couldn't control her desires.

She didn't have time for desires or sexy attractions. Yet here she was heading straight toward both.

The faux wooden doors slid open with a soft whoosh. Stella immediately took in the fitted tee stretching

across broad shoulders and well-worn jeans over narrow hips. Dane's hair was wet, making it seem even
darker than before. He'd shed the plaid shirt and, mercy's sake, this rancher certainly did the whole hands-on
thing. That body made it very clear that he didn't just
stay in some office writing checks for his employees.

Clearly Dane had freshened up while she still looked
like the haggard mess she'd been since this morning.
She should've at least changed, but she hadn't even considered removing her dress and knee boots.

She'd been too busy arguing with herself over why
she'd let this virtual stranger affect her so. Maybe
she'd been smitten by his white knight routine, but she
couldn't just dismiss how ridiculously handsome he
was, nor could she ignore how her entire body seemed
to tingle with a rush of arousal whenever he got close.

There was something rough and rugged about him.
When he'd mentioned a ranch…well, toss her a set of
chaps and mount up because that was just flat-out hot.
Plus, she'd never ridden a cowboy.

Oh, ranchers and cowboys were all throughout Montana, but none had interested her and she spent most
of her time with men in suits who only pretended to
know the ranching lifestyle. They'd never do anything
labor-related that might mess their suits or smudge their
manicures.

Dane rested his hip on the back of the leather sofa
in the living area and greeted her with a crooked grin.
"So you are a risk taker."

Stella merely held out the bottle of wine and
shrugged. "What can I say?"

"You can say that you'll stay awhile."

He didn't stand, didn't move toward her. He simply relaxed there like he was giving her total control, yet that leveled, dark gaze told her who really called the shots. Hadn't she come to him? How could he be so powerful, yet not a bit demanding or even making a move?

The way he stared at her...

Like a lion inviting his prey and she was positive she wouldn't mind being feasted on.

Stella stepped into the spacious penthouse suite. The views never got old, and even from the doorway she could see across the room and stare out the wall of windows. Even in the dark, there was a soft glow coming up from the valley and casting mysterious shadows all over the mountainside.

Lara Anderson had seriously thought of everything when she'd built Mirage on the side of the mountain. No expense had been spared and that's what made Mirage such a magical escape.

If all of these guests opted to come here and get away from their daily stresses, why couldn't she do the same...even if for a short time.

The high-beamed ceilings and dark wood floors made the space appear more like a glorified cabin than a room in a resort. The crackling fire called to her. The stunning feature of the fireplace with its stone surround extending to the high ceiling seemed so inviting...so romantic. No, that was the hot guy that seemed romantic. And she'd brought the wine.

This was too easy. Sex was easy. Seduction was easy. Giving in to hormones and not giving a damn about tomorrow or consequences would be so...liberating.

Unfortunately, she didn't have that luxury of a one-night stand. But flirting and unwinding with a sexy stranger was dangerous ground that she couldn't help but want to dance on tonight. Just one time. That wouldn't hurt anything, right?

"I didn't think you wanted to take a risk."

Stella offered Dane a smile. "I'd say this one is harmless."

Though she knew a man like Dane was anything but. Yes, this was taking a huge chance coming to his room, but, well, her father couldn't control every move she made. She didn't have to justify her personal life to him. All she had to do was prove herself worthy of keeping Mirage and having him sign the property over to her at the end of this six-month experiment. She had only three months to go.

"*Harmless* isn't a word people usually use to describe me," he countered, his dark eyes half-hidden behind lowered lids. That husky voice sent shivers racing through her.

Maybe they didn't use *harmless*, but the word that seemed to embody Dane Michaels was definitely potent. She hadn't even tried to rationalize the hows and whys of this man and her instant attraction to him. What would be the point? Nothing would come of this…whatever this was. Besides, this was fun. When was the last time she'd done something simply because she wanted to? Every move she made had a purpose and an end gain.

Dane crossed the space, keeping his gaze locked on hers. The snap of the fire behind her filled the silence and added to the allure of the moment. The mysterious man, the late hour…the sexual tension.

"Why don't you go have a seat," he murmured. "I'll take care of everything."

Everything? As in…

He slid the bottle from her grasp and she suddenly recalled why she was here. Wine. Not orgasms.

Relax, Stella. Don't make a fool of yourself.

One glass of wine and then she needed to go. Because if she stuck around much longer, she may come across as desperate and not the kick-ass, independent woman she'd fought so hard to be.

"What time will you start back to work in the morning?" he asked as he came over with two very generous glasses of wine.

She wasn't much of a drinker, so if she sucked down all of this she'd likely end up draped over the rug in front of the fire before long. And since "drunk Stella" lacked impulse control, she'd probably be posed in some "come and get me" style that would surely embarrass her once the buzz wore off.

"I'll go back down about five."

Dane settled next to her on the leather sofa and glanced to his watch. "That's in five hours. When do you sleep?"

"When I have time."

Which was rarely. If she could go through these next few months on no sleep, she totally would. There simply wasn't enough time in the day. She had to keep all these balls juggled in the air. Dropping even one could prove fatal for her goals.

"Have you always put so much pressure on yourself?" he asked, taking a drink and then putting his glass on the raw-edged table.

"I don't see it as pressure," she retorted. "There are things I want and failing isn't an option."

"You're the manager of a picturesque mountain resort. What other goals could you possibly have?"

Stella stared into her wineglass. "Not everything is as it seems."

Before she revealed too much, she took a sip and closed her eyes as the fruity flavors burst in her mouth. She couldn't suppress the sigh that escaped her. That was a great bottle she'd grabbed from the wine cellar.

When she lifted her lids, Dane's gaze had dropped to her mouth and...had he shifted closer?

Arousal churned through her and she couldn't even blame the wine considering she'd just taken her first sip. The seclusion at this late hour and the roaring fire might be impacting her, yes, but not the wine.

"Do you want something more than Mirage?" he asked.

Stella set her glass next to his. The intimate image had her biting on her lip for a just a second before shifting her focus back to him.

"Mirage is all I've ever wanted," she explained. "My father bought the resort several years ago and I'd heard the story of the lady who had built this, relentlessly pursuing her dream. A single mom who pushed through and built something so dynamic and spectacular just hit me, you know? I didn't grow up with my mother, but I just felt pulled toward this strong female, even though I'd never met her. I knew I wanted this business to be mine. My father has plenty of companies around the globe, but this is the one I want."

Dane's eyes seemed to grow even darker, his jaw clenched, but he remained silent. She'd started talking and hadn't even considered that he probably wanted a short, quick answer.

"Sorry," she said with a soft laugh. "I didn't mean to ramble."

"Never apologize for going after what you want."

Stella's smile faltered as she swallowed. "And what is it you want, Dane?"

"That's not so difficult to guess."

Oh, he wasn't subtle. And yet, something about the way he didn't quite come out and say it, but let the implication hang heavily in the air packed an even sexier punch.

"And do you think I came here for sex?" she asked.

"I think you came here because you wanted to know what would happen once we were alone."

"We were alone in the kitchen," she reminded him, clasping her hands in her lap to prevent them from trembling—or reaching for him.

"Not like this." He eased forward, never taking his eyes from hers. "You might not want to take risks, but you can't help yourself. The resort, me... You want to know what it's like to fully throw yourself into temptation and ride out the challenge."

How did he peg her so easily when she'd met him only hours ago? And why did her entire body stir with each low, rumbled word that slid through his lips?

Because she wanted those lips on hers, on her body. The need crashed through her and took hold like nothing she'd ever experienced.

"I try to have a little more control than that—I'm not as reckless as you make me sound." Or at least that's what she tried to tell herself. "And I'd never take a risk with this resort. Mirage is my life."

"You're quite the professional," he agreed. "But you still took a risk by taking it over. Business isn't for the faint of heart."

"You sound like my father," she murmured.

Dane placed his hand on her knee. "Does he also tell you what a stellar job you're doing?"

Stella eyed those tanned, rough fingers against her dark skin. The hem of her dress proved to be no barrier as the tip of his pinky slid beneath the fabric.

"He, um… No. No, he doesn't."

Mercy, how could Dane carry on a normal conversation? Her body was revved up and she was about to start begging. She really shouldn't deprive her body so long from such a basic, necessary need.

Stella reached for her glass and took another sip. "Let's not bring my father into this."

His hand inched a bit higher, then his thumb slid over the bottom button of her dress as if he would pop it open at any moment.

"Agreed. Everyone should stay out of this room except us."

Stella took another sip and set her glass back down. "We're not having sex."

"Not yet."

She couldn't stop her smile. "At all," she clarified. "I can't afford to get caught up in anything but work right now."

Dane's eyes crinkled in the corners as he smiled. "Yet here you are."

Well, he had her there. Stella laid her hand over his and for a split second—okay, maybe more—she wanted to slid it on up and show him exactly how he could alleviate her stress. But she held his hand firmly in place on her bare thigh.

"I don't even know you," she stated. "Clearly there's chemistry, but I can't get sidetracked by a sexy man who came to my rescue."

"I obviously wasn't looking to get sidetracked, either, but there's nothing more I want than to lay you out in front of that fire and give you exactly what your body is aching for."

The man knew all the right words to say. There should be some major red flags going up. A stranger coming in at the exact time she needed someone, the fact he knew precisely what to say and just how much to press without being a jerk...

No matter the flags, she honestly couldn't find a flaw here.

Stella reached for her glass and tipped it back, taking every last drop of her favorite wine. With a soft clink, she set the glass back down and came to her feet. Dane's hand fell away, and he rose, as well.

"I should get to my room and attempt a few hours of sleep."

Dane brushed her hair from her face, letting his fingertips feather across her jaw. Something flashed through his eyes a second before he curled those same fingers around the back of her neck and pulled her mouth to his.

Stella didn't even try to fight the kiss...why would she? They'd been building toward this moment since they met—did it matter that was only a few hours ago?

Besides, a kiss was harmless. Well, most of them were. A kiss from Dane Michaels was powerful, toe curling, panty melting, and instantly had her mind on sex. The way his body lined perfectly with hers, the way his lips coaxed hers apart, eager for more, only had her more than ready to take him up on his offer.

The wine had gotten to her just as she'd thought it might. She swayed against him, reaching up to clutch his bare biceps. Those were rancher arms. No sedentary job could produce muscles so firm, so…magnificent.

Dane eased back and Stella whimpered. Damn alcohol. She'd never whimpered or begged for any man, yet she'd just done the first and was closing in on the second.

"I'll check on you tomorrow," he told her. "If you need me, you know where to find me."

When he released her, Stella had to concentrate on staying upright. She hadn't had nearly enough time with him. She wanted more of that whiskey-soaked tone, that dark gaze, those lips and hands on her.

Straightening her dress, Stella pulled herself together and crossed the suite to the elevator. Dane came up behind her, practically pressing her against the doors. Stella closed her eyes and inhaled that spicy, masculine scent.

"I'll see you tomorrow."

The whisper in her ear, the warmth of his breath on her skin had her shivering and with the way his chest was pressed to her back, there was no way he missed her body's reaction to him.

Stella risked a glance over her shoulder. "I look forward to it."

And then she fled back to her room where she replayed over and over the entire evening from the moment Dane stepped into the dining room to the moment he sent her entire body up in flames.

So why didn't she just give in and let him douse them?

No. The real question was, how long would she make them both wait?

Four

Dane sipped his morning coffee and relaxed in the Adirondack chair on the expansive enclosed balcony. He'd come out at sunrise to admire the breathtaking view. He'd had a restless night, thanks in part to one seductress who'd plastered her sweet body against his and left him wondering just who was playing whom.

He'd remained in control of the situation last night, but barely. He needed to have a better grasp of just how potent Stella was before their next encounter. Coming into this whole plan, he sure as hell hadn't planned on questioning his damn sanity regarding his hormones.

Stella had certainly surprised him last night by coming to his suite. He'd written off seeing her again until today after she'd seemed to reject his invitation. Dane wasn't often taken off guard and finding more reasons to admire Stella was not helping his cause.

He didn't want to admire her, he wanted to use her for her insight into her father's sharklike mind when it came to business. Yet each moment he spent with her, he found himself growing more and more captivated.

Dane had already sent an offer to buy Mirage outright that was more than reasonable, but Ruiz Garcia had turned it down without a counter.

There had to be a way…and Dane was using the method he felt would be the most effective. If the guy treated his daughter like a peasant employee, why the hold over this resort? Why not just sell it, take the money, and cut his daughter out of the business entirely? Why string her along?

So many questions, yet none of them really mattered. All Dane cared about was what it would take for Ruiz to sell Mirage. That was the bottom line.

Dane extended his legs and crossed his ankles. He'd give his brother another hour or so before he called. Ethan was not a morning person, pretty much because he was a nighttime partier. His current state likely involved being wrapped around at least one woman.

While Dane worked here in Gold Valley, Ethan was hoping to work his own magic at the second Mirage resort on Sunset Cove. The island off the coast of California was certainly more Ethan's lifestyle. Dane preferred his secluded ranch, he thrived in being alone where he didn't have to feed a relationship and had nobody depending on him.

The bond between Dane and his younger brother had been strained since the passing of their mother, but they were still brothers and had two goals binding them together: get back the Mirage resorts and take down Robert Anderson. That bastard had stolen too much from them when they'd been helpless, but now Dane and Ethan were powerful and even more so when they put their resources together. There wasn't a place Robert could hide, not anymore.

None of this was about the money. Both Dane and Ethan could buy any resort anywhere in the world. Hell, they could build something even bigger, better, but they deserved what their mother had created.

With the twentieth anniversary of her death approaching, Dane wanted, needed to feel closer to the only woman he'd ever loved.

Tamping down the ache resonating in the void in his heart, Dane came to his feet and rested his arms on the wrought iron railing. Clutching his coffee cup, he overlooked the valley and felt like a damn king. There was nothing more refreshing than mountain air that was so crisp, so raw.

Dane wouldn't have a difficult time coming off the ranch with picturesque views like this to tempt him. He'd worried about who would actually run the place in his absence once he got Mirage in his control, but the worry seemed less potent now that he realized how comfortable he still felt here. He would be a hands-on owner. This was his mother's place, his mother's dream, there was no way he could turn Mirage over to anybody else.

So long as he kept that in the forefront of his mind, Dane knew he could push through his doubts and fears. If anyone could get him to step back out into society on a regular basis, it was his mother. She deserved for him to step up and put his own issues aside and be the man she'd raised.

Dane pushed off the rail and took the last sip of his

coffee. As he made his way through the double glass doors, he pulled his cell from the pocket of his jeans.

There was no time to waste. He needed to discuss things with his younger brother. If that meant disrupting his morning slumber and irritating his bedmates, so be it.

Dane set his coffee mug on the large raw-edged wood island between the kitchen and the dining area as he dialed. He waited for Ethan to pick up, but voice mail kicked in and Dane muttered a curse before clearing his throat and leaving a message.

They were closing in on Robert and Dane was chomping at the proverbial bit to serve a healthy dose of vengeance to his stepfather. Dane wanted to know where Ethan stood and what intel he'd uncovered since they spoke last.

Each day that went by was another day closer to the anniversary of their mother's death and another day that bastard was able to live his life as a free man. Those days were coming to an end and a new chapter in the Michaels brothers' story would begin. Maybe regaining their legacy would bring them back together, closer, like they used to be.

Dane pocketed his phone and headed toward the en suite to shower. While waiting to hear from his brother and plan their takedown, Dane had a lady to charm. And judging from her reaction last night, he wasn't too far from accomplishing all of his goals.

The vibration on the nightstand irritated the hell out of Ethan. Couldn't a guy get a good morning's sleep? If that damn thing kept going off, he'd throw it out the open patio door, not caring if it landed in the ocean.

He turned his face into the soft, warm pillow and blinked against the sunlight streaming in. He purposely kept that patio door open so he could hear the ocean crashing to the shore. Security wasn't an issue—unless a thief who could defy gravity decided to scale the high-rise penthouse. Ethan had confidence he was safe.

Besides, he thrived here. The beach, the ocean, the endless water views from his bed. He'd grown up in Montana and the mountains were fine for his brother, but the second Ethan had set foot on a beach, he knew exactly where he belonged. Everything about this atmosphere called to him and he couldn't imagine spending his life in the mountains like Dane.

The cell buzzed again and Ethan rolled over and smacked the damn thing before pulling it toward him. The screen lit up with a few texts from numbers he didn't recognize and a voice mail alert from Dane.

The texts could wait. Even though they were likely from the ladies he'd met last night and Ethan rarely kept a woman waiting—in bed or out—this business with Dane had to take top priority. They both had their own individual goals, but their joint goal had Ethan sitting up in bed, the sheet pooling around his waist as he dialed his brother.

"Did I interrupt anything?"

Dane's answer in lieu of hello had Ethan grunting and glancing to the other side of his king-size bed. The four-legged, furry feline hadn't stirred since crawling over his face to get to her spot in the middle of the night.

Not many people knew about the fur ball that he'd rescued. But damn it he'd seen the poor lethargic thing out in a storm and he simply couldn't leave it there.

Ethan had had every intention of finding a new home for it.

Two years later, they were still together.

"I'm sandwiched between two redheads," Ethan replied, instead of mentioning the real pussy in his bed. "This better be good."

"I'm at Mirage in Gold Valley."

Ethan felt a swell of pride and anticipation, quickly followed by a dose of jealousy and longing. Dane had already pushed through to the next phase of their mission to gain back what belonged to them, but timing was everything and Ethan wasn't quite ready to make his presence known at Mirage in Sunset Cove.

"I've already gotten close with the manager—who also happens to be the owner's daughter—and it's just a matter of time before I can get the angle I need to get this location back in our family."

Our family. They hadn't been a true family since their mother died. When that happened, Dane had closed in on himself, their stepfather had shown his true, greedy self and Ethan...well, he'd turned to anyone who could make him forget, even if that was for just a night.

"You're moving fast." Ethan threw off the sheet and swung his legs over the side of the bed, taking a moment to enjoy the breathtaking view. "And here I thought I was the charming, irresistible brother."

"You're cocky. There's a difference," Dane retorted. "What have you found out about Robert?"

Ethan raked a hand over his bare chest as he came to his feet. "Right now he's comfortable in Hawaii. We're so damn close. I want to lure him in. I need him at Mirage in Sunset Cove."

"You're confident you can get him there?" Dane asked.

"He's never been able to turn down the idea of making millions." Ethan had formulated a rock-solid plan, but he needed his brother's help. "If he thinks he can get this resort back and flip it again to make money on it twice, he'll break records getting there."

"Don't make a move until you tell me," Dane stated. "I want to be there when you approach him. We're a team on this deal."

Right. A team. Ethan had hinged his entire life on that...or at least the first eighteen years. But losing their mother had torn a hole through both of them, and they just hadn't been able to reach each other across the empty space. They'd stuck together until they'd both finished high school but then, motherless and penniless, they'd both joined the military and gone their separate ways.

They stayed in touch, calling and texting, randomly getting together, but nothing was the same. Ethan couldn't even blame their polar-opposite personalities. When they'd been growing up, they'd simply balanced each other.

While Dane was more studious, Ethan had been a jock. They could put down an extra-large pizza—covered with sausage of course—and one ate all the edges, the other ate the entire middle. Everything they'd done just seemed to jive.

As adults, well, they were more acquaintances than anything. Their main goal of taking back the resorts and annihilating Robert had always kept them bonded... but Ethan wanted more. He wanted his brother back. In the years since they'd split apart, no one had filled that void. He was always surrounded by people, but he was lonely for family.

"I'm hoping to lure him in within the next month," Ethan replied. "I'll keep you posted."

"I'll do the same from my end." Dane cleared his throat. "We're going to make this happen. For Mom."

The void in Ethan's heart throbbed. "For Mom," he repeated.

And for us.

Five

Stella stifled the urge to breath a sigh of relief at how smoothly the morning had gone with the part-time chef. Thankfully she'd agreed to step up full-time and save Stella's ass.

Considering it was only lunchtime on day one of the replacement, Stella wasn't about to pull out the confetti and celebrate just yet. But she did feel some of the weight ease from her shoulders.

Granted she should be relaxed after that wine and those kisses last night from a virtual stranger, but that sexual tension…

She'd had friends in college who had had one-night stands and Stella had never understood how someone could tumble into bed with a person they'd just met.

Well, now she knew exactly why they didn't let their inhibitions get in the way. Just the memory of that intimate moment had her body heated in ways she didn't think possible.

Unfortunately, as much as she wanted to replay the events and tack on her own fantasies, there was too much work to be done.

Since the lunch rush seemed to be under control, Stella headed toward the front desk. Checkout time had passed an hour ago and they were due to get a new wave of couples. Every room was booked, which was always a good thing on a weeknight.

Since Stella had taken over, she'd been trying her hardest to make sure her marketing team kept pumping out information and waving the amenities around all over social media. The previous manager hadn't been interested in growing the business, but rather staying behind his desk and remaining stagnant. All he cared about was that he got paid.

Well, that had put a damper on her father's plans to watch cash just flood in, so Stella had jumped at the chance to not only manage this remarkable resort, but also show her father she was a worthy businesswoman.

She didn't need his approval. She didn't need his money. But she wanted his respect and she had a sickening feeling in her gut that she'd never get it. This was her last chance. She was done putting herself out there, basically waving around in his face all the ways that she was worthy to be in his world, his damn life. If he didn't acknowledge her or treat her the way she deserved, then she'd be done.

Even if that would leave her officially alone. Over time she had come to the realization that perhaps she'd be better off alone than begging for attention or love from her own father.

Stella passed through the wide-open, four-story lobby. She never tired of the beauty of this place. Not only had Mirage been built with wood from the forest where the building stood, the place had been built around some of the old trees. Literally, there was a large, live ponderosa pine growing straight up through the middle of the lobby. It was quite a focal point for newcomers looking for a place to take selfies.

Besides the live trees randomly found inside the resort, there were windows absolutely everywhere. A breathtaking view was never farther than a glance in one direction or the other. Mountain views were the main reason Stella loved not staying behind her desk. She'd taken the smallest office, though she had a feeling her father had a hand in doling that area out to her.

Even though she was rushing from one crisis to another, at least she was surrounded by breathtaking splendor, so she wasn't about to complain.

After Stella registered several people, she headed toward her office just to double-check on the couples currently on fantasy dates. No matter what the couple wanted, the discreet employees at Mirage worked overtime to make it happen.

In the short time she'd been there, she'd had some strange requests and some…risqué ones, as well. It was not her place to judge or try to understand people's fetishes, but she had to admit sometimes she was intrigued.

And that intrigue only intensified when the thought of Dane Michaels flooded her mind. She couldn't help but wonder what he'd think if she invited him to the Lumberjack Room or the Campfires and Corsets Room.

No doubt she'd be in over her head, but part of her wanted to. She ached to get his hands on her.

But there would be no need for fantasy dates between her and the sexy rancher in the penthouse. That man was already like every single sexy dream she'd ever had come to life. If she wanted to try something daring, risky, adventurous, she had a feeling just sleeping with that man would embody all three.

Stella smoothed her hair behind her ears and let out a sigh as she rounded her desk. She didn't bother taking a seat, there was never any time for such things. She cross-referenced her lists of guests and their requests, feeling reassured in her certainty that her staff could handle every need that was requested and any additional ones coming in.

Well, food and fantasies were covered for the next twenty-four hours. Maybe she would get through this day without a complete meltdown or catastrophe. One could hope.

Stella rounded her desk to head back out, but Dane filled her doorway and she froze in place. Her hand rested on the mahogany desk and her toes curled in her boots.

"Didn't think you'd be someone stuck in an office."

He hooked his thumbs through his belt loops and steadied those dark eyes right on hers…right after he gave her a visual sampling. Perhaps the sampling he'd had last night hadn't been enough.

Her eyes were drawn to that belt buckle again. She'd ask him about the emblem sometime, though she already knew he'd tell her that it was his ranch. She found that she genuinely wanted to know more about it…about him.

"I'm rarely in here," Stella replied, attempting to get

her heart rate and nerves to settle. "I had a few things to check on. How did you know where my office was?"

The offices and anything considered "behind the scenes" were discreetly hidden from guests. Lara had thought of everything when she'd designed the adult retreat. She'd wanted the guests to feel like they were truly in a magical place and reality didn't exist.

Dane shrugged and offered that sexy, borderline naughty half grin. "I can be persuasive when I want something."

Wasn't that the truth. She wasn't naive enough to ask him what he wanted from her. He'd made that perfectly clear last night. In his defense, she'd also made her own wants quite apparent, even if she hadn't fully acted on them.

"Dane—"

Her cell rang from inside the pocket of her button-up plaid dress. She held up a hand to Dane. "I need to take this."

He nodded, but didn't step out to give her privacy. Instead, he actually came on in and made himself at home by going straight to the window to look out over the back of the property.

Stella smiled at his audacity, but pulled her ringing phone out. One look at the screen and that smile vanished. She resisted the urge to groan or flat-out ignore the call, but she reminded herself that she wanted this. She wanted a relationship, so she swiped her finger across the screen.

"Dad," she greeted. "I haven't heard from you for a while. How are you?"

"I've been busy working." The gruff reply wasn't abnormal or unexpected. "Have you been keeping an eye on the weather? There's a storm coming and they're saying it could be quite substantial."

Storms in Montana were always substantial. They were in the mountains so high, they were about one good stretch from touching clouds—or so it seemed most days. Snow and blizzards were nothing new here. And of course she kept her eye on the weather. Just like everything else around here. She had to stay sharp and know everything going on inside and out of her resort. Well…almost her resort.

"I'm aware," she replied, risking a glance to Dane who remained with his back to her. "Everything is under control, Dad. Our backup systems have never failed and all of our guests will remain comfortable and happy. We're actually booked up for the next month."

She couldn't help the pride that surged through her. When she'd come on board, they hadn't been completely booked up, which told her that her marketing team had tapped into something brilliant in a relatively short time.

"Only a month ahead?" he scoffed.

Stella gritted her teeth and turned to pace to the other end of the office. There was no way Dane wasn't hearing every word she said, but she couldn't focus on the handsome stranger right now.

"In comparison to last year, we're doing a remarkable job," she retorted. "It's been years since Mirage has been completely booked for more than a night at a time."

When her father had first purchased the resort, he'd had an amazing manager, but when that manager passed away suddenly, her father had scrambled to fill the spot. Unfortunately, the replacement lasted only a year and that had been enough time to see numbers start to decline.

So here she was cleaning up someone else's mess all while proving to her father that she was capable and deserved to have this property.

"One month of solid bookings won't make up for three years of dismal numbers," he replied.

"Yes, well, I'm working as hard as I can." If he was here, perhaps he'd see that. "I'm confident the numbers will continue to grow now that I'm in charge."

"And what have you done about the chef who quit?"

Of course he would know about that. He wasn't a ruthless businessman for nothing. He'd never let his investments go unsupervised—and he wouldn't consider his daughter to be supervision enough on her own. Stella had no doubt her father had spies strategically placed throughout the resort, either as employees or guests.

Dread curled through her. She'd just been half joking to herself, imaging the resort full of spies, but now that she thought about it, she realized she wouldn't put it past him. In fact, she was positive he'd done just that. There was no other way he would know about the chef less than twenty-four hours after the man quit.

"Like I said, I have everything under control," she told him.

On a sigh, she spun back around, only to lock eyes on Dane. She hadn't seen that look from him before… something akin to compassion or worry. But just as quick as she saw it, the look vanished.

"If you want to know more about what's going on here, you can ask me or maybe come check things out yourself. I think you'd be pleasantly surprised," she added. "But I don't appreciate being spied on."

Her breath caught in her throat as she continued to

stare at Dane. "I have to go," she told her dad before disconnecting the call.

Without taking her eyes from Dane, she slid her phone back into her pocket then crossed her arms.

"How long have you been working for my father?"

Dane's dark brows rose toward his hairline. "Excuse me?"

"You were sent here to spy on me, right? See if I can actually do this job and not screw it up?"

She'd been such a fool to think a kind stranger just happened upon her and saved the day, then was suddenly attracted to her.

"Does he know you want to sleep with me or is that all part of his plan?" Stella asked, suddenly sickened at the idea. "How much is he paying you?"

Before she could draw her next breath, Dane had closed the distance between them. His fingers curled around her biceps and he hauled her against his chest. The motion had her tipping her head back to keep her focus on him.

"You think I'd whore myself out?" he demanded. "I don't work for anybody and I sure as hell wouldn't take money to have sex with you."

Oh, he was angry. She didn't know Dane, but after hearing the conviction in his voice, she had no doubt he was telling the truth. Beneath that anger, Stella saw pain.

"When I get you in my bed, it won't have anything to do with your father," he growled.

When.

Her entire body heated between the threatened promise of her in his bed and the way he'd plastered his body against hers from hip to chest, and Stella couldn't do a thing but hold on.

She gripped his arms and stared back into those dark eyes, now hard with fury. But she wasn't scared. Dane wouldn't hurt her. Someone who sacrificed his whole evening to help a complete stranger, expecting nothing in return, wasn't a person who should be feared.

But he was hurt by her accusation.

"I'm sorry." Stella closed her eyes and pulled in a shaky breath, trying to rein in her frustrations. "My father... It's all complicated, but I think he's spying on me and how I'm doing here. With the timing of you showing up, I just jumped to conclusions when I shouldn't have doubted you."

Dane's grip lessened, but he didn't let her go. He eased back slightly, the muscle in his jaw clenched.

"Your father doesn't trust you?" Dane asked, his brows drawn in.

"Apparently not. I never thought that was an issue," she replied, hurt spreading through her. "But it would seem that my loyalty is in question or at least my judgment." Stella shook her head and attempted a smile. "I don't know why I find you so easy to talk to. Sorry about all that."

Dane stroked his thumbs over the curve of her shoulders. "Don't apologize. I'd say I'm easy to talk to because I don't know the dynamics here. I'm just a stranger to you."

Yes, something she needed to remind herself of. She shouldn't get wrapped up in a stranger, emotionally or physically.

Yet here she was, doing a stellar job of both.

Everyone had a breaking point and apparently Dane Michaels was hers. She'd worked so hard for so long, putting her personal life on the back burner. No, her personal life wasn't even on the stove, let alone a burner.

Maybe she should take an hour a day just for herself…and whatever pleasantries came along.

"Come to my penthouse for dinner," she told him. "I'll have everything ready at eight."

Dane's brows shot up. "You live on-site full-time?"

Stella nodded. "There's no way I'd want to commute when I'm always needed. This resort is my life, my baby. I want to always be available."

"You really do love this place," he muttered.

"Of course I do." She stepped back, needing to distance herself from the man who had her reevaluating her priorities. "So, eight o'clock?"

"You don't need to feed me dinner."

Stella smoothed her hair away from her face and squared her shoulders. "I do, so don't argue. I'll apologize and you'll be a gentleman and accept my offerings."

Once again, he got that hungry look in his eyes. Being in such close proximity with Dane made it quite difficult to remain a professional.

"Do you really think you'll be back to your room by eight?"

"I'll make it happen if you promise to be there."

Dane flashed her that smile that had her stomach tightening with anticipation. "I'll be there."

He leaned forward, not reaching for her or even attempting to touch her. His breath on the curve of her ear sent shivers assaulting her every nerve ending.

"I'm counting down the hours until I touch you again," he murmured.

Before she could regain her mental balance, Dane

had eased around her and walked out of her office. Stella remained in place, wondering how she was going to focus on work when her body was more than ready for Dane's promised touch.

And just how the hell was she supposed to concentrate on the potential storm heading toward the resort when her own storm was taking over her emotions?

Six

Damn. There was nothing sexier than an aggressive, confident woman. Stella not only embodied both of those qualities, she was so much more and Dane hadn't expected her to be the complete package.

What he had expected to be a little flirting with a vulnerable woman who would give him insight to her father was turning into so much more than he ever expected.

Dane had the flirting down and was well on his way to the seduction—a little *too* well, really. Whenever he was near her, he couldn't seem to remember why taking her to bed was anything other than an excellent idea. He was drawing her in, just as he'd intended, and yet the draw pulled just as strongly on him. This woman was a force all her own.

And as far as the insight to her father? Well, Dane's original assumptions were correct. The guy was a bastard in the same over-entitled category as his own step-father.

It was no wonder those two had done a business deal. Sharks tended to swim together. But Dane had heard a rumor the reality was that Robert had lost the resort in a gambling bet gone bad.

Never in all of his plotting and scheming did he ever think she'd assume he worked for her father. Dane hadn't lied when he told her no. He hadn't lied when he said he wouldn't whore himself out or take money for sex.

But he would take the resort.

The guilt he'd tried to ignore, the guilt he'd told himself wasn't there, suddenly grew sharp teeth and clung tight to his soul.

He'd come this far. Nothing and no one would stop him…not even Stella. He hated with every ounce that she was going to get hurt by his takeover of the resort. There was no avoiding that. But perhaps once she moved on she would see that Dane had saved her from her father. Because that man would never be happy with her running any of his businesses. Dane wasn't sure of the issues that circulated between father and daughter. That wasn't Dane's business, but that didn't stop him from wondering.

Dane left his penthouse at exactly eight and headed toward Stella's rooms on the other side of the resort. Since leaving her earlier he'd done some exploring, taking in what had been changed since his mother's passing and the last time he'd been there.

But even the remodeling, the addition with more saunas and private movie rooms in the back, the suspended decks overlooking the valley…none of that had taken his mind off the scene in Stella's office. His mind just kept circling back to the phone call he'd overheard.

What the hell kind of game was her father playing? From what Dane knew, Stella had six months to turn this resort around and pull in more money than the previous manager had lost in the past year—a manager hired by Stella's father, and kept in the position despite obvious incompetence, when her father still didn't see her as fit for the job.

Well, here she was, doing a stellar job and Ruiz Garcia still didn't see what an amazing businesswoman she truly was. Dane hadn't missed the way she'd lowered her voice when he'd been present. He hadn't missed the disappointment and the hurt lacing each and every word. And he hadn't missed the pain in her eyes when she'd realized her father had likely planted a spy.

What really pissed him off was that she'd thought that was him. But he wasn't angry with her anymore—no, he was angry with himself. She had every reason to be suspicious, given the timing. But her suspicions were pointing her in the wrong direction. He *was* a spy, but the only person he worked for was himself. Dane would never work for a backstabbing mastermind like Ruiz, but could he really claim to be that much better when he was plotting against Stella even as he headed toward her for their date?

Dane made his way through the lobby and glanced out the doors into the darkened night. Snowflakes swirled around in the beams of light. The storm was rolling in and, if the forecast was correct, they were in for a hell of a blizzard.

Living in Montana had acclimated him to snow and cold. He loved the weather, actually. His ranch was postcard worthy all blanketed with snow. He longed to be back there now, to be in his den with a roaring fire and his two golden retrievers, Buck and Bronco, asleep on the rug in front of the crackling flames.

Thankfully his housekeeper was staying in the guest quarters and taking care of the dogs while his foreman oversaw everything ranch-related. Dane trusted very few people, but once they were in his inner circle, they were there for life.

As Dane passed the hallway toward the Sleepy Forest suites, he did a quick glance and spotted a couple in their midfifties, if he had to guess. They were hand in hand and staring at each other as if nobody else existed outside their happy little bubble.

Dane couldn't imagine ever letting someone that deeply into his heart. There was only so much brokenness a man could take and Dane truly felt he'd had his fair share over time. With the loss of his mother, the distance with his brother, the loss of friends in the war...

He didn't even want to pretend to play the game of feelings and emotions and hoping for a successful long-term relationship. Living on his own and worrying only about himself and his ranch was more than enough to make him happy in this life.

When he took the private elevator to Stella's penthouse, he forced himself to calm down and regain his focus. Getting wrapped up in her personal struggles with her father was definitely not Dane's place. The only reason he needed that information was to use it to obtain everything he wanted.

And the damn guilt? He couldn't get wrapped up in that, either. Not only was his brother counting on him, Dane owed this to his mother who never, ever had any intention of selling her businesses...let alone to the devil.

Stella may think she wanted to be here and manage Mirage, but until she was out from her father's thumb, would she truly be happy?

She was brilliant, she had a drive not many people had. Stella would go on to do greater things, on her own, without her father.

Ready to get this night going, Dane tapped his knuckles on the door and waited. He didn't have to wait long. The double doors swung open and Stella stood before him looking just as stunning as she'd been this morning. Even working herself ragged, somehow she managed to come across as in control and put together.

If it hadn't been for that brief moment in her office when she'd looked so hurt while on the phone with her father, Stella would have convinced him not a thing was wrong in her world. He knew better.

The nugget of guilt grew, taking root.

"Perfect timing," she stated with a smile as she gestured him in. "I just got everything set up and sent the cook away."

Dane stepped in and instantly fell back into his past. Nostalgia hit him hard as he scanned his eyes over the open space. He'd been a preteen when his mother had opened Mirage. This had been her on-site room and Dane and Ethan would take turns getting the fire going on cold, snowy nights...just like tonight.

He swept his gaze back across the spacious room, taking in all the familiarity and noting each change since he'd been here last. Little touches made the room all Stella. The pictures across the mantel, the bright red throw over the leather chair, a pair of worn boots next to the sofa.

But so much was still the same. That stone around the fireplace he'd helped choose with his mother, the dark kitchen cabinets and raw-edged countertops… The leather sofas were the same, the lamps were the same, the chocolate fur rug in front of the fire was the same.

So much reminded him of his mother, which only added to his steely structure and mental drive to finish the job he'd started.

Lara had loved her boys with her entire being. She'd done all of this for them, for their future. She'd taken the inheritance from her grandfather and invested every single penny first into this resort and then, just as soon as it started showing a profit, she'd opened her second Mirage location.

Nearly twenty years had gone by since Dane had seen her or even heard her voice, but she was still here. This room, this resort, they were all pieces of her and he wasn't going to stop until he got them all back…no matter who he had to use to serve his purpose.

"You didn't have to send up wine and flowers this afternoon."

Stella's sweet voice pulled him from the tunnel of thoughts. He turned to face her just as she closed the door and leaned back against it.

"And the basket of spa and bath items was too much," she added. "But that robe and those slippers feel like heaven, so thank you."

Dane nodded. "I figured you don't take the time to pamper yourself, so I thought you might need a reminder."

Stella pushed off the door and closed the distance

between them. "I don't even know how you managed to get everything delivered to my penthouse because I know you didn't purchase the flowers from the gift shop and those lotions in the basket are from France."

"And how do you know that?" he asked.

"Because that is my favorite brand, right down to the scent." Stella crossed her arms and tipped her head. "Apparently you have some incredible resources if you could manage all of this in a short amount of time."

She didn't need to know that it took only one phone call to make all of this happen. He'd spared no expense on the items themselves and had paid another hefty sum to get everything delivered without Stella sensing a thing.

And yet he got the oddest sense that it was the fact that he'd made an effort, that he'd tried to treat her, to spoil her a little, that pleased her the most. Did she ever have anyone do something just for her? Or was she too busy worrying how to please everyone else and still reach her goals?

Ignoring her statement, because she didn't need to know just how far his reaches were, Dane took a step back and glanced toward the fireplace where a table had been set up.

"Did you order all of this or did you have them send up some leftovers?" he asked, turning his focus back to her.

Stella's dark eyes narrowed as she swatted at him. "Leftovers? You think I invited you to my room for leftovers?"

Dane reached for her hand and had her tumbling against his chest, earning him a small squeak from her lips. She tipped her head back and met his gaze.

"What *did* you invite me here for?" he murmured, mesmerized by the thick black lashes framing her expressive eyes.

Damn it. If he wasn't careful he'd find himself lost in Stella and ignoring all the things he actually should be doing.

Like getting her to open up and trust him...

"I wanted to see you," she whispered. "To...talk."

Dane couldn't stop the twitch of his lips. "Talk? When I kissed you earlier you didn't seem so eager to talk."

"Maybe that kiss affected you more than it did me."

Dane didn't even think before he crushed his lips to hers. Like hell she wasn't affected. And so was he, whether he wanted to be or not. He'd been waiting too long for another sample. Nine whole hours and every minute that went by, he could still taste her. Well, now he didn't have to fantasize because she was in his arms.

Or more like plastered against him, which was exactly where he wanted her. He hadn't expected to physically ache for her. Never once did he consider that he would have an issue with self-control. Dane was always in control—except when the nightmares came. But with women? When he'd gone to bed with the few women he'd had since coming home scarred and broken, he'd never relinquished his power or felt out of control.

Dane wrapped his arms around her, settling his hands over her round backside and urging her hips to align with his.

Stella let out a little moan as he coaxed her lips apart and thrust his tongue against hers. There was no hesitation on her end, and much to his surprise, she reached up with her free hand and threaded her fingers through his unruly hair. That slight tug had even more arousal pumping through him.

He turned her toward the back of the leather sofa and lifted her to sit on the top of the cushions. Dane stepped between her spread legs and raked his hands up her bare thighs and beneath the hem of her skirt.

Pulling her hand from between their bodies and out of his grip, Stella reached for the buckle on his belt and gave a swift jerk.

Dane pulled away and worked on taking deep breaths and getting this situation back under his control. He still needed information and it was damn difficult to think with her mouth all over his.

"Why don't we eat?" he suggested.

Stella blinked and dropped her hands. "Right…um, that is the reason I invited you."

"And to talk," he reminded her, because hearing all about her life with her father was of the utmost importance…despite his arousal.

Stella slid off the couch and straightened her dress. Every part of Dane wanted to finish what they'd started—but that just proved that he needed to back away. He had to stay in control, had to keep his eye on the prize and not get distracted by how good she looked. And smelled. And tasted…

Everything about Stella had become more complicated than he'd initially thought. Each moment had to be assessed and plotted.

Dane followed the sway of Stella's hips as she led the way toward the table for two set up in front of the fireplace. But when she just stood there, looking down at the setting, Dane came up beside her.

"Something wrong?"

Her eyes shifted to him and she smiled. "Let's take dinner onto the balcony."

The climate-controlled, glassed-in balcony off the bedroom would be less intimate.

"Sounds good to me."

They both filled their plates and grabbed their wine-glasses before heading out to the cozy, spacious area high above the valley. This was just another area he and Ethan had enjoyed when they came to stay with their mother. They'd pretend they were military spies looking over enemy territory.

Dane glanced to the L-shaped sofa and pushed aside the memories of when the space had three plaid upholstered chairs for Ethan, their mother and Dane. Their stepfather was often out doing business, leaving the three of them alone, which had been just fine with Dane. From day one he'd had an odd feeling about the guy his mother had married, but it hadn't been until after his mother's death that that feeling had grown into full-fledged hatred.

Stella took a seat in the corner of the sofa and extended her legs out, propping her plate on her lap. Dane sat on the other end and balanced his plate on one leg and sat his wineglass on the maple table before him.

"Is this the first time this week you've made it back to your room at a reasonable time?" he asked, stabbing the steak with his fork.

"Yes." She took a sip of her wine and leaned to the side to put her glass next to his. "The first time in a lot longer than a week, actually. I've never had a reason to get back to my room by a certain time. Nothing seemed as important as being with my staff and ensuring all the guests' needs were attended to."

"I'm flattered I ranked above that," he commented.

"Oh, if I get a call, I'm heading back down," she stated with a laugh. "Nothing comes between me and my goals."

Dane shot her a side glance and found her looking back at him. Apparently he'd been added to her goal list, which was fine with him. But then the scars would come up and that wasn't exactly a point he wanted to discuss.

And yet another niggling speared at him. She had no clue why he was here, what he was capable of doing… what he would ultimately take from her.

Guilt could be all-consuming, but he had to remain focused. He had to see this through.

Dane forced his eyes back to his plate and focused on the meal. Guilt had no place here, not if he wanted to complete this mission. It wasn't his fault that she'd ended up in this situation, nor was it his duty to protect innocent people.

Dane had been innocent, too, but his life had still been ruined and he'd been left to his own devices.

None of this was what his mother would've wanted. She'd had her own plan of passing these resorts to her boys and Dane and Ethan were going to see that plan through…no matter the cost.

"This place is rather remarkable," he said after a while. "You've got to be proud of what you've done."

"I am, but it's not my opinion that matters."

"Your opinion should be the only one that matters," he countered, trying to rein in his anger. "If your father can't see how amazing you are, then maybe he's not worthy of your loyalty."

Stella set her plate on the table and grabbed her wineglass. "I'm not sure anything can impress my father, to be honest. He sets a level of standards that no one could possibly reach."

Dane finished his meal and set his plate next to hers. He reached for his own glass and scooted down to sit next to her. Stella took another drink, then let out a clipped laugh.

"I should've learned my lesson when I was nineteen. I got the silver medal in a national competition for cross-country skiing and he was angry that I hadn't lived up to his expectations and placed first."

Dane recalled her medal mention in the background check he'd had done. He shouldn't be surprised at her father's lack of enthusiasm or praise. He didn't deserve her loyalty.

Dane knew all too well what it was like to be alone like Stella was. Having a bastard father was the same as going through life without one. While he had his brother, he and Ethan had never been the same since their mother passed, and he knew that emotional gap was partly his fault.

When he came to Mirage, Dane never expected to have so much in common with Stella, yet he found himself drawing closer to her in ways that could and would get him into trouble if he didn't stay emotionally detached.

Dane set his glass down before plucking hers from her hand and placing it back on the table. He shifted toward her, placing one hand on the cushion beside her head and the other near her hip.

"Maybe for the next several hours we forget everything outside of this room," he suggested.

Stella's eyes widened as she eased farther back onto the cushions. "Hours? You think quite a lot of yourself."

"When I get your clothes off, I intend to take my time," he promised.

He very deliberately said nothing about shedding his own clothes. Maybe there was a way they could make this work without him baring too much—of his skin or anything else. There were so many ways to make a woman feel good. Stella deserved every single one of them.

Stella's chest rose and fell with each breath. The little button at the top of her dress strained against her chest and Dane didn't take his eyes off her as he reached for the closure and freed her.

When she smiled, he slid his hand down to the next button and slid it through the slit. A flash of red lace teased him, mesmerized him. That was exactly the lingerie he'd imagined she'd be wearing. Nothing plain or simple for this bold, assertive woman. Of course she'd have red. The power color suited her.

"Are you starting that time now?" she asked, her voice breathless with want.

Dane ignored her question and slid a finger between her breasts. Such silky skin against his rough, ranch-hardened hands. He'd always been a hands-on guy—in and out of the bedroom. And he couldn't remember the last time he'd wanted to get his hands on someone this badly.

He knew he should resist. But she made it so damn hard…in all the best ways. He needed to slow this down. Regain control. Focus on what she needed, rather than what the craving in his blood demanded.

"I'm still exploring." Up, down. He continued to let his fingertip glide over her. "Trust me, you'll know when I get started."

Stella covered his hand with hers and pushed down. "I still have more buttons."

Yeah, he'd noticed. The damn dress had little buttons that went from chest to just above her knees. She'd looked like an adorable little package just waiting to be unwrapped.

He placed her hand on the next button and let go, silently urging her to continue. With a naughty smile to match the gleam in her eyes, Stella kept her focus on him as she finished revealing the rest of her curvy body.

And then a shrill ring pierced the moment.

With a groan, Stella sat up, forcing Dane back.

"I have to get that," she stated with an apologetic tone.

Dane let her up and watched as she covered her body and made her way back into the penthouse. A large part of him wanted to take that phone and smash the hell out of it, but the other part of him, the businessman in him, understood her commitment to her work.

He'd fallen into his ranch by sheer luck. He'd purchased it during a foreclosure and made one wise investment and purchase after another. He'd worked damn hard to get where he was today.

Honestly, Dane hadn't known just how much he would appreciate Stella until he arrived and saw her in action. He'd never taken into account just how much she did for Mirage. Because of her, his mother's business was back to thriving. The resort was moving into a stronger year of sales and coming back from the brink of near financial ruin.

Dane went to the window and shoved his hands into his pockets as he looked out onto the fat flakes coming down. The storm was going to hit hard and fast. People accustomed to Montana weather wouldn't be fazed by this blizzard, but those who had traveled in from places that didn't measure snow by the foot might be in for a surprise.

The mountain would be cut off to all traffic if the storm came in as wild and ferocious as predicted.

Dane blew out a sigh and cocked his neck from side to side. Even analyzing the damn weather did nothing to squelch his arousal. He'd had Stella spread out before him, arching against his touch, and—

"I have to go."

Dane turned to see Stella pulling her hair back into a low ponytail, her dress now all buttoned back up as if nothing had ever happened. His heart rate was still accelerated and now that he knew exactly what she hid beneath that dress, he couldn't shut down quite so quickly.

"What's wrong?" he asked.

Stella turned and headed through the penthouse, pocketing her cell and charging toward the door. Dane followed behind her. "Emergency with one of the rooms. I'll tell you more later. Stay and have more to eat or… whatever."

And then she was gone.

Dane could search her entire penthouse if he wanted, but he knew there would be no hidden secrets kept here. Everything he hoped to learn would come from the tidbits he picked up from Stella herself.

And from the little time he'd spent with her, he'd learned a good bit about her father. Other than the fact Ruiz was a bastard, something Dane already knew, he also discovered there were very likely spies in place throughout Mirage, which meant Dane had to be careful.

Ruiz was stringing his daughter along, making her

do his grunt work at this resort, all while waiting to bring in the extra cash.

Dane was willing to up his offer, but there had to be something he was missing. A man like Ruiz Garcia let his entire life revolve around money. The first amount Dane proposed had been turned down flat without so much as a counter. What was it that Ruiz was holding on to? And why?

That was what Dane needed to find out and he wasn't done with Stella until he did.

Seven

After three hours of trying to calm down the newlywed couple in the Summit Suite, Stella was beyond exhausted.

She'd run out so fast on Dane that she was a little embarrassed—but she'd been nothing less than honest with him about how married she was to this place. Everything fell in line behind keeping Mirage in the best standings with each guest that came through.

Good thing she wasn't looking for a relationship because she was not the prize any man would want. Every man she knew had an ego that was too large for him to stand behind her career. That was fine with her.

Stella stepped off the elevator and crossed the hall toward her penthouse. Once she was inside, she closed her eyes and leaned back against the door. She wasn't sure what time it was, but she knew she was dead on her feet. She also was well aware the storm outside was raging and come morning, the mountain road would likely be shut down.

One worry at a time.

"You look worn-out."

Stella startled and blinked as she focused on the man across the room. Oh, what that man could do to a simple tee and a pair of jeans.

"Dane." She pushed off the door and bent down to pull off her knee boots. "I never thought you'd still be here."

Dane remained across the room near the fireplace. Clearly he'd made himself at home because he held a tumbler of the bourbon she knew had been tucked away in a cabinet when she'd left. Stella didn't care for the stuff, but when her father came, she tried to have his favorite brand on hand.

"I wanted to make sure you were taken care of," Dane replied. He tipped back the last of his drink and crossed the room to her. "Go soak in the bath and I'll bring you a glass of wine."

Stella dropped her boots next to the door and laughed. "It's after midnight. I don't have time to sit in the tub no matter how amazing that sounds."

When he came to stand in front of her, Stella let out a sigh and that pretty much stole the little bit of energy she had left.

"Dane, if you came for—"

He framed her face with hands that held her so very gently, all while looking at her like she was made of glass. Right now, that wasn't too far from the truth. The days were catching up with her and she was starting to worry maybe she did need help and couldn't do this all by herself. But if she admitted any type of weakness, her father would immediately deem her unsuitable to run his business.

It would be the national championship all over again. Never coming in first, always falling short.

"I knew you'd argue."

Dane's words barely registered before he bent and picked her up. With one arm behind her back and the other behind her knees, he headed toward the master bath. Stella laid her head against his chest and closed her eyes.

"You should go," she murmured. "I'll take a quick bath to relax, but you should already be in your room sleeping like the rest of the guests."

Dane eased her onto the edge of the Jacuzzi tub. "If I left, you'd fall asleep in the bathtub and drown. Now get your clothes off."

He started the water, testing it with his hand and completely ignoring her as she started working on each button.

"You really didn't stay for sex?" she asked, shrugging out of her dress.

Dane's focus turned to her, his dark eyes raking over her bare skin. The hunger just as apparent as when he'd been touching her earlier.

"You'll be wide-awake when I have you."

He stood straight up and glanced around the spacious bath. He went to the vanity and searched through the basket he'd had delivered, pulling out products before settling on one. He flicked the top, sniffed, seemed to nod in agreement with himself and dumped the entire bottle into the bath.

Stella laughed. "That's a bit much and one hell of an expensive bath."

He set the empty bottle back on the vanity. "I'll buy you more."

Stella couldn't wrap her mind around this guy. Who was he? Other than a perfect stranger who'd swept into her life just as fiercely as the storm threatening the mountain.

But...was Dane a threat? He hadn't shown any sign of that and she truly didn't believe he worked for her father. That idea had popped into her head due to stress and exhaustion from dealing with, well, everything.

Stella removed her bra and panties and slid into the warm bath. She didn't even try to suppress the moan as she let the heat and fragrant bubbles envelop her. She leaned back against the cushioned bath pillow and closed her eyes.

"Don't let me drown," she muttered.

Dane's chuckle carried from the room, as did his footsteps over the hardwood floor. Maybe if she just relaxed for a few minutes and let someone else take care of her she could revive herself.

Letting someone else have control certainly wasn't the norm for her. Since her mother passed during childbirth, Stella had spent her whole life figuring out how to take care of herself.

Her father often blamed her for her mother's death. He punished her with a strict childhood that always kept Stella in line. By the time she was a teen, she realized that he was an angry, bitter man, lashing out over the loss of his wife. Being left with a daughter when he'd wanted a son hadn't helped matters.

Still, he was the only parent she knew and she

wanted…something. At first she wanted acceptance, then she wanted acknowledgment. Now…

Stella opened her eyes and blinked against the burn. She hadn't cried in so long and she certainly didn't like feeling so vulnerable. But was it too much to ask to just be loved by a parent? Was she that hard to accept and let in?

"Here you go." Dane strode back into the room and set the stemless wineglass on the edge of the garden tub. "Oh, no."

He stared down at her as he took a seat next to her glass. "Why the tears?"

Dane reached out and swiped the pad of his thumb over her cheeks and Stella's heart thumped. She'd known him such a short time, yet she felt some strange connection to him, yet she truly didn't know him all that well.

"It's just been a long day," she replied, offering a smile. "The bath does help and the wine is a definite perk."

"I'm not sure how much this is helping if you're upset." He cocked his head and continued to look at her with worry etched over his ruggedly handsome face. "I only stepped out for a minute."

Stella curled her fingers around her wineglass and lifted it to her lips. Bubbles slid down her arm and dripped back into the water. She let the cool, crisp, fruity blend calm her and make her think of happier times. There were happy times…weren't there?

"Have you ever wanted something so badly, living your whole life for that moment when you'd get it, but once you got there, you realized maybe you're just a fool and it was never in your reach at all?"

She was babbling, she knew, but she risked a glance at Dane and noted the sympathy had turned to understanding and maybe a dose of anger. The muscle in his jaw clenched and he merely offered a clipped nod.

"I don't know that I'll ever be what my father wants," she went on. "I'm not sure *I* want to be, honestly. I'll never understand how he couldn't just love me for me. Why we can't just be father and daughter. But after all this time, it's just not going to happen. Is it?"

She shouldn't have tacked on that question, but part of her wanted him to counter and tell her she was mistaken. She wanted someone on her team, in her corner, cheering her on. Damn it. When did she get so wimpy and weak?

"I don't know your father," Dane stated slowly as if choosing his words carefully. "But I do know we don't always get great parents. My mother was the best. She raised my brother and me as a single mom and we were always her top priority. Then she remarried and my stepfather was…well, he wasn't parent material. When she passed, we were stuck with him and that's when we realized what a true bastard he was."

Stella set her glass on the edge and sat up in the water. Dane's eyes instantly went to her chest and her body immediately responded.

"Sounds like we both had to pave our own way."

Dane reached into the water, keeping his eyes on hers the entire time. "You're not relaxing."

His hand found her thigh. That firm grip held her for a moment before he trailed his fingers up. Stella instinctively spread her legs and let her head fall back against the bath pillow.

"Drink your wine," he demanded in that husky tone dripping with arousal. "I've got this."

Stella reached for her glass, but had to hold it with two hands to prevent herself from dropping it into the bubbles as those clever fingers parted her. Stella took a sip, her eyes locking on Dane's over the top of her glass.

That dark unruly hair, the heavy-lidded gaze, the black stubble along his jawline all joined together to give him that mysterious, alluring factor. She'd never been reckless with anything in her life, let alone with her body. She'd been too focused on work, on moving forward to prove herself.

Letting a near stranger touch her this way felt wrong…yet oh so right.

Dane slid one finger into her and Stella arched her back, biting her lip to keep from crying out. As wave after wave of pleasure slid over her, she closed her eyes and let the moment capture every bit of her.

Nothing existed but Dane's touch. She gripped her glass and clutched it against her bare chest. Water rippled, almost providing soft music to frame the intimate moment. She hadn't expected this, hadn't known he'd still be here when she came home.

As her body jerked, the wine sloshed from the glass and over her chest.

Suddenly the glass disappeared from her hands and Stella focused her attention to Dane. He'd leaned down, his free hand resting on the ledge beside her head. His other hand continued to work her and her hips rose to meet each pump.

Dane dipped his head and ran his tongue along the trail of wine. He made a satisfied purring noise low in his throat. "I never thought I'd crave white wine, but damn. That's good."

He slid his lips along the path again and took his time, quite the opposite of the frantic movement of his hand beneath the bubbles.

Once the wine was gone, he lifted his head and simply watched her. Watched her as if this would be enough to satisfy him.

Stella had never been on display like this, never realized how arousing it could be to have someone watch you so intently with such determination and fixation in their eyes.

The touch, the stare, the intensity of being utterly consumed by a man she barely knew…it all became too much.

Stella reached up and curled her fingers around Dane's biceps, her other hand went to his wrist beneath the water. She didn't know if she wanted to help him or if she just didn't know where else to put her hand, but the way his muscles and tendons were flexing beneath her touch, working so hard at bringing her pleasure, had her body spiraling out of control.

Bursts of euphoria pulsed through her, her entire body tightened around him, and he murmured something as he leaned down and captured her lips. Every part of her continued to quiver as the release flowed.

Dane consumed her, but still, she wanted more.

Stella's body started to settle, leaving her sated, exhausted, and most definitely relaxed.

When she regained control of her breathing and returned to reality, Stella opened her eyes. Dane's hand rested on her thigh and that cockeyed smile matched the hunger in his eyes.

"Ready for bed?"

Stella started to sit up.

"Not sex," he added. "I already told you that's not why I'm here."

Confused, she stood, her legs trembling more than she'd expected. "Then what do you call this?"

In that slow, easy manner of his, Dane rose to his feet and reached toward the heated towel bar. He pulled off a fluffy white towel and with an expert flick, he wrapped it around her.

"I call this getting you to relax and maybe being a bit selfish in taking what I want, too." He shrugged and clutched the towel together between her breasts. "I'm human."

Her eyes darted down to just below his silver belt buckle. "I see that and you're also miserable."

"After what I just saw?" He smiled even wider and shook his head as he scooped her up and out of the tub. "I'm far from miserable. Turned on and aroused? Absolutely. But watching you like that is something I'll never forget."

Yeah, she wouldn't forget it, either. Dane had a touch like none other...at least none she'd ever had. Those rough hands could certainly do more than run a ranch—or whatever it was he did.

Mercy's sake. She'd just let a man she barely knew pleasure her in such an erotic way. When did she become that woman?

Stella rested her head against his shoulder. Perhaps she'd always been that woman—the type who deserved more than she allowed herself to have, the type who should take more of what she wanted out of life and not work herself to death, and the type who knew when a fling was too good to turn down.

"I really can't sleep long," she murmured.

As he carried her, a wave of dizziness overcame her. The hours on her feet, the warmth from the bath, the lethargy from the greatest orgasm she'd ever had... everything made her feel as if she was caught in that world between being asleep and awake.

"Stay." The single word slipped from her mouth before she could stop herself. "I don't want to be alone."

She cringed at her own words. That sounded like begging and after coming undone all around him a moment ago, she'd better watch out or he'd think she was getting attached. There was no room in her life for attachments.

Honestly, she wouldn't know how to do a relationship or commitment anyway. It wasn't as if she'd grown up with a good example. Stella wasn't sure she could ever have a normal or real relationship. Most little girls dreamed of their wedding day, but she'd only dreamed of the day her father wrapped his arms around her and told her how proud he was of her.

Tears pricked her eyes again as Dane settled her onto her bed. Before she rolled over, she thought she felt a dip on the mattress behind her.

He'd stayed. After giving so freely of his passion, expecting nothing in return, and after she'd accused him of horrible things earlier...he'd stayed. For her.

Eight

Dane stared out into the darkness. Swirling snow-flakes fluttered through the soft beam of light coming off the patio. He did his best thinking in the middle of the night, in this stretch of time when the world seemed to be calm.

After his years in the military, sleeping never came easy. Nightmares plagued him night after night, but he figured that would forever be an issue. In truth, it didn't seem to be as bad lately. He didn't know if his memories were getting better or if he'd just grown accustomed to living with the horror that was his new normal.

Dane glanced over his shoulder toward the king-size bed. The navy sheets and duvet were all twisted on one side where he'd tried to rest, but perfectly placed on the other where Stella slept beneath them.

And that sight right there perfectly summed up their

differences. He was restless and edgy, never quite feeling settled with anything in his life…not since his mother's death. One would think after nearly twenty years he would find some calm center inside of himself, but one life event had rolled into another and Dane had never quite found his inner peace.

Now that Dane had a bit more insight to Stella, he had to assume she never had, either. Perhaps she didn't even know she was chasing a dream that would leave her only broken and angry.

Dane hadn't lied when he said he didn't know her father, but he was well aware the type of man Ruiz was. It didn't take much digging to find out the guy wasn't the most honest and loyal to his associates or with business deals. He looked out only for one person…himself.

So where would that leave Stella? Her father treated her like nothing more than a piece on a chessboard…and then Dane came along and did the same thing.

Guilt clawed at him as he turned his attention back to the blizzard raging outside. He caught his reflection in the darkened part of the window and muttered a curse.

How the hell did he obtain his ultimate goal and not run over Stella in the process? That's not what his mother would have wanted. She hadn't raised them to be selfish and scheming. Yet here he was, excelling at both.

He hadn't expected to care about what was going on with Stella's personal life. When he'd planned and plotted all of this to get Mirage back, he'd only had his family in mind. Somehow, he wanted to get back what he and his brother were supposed to have and if gaining back the two resorts pushed them closer together, then that was just another reason to keep moving forward.

No matter who stood in his way.

Rustling sheets had him glancing over his shoulder. Stella sat up, the duvet pooled at her waist, her breasts on display and her midnight-black hair all around her shoulders.

The crackling fire sent a glow throughout the open room, putting out a romantic ambience that shouldn't affect him, but had his body stirring as he made his way toward the bed.

Stella raked her gaze over his bare chest. When he'd gotten up, he'd removed his shirt, but kept his jeans on. He'd like to blame his lack of sleep on the confining garment, but the truth was that PTSD and the guilt over his current situation were gnawing at him.

When she eased the covers aside and swung her legs over the bed, Dane stopped. She came to her feet and without a care to her nakedness, she crossed to him. That curvy body approached him and had his arousal pumping.

Her bare feet left whispered sounds as she seemed to glide across the wood floor. There was something so mystifying, so captivating about this woman. That was the only explanation for why he kept allowing himself to be pulled in deeper.

He'd set out to seduce her, but somewhere along the way, the roles had reversed.

Without a word, Stella reached out as she came to stand before him. Her fingertip went to the tattoo of the eagle on his chest that crept over his shoulder. His muscles tensed beneath her touch and he clenched his fists at his sides to keep from picking her up and taking her back to bed, finally having what his body craved.

Those fingertips left the ink and started traveling

downward. His abs tightened as he kept his eyes locked on hers.

"Stella," he growled in warning.

The warning was more for himself, though. If he ultimately went through with this seduction, he would be just as much of a bastard as the men he hated.

Her fingers went to the snap on his jeans, pulling it loose. The zipper slid down next.

Damn it. He was human with temptation staring him right in the face. He wanted her too badly to care if it made him a bastard.

Something snapped, likely his sanity, but he circled her waist with his hands and lifted her against him. Dane crushed his mouth to hers and Stella opened for him as she wrapped her arms around his shoulders and her legs around his waist.

Dane wanted to completely consume her, to strip away everything—the clothes, the lies. The damn world outside. He wanted every bit of it gone.

Taking long strides, he headed toward the bed. He wasn't waiting any longer. Guilt had no place in business…or the bedroom. Only desire belonged here. And he desired the hell out of her. From her pants and moans and the way her fingertips dug into him, she was just as achy.

When he reached the post at the end of the bed, Dane eased her down to her feet. She blinked up at him, but he took a step back. He continued to watch her as he rid himself of his jeans and boxer briefs.

Dane stepped out of his things and kicked them aside.

"Turn around," he demanded. He couldn't risk her seeing his back, but if she wanted to believe he just enjoyed this position, that was perfectly fine...because he did.

Stella quirked a brow before obeying. Dane shifted behind her and slid his hands down her arms until he reached her wrists. He circled her delicate skin and lifted her hands, wrapping them around the thick, wood bedpost.

Dane tucked his body up against hers as he trailed his lips across her shoulder, up her neck, to the curve of her ear.

"Hold on."

He quickly grabbed a condom from his wallet and covered himself as he stepped in behind her once again. With his hands gripping her hips, he pressed his body into hers.

"Spread your legs," he murmured.

Stella stepped wider and Dane used the opportunity to ease his hand to the front of her body, pleased to discover she was more than ready to take him. He slid the tips of his fingers through her, fighting the staggering need to take this final step.

"Dane."

His name coming off her lips in a cry of pleasure was all the motivation he needed. Dane slid into her and had her crying out once again. He, on the other hand, stilled.

She. Was. Perfect.

Closing his eyes against any emotions other than lust and raw, primal need, Dane concentrated on just how amazing they were together. For this night, and maybe the duration of his stay, he wanted to be here in her bed. And out of her bed? Well, that was a space he couldn't think about right now.

Stella's knuckles whitened as she gripped the post.

Her head fell back against his shoulder. As Dane continued to pump his hips, he kept his hands firmly on her thighs, his fingertips digging in to keep her in place.

He leaned down and sucked on that curve of her neck, earning him another pleasure-filled groan. Damn if he didn't know her body already and that was one of the most powerful tools he had in his arsenal.

Stella reached up higher on the post and sank back against him even farther. Within seconds she was coming undone and panting his name. Dane couldn't hold back another second and he was done trying. He followed her release, pressing his forehead against her shoulder as he gritted his teeth. He held on to her until both of their bodies ceased trembling and even then, he didn't let go.

"I think my legs are going to give out." Stella's breathless words broke the silence. "I don't know how we're still standing."

He nipped at that curve in her neck again, suddenly realizing he liked that spot because each time he touched her there, she trembled. He liked having that control over her, just that little kernel that was all his.

"We're still standing because I wasn't about to miss a second of this sweet body by falling down," he countered.

Dane spun her around and lifted her up before circling the bed and laying her back down on her side. He rested a hand on either side of her head and stared down at her dark eyes, that midnight hair spread all around her.

A sheen of sweat had broken out on her chest and Dane couldn't resist. He leaned down and took one breast into his mouth. How could he want her again when his body hadn't even recovered from the last time?

When she arched against him and let out something akin to a purr, he knew exactly how. Stella Garcia was magnetic and there was no way he could say no or deny either of them what they both needed.

"You're not going to get any more sleep."

She smiled up at him. "Is that a threat?"

He palmed the other breast. "No. That's a promise."

Nine

She didn't know how she was doing it, but somehow Stella was going from one part of the resort to another, checking on staff, guests, food, and anything else she could. She tried to stay calm and competent, but it was much more of a struggle than usual. This storm was raging like nothing she'd ever seen and she was running on next to no sleep.

And yet in spite of that, the memories from last night had her smiling as she made quick strides to one of the theater rooms. If the power went due to the blizzard, she knew her generators would kick in and there would be no worries. But she still wanted to make sure everything was in good shape and that all of her guests were as comfortable as possible. They'd likely be stuck beyond their projected date, so she planned on offering discounts and extras to make up for their inconvenience.

As much as she hated the idea of stranded guests,

Stella couldn't help but feel a little giddy about one guest in particular.

Once she checked on the theater rooms and the fantasy suites, she breathed a sigh of relief. So far this day was going better than most. Each guest was quite understanding of the fact the mountain road would likely close. Each guest was also given the choice to check out now and get a discount on their next stay or continue their vacation at a lower rate. Everyone had decided to stay and she couldn't help but feel a burst of pride. Thankfully they had just enough rooms and they were full.

She was actually doing this. She was kicking ass at being the manager of Mirage, one of the most spectacular adult resorts in the world.

Stella hoped like hell whoever her father had planted here saw that. She only wished she knew who the culprit was, but she wasn't wasting her time trying to find out. Whoever it was, there was nothing she'd be doing any differently even if she knew. Her guests always came first and losing sleep, skipping meals, and having achy arches in her feet were all worth it to have happy guests.

Stella pulled her cell from her pocket to check the radar once again. Not that anything had changed since she looked at it thirty minutes ago, but she just wanted to see…just in case.

The bright blue blob right over Gold Valley stared back at her. Okay, well, she would get through this. Blizzards were expected in this part of the country and there wasn't much she could do to fight Mother Nature. If the mountain closed, at least her guests would be safe right here and she would play the dutiful host and make sure each need was met.

Perhaps she could include her own needs in that mix. Her cell vibrated in her hand and she glanced back down to see her father's number.

Quickly swiping the screen, she answered, "Hello."

"Stella. How are things with my resort?"

His resort. She didn't roll her eyes, but she just barely suppressed herself.

"Every room is still full and the guests are all staying through the storm."

"Of course they are. Why would they leave?"

No reason to give her any credit. Really, no problem.

"I will be arriving in two weeks to check things out," he went on. "I trust the penthouse will be ready for me."

Stella gripped the cell. "We are booked up. I wasn't aware you wanted a room."

"You don't think you should always have a handful of rooms at the ready for special clients or your own father?"

Stella smiled at a young couple strolling through the hallway. Once they passed, she still lowered her voice as she made her way toward her office.

"I think that every client deserves the same treatment no matter their financial status," she stated. "I wouldn't turn someone away in the hopes that some millionaire needed a room. I maximize on every profit possible."

"That line of thinking will get my doors closed," he growled. "If you're running my resort, then you'll do it my way."

Stella finally slipped into her office and closed the door at her back. Fury pumped through her.

"*Your* resort. *Your* way." The words slowly slipped through gritted teeth. "And here I was under the impression this resort would eventually be mine."

"That's my call and for now, Mirage is still mine. I'm sure in the next two weeks you will figure out a way to have my suite available."

"You can stay in mine," she offered. "I'll sleep on the sofa."

"Don't be absurd."

Stella took a seat in her chair and immediately realized her mistake. Now that she was down, she didn't want to get back up.

"If someone cancels, I'll be sure to put your name on that room," she promised. "But for now I need to go unless there's something else you needed."

"There is one more thing."

Stella's eyes scanned the security cameras at the front desk, the lobby, the public decks, and the front entrance. The security cameras in her office had all angles of the resort, save for the suites and the fantasy rooms.

"What's that?" she asked.

"I was offered a great deal of money to sell."

Stella's heart clenched, her breath caught in her throat and she stilled, afraid to move, desperately praying she'd heard wrong.

"I've turned the would-be buyer down," he added. There was something akin to gloating and arrogance to his tone. "But I've been wondering if you'd rather have a nest egg than a business. You could always take the money and invest, travel around the world, or even start up your own place."

Stella rested her elbows on her desk and rubbed her forehead as she pulled in a shaky breath. So that's what all of this was. Everything in his life was still about money. He'd never change, likely he never intended to give her this property. But that wouldn't stop her from pushing forward and making sure her reputation remained impeccable.

She owed that to the single mom who'd started this. A strong woman who had a vision, a passion. Stella might not have much in common with Lara as far as family life went, but she understood drive and determination.

"I don't want the money," she explained. "At the end of this six-month experiment, I want the resort. I know I'm not the son you wanted, or the perfect business partner, but I've never given up on us."

She bit her lip the second she realized it was quivering and she was close to losing it.

"I just want a chance," she stated, once she got control of her emotions. "I've tried for so long to please you. What will it take?"

Silence on the other end had her glancing to the screen to make sure they were still connected.

"I never said you didn't please me," her father finally said. "And rehashing the past won't change a thing."

"Rehashing the past? You mean discussing my mom? Because anytime I try to talk about her, you shut the topic down."

"Stella, I will not discuss this now," he reprimanded. "I believe you have things to do. I will see you in two weeks."

He disconnected the call, leaving her emotions in even more of a jumbled mess than before. She hadn't meant to bring up her mom, but sometimes it just happened. She'd always wondered about her, wanted to see photos of her, hear stories about what she'd been like. But there had been nothing. No photos, no stories. Ruiz had shut completely down.

How did the man deal with grief or pain if he never faced it?

Laying her phone down, Stella ran her hands over her face and took long, slow breaths to calm herself down. Leaving her office upset was not in keeping with the professional front she wanted anyone to see.

She smoothed her hair back from her face and started to stand, but stilled when she spotted Dane on the screen. He was actually outside on one of the covered patio areas. He wore a pair of jeans and a thick, wool coat. He was talking on his cell and staring out at the swirling snow. Whoever he was talking to had him shaking his head and gesturing with his free hand.

This was none of her business. She had no real ties to him, no reason to expect to be allowed some insight into his life. Yet she continued to stare. When he raked a hand over the back of his neck, Stella sank back into her chair and wondered who or what had him so upset. This wasn't the laid-back man who had pleasured her multiple times. This certainly wasn't the guy who had a life motto of "it will all work out."

She'd seen only the very sexy, very giving side of Dane Michaels. Who was he really? A rancher and ex-military, but that's all she knew.

On the screen she watched as he ended the call and pocketed his cell. Realizing she'd been staring for quite a while, Stella grabbed her own phone and came to her feet. Lunch had just passed and she hadn't grabbed a bite. She'd swing through the kitchen, make sure they were all set for dinner and the wine and cheese hour and pick something up for herself really quickly.

Maybe she should go ahead and plan a dinner for her room again. They had nowhere else to go and she wanted to take time for herself. If her father was seriously making a visit in a couple weeks, Stella was taking her reward now for the headache she'd have later.

Her cell chimed again, this time a text from the employee who kept the private hot tub areas maintained between guests.

Apparently the guests were requesting a special bottle of pinot noir and not the regular house white that was kept in that area.

Stella went to grab a bottle of the preferred wine. She of all people knew the importance of wine and a nice relaxing soak.

And once again, even in work, her mind circled back to Dane. What was she going to do when his time here came to an end?

Ten

Ethan stared at the phone and wondered what he'd said to make Dane so angry. His brother wasn't one to let his emotions drive him...or he never had been. Had that changed? Considering they hadn't spent too much time together in the past, oh, couple of decades, Ethan couldn't really consider himself an authority on his brother anymore.

All Ethan had said was that if Robert showed up at Mirage in Sunset Cove, then Ethan wasn't sure he could wait for Dane to tie up loose ends and get down there to join him. They'd waited all this time, years, to build up their resources, their finances, their power. The time to strike was now and there wasn't a chance in hell Ethan was going to let Robert slip out of their grasp again.

Ethan didn't mention that he happened to already be at Mirage. Dane thought he was just in California, but

Ethan figured he should keep his plans to himself. He trusted his brother—even with the distance between them, there was no one he trusted more than Dane. They may have grown apart, but they would always have a bond like nothing else in the world. But that didn't mean his brother needed to know everything.

Shoving his cell back into the pocket of his shorts, Ethan strolled out of the open lobby area and straight toward the beach. While he was waiting on dear ol' stepdad to make his appearance, there was no reason he couldn't take in the sights while he waited…and by sights he meant that sexy, lush lady sporting a red bikini. Suddenly he had a new favorite color.

Who said he couldn't enjoy himself while on the hunt for Robert? Besides, Ethan planned on being at Mirage for a while—like forever.

As soon as he secured this place in his name, as his mother had originally intended, he planned on living right here where he belonged to manage the place and keep it prosperous. The beach, the ocean, they were home. Ethan may have grown up in Montana, but there was nothing like that salty breeze and the sand between his toes.

And the views. Had he mentioned that already? Because he never could understand why anyone would rather be bundled up around a fire when they could be showing off sun-kissed skin and enjoying their favorite beachside beverage.

The lady in red sprayed herself with sunscreen and tossed her bottle back in her striped beach bag. He glanced up and down the shoreline. With this as an adults-only resort, there was a peacefulness not many beaches had. There were no screaming, running children since this was a private island.

Family vacations were great, but Mirage was not that type of destination. His mother, a lifelong romantic, had built two stellar resorts all with couples in mind. Her sense of romance had led to her commercial success, but also her personal downfall. She'd wanted to marry for love, she'd wholeheartedly believed in it, and she had married...but Ethan highly doubted love had entered anywhere in that equation.

Her father had passed and Lara had been left raising two boys on her own. The scenario seemed to be tailor-made for Robert because he obviously preyed on the weak and vulnerable.

The Michaels boys were neither weak nor vulnerable now. They were angry, they were still hurt, and they were ready to fight back. There was nothing Ethan wouldn't do to honor his mother, and she'd raised strong boys. This was what she would've wanted.

Ethan slipped off his flip-flops and looped his fingers around the straps as he made his way across the warm sand.

Walking along the edge of the water always relaxed him, always helped him see a clearer picture. That was why he'd come out to Mirage instead of waiting. He needed to be here to sort through all the mess in his head, to figure out the precise steps he needed to take. He had to act fast, but he also had to be smart about it.

The sexy, curvaceous woman in red glanced his way and Ethan didn't even try to hide his smile...and he didn't move when she made her way over. A woman who knew what she wanted was one of the sexiest qualities.

Considering her smile widened as she crossed the sand toward him, well, apparently they wanted the same thing.

"I'm sorry, sir. Who did you say you were again?"

Dane didn't fault the young male for questioning the stranger who was in the midst of checking on the generators in the maintenance area. No guest should know where this room was, as rooms dedicated to the staff or the maintenance of the resort were hidden from the guests.

The entire resort had the illusion of running on fairy dust or some other magical oddity. That had been imperative to his mother who wanted couples who came here to only see the perfection, the fantasy, the beauty. "Real life" shouldn't exist on vacation, she'd always said. And she was correct. People wanted to get away from all cares and responsibilities, and she provided exactly what patrons wanted.

"Dane Michaels," he stated again as he settled his hands on his hips. "Miss Garcia asked me to check on this and she said you might be down as well since you're so thorough with your job."

The BS just rolled off his tongue, but hit the mark as the twentysomething puffed his chest with pride.

"I wasn't aware we had a new maintenance guy," the other man said. "But I checked on these yesterday."

Dane wasn't about to get into an argument or contradict the guy's mistaken assumption. But Dane would feel better if he checked on all of the "behind the scenes" things himself. After all, he had to keep up with all sides of his property.

"The storm closed the mountain." Dane purposely

dodged the questioning stare from the other guy. "It's not going to let up for a few days. These generators will likely be put to use very soon."

The worker nodded. "That's what I was thinking, too."

The radio clipped to his hip crackled and a female voice came over the airwaves. He knew that voice and she may not like knowing he was in here checking things out. He listened as she requested any available hands to get to the dining area to set up for the lunch crowd.

With the storm, so many employees were unable to make their shifts, which meant the ones stuck here were pulling overtime for the foreseeable future.

And that meant Stella would be running from one end of Mirage to the other, taking little time for herself—if any. He'd make sure his mother's resort was running just fine, the guests were happy, and Stella's needs were met…every single one.

The worker turned his radio down and started looking over the area with the generators. Dane stood back and crossed his arms over his chest, calculating and contemplating.

"These are all set to go," Dane assured him. "Aren't you going to the dining area to help?"

The boy shrugged. "Other workers will help out."

Dane stared at the back of the guy's head and clenched his jaw to keep from yelling at the boy for his lazy, entitled attitude. In due time. This jerk had no clue who Dane was or that he'd be fired for that earlier comment as soon as Dane was in charge.

"This is all covered," Dane stated once again. "You and I can both pitch in. This is a nasty storm and every employee here needs to help anywhere they can."

The other guy stood up and turned, his brows drawn in. "I thought Mitch was over maintenance. What's your position?"

Higher than yours, asshole.

"Miss Garcia is waiting on help." Dane gestured toward the doorway. "Let's go."

Dane thought there was going to be an argument, but the guy finally nodded and headed out the door. There was need to let Stella know about her lazy employee, but Dane wouldn't forget the kid.

By the time they got to the dining area, several employees, all dressed in black, were already bustling around and setting sprigs of evergreen and simple white votives on each of the tables. The lunch decor was quite a bit different than the dinner ambience. For one thing, it was a lot busier. Many couples chose to eat in their room or one of the fantasy rooms during the evening.

There were little changes Dane saw that hadn't been implemented while his mother had been here. The changing of decor being one of them. He liked the touches Stella put on the place—no doubt with her father's permission. The idea of giving the guests a different restaurant feel each time was smart.

The more he saw of Stella—the way she ran this place, the way she actually cared and wasn't just in this for money or recognition—the more he wondered what his mother would've thought of her.

Not that there was any reason to wonder, really. He knew exactly what she'd have thought.

Lara would've loved Stella.

Dane crossed the dining room and cursed himself. What the hell did he care what his mother would've thought of Stella? The thought was absolutely irrelevant. Stella and her father weren't going to be part of Mirage much longer and Lara would be proud of Dane for getting back what belonged to him.

There she was. Across the room against the two-story windows encased with stone. Stella had on another one of those sexy little dresses that stopped at her knee…this one in red that made her look only more exotic with that dark skin and hair.

Instead of her usual brown boots, she had on black. There were several inches of bare skin between the top of her boot and the hem of her dress. He clenched his fists, aching to touch her.

Soon, he promised himself.

Stella turned to talk to an employee, pointing in the direction of the kitchen, then she nodded and spun back around. He watched for only a minute before she shifted that dark gaze to him. Even from across the room he could read her body language. She was exhausted, but running on pure determination.

She offered him a soft smile and the gesture hit him square in the gut. Out of this crowd of people she focused on him and the unspoken bond that they shared shouldn't have his heart clenching, but damn it…

There was no room for distractions, no matter how tempting and captivating. He wanted her physically, something he hadn't expected. But he could at least control the passion. Desire and sex were easy—as long as he stayed in control, kept himself from getting too attached and kept her away from his ugly scars.

The true problem came from all the other unwanted, unexplained feelings that were flooding in before he had a chance to shut the damn door on his emotions.

Hadn't he locked that once already? How the hell had this woman, in such a short amount of time, managed to kick it down?

Dane made his way across the room, circling the tables and weaving through chairs not quite set in place yet. Once he reached her, Dane used every ounce of his willpower not to reach out and touch her or to pull her out of this room so he could force her to rest.

But resting wasn't Stella's style. They were cut from the same proverbial cloth in that they didn't rest when there was still work to be done.

"All hands on deck, huh?" he asked when she came to stand right before him.

With a smile and a nod, she replied, "Something like that."

"What do you want?"

Stella quirked her brow. "That's a loaded question."

"It was meant to be."

He might not be able to touch her, but that didn't mean he couldn't let her know exactly what he wanted.

"In that case, I wouldn't mind being away from here, somewhere secluded so I could do anything I wanted for just one day." She closed her eyes and sighed before meeting his gaze again. "But since that's not happening anytime soon, maybe you could check in at the front desk and make sure everything is okay?"

Dane nodded. "Not a problem."

When he started to turn, she called his name. "Be in my room at eight."

Already turned on by her demand, Dane leaned toward her to whisper, "You'd better be ready for me."

Her visual tremble had him whistling on his way out. Damn if she wasn't sexy. She'd been all authoritative, but then when he'd turned the tables, she practically melted to a puddle.

Dane had every intention of doing whatever he could to help her make sure this storm went unnoticed by the guests. But tonight, well, Stella would be his and there was no better recipe for seduction than to be snowbound with a sultry vixen.

Eleven

Stella stared at all the food and the special bottle she'd had brought up just for Dane. Was she a complete and utter fool? How could she feel so strongly for a man when she'd only just met him a few days before?

Yet he'd proved time and time again that he was selfless—both in the bedroom and out. He'd jumped at the chance to help her and pitch in around the resort since some employees couldn't make their shifts. He'd helped work in areas she hadn't even asked, putting in hard labor during what was supposed to be his vacation.

Was that why it was nearly quarter after eight and he still hadn't made it to her penthouse? Perhaps he'd fallen into bed like all the other workers she'd put on sleep rotation.

There had been some serious shuffling of cots and

blow-up mattresses in order to fit in the staff members who would be resting while others filled in.

She'd already made a mental note to give each employee a bonus for all their hard work. She hadn't heard one complaint and anything she'd asked, they'd gotten right to handling.

Yet now she stood with her thoughts and her concerns. Not over Mirage or the raging storm. Those two were easy to manage. But Dane proved to be a much more unpredictable beast.

Stella padded through her penthouse and went to the fire. There was nothing like coming back here at the end of a long day and staring at the flickering red and gold flames. A glass of wine in her hand never hurt, either, but she was waiting on Dane.

"Stupid," she muttered to herself and turned away from the fire. Even that wasn't calming her nerves.

Dane was likely just as worn down as she was. Maybe he'd even had enough of her. Why was he busting his ass so much anyway? What was he getting out of all of this? Nothing here was his responsibility, his future didn't hinge on how well this resort ran if the power went out and the road didn't open for several days.

Jerking the rubber band from her wrist, Stella pulled her hair atop her head and twisted it into a knot. She should eat something since she'd brought leftovers from the kitchen up to her room. She hadn't had much time for eating earlier, between bustling from common rooms to suites to fantasy rooms and thinking about her night with Dane.

Just as she popped a cube of smoked gouda into her mouth, the buzzer on her private elevator echoed through the penthouse. Nerves curled together in her belly, which was so silly. Dane was just a man and he was a temporary man at that. Their time would likely draw to a close as soon as the road opened and he was on his way. He had already overstayed his time here and his reservation was technically up. Not that she cared or would kick him out at first chance.

Was she an even bigger fool because she felt a little sliver of emptiness at the thought of him leaving?

Honestly, she didn't care that she was getting in over her head. Dane had shown her so much compassion and support during these past couple of days. And the things that man could do in the bedroom? Her body tingled just thinking about his talents. Even if she got to keep him for only a short time, it would be worth it. That man would certainly fuel fantasies for years to come.

The elevator door slid aside and there he was. A man in a bespoke suit couldn't have looked more powerful, more confident and in control. He had that whole rugged rancher look down to a perfectly imperfect manner. The plaid shirt, the worn jeans, the scuffed cowboy boots.

And those eyes. Dark as midnight surrounded by inky lashes any woman would envy.

Dane came toward her, but his eyes scanned the room before landing back on her.

"You worked all day and came back here to set up dinner?" he asked, obviously shocked.

Stella shrugged, not sure how to take his tone. Was he surprised in a good way or a bad way?

"I may not be able to escape to that remote location I dream of, but this is close enough."

She took a step toward him, closing the gap. Stella reached up, flicking his top button until it slid through the hole. She glanced from her fingertips on his shirt up to his coal-like gaze.

"And if you're here, I don't really care where I am," she added. "Maybe for tonight, we can pretend we're just like any other guest and…"

His hand covered hers. "And what?"

Stella laughed and shook her head. "I'm being silly. You *are* a normal guest."

Dane tipped her head up, framing her face with those rough, firm hands. "I'm a guest, but nothing about this stay has been normal."

"No, I guess not." Stella sighed and took a step back. "I probably shouldn't throw myself at a man who just came off an engagement."

The corner of his mouth tipped up. "No, maybe not, but I never asked you to stop."

"You didn't," she agreed. "But before you rip my clothes off—"

"I believe that was you working on my clothes when I'd barely taken a few steps in."

"Details." Stella waved her hand in the air. "Anyway. I have something for you, something other than leftovers from the kitchen."

She turned toward the bar area separating the living room and kitchen. Tucked perfectly on the other side of the domed lids, she pulled out the white bag and presented it to Dane.

He eyed the gift she clutched in her hand, but he didn't take a step to get it.

"You found time to get me something?" he asked. "In the midst of a raging snowstorm and running a resort full of anxious guests with cabin fever?"

"You're not the only one with pull," she stated.

Dane quirked one thick, dark brow and reached for the bag. "You didn't have to get me anything."

"I didn't do it because of the lotions you got me," she told him. "I did it because I wanted to thank you for everything you've done. You didn't have to be so amazing."

"It's a character trait I can't shake."

Stella couldn't help but laugh at his dry humor as he reached into the bag and pulled out the bottle she had procured from a secret stash that only certain employees knew about.

"Stella." He turned the bottle around and stared at it for a long moment before turning his attention back to her. "This is... I've never had anyone give me a gift like this."

Seriously? He'd been engaged, he had a brother, and a bottle of rare bourbon had him struggling to find words? Even her selfish father gave her gifts—granted, the gifts were given only on birthdays and Christmas and always delivered by his assistant or, in the early years, the nanny. But still...

"It's just bourbon," she muttered, suddenly wondering if she'd gone too far. They were just casually involved and she'd had no clue this would be so emotional for him. "I knew we had a couple bottles of important liquor hidden for special guests or clients who had requests."

He continued clutching the bottle. "I didn't request it."

"It's a gift."

Dane stared down at the bottle, the muscle in his jaw ticked as he remained silent. She'd definitely done something wrong because she'd thought he'd be a bit happier.

"If you'd rather another brand, I know we have several bottles of—"

His eyes snapped to hers. "No. This is… This is more than thanks enough. I'm just surprised since these bottles are hard to come by."

Stella smiled. "Not so difficult."

He raked that dark gaze over her and she knew full well he knew just how powerful that visual caress was.

"I don't need to be paid, or to get lavish gifts," he told her as he set the bottle on the table and closed the distance between them. "I already told you I'm a simple man."

"The way you're looking at me proves how simple you are."

Dane snaked an arm around her waist and hauled her flush against him. Stella flattened her palms against his chest and tipped her head back to meet his hungry gaze.

"You deserve better," he murmured against her lips. "But I can't pull myself away."

Stella threaded her fingers through his coarse hair. "I never asked you to go and I'll decide what I deserve. Right now, I deserve for you to make this ache go away."

Dane's hands slid down the curve of her body, those talented fingers slid beneath the hem of her skirt and teased along the edge of her lacy panties. So close. So, so close. She wanted him, she didn't care about anything else right now. She didn't care about what was happening between them, because she was positive there was more going on here than sex. Though at that moment, sex was all she wanted.

As for the long term, she had her goals and Dane…
well, she assumed his were substantial since he'd been
so tight-lipped about them.

"I feel a little guilty." She arched into his touch,
barely suppressing a moan. "Doing this while everyone is trapped here."

Dane's low chuckle vibrated against her chest. "I
assure you, nobody is complaining they're stuck at a
couples' resort with fantasy rooms. And they're doing
the same thing we are."

"Does that mean I can take a minute off?"

Dane eased back, drew his brows in and gripped
her backside. "I assure you, this will take more than
a minute."

Stella sure hoped so because she wanted as much of
Dane as she could get. She'd never felt more alive, more
powerful than when she was with Dane.

The way he held her, looked at her, worshipped her,
were all so new, so exhilarating. There was no reason
not to just take what she wanted.

Being stranded with a sexy stranger wasn't something that happened every day, right?

Before she could continue her justifications, Dane
palmed her backside and lifted her up as he carried her
toward the balcony.

"My bedroom is the other way."

Lips trailed down her throat. "I want you out in the
open, where I can see everything."

He stepped out onto the glass-enclosed patio. The
one-way windows allowed them to see down to the
valley below, but nobody could see in. Still, the idea of
being exposed was erotic and thrilling. She knew her
guests took full advantage of the various hot tubs po-

sitioned on the glass balconies, but she'd had no reason to come out here for anything like this before.

Dane eased her to her feet and made quick work of stripping her of her clothes. When she reached for him, she fully expected him to push her away.

And he did, but he grasped her hands in his. Dark eyes held hers and something other than passion looked back at her. There was that heaviness of pain once again. She'd seen that emotion in his eyes before, but never when they'd been on the brink of driving each other out of their minds with want and need.

"I need to tell you something."

His words were coated with a raw, emotional tone she'd never heard from him. Stella turned her hands over beneath his. She might be standing before him completely stripped, but Dane was much more exposed, much more vulnerable.

"I… I have secrets." The muscle in his jaw clenched as he glanced down to their joined hands, then back up to her face. "Before this goes further, you need to know that I never expected this."

"I never expected finding a sexy stranger, either," she countered with a slight smile, hoping to put him at ease. "You don't have to tell me your deepest, darkest secrets. We have no strings."

"I know, but…"

Dane released her hands and stepped back. Stella wished she'd left something on now that she stood there without him so near. But she realized he wasn't staring at her, he was reaching behind his back and gripping his shirt. With a quick jerk, he had it off and then fisted the material in his hands.

"When I was in the army, I lost some buddies." He

stared down as he continued to twist his shirt. "There was an accident. Details aren't necessary here, but the scars are—"

"Stop." Stella reached for him and pulled the shirt away. She dropped it to the floor and raked her eyes over his chest. "I don't care about scars and you don't owe me any type of explanation."

The dark hair covering his chest and abdomen, the tattoo curving over his right shoulder...none of that seemed to hide any imperfections that she could see. She ran her hands over him, up his arms to his chest, down toward the top of his jeans.

"You feel fine," she murmured. "You look fine."

Without a word, she moved around to his back. Stella's breath caught in her throat, instant tears burning her eyes. She slid her fingertips over the puckered scars and obvious burns.

"You don't have to—"

"You look and feel fine here, too," she affirmed, not wanting him to offer her an out. She didn't *need* an out. She needed to make him feel that he was worthy of her, that she appreciated the fact he trusted her enough to tell her, show her.

Dane's entire body remained rigid beneath her touch. Ignoring his obvious discomfort, Stella stepped into him, resting her cheek against his back and wrapping her arms around his waist.

"Did you think this would turn me off?" she asked.

"I've never shown anyone," he murmured. "It's not exactly a time I want to talk about."

Stella pressed her lips to his back, then moved on and placed another kiss, then another. "I wasn't in the mood to talk anyway, cowboy."

Her lips traveled all over until she moved to the front and placed them on that ink over his chest and shoulder. Taking his face between her hands, Stella forced him to meet her gaze.

"You're still wearing too many clothes."

He kept that dark, pained gaze locked on her. "You don't deserve this."

Stella threaded her fingers through his hair and pulled his lips to hers. "I know what I want, Dane. Now stop talking."

Dane surprised her by nipping at her lips, then easing back to slide his fingertip down the valley between her breasts. "Have your way with me."

The low, rumbling words filled the space between them and Stella wasted no time in removing those jeans that hugged his lean hips so deliciously.

Dane may be imperfect in his mind, but to her…well, he was the most perfect, stable, comforting aspect of her entire life.

Now she had to figure out what to do when he chose to leave.

Twelve

"Get down!"

Dane fell to his stomach, using his elbows to crawl away from the knoll. The blast shook the ground. The air was filled with the sound of men screaming in pain. And then something hit his back so hard, the air left his lungs.

One second everything was chaos and hell, then it was quiet and hell. His back burned like nothing he'd ever experienced, but he couldn't lose himself in the pain. He needed to get to his buddies. Reese and Bagger were on the other side of their Humvee. If he could crawl to them, they could somehow get out of here.

With each pull he took to move himself forward with his arms, the pain in his back seemed to intensify. There was something heavy pressing against him. If he could just get to his buddies, maybe they could help each other.

But the quiet seemed to grow. Being out in the open, shouldn't he hear something? Those cries moments ago had stopped, leaving only his own grunts as he dragged himself to the front of the vehicle.

Dane looked around the front, fully expecting to see his comrades, but there was only one person. Stella. She smiled at him.

"Help me," he cried. "Help."

She squatted down and smirked. "Help you? Like you helped me lose everything? You're on your own, Dane. That's how you like it anyway."

"Stella, please." He just needed this weight gone. He couldn't breathe, and the pain had him fading fast. "Stella. Stella."

He kept calling for her. Why wasn't she answering him?

"Stella!"

That weight on his back finally shifted, then something kept pounding against him. Over and over. Dane pushed away, tried to pull in a breath, but he wasn't getting enough oxygen. He was dying and Stella had walked away.

"Dane."

He jerked up, panting. The frantic tone in Stella's voice had him blinking against the darkness. With the sheet pooled around his waist, Dane gripped the edge of the fabric and attempted to regain some normalcy to his breathing.

Her hand went to his back and Dane cringed, still not used to the touch there and not ready to be consoled after the same damn nightmare that had plagued him for years.

No. Not the same. This time the ending was quite

different and almost more disturbing than the usual horrendous scene.

He didn't have to be Dr. Freud to understand what the dream meant. In it, she'd obviously found out about his plan. She'd discovered he'd been lying to her, that he'd stolen her business from her.

But it wasn't hers. Not now, not later. Mirage could never belong to her and he shouldn't feel guilt when he wasn't the one who put her in this position.

Yet guilt still gripped him by the throat and made it damn near impossible to breathe.

He jerked the covers aside and rose from the bed. His eyes adjusted easily to the dark; he'd been living in darkness for years so this wasn't new.

"Dane."

That soft voice, the voice that belonged to a woman who cared for him, who saw his scars and wasn't bothered by them.

"I can't stay." He searched for his clothes and didn't look back at her when the sheets rustled. "I shouldn't have fallen asleep here to begin with. I know what happens."

He scooped up his shirt, but couldn't find his damn pants.

"The nightmares?" she asked. "You weren't dreaming of the war. You were screaming for me to help you. So let me."

Those slender arms came around his chest, pinning him in place before he could put his shirt on. She wanted to help, but if she knew the truth she'd turn away from him, just as she had in the dream.

Dane didn't want to hurt her. Hell, he didn't purposely want to hurt anybody, except for Robert, but he wanted what belonged to him. Why did all the paths leading to his goal get more twists and turns and road-blocks?

"I never stay with a woman," he admitted. "Not since the accident. But you're...different."

"All the more reason for you to quit running." She circled around to the front and gripped his biceps. "I'm here. I'm not asking you to leave, I'm not asking you to talk about anything if you don't want to. But I am asking you to give me a chance. Don't shut me out."

Give her a chance? That's not what he'd come here for, but damn it. He couldn't help himself and now anything they had was based on a foundation of deception.

"I wasn't lying when I said you don't deserve this." He fisted his shirt and wished like hell he'd found some other way to get what he wanted. "I won't be here long and you're dealing with your father—"

Stella's soft laugh filled the room, her warm breath tickled his bare chest. "You know how to ruin a mood. Yes, I'm dealing with my father, but right now, I'm dealing with you."

"I'll go back to my room," he offered. "It's best that way."

"Best? For you?" she asked. "Because the best thing for me is for you to stay. You obviously trusted me enough to show me your scars. Let me see the ones you're hiding on the inside."

There was nothing else he wanted more than to let her in completely. But they were at odds with each other, though she had no idea who he truly was. This seduc-tion had gotten out of hand, his guilt had grown more and more, and damn it, he actually cared about her.

There was no way he could prevent her from being

hurt. None. Even if he walked away and gave up on Mirage—which he could never do—she'd still be hurt by her father's callous treatment and failure to keep his bargains. All he could do at this point was either keep going and enjoy this time with her while it lasted, or start to put some distance between them. She would hate him in the end anyway. Did it matter when that started?

"You can't want more," he warned. "I'm leaving when the mountain clears."

Stella's hands fell away. "I know you are. I guess I was just hoping you would stay a little extra time."

If only she knew the irony in her statement.

"I don't want to get too deep," he added. "There's so much we both have going on and this fling…"

"Doesn't have to end."

She reached for the shirt he held on to and dropped it onto the floor. Taking him by the hand, Stella led him toward the bed. He was utterly defenseless. He was also a bastard. Going back to his room was the smart move, but clearly he'd not been making smart decisions since coming to Mirage because now he had a sinking feeling Stella was falling for him.

As she lay next to him, with her arm over his chest and leg over his thighs like she dared him to leave again, all Dane could think of was that he'd been too busy enjoying her to pull out the secrets he'd come here to discover.

Darkness transitioned into light and Dane continued to stare up at the ceiling. Stella had fallen asleep, but now she stirred. He'd been lying here too long with his thoughts, with his damn guilt that gnawed a hole in his gut.

How was lying to this innocent woman honoring his mother? That's not the type of person Lara Anderson had been. She'd been kind and caring and so giving and loyal. She'd been perfect and Dane, well, he was anything but.

"I want to buy Mirage."

The words were out before he could talk himself out of admitting the truth—or at least a partial truth.

Stella's hand pressed against his chest as she lifted slightly to look down at him. Her hair flattened against one side of her head where she'd slept against his side, her heavy lids shielded half her eyes.

"What?"

Dane swallowed and tucked one arm behind his head. "I want to buy Mirage."

"Yeah, I heard you." She shook her head as she sat all the way up and shifted to face him. "But it's not for sale."

"Everything is for sale for the right price."

She stared back at him as if seeing him for the first time—as if she was finally seeing the man beneath the facade. But she still didn't know the truth.

"My father is turning this over to me," she told him as she let out a laugh. "And I'm certainly not selling it."

Dane remained still. "Are you *certain* your father is going to give this place to you?"

A flash of irritation followed by determination crossed her face. Stella tipped her chin and shoved her hair away from her face. "I won't settle for anything less. I know I'm not what he envisioned for this business or any business of his, really. A son would've already had his choice of companies. I ask for one and I'm jumping through damn hoops to secure it."

So her father's issue was that his only child was a girl? What the hell kind of backward thinking was that?

Dane clenched his teeth and eased up onto one elbow. "Your father won't be the one keeping this resort," he vowed.

Stella's brows drew in. "I'm not following you this morning. You didn't get any sleep, did you?"

He reached for her hand and gave it a reassuring squeeze. "This has nothing to do with last night."

A total lie. This had *everything* to do with last night. He'd let her in, deeper than he'd let anyone. He'd seen a side of her he hadn't expected and damn it, he respected her.

None of this was going according to plan and now he was just winging everything and he hoped like hell his goals didn't vanish forever now that they were finally within reach.

"Your father will not be the owner of Mirage for much longer," Dane reiterated. "I promise."

"I still don't get it," she muttered. "Do you know something I don't? And if you say you know my father, that you actually do work for him, I will throw you out into that blizzard—"

"No. I don't know him." Not personally anyway. "And I certainly don't work for him. But I've dealt with men like him before. He won't hold on to this place and he won't turn it over to you because all he cares about is money."

If he cared half as much about his daughter, that would be a nice step in the right direction.

Dane didn't want to ask more questions, didn't want

to get more involved emotionally than he already was. But he couldn't stop himself.

"Were you two always at odds?" he asked. "When you were growing up, what was he like?"

Stella shrugged and took her fingertip to the back of his hand. She drew imaginary circles around his knuckles as she seemed to be contemplating her words.

"He wasn't around much. My mom died when I was born, so he hired a nanny." She chewed on her bottom lip as she went around another knuckle. "When he was there, I was never good enough at anything I tried. I loved skiing and would take my thoughts out to the slopes. One lesson turned into another and years later I found myself competing at national levels."

Dane knew that was the extremely shortened version because anyone who competed at that level had worked their ass off for years, giving up most of their social life for the ultimate goal.

"I think he blames me for her death," she went on, emotion lacing her tone. "He's never come right out and said so, but he's hinted enough."

"It wasn't your fault. You know that, right?"

Stella remained silent as she glanced away.

"You're not responsible for her death," he stressed as he sat all the way up. "Listen to me."

Dane took her bare shoulders and turned her to face him before he framed her face and forced her to hold his gaze.

"Whatever you grew up believing, whatever he said or just implied, you know nothing was your fault."

Stella stared back and shrugged. "It was not exactly my fault, but if I hadn't been born maybe she and my dad would still be married. Maybe they would've had other children. Boys—to fulfill all the requirements to be a Garcia heir."

Dane couldn't wait to take this resort back and get Stella out from under her father's ruling thumb. She might hate Dane in the end, but at least she'd be saved from one bastard.

"You don't really believe that." Dane wanted to shake sense into her, but he'd only known her a handful of days and he couldn't exactly reprogram her from over twenty years of dealing with her father. "You're stronger than your father. You wouldn't be here if you were weak. Being a woman is actually your strength. Women think in a different way than men and this resort needs you."

Stella attempted a smile. "Nobody has ever acted like I'm needed here or at any other business, for that matter."

"Then everyone is a damn fool."

He meant every word. She was valuable, and she'd done wonderful work here. The only problem was that he just couldn't have her take his resort.

"You're a sharp businesswoman and if your dad can't see that, then stop beating yourself up and go out and make something of your own without worrying about how he'd react."

"That's easy for you to say," she retorted. "I don't have unlimited means of income. Everything I have is from my salary, but it's not a lot. My father considers room and board enough. This resort, this little piece of his life is all I've ever wanted. I gave up on his love a long time ago, but getting his respect is something I may never give up wanting."

"Why?"

"Because he only deals in business," she explained. "Respect for my business abilities may be the closest thing to love that he can give. I don't know that he's capable of love in the way that I need it."

Not likely, but since Dane didn't know how to love anyone like they needed, he wasn't the person to offer advice on this matter.

His cell rang, breaking the tension and giving him the out he needed.

"I need to take that," Dane explained as he eased off the bed.

He scooped up his jeans and pulled the cell from his pocket. With a quick glance to the screen, he saw it was Ethan.

"I'm just going to step out here." He started for the patio when her words stopped him.

"That's not your ex-fiancée wanting you back, is it?"

Ex-fiancée. Damn it. Dane had gotten so swept away in this whole charade, he'd forgotten about the fictitious woman.

"I promise, it's nobody wanting me back."

Possessive girlfriends had never been an issue in his life because no one had ever been allowed to get that close. He was fine with that. There was no need to chance having your heart ripped out again. Once was more than enough for him when he lost his mother. The ranch kept him busy and that was all he needed. Well, that and Mirage.

Dane swiped the screen and glanced over his shoulder to see Stella sliding beneath the covers, her hand going to the dent in his pillow.

Swallowing the guilt, he answered. "It's awfully early for you, isn't it?"

"I haven't been to bed, yet," Ethan replied. "I figured being a rancher you're always up at this time anyway."

"I'm not on the ranch."

"I'm aware," Ethan growled. "Shut up and listen. Robert is due to be at Sunset Cove in three days."

Dane gripped his cell. "How do you know? And are you positive?"

"My sources confirmed his travel arrangements. How soon can you get here?"

"You're already there?" Dane shook his head and glanced to the hot tub where hours ago he'd pleasured Stella until she cried out his name.

The memories of her would last him a lifetime, which was good since she'd hate him in the very near future.

"I'm here," Ethan confirmed.

"Just make sure you keep the goal in mind—and I don't mean bikini-clad women."

His brother chuckled. "No reason I can't enjoy myself while I wait."

There was static on the line and Ethan's muffled voice a moment before he said, "I'll text you updates. I gotta go."

The call ended, leaving Dane wondering just how quick he could wrap things up here. Ruiz needed to be dealt with here and now. The next number Dane would have his broker throw out would be impossible to turn down. Maybe he could make things move faster by appealing to Ruiz's male chauvinist side.

Dane stared out the window as the sun started peeking over the mountaintops. The snow had stopped sometime during the night, which was good news for the stranded guests.

  With another quick glance over his shoulder, Dane
sent a text to his broker with the new offer and stipu-
lations. There was no way this would be turned down.
Ruiz was a smart businessman. If all went as planned,
this resort would be his in thirty days.

Thirteen

Stella had never taken advantage of a fantasy suite. She had her own penthouse for one thing, but the main reason was she'd never had a need or a man.

Well, now she had both.

Butterflies fluttered in her stomach and she had no clue why she was nervous. It wasn't like she was a virgin or hadn't slept with Dane before. Over the past several days, they'd been all over each other.

The blizzard had calmed down to Montana's usual snow accumulation and guests came and went, still cautious of slippery roads. All was mostly back to normal.

Except Dane stayed. His stay was technically up two days ago and his penthouse had been taken by a couple celebrating their tenth wedding anniversary.

So she moved his stuff into her suite.

Stella jerked on the tie of her shirt. She couldn't believe she had donned this outfit, but she figured Dane would like it. At least, she hoped he went for that whole lumberjack girl vibe. She'd taken one of her plaid flannels and left all buttons undone, simply tying the bottom in a knot just below her breasts. She figured the bright red lacy bra beneath was a nice touch.

Then she'd found an old denim skirt and ended up taking a pair of scissors to it to make it about four inches shorter. Dane would love the present beneath the skirt.

Of course she couldn't exactly parade through her resort looking like she was about to take the stage as a strip club's version of *Twin Peaks* with her boobs on display. That wouldn't be professional at all and her father's minion, whoever that might be, would certainly be all too eager to tattle.

Stella had put a fake name into the computer system to block off the room for the night and she'd sneaked in with her costume in her purse. She still wore her knee boots, but she had pulled her hair from the twist and left it in a wild mess around her shoulders.

She pulled her cell from her back pocket and checked the time. Dane should be here any minute. She'd told him she needed help moving something in the Lumberjack Room and he'd said he'd be right there.

Now she waited.

Stella crossed the hardwood floor and put the cell in her bag in the corner. A click of the door had her spinning back around.

Dane stepped through the door, took in the lanterns all around the room, the hanging tent, and the bourbon bar.

Then his eyes scanned back to her. The dark gaze

raked over her, up and down. Then another slow, visual perusal.

"So I'm assuming you don't want to move anything," he said as he reached behind him, flicking the lock into place.

He crossed to the middle of the room and put his hand on the small wooden steps leading to the tent. He peered inside and back to her.

"This thing hold people?" he asked.

Stella smiled. "It's secure for up to eight hundred pounds."

Dane hooked his thumbs through his belt loops as his gaze took another travel down her body. "Then I guess we're safe."

Safe? She was anything but safe with him. At least not emotionally because she was pretty sure she was falling for him, which was ridiculous considering she'd known him just over a week. The level of feelings she *thought* she had couldn't be developed in such a short time...could it?

"Something is rolling around inside that head of yours," he stated, pulling her from her thoughts. "Maybe you need a distraction."

"Oh, believe me. You've distracted me since you got here."

Dane kept that dark gaze on hers as his mouth kicked up in a grin and he pulled on his belt buckle. "That's the nicest compliment I've ever received."

"You *would* take that as a compliment."

Dane stood before her with his jeans unfastened, belt dangling, and reached for the hem of his shirt. "Why did you go to this trouble? We could've just stayed in your penthouse."

Stella shrugged. "I wanted to change it up a little. I never know when you're going to leave, so I guess I wanted to—"

"Give me a going away present?" he asked.

When he whipped his shirt over his head, she felt a warm glow of satisfaction at the realization that he'd gotten so comfortable with being bare around her he no longer even hesitated to take off his shirt. Everything about being together had become natural and effortless. They'd fallen into an easy pattern of making love at night, and when she worked during the day he would text to check on her or he'd make himself scarce and let her work. He never tried to tell her how to do her job and he'd never mentioned buying Mirage again and she certainly hadn't brought it up.

"Let's not talk about you leaving," she added. "I'd rather focus on you and this fantasy of mine."

Dane quirked a brow. "Did you have any man in mind for this fantasy?"

She took a step toward him and toyed with the tie between her breasts. "I didn't even think of this fantasy until I saw you."

He reached out, easing her hands aside, and slid apart the knot holding her shirt closed. Dane's fingertips grazed over her skin as he pushed the material from her shoulders. Stella shrugged until the shirt fell to the floor.

"I do like this outfit you came up with." He caressed the line on her skin just above the lacy edge of her bra. "I don't think I've seen you wear this around the resort before. Is this special for me?"

"You know it is."

His hand slid down and he curled his fingers inside

her waistband, tugging her toward him. "I like knowing you thought of me, of this. Nobody has ever done
anything like this before."

Which would explain the lack of fiancée now.

"First the bourbon and now the fantasy room." Stella
smiled. "This has been quite the week for you."

"You have no idea," he murmured. "But let's get to
this fantasy."

"Well, as much as I'd love to escape to the middle of
nowhere and just chill, that's not possible for me now.
So, I thought I'd bring you here and we could at least
pretend to be somewhere else."

Dane unfastened her skirt and sent it down her legs.
She kicked it aside, leaving her in her matching red bra
and thong set, and her boots.

"I don't care where I am if that's what you're wearing." Dane finished undressing and wrapped an arm
around her waist. "Tell me you've never brought another man in here."

Stella rolled her eyes. "What do you think?"

He dipped his head and feathered his lips over the
swell of her breasts. "I think I'm damn lucky and I'm
done talking."

She fisted his hair and arched her back as he jerked
her bra cups aside and feasted on her. His hands
gripped her backside as he lifted her off the ground.
She wrapped her legs around his waist and let him take
total control.

Dane spun toward the suspended, oversize tent and
sat her on the open edge. When he eased back, Stella
nearly whimpered. But he didn't go far. He reached
down to her boots and slid one, then the other off, letting them thunk to the floor.

Stella spread her legs, making room for him. He stepped up onto the bottom rung of the small ladder and curled his fingers around her waist.

"I want to see and taste every damn inch of you," he told her as he scooted her back into the pile of pillows. "I'll ruin you for another man."

Stella stilled, her eyes darting to his. Ruin her for another man? What was he saying? Did that mean he wanted more? That he wanted to stay and see what happened?

Little did he know, he'd already ruined her for anybody else. There would never be another man like Dane.

But that was something they'd have to discuss later when he wasn't making her toes curl with passionate promises.

Dane trailed his lips over her chest and down to her abdomen. "You're so damn sexy."

He made her feel that way. She never would've taken another man to the fantasy suite. Sex with Dane was, well, indescribable. She wanted to experience everything with him.

Hooking his thumbs in the silky material of her panties across her hips, he didn't tear them off or jerk them down. Instead he drove her out of her mind with sliding those rough, calloused hands over her heated skin as he slowly eased the material down her legs.

His mouth seemed poised to follow the path of his hands and Stella couldn't control her restlessness. She ached, she needed, she craved.

When he held her knees apart with the width of his broad shoulders, Stella couldn't suppress the groan that escaped her. And then his mouth was on her. Those big, firm hands gripped her inner thighs as he pleasured her in a way she'd never known before.

Stella threaded her fingers through his hair and arched her back. Dane's relentless urge to please her had her body spiraling out of control and she didn't even try to hold back her cries.

The climax hit her so fiercely, Stella shook against him for what felt like hours until her tremors began to slow. Before she could fully recover, he was putting on a condom and climbing up to her.

"I'm not nearly done with you."

He gripped the backs of her thighs and slid into her in one slow, delicious thrust. Then he flipped them so she straddled him and he smiled up at her.

"Do what you want, cowgirl."

Why did he have to be so sexy? Was there anything about him that didn't turn her on? The relinquishing of power right when her body still zinged and tingled made her feel dizzy and overwhelmed. She wasn't sure she could even move right now.

Dane playfully smacked her hip. "I'm waiting."

Bracing her hands on his chest, Stella smiled as she started to move. Dane's fingertips dug into her thighs as she rocked against him. From the way his jaw was set, his nostrils flared, and his lids lowered, she'd guess she was doing just fine.

As she quickened her rhythm, her body started climbing again. The pleasure became too intense and she leaned down, capturing his mouth with hers.

Dane palmed her backside and urged her faster while he made love to her mouth. He seemed to touch her everywhere all at once, causing that familiar tingling to build and grow until she exploded all around him.

He tightened his hold as he stilled beneath her. His lips moved over hers almost as if he couldn't get enough.

Yeah, he'd definitely ruined her for any other man.

Stella waited until they both stopped trembling before she sat back up and smiled. "Well, I should book this room more often."

Dane reached up and cupped her breasts. "You'll only be booking it with me."

When he said things like that, she couldn't help but think…

"What do you say we take that bottle of bourbon and go upstairs?" he suggested. "I have a few more things I want to do to you."

Mercy. Was he serious? She wasn't sure she could walk on these shaky legs, let alone head in for round two…or three in her case.

Within minutes, though, they were dressed and heading the private back way toward the elevator exclusively for her.

Dane laced his fingers through hers and Stella couldn't help but smile. She hadn't held hands with a man in, well, years. There was something so innocent, yet so…was *bonding* the right word? After all they'd done together, the fact he led her back to her suite by her hand was so damn adorable.

There was no denying she'd fallen in love with him. What would he do if she actually came out and told him? Would he vanish? Would he tell her he felt the same?

Part of her wanted to be completely honest and open with her feelings. The rest of her wanted to keep her feelings locked away inside her heart where they couldn't be hurt or crushed. She'd never told someone she loved them before.

Maybe she couldn't trust her feelings. What did she know about love? She'd never known her mother, her father was about as loving as a tree stump, and the only other time she'd thought she was in love, the man had been a cheating scumbag who had been using her only to impress her father.

Maybe all this amazing sex had her emotions and thoughts too scattered.

"You're awfully quiet," Dane stated as he punched the code in to take them up to her penthouse. "Maybe I wore you out."

Stella squeezed his hand and rested her head on his shoulder. "I'm not even going to deny that because it's true."

He kissed her forehead. "I'll let you sleep a few hours before I take you again."

Her body stirred. Just those simple words had her imagining them together again. Each time was just as thrilling as the first. She was half-dressed, and they were entirely alone, so he could have her right here and now and nobody would ever know.

But she really needed to figure out what she was going to do about her feelings…how to tell him.

Maybe she should actually put some clothes on to have the talk because it didn't seem appropriate to have a serious conversation when her underwear was gone, her shirt was tied over her bare breasts and her skirt was so short her nether regions were nearly showing.

The elevator door slid open and Stella took in everything all at once. The roaring fire that she hadn't started, the overwhelming scent of a pipe and the robust man wearing a suit at nearly midnight.

"Dad. What are you doing here?"

Fourteen

Dane released Stella's hand and stared at the man across the room. So this was Ruiz Garcia. The businessman was clearly all business. Who the hell stayed dressed up at this time of the night?

"I told you I was coming."

Ruiz turned to face them and his eyes widened at the sight of Stella's outfit. "I don't have to ask what you've been doing. Is this typical behavior at my resort for you?"

"Dad, I just—"

"Decided to take advantage of a fantasy suite," Dane chimed in, earning him a glare from Stella. "She's been working her ass off," Dane went on, ignoring her wide eyes. He stepped around her, mostly to shield her half-naked body, but also to shield her from the proverbial big, bad wolf. "This is an adult resort, and it's beautifully managed and maintained, with everything a couple could want. No reason she can't take advantage of the amenities."

Ruiz narrowed his eyes as he slid aside his suit jacket and slid his hands into his pockets. "And you are?"

"He's with me," Stella answered before Dane could.

Ruiz wouldn't recognize Dane's name because each deal that Dane had his broker send had been listed under a business name. Ruiz had no clue who he was really dealing with. But Dane knew exactly what he was up against, which gave him just another edge he needed.

Stella came to stand beside Dane as she crossed her arms over her chest. "You told me the other day that you were coming in a couple weeks. Why are you here now?"

"I had news I wanted to deliver and didn't want to discuss over the phone." Ruiz glanced to Dane. "Perhaps your friend could give us some privacy and you could put some decent clothes on."

Stella stepped forward and Dane remained rooted in place. This was her fight, but he wanted her to know he had her back. If her father started mansplaining or talking like he had the impression he was above her, she could know Dane was there and was totally on her side.

"Dane is staying here with me, so say whatever you need to say."

Ruiz's brow quirked as he glanced between the two. "Well, whatever you have going on is irrelevant to the news I need to pass on. I'm selling Mirage."

Stella gasped. "Does that mean you're giving me the chance to—"

"No." Ruiz pulled in a deep breath and took a step

toward his daughter. "I received an offer just today and I'm accepting it. The terms were too good to pass up."

Dane didn't know what to feel, how to react. Clearly he couldn't show any sign of knowing about the offer, even though he had no doubt the offer Ruiz spoke of was his.

After all this time, Mirage would be his. Dane swallowed the lump of emotions at the thought of getting his mother's place back where it belonged.

But he glanced at Stella and all of his elation simply vanished. The look on her face, one of betrayal and pain, sliced right through him.

"You—you're just selling this when you've known how much I want to have it?" she asked.

"Business is business," Ruiz stated with a shrug as if that summed up crushing his daughter's entire world. "If you didn't get so emotionally involved, you would know that and you'd already have a plan B instead of investing your entire future here."

"Plan B?" Stella asked, her voice cracking, revealing just how close to the edge she was. "You're my family— I shouldn't need a plan B for how to prove myself worthy of your time or attention. My entire life I've wanted you to notice me, to make a point to acknowledge that I'm your daughter. Your employees and stockholders rank higher on your priority list than I do."

Ruiz's eyes darted to Dane. "You care to give us a minute?"

"Yeah, actually I do care."

Dane folded his arms over his chest and glared back at the man who was used to people jumping at his every command. The muscle in Ruiz's jaw clenched. Clearly he hadn't expected Dane's response.

"Just tell me why?" Stella demanded. "Why would you do this? Why even give me hope when you planned on selling?"

Ruiz focused his attention back to his daughter and Dane took a step toward her. She stood there not caring about her precarious state of dress as she fought for her future...a future he had stolen from her.

Seeing her pain firsthand was sure as hell nothing he'd planned on. He'd thought he'd be gone before the ramifications of his actions kicked in...and back when he'd made the plan, he honestly hadn't cared enough to even consider how someone else might feel at that moment in time.

Her pain, her obvious anger, couldn't deter him. He still had a goal, he still had to get his mother's resort back where it belonged, and once he had that...well, then he could deal with Stella without her father prying into their business.

Because now Stella was his business. He didn't want her hurt, so all he could do at this point was try to make things less crushing. He had no idea how, but he'd damn well figure out something for her because unlike her bastard father, Dane actually cared about Stella's future.

"What was the offer?" Stella asked.

More than you have, sweetheart.

Yet Mirage was all he'd ever wanted. Money was just paper, not what kept him driven. Revenge and justice kept him pushing forward each and every day of his life.

"The offer was well over what I paid for this resort, so the profit will be a nice chunk in my pocket," Ruiz replied with a smug smile. "I'm sure we can find something else for you to do."

"I don't want anything else," Stella growled. "You

know this is what I wanted. I love the story behind it, I love the setting, the idea. I love every aspect. Do you even know that kind of passion?"

Ruiz narrowed his gaze at his daughter. "Don't preach to me about passion. It's my passion that gave you any opportunity you ever had. Money is the greatest passion of all."

"That's sad if that's truly how you feel," Stella told him.

Dane pressed a hand to the small of her back. Of course Ruiz would hang his black heart on his finances. He probably slept with a bag of money as a security blanket.

"I never cared about money growing up," Stella cried. "I wanted you there. I'd lost my mother and I never really had a father."

"You had opportunities most kids dream of," Ruiz spat back. "So maybe you should be thanking me instead of whining. Without me, you would've been in the foster system and then what would've happened?"

Stella gasped. "Foster care? What are you talking about?"

Ruiz sneered and dread curled through Dane.

"Your mother had an affair. I'm not your father."

Stella reached out for something stationary to hold on to, to help her remain standing. But her knees shook, buckled, and only Dane's strong, familiar arms wrapping around her kept her from collapsing.

She leaned back against him as she stared at her father.

No. Not her father. A man who wanted accolades for his half-hearted efforts in keeping her out of the system.

"You're lying," she accused, not really knowing what else to say. Dane's strength kept her up, but she held on to his forearm for fear he'd let her go.

"I'm not," her father said. "She cheated on me and her lover was your father."

How could he just now be dropping this bomb on her? Why after all of these years did he want to purposely continue hurting her?

"I want his name." She straightened her shoulders and stood straight up, but didn't let go of Dane. "I want to know who my real father is."

"He's dead."

Stella stared at him for a moment before she let out a laugh. "You're such a liar. You're going to great lengths to ensure I hate you forever."

"Fine, if you need to know, then his name was Martin Hernandez. He was killed in a small commuter plane crash when you were two. Look him up if you don't believe me. Use my investigator. I had a paternity test done to prove in case I needed it for future reference, but he died before—"

"What? Before you could blackmail him or hold me over his head?" Stella snarled. "Why did you even keep me? Why not just give me to him when I was born?"

"Because he hit your mother when she told him about the pregnancy." Ruiz might have had a flash of remorse in his eyes if he had a heart. "I might be a bastard, but I don't condone hitting a woman. Besides, I grew up in the foster system and I didn't want that for Maggie's baby."

Stella fisted her hands at her sides and had no clue what to do next. How did anyone react when their entire world was ripped away? First her mother passed, then her father—who wasn't her father—kept her out of some semblance of pity, only to pawn her off on nannies and teachers and coaches. And now? Well, now that she thought she could get somewhere with her life, somewhere that might make her father take notice and maybe see her as a worthy businesswoman, that opportunity was stripped away.

As much as she wanted to scream and shed tears, Stella wouldn't dare show Ruiz any emotion. He didn't deserve to know that he could affect her. All of these years and she'd never gotten anything from him by way of feelings. That's all she'd wanted, but apparently because she hadn't been his by blood, she hadn't deserved even the slightest hint of true affection.

"I want you to leave."

The words slipped through her lips before she realized she was even thinking them. But as soon as they came out, she realized she really did want him gone. Stella didn't want to look at that smug smirk another second.

"Listen to me," he started, taking a step toward her. "I didn't purposely set out to hurt you, but things fell into place, both in the past and now. It's out of my hands."

Stella gritted her teeth and used up every ounce of energy not to haul off and hit him. If he wanted her to truly hate him, he needn't say another word.

"All of this was in your hands," she fired back. "You could've told me about my father, you could've told me you had no intention of ever letting me take over this resort. You spied on me because you didn't think I could handle running this place, and then you went behind my back to sell to the highest bidder. Don't act like you

couldn't have done anything about this. You've manipulated my life from the start without a moment of care
or concern for me. You never had time for me—well,
now I have no more time for you. So get the hell out."

Ruiz smoothed his suit jacket down and cleared his
throat. "Actually, this resort belongs to me until the
new owners take over. So if anyone is leaving it's you.
But, since I'm kind enough, I'll give you two weeks to
move your things."

Stella glanced around her space. She'd already gotten
so used to being here, in this space she called her own.

Swallowing the lump of pain and remorse, Stella
focused her attention back on Ruiz. "Who bought Mirage?"

"My assistant handled most of the details, but I was
told Strong L Ranch is going to be the new owner."

Stella chewed on her lip to keep it from quivering.
Whoever bought this place couldn't love it near as much
as she did. There was no way they had the emotional
connection she did. Stella had wanted this place for
years and had been so close. So damn close.

"Stella asked you to leave."

Dane's low, commanding tone reminded her he was
still here, still supporting her. He'd been quiet, letting
her handle things, but she was damn near to the point
of breaking. She wanted her father—no, Ruiz—gone.
She *needed* him gone.

"I hate that things came to this," Ruiz stated. "You've
actually surprised me with your determination and work
ethic. I'm sure there's another business that I can—"

"I don't want your businesses and I don't want your
pity." Stella pulled in a deep, shaky breath. "I'm done
waiting for approval from you. I'm done hoping you'll

see me for the woman I am. I'm not a failure, I kick ass at what I do and someone will see that…even if the man who supposedly raised me can't."

Stella turned and crossed to the elevator. She punched the button with more force than necessary, but she had nowhere else to channel all of this anger.

Ruiz stepped into the elevator and Stella forced herself to look at him. She wanted him to see that she wasn't weak, no matter how many times he had continued to knock her down. He may have shown a sliver of nobility by raising another man's kid, but Stella knew he regretted every day he'd been stuck with her. She'd never truly been his daughter, and as much as that hurt, she was glad she knew the truth.

He continued to hold her stare as the doors slid closed.

And then he was gone.

All the energy, all the emotions from the last hour took their toll. Stella flattened her hand over the elevator keypad and dropped her head. Tears burned her eyes, every word she didn't know to say got caught in her throat.

Strong arms wrapped around her. Dane eased her around until she faced him, then he scooped her up without a word. Stella looped her arms around his neck and shut her eyes as he carried her away. As strong as she prided herself on being, there were times she just couldn't hold it together anymore. Everyone had a breaking point and Stella had more than reached hers.

Dane set her on her feet and Stella blinked up at him. He'd carried her to the bed and he started undressing her.

"I don't have the—"

Dane placed his finger over her lips, cutting off her words. "You're going to rest. That's all you need to do right now. Nothing can be done about the resort or Ruiz right this minute. Just let me care for you."

Tears continued to slide down her cheeks. Stella swatted at them. "I'm not weak," she defended.

Dane framed her face with his hands and forced her attention on him. "Baby, I never thought you were. You just got the wind knocked out of you. I'm here and I'm not going anywhere."

Stella lifted one foot, then the other for him to remove her boots. When he straightened back up, Stella rested her head against his chest and inhaled that masculine, woodsy scent she'd come to associate with Dane.

"Why haven't you left yet?" she muttered.

She thought he murmured something about "not being done" but she wasn't sure and she was too tired to ask him to repeat it. All that mattered was that he was there and she knew he would stay for as long as she needed.

Fifteen

"I'll wrap up a few things and then be right there," Dane explained. "I've verbally secured the deal. I need to get back to the ranch and finalize the sale, then I'll pack a bag."

Ethan gripped the cell as he stood on the balcony of his penthouse resort room, overlooking the ocean. He glanced over his shoulder to the owner of the red bikini he'd met on the beach. She'd been in his bed since.

Harper. Her name was Harper and she had been filling his time and keeping him relaxed while he waited on Robert to get to the island. He hadn't planned on finding the distraction, but there was no way in hell he was turning her down.

"Leave the flannels at home," Ethan replied, turning his attention back to the view of the beach. "Do you even own swim trunks?"

"I'm not coming to work on my tan," Dane growled. "We're halfway to our goal. Do you think you can stay focused?"

Memories of the past few days and the curvy woman in his bed flashed through his mind in vivid detail.

"Oh, I'm focused."

Dane let out a sigh. "I'm going to the ranch later today. I'll text you when I'm on my way to Sunset Cove."

Something in his brother's tone had Ethan turning back to make sure the patio door was closed. He crossed the balcony and took a seat on the club chair.

"You don't sound near as thrilled as I thought you'd be."

"I finally have Mirage," Dane muttered. "What more could I want?"

"I don't know. That's why I'm asking."

The line went silent and Ethan waited. He stared out at the horizon as the sun started creeping up. A new day, and another step closer to finalizing their goals.

So why was Dane so…monotone?

"It's the manager, isn't it?" Ethan guessed. "Is there something going on there?"

"Don't worry about me."

Ethan clenched his teeth, but ultimately decided he was done being pushed aside.

"I've worried about you every single day since Mom died," he stated. "You might have dealt with grief your own way, but I needed you. Damn it. Don't push me out now."

More silence and Ethan wondered if he'd gone too far, revealed too much. He was human and sometimes those emotions just came out. He wasn't sorry he'd finally said something, but he was sorry that this conversation was over the phone.

"I'm not pushing you out," Dane finally said. "Not on purpose anyway. I'm just... Let me get things wrapped up here. This isn't all about the resorts. It's about us."

For the first time in nearly two decades, Ethan had a blossom of hope that he and Dane could get back to where they'd been before their world got ripped to shreds.

"I've got a room booked for you," Ethan assured him. "See you soon. And, Dane? Great job getting your resort. Mom would be proud."

The line went dead.

Ethan stared at his phone before dropping it to his lap and raising his gaze to the sky. Maybe he and Dane had further to go in repairing their relationship than he'd thought. Perhaps the mention of their mother triggered something in Dane.

Ethan didn't know. What he did know was that there was a vivacious woman in his bed, more than eager to continue this fling for as long as she was in town, and he was *this close* to securing his future and his legacy... and claiming revenge on Robert Anderson.

Dane had packed his meager bag, touched base with his broker and was all set to head back to his ranch.

But he didn't want to leave Mirage. He'd just acquired it—technically. All that was left was to sign the papers, but this was a done deal.

He wasn't frustrated and cranky because he was leaving Stella. No, they'd decided at the beginning this connection or whatever they had would be temporary. Just because he was leaving her while she happened to be already emotionally crushed and shattered because of Ruiz, well…

Damn it.

Dane ran a hand over his stubbled jaw and glanced around the penthouse. His eyes landed on the note he'd left for Stella. She was working and he didn't want to interrupt. Even though she had been dismissed by her father, she was downstairs right now making sure each and every guest had what they needed to ensure a get-away they'd never forget.

And Dane was a damn coward for sneaking out without saying goodbye. He could freely admit it, but there was no way in hell he could stay any longer. He'd gotten what he came for and hanging around would only prolong the inevitable. Stella needed to move on, and so did he.

So why was there so much pain? Why did that heaviness on his chest leave him feeling like a complete jerk?

Because he was. At this point, Dane was no better than the man who'd raised her. They'd both lied to her, deceived her, betrayed her.

She was still dealing with learning the truth about Ruiz. He couldn't unload more secrets on her. Leaving was the best option—for both of them.

Keep telling yourself that, buddy. Maybe you'll believe the lies.

Gripping the handle of his suitcase, Dane headed toward the elevator. He'd be back. This would be his suite when he returned, but he knew in his heart things wouldn't be the same.

When he'd first arrived he could see only one woman here—his mother. Now he knew when he returned, he'd see only Stella.

She'd left an imprint on his life and on this place that would never disappear. There was something so permanent about her. They'd forged a bond whether he wanted to admit it or not.

And he didn't want to admit any such thing.

Since he knew the layout of this place better than his own home, Dane slipped out in such a way that he knew Stella would never see him. He could be honest enough with himself to admit that if he saw her and attempted to explain why he was leaving, the guilt would consume him.

Dane had to push that aside. He couldn't allow anything to steal the moment he'd been preparing for. Once this was all officially his, he'd feel better. All he had to do was finalize the sale, and get to Ethan. Working with his brother to bring down Robert would only add to the euphoria of finally reclaiming everything they'd been robbed of.

Once they came in contact with Robert, well, there would be a little surprise waiting for him. Their miserable bastard of a stepfather was done stealing and being deceitful. He wouldn't be free to ruin anybody else's lives or rob futures.

Dane started to head toward the back hallway from another hallway he'd sneaked through, but a familiar voice through the door leading to the back office stopped him.

"Come to me for any specialty needs for the fantasy rooms," Stella stated.

"What about Savannah?" an unfamiliar voice asked.

"Her daughter has her first dance recital tonight and tomorrow. I told her to take the days off. Family is too important."

"You know the staff talks. We like that you're much different than our last manager," the worker said.

"Yeah, well, that was my goal."

Dane heard the hurt in her voice. He knew every moment she spent working here had to be absolutely soul crushing now that she knew the place would never be hers. She was a damn good manager and had compassion for her staff. She truly cared about this place, these employees.

Stella had just been dismissed in the most uncaring of ways only hours ago. But this morning, she went on with the business-as-usual attitude. She had her pride, sure, but she did this because she didn't want the staff or guests to suffer.

How could he just take everything from her? How could he not want her to be part of this once he took over?

But she wanted the resort to be hers and he simply couldn't allow that to happen. Mirage belonged to him.

Damn that guilt. Not only did the guilt threaten to choke hold him, he didn't know what he'd do once he got home and she wasn't there. She'd been the only person in his entire life to know what he fully suffered from. He'd never let anyone in like he had with Stella. She'd been so easy to talk to, so...

He couldn't find the words. She was everything he didn't know he needed. There was something so therapeutic about her, in the way she genuinely cared, in the way she made everyone else feel like they were the top priority in her life.

But when had anyone made her a priority?

Dane clenched his jaw and shoved the door open to the hallway. He needed to get out and get back to his ranch. An evening with his dogs, his horses, and a ride out in the country would help him think more clearly.

There had to be a way to not ruin Stella's life and still keep everything he'd worked so damn hard for. He just needed to find it.

Dane left the resort, left the mountain, and didn't look back in his rearview mirror. He'd learned the hard way that looking back only kept you in the past. Dane knew only one way to go and that was forward.

From this second on, he'd take charge of Mirage, work with Ethan to destroy Robert and find out some way to make things right for Stella.

Sixteen

After three days of riding horses, drinking bourbon on his enclosed back porch with his dogs at night and messaging back and forth with Ethan, Dane still wasn't calm.

His nerves were on edge. He still hadn't come up with a way to make things right with Stella. He had heard from her—she'd texted him, but he'd replied that he'd have to talk later.

Still taking the coward's way out.

He wanted to offer her the manager position, but deep in his gut he knew she'd turn it down and likely tell him exactly where to take his offer once she realized he was the new owner.

But Stella was exactly the type of person who should be running the resort. Dane was in no position to be hands-on every day—not if he wanted to keep his ranch. Moving permanently to the resort was something he'd have to ease into, even though ultimately that was his goal.

Dane relaxed forward in the front porch swing and rested his elbows on his knees. Buck lay at his feet all curled up, but Bronco sat obediently on the other side waiting on affection.

As he rubbed the soft fur between his dog's ears, Dane ran over and over through his mind what he would say to Stella when he saw her again. There would be no avoiding her, and he didn't want to, but he needed space to sort things out. Even before he left the resort a few days ago, he'd known he needed Stella in the business.

And as much as he wanted to keep thinking of her in that capacity, Dane knew that trail of thoughts barely scratched the surface of everything he remembered when Stella came to mind.

Oh, hell. Who was he kidding? The woman never left his mind. Everything about her clung to his skin even as he dealt with every aspect of daily life. When he'd come home, he'd imagined her here. She'd said more than once that she wanted to escape to the middle of nowhere and unwind. His ranch certainly fit that criteria and now that he was back, he realized just how much he wanted to show her his place.

As the sun set behind the mountain peaks, Dane was glad he was alone. He wasn't in the mood to talk or handle any issues. He just wanted the simplicity of swaying on the swing on his climate-controlled wraparound porch and petting his dogs. His mind was too full of worry and possibilities to consider adding anything else to the mix.

The past few nights since coming home he'd been so damn restless. Sleep hadn't been his friend since returning from the war, but now the dynamics were completely different. He wasn't afraid to go to sleep, he was afraid to wake up without Stella by his side.

When the hell had his heart gotten involved in this charade? That had never been part of his grand plan.

Knowing Stella, as soon as she found out the truth, she'd verbally attack him and make him feel like he wasn't even worthy of being in the same vicinity as her. She had every right to annihilate him, and she would as soon as she learned he was Mirage's new owner. He needed to tell her before she found out some other way.

He needed to be clear where he stood, as the owner, and that he wanted her to remain on board as the manager. Compensating her with a raise and a bonus might go a long way in securing her staying at Mirage. He had to find a way to convince her.

Dane's cell vibrated in his pocket. When he went to grab it, Bronco jerked his head back, giving a glare from the instant lack of attention.

"Hang on, boy."

The alert on his phone was from the gate announcing a visitor. From the video image, he knew who that unexpected guest was and there was no hiding from her anymore.

Dane typed in the code to access the gate and watched as Stella drove her SUV onto his ranch. The drive from the gate to the main house was just over a minute. Not nearly enough time to fine-tune the speech he'd rehearsed because the second she drove through the iron arch with his ranch name, she would know the truth.

A gut-sinking feeling rendered him motionless. His eyes stared off down the driveway, knowing any second he'd see headlights cut through the dusky night.

As dark gray clouds shadowed the sunset, Dane knew another storm was brewing...from all aspects of his life right now.

Dane came to his feet and snapped his fingers, immediately getting his dogs' attention. He opened the front door and put them inside just as those lights cut across his porch.

The knot in his gut tightened, but he remained on the edge of his porch and waited for her to get out of the car. She'd come here for a reason, and had he not deceived her and lied to her face, stealing everything she'd worked for, he might believe that she had come to him to see if there was a chance for them.

Dane wasn't that naive or stupid to think that anything good could come from a fling and a trail of deception. But now that she was here, he had to keep things businesslike and make her understand where he came from. It was time to put all his cards on the table and explain his past with Mirage. Surely she would understand the importance of family, considering that's all she'd wanted for herself.

Sliding his hands into the pockets of his jeans, Dane stared out at the drive as Stella killed the engine. He couldn't see into the windshield that well, but he knew when he looked into her dark eyes, he'd see...

Hell, maybe he didn't know what he'd see. Pain? Regrets? Rage? Likely all of the above.

She didn't get out immediately. Keeping him waiting and wondering was the least that he deserved.

Unable to wait a second longer, Dane made his way down the wide stone steps. The first fat snowflake hit his cheek. His boots scuffed against the concrete drive, but he kept his eyes on that door, waiting.

When he reached the side of her SUV, Dane peered in to see Stella with her head in her hands, her shoulders shaking. Dane jerked on the handle and opened the door. More flakes fell, but he ignored the chill.

"Stella."

Dane started to reach in, but she jerked her head up and slinked back.

"Don't touch me," she commanded as she held him with a watery gaze. "You're nothing but a liar and I'm a damn fool for even coming here."

He didn't know that someone could look so broken, yet so angry at the same time. But Stella was definitely both.

"I *am* a liar, but you're not a fool," he corrected.

Ignoring her plea to leave her alone, Dane reached for her arm and urged her from the vehicle.

"Don't," she cried, tears streaming down her cheeks. "Don't try to make this better. You can't."

No, he couldn't. Stella had taken hit after hit, but this was the first time he'd seen her so broken and completely vulnerable. He'd done this. He'd crushed her more than her father had...which was truly saying something.

The air seemed to turn colder, icier.

"Come inside," he told her. "You can hate me and cry and anything else you want, but we need to get out of this weather."

"I'd rather drive back to Gold Valley through a snowstorm than to be here with you." She pulled her arm away and took a step back. "To think I came here because..."

Dane's heart clenched. There was no way to keep his heart out of this because likely it had been involved from the beginning. Stella drove all this way for him—well, she drove for the man she thought he was.

"You're the new owner," she muttered, then let out a mock laugh. "My father is one hell of an actor because he pretended not to know you."

"He *doesn't* know me," Dane confirmed. "The sale went through my broker and was done in the name of the ranch."

"I'm aware of the ranch name," she scoffed.

The snow came down so thick and fast, the entire area seemed to be blinding white. Dane didn't wait to hear what else she had to say and he didn't ask for permission. She already thought he was a bastard. Might as well go whole hog.

He scooped her up and ran toward the porch. She smacked at his back and cursed him the entire way. Damn she was sexy fired up like this. Not that he'd ever be worthy of having her again. Those memories of their time together were all he'd ever have.

Once he set her down on the porch, Dane kept his hands on her shoulders. He didn't want to force her to do anything, but he didn't want her to bolt before she could hear him out—especially if bolting meant trying to drive in blizzard-like conditions when she was crying and upset. That just sounded like a disaster in the making.

"Why?" she demanded as she stared up at him. She didn't bother swiping at her tears, likely so he'd see the full impact his actions had on her. "Why did you lie to me? Sleeping with me was, what? Just a way to pass the time until you stole my future?"

"No," he defended with a shake of his head. "I… Damn it."

Dane dropped his hands, unable to ignore the agony on her face.

"You came to Mirage purposely to find me," she accused. "Did you laugh when you got me into bed so quickly? I must've made this all so easy on you."

When the wind kicked up and trees cracked outside the window, his dogs started barking their fool heads off. Stella jumped and glanced toward the front door.

"They're not scared," he explained. "When it thunders or gets too windy, they think someone is knocking."

"I can't imagine you get many visitors out here in the middle of nowhere."

He didn't, but his staff would always knock before entering. "Let's get inside," he told her. "You can yell at me all you want there, but I need to get in there before my boys tear up my front door."

"I should leave," she muttered, barely audible over the wind. "I came here thinking we'd see where things went. Now, I want to be anywhere else."

"I get that," he replied. "But it's nasty out there and it's a long drive back to Gold Valley. Might as well stay at least a little longer."

He turned and reached for the door, ready to hold back his dogs so they wouldn't lick Stella to death.

"I don't want to stay," she repeated, but the fight had left her tone and Dane knew she wasn't going anywhere yet.

She'd never admit her vulnerability, and he admired her for that, but he also knew if he was ever going to get through to her to fully understand his side, then now was the time to explain himself. And Stella deserved an explanation.

Dane stepped over the threshold and gripped his

dogs' collars as he hustled them back from the door. Two overly excited golden retrievers wasn't something Stella needed to put up with right now.

Once she was inside and had closed the door, Dane let go of the dogs and snapped his fingers. The boys immediately sat at his side.

"You don't have to stay long, but I need you to hear me out." He stared back at her, knowing she could bolt out of that door at any time, knowing he deserved exactly that. "It's not safe to try to drive right now. You know how Montana weather can be."

Stella's eyes darted down to the dogs and back up to him. "You're used to everyone doing exactly what you want, aren't you?" she sneered. "I'm not going to be that person."

Yet here she was, standing in his foyer.

"Mirage was always meant to be mine," he explained, needing to get to the heart of the issue. "My brother and I both have resorts that were stolen from us before we were old enough or had any power to stop it."

Stella narrowed her eyes. "Stolen? That doesn't even make sense."

Dane ran a hand over his jaw, the stubble raked against his palm. "My mother was Lara Anderson. She built Mirage in Gold Valley and Sunset Cove."

Stella's eyes widened. "That's why you were so determined? Because you think this is owed to you?"

"It is owed to me," he demanded. "Robert Anderson was a complete bastard who took advantage of my mother by marrying her when she was vulnerable after her father's death. When she passed, Ethan and I were still in high school and Robert underhandedly gained rights to those properties and left with our money."

Stella stared at him for a minute before shaking her head and pressing her hand to her eyes. "I can't grasp all of this," she muttered. "I can't figure out how any of this is my fault and why I'm being punished when all I wanted was to have a place of my own, to stand on my own."

Dane took a step forward. "I can help you. I just can't give you Mirage."

Taking a step away from him, Stella leveled his gaze. "I don't want your help. I don't want pity and I don't want…"

Her voice cracked as she trailed off and ultimately turned her back. Dane fisted his hands at his sides, knowing she wanted nothing at all from him at this point. The only thing she'd ever wanted had been ripped from her life…just like it had been ripped from his.

They both wanted Mirage. They both had had the resort pulled away from them when they were so close to obtaining it.

"I know how you feel," he stated. "I've been there. I didn't want to hurt you. I never wanted any of this to harm you in any way. I just wanted what belonged to me."

Stella spun around, her eyes full of fury and unshed tears. "Didn't want me hurt? What did you think would happen? Did you think I'd be so totally blown away by your seduction skills that I'd overlook you jerking my life from me?"

"I never thought that." Though the way she worded it made him sound like an even bigger bastard than he already felt. "I just wanted to find a way to get the resort back in my family like my mother always planned."

"You didn't have to lie to me," she threw back.

Dane gritted his teeth as he tried to find words to defend himself. But she was right. Now that he looked back, now that he realized the impact he'd had on her and how much she'd already been through with her father, she was absolutely right.

The wind kicked up so much the windows rattled. Stella jumped and the dogs started barking again.

Dane snapped his fingers and turned to the dogs. "Bed."

The one-word command had them darting toward the wide stairs and they raced each other up to the second floor. Once they were out of sight, Dane turned back to Stella.

"Come into the living room."

She crossed her arms over her chest. "I'm not staying or obeying your commands."

"You're being ridiculous right now," he growled. "Are you just going to stand in my foyer all night?"

"If I want."

Dane raked a hand over his hair and blew out a sigh. "Don't be so damn stubborn."

Stella stared at him for another minute before she turned her attention around the open space and ultimately went in the opposite direction of the living room.

He glanced up to the ceiling and willed himself to remain calm. This woman had been through hell, at the hands of her father and then him. She was strong willed and angry, and totally entitled to all her frustration and rage.

Having her here at his ranch seemed perfect in all the wrong ways. So as she set off, Dane had no choice but to follow.

Seventeen

Stella figured the storm inside was better to deal with than the storm outside…or at least that's what she told herself as she explored the first level of Dane's ranch.

She wasn't actually focusing on anything, more just wandering aimlessly through the oversize rooms. One area seemed to flow to the next and everything looked like something from a magazine. The high beams, the worn wooden floors, the plush leather sofas, and stone fireplace.

Everything about this house reminded her of the resort. The dark wood, the way everything from the furniture to the size of the rooms just screamed power and money. His mother might have built Mirage, but Dane was clearly his mother's son. Stella was not only fighting her father, but she was also up against a family lineage. Dane wasn't just going to let her have the resort, and she wouldn't expect him to if what he told her was true.

Still, that didn't mean he had gone about things the right way. She wasn't sure what the right way would have been, but she sure as hell knew he'd made the wrong choice.

"Looking for another escape route?" Dane asked as he came up behind her.

Stella turned her attention from the photos lining the mantel to Dane. He stood behind her, just close enough she could reach out and touch him, but far enough to give her a bit of space.

"I'm trying to wrap my head around all of this," she replied honestly. "I mean, what the hell were you thinking coming into all of this? That you deserved Mirage, that you'd get it no matter what and that anything that wasn't your feelings or your end goal simply doesn't matter? Did I sum it all up?"

The muscle clenched in his jaw as he shoved his hands into his pockets. Those dark eyes narrowed.

"Don't even try to be offended," she went on. "You brought all of this upon yourself."

"I had no time," he demanded. "It's not just Mirage in Gold Valley. There's more going on and I had to move when I could."

"More what? More businesses you're trying to steal from unsuspecting women?"

He stared at her for another minute before cursing under his breath and turning to pace toward the wall of windows. The harsh conditions continued to rage outside and honestly, it wasn't much prettier inside. She wished she'd never come. She wished she'd never met Dane Michaels. And she wished like hell she'd never put stock in thinking her father would finally give her something—anything—she truly wanted.

She'd felt so damn isolated for so long. Even training for the competitions she'd felt alone because not many people understood that willpower and determination.

Now here she was alone. Stella knew she needed to dig deep and find that drive and determination all over again. She would, too. Nothing would keep her down. Life may knock her, but she couldn't let the hits deter her.

Stella stared at Dane across the room. He'd not answered her and from his rigid shoulders and silence, she had a feeling he wasn't planning on it, either.

She turned back to the photos on the mantel. There were only three. There were two on each end and each picture was a teenage version of Dane with another boy who she assumed was his brother, and their mother. The photo in the middle of the mantel was a snapshot of his mother alone. Her head was thrown back as she laughed and there was so much happiness, so much life in that image.

Tears formed once again and Stella wished she didn't feel for this woman, this man. But Lara Anderson was the woman Stella had admired for years. Stella had loved hearing the story about Lara and how she'd started the resorts for couples…yet she was a single mother with two boys.

There was a family here in these photos, a family Stella had always wanted and craved. But this family had been torn apart by an untimely death and Dane just wanted to reclaim what he believed belonged to him.

She turned back to find him staring directly at her. Her stomach tightened. That darkened stare had her nerves on edge. She didn't want to see this side of him. She didn't want to see him as a human with real feelings. From the second she turned into the drive and saw that iron arch with the ranch name, Dane had become a complete stranger. She didn't know where the man was from the resort, but damn if her heart didn't have a hole in it that was just his size.

She could walk away, no matter how much it hurt, if she could convince herself that everything about that man she'd thought he was had been a lie. But the longer she stayed, the more she realized the truth was complicated—and so was Dane.

"I realize we're not that different," she stated. "We both want the same thing for justifiable reasons."

Dane started forward, but Stella held up her hands and kept going. "Your methods are clearly what sets us apart. I never would've used someone, blindsided them, and then stolen their life."

"You really think your dad was just going to turn the resort over to you?"

Stella's heart clenched. "Maybe not, but I had a fighting chance before you came along throwing your money and whatever else at him."

Dane crossed his arms over his chest and clenched his jaw. "I gave him two of my businesses on top of the money."

Part of her admired the lengths he would go to in order to reclaim his mother's legacy. The other part of her, the part that had been manipulated, hated every part of Dane Michaels for going behind her back to steal what she'd thought could be hers.

But damn if she wasn't still attracted to him. Her

body still responded to that midnight gaze, those broad shoulders...one glimpse of those talented hands.

Why couldn't there be some switch to turn off emotions and tingly reactions? Sex messed with her head. Great sex somehow managed to mess with her heart because there was no way she'd fallen for him. Stella refused to believe that she could have in such a short time.

"You're thinking."

Dane's words settled between them. That low tone always got to her in ways she'd never been able to explain. How could a voice cause arousal?

But, yes, she was thinking. Thinking how she was stuck here waiting for the storm to pass. Thinking about how she'd been used. Thinking about how the past few weeks had been out of her control and she wanted to take that control back.

Stella took a step toward Dane before she could talk herself out of this. If she thought too much she'd find every reason not to take this leap. But for now, just for this moment, she was in charge and she'd be damned if anyone else would ever take the decisions from her again.

"I hate you," she told him as she started working on the buttons on her dress. "I hate how you stole my world from me. But you're right. You are the same man who stayed in my bed when I was exhausted and alone, who helped me when I didn't even ask. You're the same man my body craves and the man I can't stop wanting."

"Stella—"

"No." She shrugged out of her dress, sending it to the floor in a whisper. "I call the shots now. You used me, right? Well, I'm about to use you. I want you and I'm going to have you."

Dane's eyes widened, his jaw clenched and his nostrils flared. She recognized his signs of arousal and desire. His gaze raked over her nearly bare body. She had on only her knee boots and her matching nude lace bra and panties.

"This isn't a good idea," he told her. "You know it's not. Are you doing this to get back at me?"

Stella shrugged. "Perhaps. But I'm also doing it because I want you. I wish I could turn that off, but I see you and my body responds."

She quickly rid herself of her boots before focusing on him again. "Unless you've decided you've gotten all you wanted from me."

Dane muttered a curse before he was on her. "I should turn you away, but damn if you don't have some power over me."

He scooped her up and started back toward the entryway, back toward the steps.

"Not your bedroom," she commanded.

There was no way she'd go somewhere that personal, that intimate.

"This isn't anything more than sex," she added.

Dane set her back on her feet and backed her against the wide door frame leading from the living room. For a half second, he merely stared, seeming to take in her entire body with one hungry sweep.

Then he thrust his hands through her hair and captured her lips. Stella arched her body and found the edge of his T-shirt. With frantic motions, she jerked it up, pulling her lips away long enough to get the shirt up and over his head. Then he was on her again as she went for his belt and the snap on his jeans.

She'd barely gotten them unzipped when he pulled

away. Dane kept his eyes on her while he reached into his pocket and pulled out protection. He covered himself and stepped back toward her.

Stella opened for him, threading her fingers through his hair, and taking everything he gave. Part of her knew this was wrong, but the devil on her shoulder thought it was a great idea. There was nothing wrong with taking charge and allowing pleasure. There was nothing wrong with going into this moment with her eyes wide-open and her heart shut tight.

When Dane gripped her waist and lifted her, Stella's thoughts vanished. All she knew was passion as she wrapped her legs around his waist and sank onto him. Clutching his shoulders, she closed her eyes and pressed her back against the solid door frame. Dane's lips trailed over the column of her neck, over her sensitive breasts. He palmed her backside as he pumped his hips and Stella just let the euphoric sensations wash over her.

Dane muttered something as he traveled back up to the erogenous area just below her ear.

That was all it took for her body to respond and spiral out of control. All of her emotions balled up together and she gave herself over to the climax. This was why she'd decided to surprise him. She'd needed to be with him, needed to feel him.

Stella's entire body shook and all thoughts vanished. She kept her eyes shut, needing to keep her emotions locked inside and not look too closely at him. She just wanted to feel.

Dane murmured something in her ear, she only made out the word "need" but she ignored it as he jerked his hips harder. His body tightened, his fingertips dug into her backside, and Stella dropped her head to his shoulder as he took his own pleasure.

His heated body stuck to hers, and Stella didn't want to lift her head. She didn't want to face reality.

But she knew this was it. She and Dane were done... if they'd ever really started. They'd had a fling, that was all. Though she'd thought there was more, there couldn't be. He'd deceived her, slept with her under false pretenses and then left without a word. At any time he could've given her the truth, but he'd chosen to keep his true self hidden away.

The same way she'd have to hide away the fact she'd fallen in love with the man she thought he was.

Pulling together all of her strength and resolve, Stella extracted herself from the warmth and strength she'd only experienced from Dane. She hated him for making her hate him. That sounded so messed up in her own thoughts, but he'd damaged something inside her. Something she didn't know if she'd recover from.

He didn't say a word as he stepped from the room. Stella dressed in a hurry, not caring if her buttons were straight or her hair was in knots. She had to go. Staying here, waiting on him to state another defense, would only make her thoughts, her heart, even more muddled.

Just as she zipped up her boot and came to her feet, Dane stepped back into the room.

"You want to talk about this?" he asked.

"Nothing to discuss." Did that even sound convincing? "You used me, I used you."

"Is that what this was?" he asked, crossing his arms over his chest and leaning against the very spot he'd just taken her. "You wanted to retaliate? Doesn't seem like you."

Stella swallowed and tipped her chin. "Seems we didn't know each other as well as we thought."

She crossed to the doorway, easily moving past him in the large opening.

"Where are you going?"

Tossing a look over her shoulder, she replied, "The storm has passed."

"What about us?"

Gripping the doorknob, Stella turned away and whispered, "That's passed, too."

Eighteen

Mirage wasn't near as inviting as it had been.

For the past month, he'd been back and forth between the resort and the ranch. More at the resort, though, since he needed to acclimate the staff to his management style and get up-to-date with the various systems.

Ethan had told Dane to hold off on coming because something had held Robert up and it looked like he wasn't going to be coming for a bit. Dane certainly had things he could be doing here to bide his time.

His first order had been to fire the asshole who'd disrespected Stella. Apparently he'd also been the spy, hence the cockiness since he worked directly with Ruiz.

Dane's second order had been to get his attorney and accountant on-site to see what the hell he could do to get Stella back here—where she belonged.

That had been over three weeks ago and he'd still

not heard a word from her. He'd known full well she'd received the employment offer and he didn't know what was taking her so damn long to respond. Though her silence was nothing less than he deserved.

Damn it. Nobody just flat-out ignored him. Never. Not even when he had it coming. He might be a recluse, he might shy away from getting too involved with crowds of people, but that didn't mean he was soft or ready to just give up.

Dane knew he had to give Stella time. Her entire world had been shattered and he'd precipitated it all. Now he was trying to piece all those shards back together and without seeing her, he had no idea if his tactics were even working.

Since she'd walked out of his house after using him, he'd been destroyed. He didn't care that she'd wanted to use his body. Their physical connection couldn't be just ignored or brushed aside. There was no way someone as caring and loving as Stella could just walk away and not think or feel anymore.

And there was love looking back at him when she'd been in his home. He'd seen it, felt it.

And he knew he'd fallen just as hard.

Dane turned the corner heading to his office at Mirage. He nearly ran into one of the receptionists, but quickly put his hands out to stop her from plowing into him.

"Oh, Mr. Michaels," she gasped. "I'm so sorry."

Dane might still be struggling with some names of his new employees, but not Lola. He remembered her quite well.

"I've told you to call me Dane," he reminded her,

as he'd done every single day he'd been there. "You worked for my mother."

Lola smiled and smoothed her cropped, gray hair from her forehead. "That may be, and I may remember you as a thirteen-year-old boy, but that doesn't mean anything now. You're my boss and I respect that."

"I appreciate the respect, but Dane will be just fine," he confirmed. "You've been here since the beginning. I hope you'll stay on."

Lola nodded and patted his arm. "I wouldn't dream of leaving. Your mother would be so proud of you."

Guilt threatened to choke him, but so did a rush of warmth at the kind comment. Story of his life lately. He'd destroyed one woman he loved while honoring the other.

"Oh, Stella is in your office," Lola added.

Dane jerked. "Excuse me?"

"Stella Garcia," Lola repeated. "She said she had an appointment, so I let her in. I was getting ready to call you. I hope that was okay."

The worry in her tone had Dane offering a smile. "That was more than okay. Thanks, Lola."

He skirted around the faithful employee in an effort to get to his office. Dane didn't care that he looked like a madman racing down the hall. There was only so much control a guy could have and he'd waited long enough for Stella to get back with him about his offer.

Granted, he'd thought she'd call, but an in-person meeting was sure as hell something he wasn't about to turn down.

Dane opened the door to his office and stepped inside to find Stella in his new leather office chair behind his desk.

She glanced from his computer screen to him as she propped those long bare legs up on the corner of his desk.

Just the sight of her had his gut tightening, his heart pumping faster. He leaned against the door and closed it with his back. She didn't have on boots today like she typically did with her dresses. No, today she had on heels meant for the bedroom and a little red suit that looked like it was made of wrapping paper it was so damn tight…in all the right places.

If he needed to hire someone to torture guests, she'd be the woman for the job. She was killing him.

"Your minion gave me the message," she stated. "Was that some type of a joke?"

Dane hooked his thumbs through his belt loops and shook his head. "Not a joke at all. I just didn't confront you myself because I knew you needed time."

"Time?" Those legs slid off his desk with grace and Stella came to her feet. She smoothed her skirt down to mid-thigh and circled the desk. "You proposed marriage through a damn letter that my attorney delivered from your attorney."

Dane swallowed. "I guess the proposal could use some work, but I figured if I asked in person you'd punch me—and then you'd say no. I can take a punch, but I didn't want you to turn me down."

Stella stared across the room. With her brows drawn in, her hands on her hips, her jacket pulling across pert breasts…she was damn breathtaking.

"Turn you down?" she repeated. "Of course I'm turning you down. You're insane. I'm not marrying you."

"Did you read the entire letter?"

"The part where I'd be part owner of Mirage? Yes."

She licked her lips, probably not knowing how arousing that was. Now was certainly not the time to bring it up. "I don't know where this came from, but I'm not marrying you. If you feel guilty for taking all of this from me, that's on you. You can't just ask someone to marry you because your feelings are all out of whack."

Dane took a step toward her, then another, until they stood toe-to-toe. "You could've ripped up the letter and ignored me," he told her, reaching to brush a strand of hair from her cheek. He let his fingertips feather across her jaw as he continued. "You could've texted or even called. Yet here you are."

"I needed to—"

"See me?" he asked, sliding his other hand up to frame her face. "Damn, I've missed you."

Stella closed her eyes. "Don't say that. We are nothing, Dane."

He remained silent, waiting for her to finish the silent war no doubt waging in her head. After a moment, her lids fluttered and she focused on him.

"You don't want to marry me, you want to sleep with me," she told him.

Dane couldn't suppress the smile. "Why can't I do both?"

On a groan, Stella backed away and shook her head. "Because this is reality and the reality is I can't be with someone who lied to and deceived me."

Dane pulled in a shaky breath. He deserved that, but the words still hurt. He reminded himself that she was here, in his office, so not all hope was lost.

"You came to my house and slept with me," he started. "I know you claimed you were using me and it was just physical, but that's not the Stella I know. You love me."

Her eyes widened, her mouth opened, but nothing came out. She quickly snapped her lips shut and set her jaw.

"Even after you realized who I was," he went on, "you still wanted me. That's not ego, that's facts."

Stella shrugged. "So what? Yes, I fell in love with you, but that's not real. I fell in love with the person I thought you were. I don't even know the real you."

"You know me more than anyone else in my life. I've told you things, opened up about my past. I wouldn't do that with someone I didn't care about or someone I was just casually sleeping with."

When she didn't snap back with an answer, Dane hoped there was some part of her that believed him. He couldn't stop this momentum now.

"I fully admit I sought you out as part of my strategy to retake ownership of this place," Dane admitted. "I didn't set out to purposely hurt you and once I got to know you..."

"What?" she demanded. "You magically grew a soul?"

Dane couldn't hide his emotions and quickly realized Stella didn't want him to. She deserved to know exactly how he felt, his every thought on this matter.

"Once I got to know you, I realized deceiving you wasn't how my mom would want me to go about getting the resort back," he explained.

Unable to stand still or to look at that hurt in Stella's dark eyes, Dane started walking around the spacious office. He went to the wall of windows that overlooked the snowy mountain peaks.

"My mom wanted this place to be mine. There was no doubt about that. When I lost it, I knew that one day when I had the money and the power, I'd get it all back. This has been my goal since I was eighteen."

Dane turned back around and leaned against the cool glass. "Now that it's mine, I'm not near as happy as I thought I'd be. Everything is empty without you—the resort, my life. My heart."

Unshed tears swam in her eyes and he couldn't keep this distance between them another second. Dane crossed to her and took her by the shoulders.

"If you believe nothing else, you have to believe that I love you."

Stella reached up and swiped at his cheek and Dane realized he'd let his emotions show a little too well. He hadn't even noticed the tear. His only concern had been getting her to see that he hadn't lied about everything.

"I'll give the entire place to you," he told her. "If you still want it, it's yours."

Stella gasped and jerked back. "What?"

Dane's hands dropped to his sides. He couldn't believe after all of these years, all of this work, he was saying this, but he meant it.

"My mother was proud of this place, she had a goal of passing it to me." Dane raked a hand over the back of his neck and sighed. "But she wouldn't want me ruining lives in order to reclaim it."

"Dane."

"She would've loved you," he murmured, the damn emotions threatening to strangle him. "She would've loved you not only because I love you, but because you're a kick-ass businesswoman."

Stella laughed and closed the distance between them.

Those tears swimming in her eyes threatened to spill at any moment.

"Say it again," she demanded.

"I love you, Stella." He smoothed her hair from her face, sliding his thumb along her bottom lip. "I thought I did before you found out who I was, but I was too afraid to admit it—I knew you'd eventually learn the truth and that it would ruin everything between us, so I tried to convince myself it wouldn't wreck me to lose you. I want you to have this place. You may not be ready for marriage, but you deserve this."

Stella fisted his hair and pulled his mouth to hers. Dane didn't miss a chance to wrap his arms around her and pull her in. It had been too damn long.

When she broke the kiss and leaned back, her eyes shone bright with tears and her smile filled those cracks in his heart.

"I want the resort, but I want you, too," she told him. "Do you think your mother would be on board with both of us running this? I'm not sure that marriage is our next step. We probably should slow down a bit so we don't mess this up again, but that doesn't mean we have to be apart."

"I'll go as slow as you want," he told her, smacking her lips with his. "And I'm the one who messed up before. But I sure as hell won't take you for granted ever again. We're equals, Stella. In business and in life."

"Can I make a confession?" she asked.

"What's that?"

"I don't have anything on under my suit."

Dane's body instantly responded. "Miss Garcia, is this how you plan to conduct all of our business meetings?"

She stepped from his arms and went to the door. With a flick of her wrist, the dead bolt clicked into place. Stella turned back around and started working on the buttons of her jacket.

"I hope that won't be a problem," she asked. "I didn't think my new business partner would mind."

Dane closed the distance between them and finished unwrapping his woman. "Oh, he definitely doesn't mind."

As he pulled her into his arms, he realized that the emptiness in his life that he'd felt ever since losing his mother had healed at last. Here in this place, with this woman beside him, he knew he was exactly where he belonged.

He was finally home.

* * * * *

COMING SOON!

We really hope you enjoyed reading this book. If you're looking for more romance, be sure to head to the shops when new books are available on

Thursday 8th August

To see which titles are coming soon, please visit

millsandboon.co.uk/nextmonth

MILLS & BOON
Desire

Indulge in secrets and scandal, intense drama and plenty of sizzling hot action with powerful and passionate heroes who have it all: wealth, status, good looks... everything but the right woman.

LET'S TALK

For exclusive extracts, competitions
and special offers, find us online:

🅕 facebook.com/millsandboon

🐦 @MillsandBoon

📷 @MillsandBoonUK

Get in touch on 01413 063232

For all the latest titles coming soon, visit
millsandboon.co.uk/nextmonth

MILLS & BOON

THE HEART OF ROMANCE

A ROMANCE FOR EVERY KIND OF READER

MODERN

Prepare to be swept off your feet by sophisticated, sexy and seductive heroes, in some of the world's most glamourous and romantic locations, where power and passion collide.
8 stories per month.

HISTORICAL

Escape with historical heroes from time gone by. Whether your passion is for wicked Regency Rakes, muscled Vikings or rugged Highlanders, awaken the romance of the past.
6 stories per month.

MEDICAL

Set your pulse racing with dedicated, delectable doctors in the high-pressure world of medicine, where emotions run high and passion, comfort and love are the best medicine.
6 stories per month.

True Love

Celebrate true love with tender stories of heartfelt romance, from the rush of falling in love to the joy a new baby can bring, and a focus on the emotional heart of a relationship.
8 stories per month.

Desire

Indulge in secrets and scandal, intense drama and plenty of sizzling hot action with powerful and passionate heroes who have it all: wealth, status, good looks…everything but the right woman.
6 stories per month.

HEROES

Experience all the excitement of a gripping thriller, with an intense romance at its heart. Resourceful, true-to-life women and strong, fearless men face danger and desire - a killer combination!
8 stories per month.

DARE

Sensual love stories featuring smart, sassy heroines you'd want as a best friend, and compelling intense heroes who are worthy of them.
4 stories per month.

To see which titles are coming soon, please visit

millsandboon.co.uk/nextmonth

JOIN US ON SOCIAL MEDIA!

Stay up to date with our latest releases, author
news and gossip, special offers and discounts, and
all the behind-the-scenes action
from Mills & Boon...

 millsandboon

 millsandboonuk

 millsandboon

It might just be true love...